FYREBIRDS

ALSO BY KATE J. ARMSTRONG

Nightbirds

FYREBIRDS

KATE J. ARMSTRONG

 Nancy Paulsen Books

NANCY PAULSEN BOOKS

An imprint of Penguin Random House LLC

1745 Broadway, New York, New York 10019

First published in the United States of America by Nancy Paulsen Books,
an imprint of Penguin Random House LLC, 2024

Text copyright © 2024 by Kate J. Armstrong
Map illustrations copyright © 2023 by Sveta Dorosheva

Nancy Paulsen Books & colophon are trademarks of Penguin Random House LLC.
The Penguin colophon is a registered trademark of Penguin Books Limited.

Visit us online at PenguinRandomHouse.com.

Library of Congress Cataloging-in-Publication Data is available.

Printed in the United States of America

ISBN 9780593463307

1 3 5 7 9 10 8 6 4 2

BVG

Edited by Stacey Barney
Design by Suki Boynton • Text set in ITC Galliard Pro

For Kaitlin, my Fyrebird sister

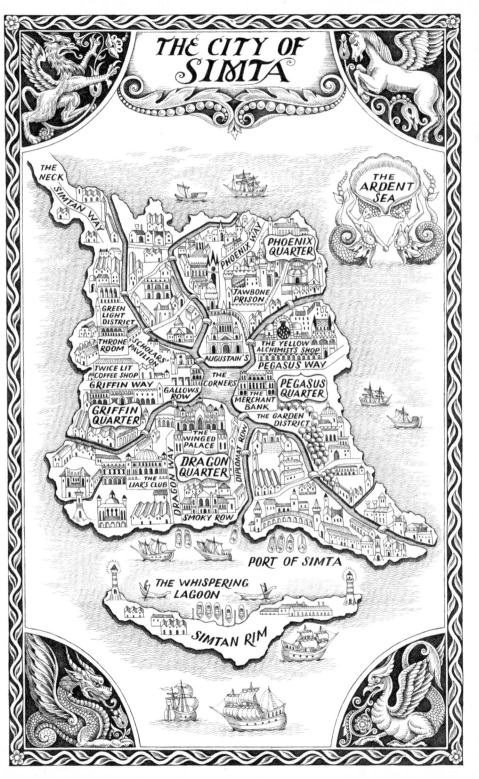

— PROLOGUE —

A TASTE OF THINGS TO COME

LL HIS LIFE, King Joost has heard tales of magic. His father spooled them out on cold nights on their hunting trips in the Pinelands, adding flourishes with every spin of the yarn. He spoke of enchanted potions and clever witches, but the ones about the Fyrebirds were Joost's favorite. *They commanded the elements,* his father would whisper. *Conjuring storms, leveling forests. Those women brought whole armies to their knees.* The stories never failed to warm him. He would lean closer to the frost-ringed fire, enthralled.

And then, at thirteen, he went to Simta with his father. The trip was full of endless meetings in uncomfortable formalwear and shaking hands with people he knew his father would rather conquer. But one night they slipped past their guards and went in search of magic. Joost will never forget his first taste. The drink, sweet and opalescent, made time run slow, like chalkpine resin. It's a feeling that, a decade later, he can still taste.

Joost sips his wine, leaning into the furs draped over his father's throne: his now. The vintage is from the Stonefields, deep and rich, but it doesn't satisfy. Every drink since those heady nights in Simta has been less satiating than the last. Joost's woodland nation is rich in many things—marble, timber, silver—but not magic. Eudea has always been the only place that power bears fruit. Trellians have smuggled magic-laced plants out of their nation before, but all have withered. They only seem to thrive in Eudean soil.

But Nightbirds, now. They might prove more resilient. Joost still can't believe such girls are real. It's said witches have risen again in Eudea, and that they can gift their magic with a kiss: a tantalizing promise. When the news first trickled in, it seemed too good to credit, but Joost's ambassador saw some of their feats with his own eyes. He wrote to Joost of fiery wings, indoor storms, and waves lifting warships. They sounded like the Fyrebirds from his father's stories. How he longs to see them for himself.

He lifts two fingers, gesturing to one of his galgren. She steps away from the wall and the tapestry of a Trellian forest, eyes downcast. Her sable velvet gown is the same color as the fawns he and his father used to hunt. Trellane has many types of slaves, but her kind are the finest. As she fills his cup, his gaze falls to her pershain: All his galgren wear them. The silver chain sits close against her throat, its end fed through a clasp carved to look like the head of a mountain lion, then left to hang in a thin line down her back. Its loops are delicate but strong, unbreakable. Not that she would try: His *beautiful chained* are sweet as budding flowers, and as obeisant. He could take it up and she would follow wherever he wills.

On that trip to Simta, the suzerain's odious son made a joke to Joost about the pershain. *I suppose you Trellians don't need to learn courtship. You'd rather tug your women around on a leash.* Interesting, then, that Dennan Hain is said to be keeping one of the witches close, sequestered in his Winged Palace. Perhaps now he understands the pershain better. Some were meant to lead, and some to serve.

There is a shuffle near the doorway. It is probably another group of farmers come to complain about this year's failing harvest. Joost isn't in the mood. Since he ascended, it feels as if their empire has been shrinking, shriveling. He grows bored of his subjects' complaints and weary of his father's judging ghost. But no: His guards have brought in his Eudean ambassador, who is walking toward him with a chained girl in tow. She looks about sixteen, her large eyes wide and wary. Joost puts down his wine, intrigued now.

"What have you brought me, Lleyn?"

"A present, my king," his ambassador says. "I bought her in Simta. The little bird came dear, but I think you will agree her worth the price."

The little bird. Joost looks at the girl with fresh eyes, heart racing.

"What is your name?" he asks.

She looks away and doesn't answer. Lleyn yanks on her chains until she speaks.

"Phryne."

"Phryne." His Simtan isn't smooth, but it will serve. "I am King Joosten Tharda. Welcome to the kingdom of Trellane."

She does not bow, as she should in his presence. He is too eager to chastise her.

"No need to be afraid," he says, soft as silk. "You are a guest here."

Her voice wobbles. "Then why am I in chains?"

He gestures to Lleyn to unlock her irons. She rubs at her wrists, eyes darting to the stony-faced guards and the girls in their pershains. The girl looks poised to run, but seems to think better of it.

"We have a custom in Trellane," Joost says. "That visitors kiss the king in welcome. I have the feeling your kiss holds more . . . magic than most."

Her jaw tightens. "I don't know what you mean."

"Do not lie. It makes me think we are enemies. I would rather you and I become friends. I am kind to my friends, and to those who obey me."

He reaches toward her, beckoning softly. It takes a long moment for her to place her hand in his. Joost's eyes fall to her neck. She will look beautiful in the pershain.

"So tell me, Phryne. What is your magic?"

Again, she hesitates. Again, he tells her those who follow him are treated kindly. At last, speaking so low it is almost a whisper, she tells him what sort of magic she holds. It is a power that makes him shiver. He fights the urge to lick his lips.

"If you give me a taste, I will ensure you are happy here. You can have anything."

She swallows. "I want to go home."

"Anything," he says, "but that."

After a moment, she nods. He pulls her closer. Slowly, reluctantly, she presses her lips to his. He feels something tingle on his tongue, tasting not unlike that long-ago cocktail. It's sweeter, though, with a hint of blood or metal. An intoxicating taste of what's to come.

When she pulls away, Joost flexes his fingers. He can feel the magic thrumming through him, rich and heady. Then he reaches out toward one of his guards. He can feel the threads of the boy's veins ready to bend to him. His heart seems to sit like a frightened bird in Joost's hand. He wraps his will—and the magic—around it, ceasing its rhythm. The boy clutches his chest and falls to his knees. With just a push, Joost could crush his life, end it. But he lets go of his grip. The boy gasps.

Joost is a king and was a prince before that. He has experienced many kisses, but none that could thaw his frozen heart. This girl's kiss is not just the glow of the fire, but the flames themselves, warming him through from the inside. And she is only one witch. Imagine what other vintages he might sample, what other flavors of magic there might be. *This,* he thinks, *is a treasure worth invading for.* To own such power, he will pay any price.

PART I

DANGEROUS
TIDES

Twisted ring, crooked tooth,
Nightbirds help you see truth.
Jewel and coin, shining light,
Nightbirds make your fortunes bright.
Spark and fire, rope and burn,
Nightbirds let you skip a turn.
Lips and kiss, quick and sly,
Nightbirds drink your soul bone dry.

—A NEW SIMTAN CHILDREN'S RHYME

– CHAPTER 1 –
MANY FACES

MATILDE DINATRIS IS a girl with many faces. She changes them the same way she might her lip stain, wearing whichever one suits an occasion best. Coming from a long line of Nightbirds, she learned such deceptions early. She was raised to know how to hide, dissemble, and evade. *A girl must learn to be two things,* Gran used to tell her. *The person she is behind closed doors, and the version of herself she shows the world.* She never warned Matilde how easy it can be to lose track of one's true self. She wears masks so often, she isn't sure which face is hers.

She walks through the party, weaving around potted shrubs and under arbors full of night-blooming vines. Flamemoths love moonflower nectar, and she's had thousands of them released for the evening. They cling to the petals as if hiding from the depthless sky. The Winged Palace's roof is filled with people, all marveling at the garden few of them knew existed. Dennan showed it to her years ago, during a game of hide-and-seek.

Tonight, two versions of her are on display: House daughter and Fyrebird. Her dress, a drop-waist copper silk number, flashes red and orange as she moves: fire colors. She has paired it with a smile that says *no need to fear me*. Still, some guests step out of her way as if she makes them nervous. As a Nightbird, she used to find winning hearts much easier. Now that they know what kind of power she wields, they seem less willing to be charmed.

It's strange to think that months ago, she was a prisoner here, a captive of Epinine Vesten. Now she is the guest and adviser of Dennan Hain, though these days he goes by Dennan Vesten. No one here would dare call their new suzerain the Bastard Prince . . . at least, not aloud. Tonight, she serves as his hostess as well. This party was her idea. It would feel more intimate here, she argued, less stuffy than the pomp and circumstance of the ballroom. A setting that might tempt their guests to lower their guards. She presided over the guest list, selecting influential Great House lords and ladies, wealthy merchants, and popular naval captains, all of whom she wants to win over. Since finding out that girls with magic aren't extinct, her city has remained divided over what to do about them. Some see them as a gift from the Wellspring, meant to be treasured—or exploited. The church believes they are an evil to be quelled. Many see them as dangerous, one way or another. Matilde aims to convince them that none should be caged.

She picks up a glass of blush wine from one of the refreshment tables. Heads turn and watch as she sips, following the libation as it slides down her throat. She used to bask in the feeling of a room's eyes on her, but there's a heat to these stares now—a bite. It has been like this since Leastnight, when she, Sayer, Æsa, and Fen did feats of magic that continue to be whispered about. Such power hasn't been seen in centuries, earning the four of them charming nicknames. Her maid revealed hers, the Flame Witch, with a wince, but Matilde likes its fierceness. It's certainly better than what some people call her when they think her back is turned. But one title unites them all: Fyrebird, a word once used for only the most powerful witches. *Fyre* means "wild" in Old Eudean, and that is how many see them. She has made sure, these past months, to show them nothing but restraint and control.

But still, it's clear an old power is rising, and some want to worship it. Shrines have been built on the ruins of Krastan's shop, at the base of the vine Fen made grow in Phoenix Quarter, and within the bowels of the beached ship Æsa left on the Rim. The Wardens tear them down, but the things simply crop back up. She hears people leave lit candles and paper wishes on her shrine, asking for protection. These past few months, she has done her best. But the paths of power are thornier than she imagined, full of tangles. Men are forever getting in her way.

Speaking of . . . She makes her way toward Lords Giles Abrasia and Sand Deveraux, two members of the Simtan Table. They stop talking abruptly as she sashays into their sphere.

"My lords. I hope you're enjoying the party."

"Indeed," Sand says, lips thinning. "Though such a thing seems a bit reckless, given the unrest about your position here. And your . . . growing closeness with our suzerain."

There are those who suspect her of controlling Dennan. She overheard the new Pontifex call him bewitched. What flotsam. If that were true, she would have had him kick the church off the Table, and she would now occupy the Pontifex's empty chair. But those men still won't allow her a place amongst them. She is forced to sit instead behind a grate and eavesdrop on their meetings. To listen in silence as Dennan speaks for her.

"Come now," she says. "Such gatherings are even more important in times of trouble. It can only help unite us."

"Not when you openly flout the law."

She taps a nail against her glass. "You will find nothing illegal here, my lord. Unless you count me as contraband."

"Some do," Sand says. "As you are well aware."

She stifles a frustrated sigh. The Prohibition against all magic is still in effect, despite her best efforts to convince those in power to abandon it, or at least amend it to exclude magical girls. How can you arrest someone for something that lives inside them? How can you legislate a thing that flows through someone's veins? And yet many view them as criminals simply for having magic—the four Fyrebirds especially. Some say she is lucky to still be walking free. The church put a warrant out for Æsa after she escaped Jawbone Prison. Dennan has refused to send the navy out looking for her, but the Wardens would happily arrest her friend on sight.

"I'm surprised at you, Lord Deveraux," she says. "Magic runs in your bloodline. Surely you do not see it as an arrestable offense."

"I do when it is used for ill," he snaps. "We cannot help girls who use such power to wreak havoc. Just look at the Storm Witch."

At the mention of Sayer, Matilde's pulse quickens. "What about her?"

Giles's bushy brows rise. "Your little friend runs amok, assaulting paters and threatening lords as if our laws don't apply to her. You abet her by refusing to tell us who she is."

"It seems to me that she is simply trying to protect girls with magic. If the law did the same, perhaps she wouldn't feel the need."

"You must see how difficult she makes any such efforts. Everything she does underscores the church's claims."

Dash it, Sayer. Why can't she see that her actions make Matilde's mission harder? She would tell her so if they were still speaking.

"I understand your passion," Giles says. "Women are so often ruled by it. This is why we had the Nightbirds system. To protect you not just from the law, but from yourselves."

No, they had the Nightbirds system so that they could use the girls' power however they liked, so they could own it. Lords like these seem to want things to go back, not forward.

"Keeping us caged did not protect us. It simply contained us. But we are out now, my lords. I would think you would want to stand with us. Not stand by while someone plucks girls off the streets."

"I don't know what you mean." Sand sniffs.

"You must have heard the rumors of the specters."

She knows they have. Matilde eavesdropped on the Table discussing the shadowy figures said to be abducting magical girls. No one knows who they are or where the girls are being taken. And yet, when Dennan pushed for an inquest, these lords did not support him. The Pontifex went so far as to deny the claim outright.

"We do not legislate gossip," Giles says. "And we have our hands full with other matters."

Matilde's hands grow hot. "Perhaps you would feel differently if one of them were your daughter."

Giles's cheeks grow mottled. Sand puts out a staying hand.

"Come, Young Lady Dinatris," Sand says. "This is no conversation for such an occasion. Best you enjoy your party and leave the politics to us."

The words, said so mildly, make her magic rise, desperate to scald him. She's about to say something ill-advised when Gran arrives.

"There you are, Matilde. I need you. Please excuse us, my lords."

The men bow their heads, but Matilde doesn't return the gesture.

"Breathe," Gran says as they walk away. "You look like you might burst into flame."

"Perhaps I should. Then they would listen."

Gran pats her hand. "Remember, darling. One must make compromises. Sometimes we need to lose a few battles to win the greater war."

"You know how much I detest losing."

It feels like all she does, lately.

"Our family is safe. That is something."

Gran is wearing blue tonight, though in private she wears red, the color of widows. She's mourning Krastan, her old love. Shadows hang like crescent moons under her eyes. None of her family have been the same since Epinine Vesten held them hostage. Sometimes she catches Dame staring at her hands, expression haunted. After being starved, Samson seems to want to eat himself into an early grave. And they still cannot go home. The Dinatris mansion has become a popular spot for Wardens to throw things: eggs, paint, flaming bottles. Dennan argues that none of them can yet leave the palace's confines. *Here,* he says, *my power keeps you safe.* Gran, Dame, and Samson haven't complained, but it feels as if the walls are closing in around her. She is forever trapped behind grates, her wings tied down.

Matilde reaches for her locket. It used to be filled with a potion Krastan made. Now it's empty, but she still finds comfort in its familiar weight. As she pulls it free of her dress, her fingers brush the embroidered flames on her bodice. The work is finely done, stitched by a seamstress not much younger than she is. Matilde knows this because the girl's dame delivered the dress, refusing to hand it to anyone else.

"I keep thinking about that woman," she says, low. "And her daughter. Phryne."

They took my girl, the woman said, gripping Matilde's hands. *The specters.* The look in her eyes, so haunted, still makes Matilde shiver.

The woman pressed a drawing of Phryne into her hand before she left. With a start, Matilde recognized her face. She was one of the girls from the Underground, one of their fledglings. The sketch is tucked into her pocket now, burning a hole.

"I know, dearest," Gran says. "But we have enough difficulties to contend with. This problem is not yours to fix."

But isn't it? She, Sayer, Æsa, and Fen are the ones who brought girls like Phryne to the public's attention. She painted the target on their backs.

"My maid told me the specters are rumored to wear grey. *Grey,* Gran." She doesn't say En Caska Dae aloud. She doesn't need to. The name of the religious cult that terrorized her family, killed Krastan, and almost ended the Nightbirds need not be voiced.

"It might not be them," Gran whispers. "No one has seen the Red Hand since Leastnight."

"That doesn't mean—"

Gran hushes her. "Not here. Too many people might be listening. Best put it out of your mind for now."

But Matilde can't stop thinking about Phryne and the missing girls. She was meant to protect them. Isn't that why she stayed, why she is here? *Find her*, the woman pleaded. *Find my Phryne.* Matilde feels the weight of that girl's fate weighing her down.

"Smile, my love," Gran presses. "Tonight is a happy occasion. Soon, our family will have much to celebrate."

Before she can ask what Gran means, she points to a girl passing under an arbor.

"Isn't that Petra?"

It *is* Petra, walking with Sive and Octavia. Her old best friends and Nightbird sisters—the ones who have been avoiding her.

"Go and see your friends," Gran urges. "You must miss them."

Matilde sniffs. "Not really. And I would rather be chased than do the chasing."

And yet, when Gran shoos her away, she walks toward them. They do not seem to see her or are pretending they don't. She should return the favor. After all, she has bigger fish to fry. But as they turn onto one of the hedge-lined walkways, Matilde finds herself going after them. Petra steers the group toward an alcove at one of the roof's outer corners. They push through the gauzy curtain, and Matilde follows them through.

For a moment, her old friends only stare at her, silent. When they were Nightbirds together, it never felt like this. After seeing clients, they would pile into one of their rooms with treats and wine and rate the evening's kisses, giving clients titles like Lord Listless Lips, the Cranky Crone, the Loud Lecher. Conversation between them used to flow, almost effortless. Now none of them seem to know what to say.

"Hello, strangers," she says at last. "I was beginning to forget what you all looked like."

"Yes, well," Petra says, tugging on a glove. "It was a busy summer."

A busy summer? Matilde was forced to go on the run by a religious zealot, her family was kidnapped, and she was almost stabbed by the Pontifex. And they didn't so much as send her a note.

"Too busy to check on your friend? Or have you officially decided to disown me?"

"Don't be dramatic," Sive says, crossing her arms over her generous chest. "Of course we are your friends."

Something in Matilde's stomach twists. "You could have fooled me."

"That's not fair," Octavia says. Her large eyes shine like jewels. "You know the pressure we are under."

From their husbands, she means, and their families, who she's sure have warned them to keep their distance. Spending time with Matilde might make people suspect they were once Nightbirds, and no one wants the world knowing *their* girls have magic. The Houses don't want to share the ones they still keep close.

"Don't be angry." Petra squeezes her hand. "We have been dying to see you. We have so many questions."

"Such as?"

She waits for them to ask about Leastnight, or the rumors of girls being abducted, or at least about the newest Nightbirds.

Octavia tugs at a loose curl at her neck. "How did you do it?"

"Do what?"

"Call up those fiery wings on Leastnight."

Elemental magic, she means. The kind Nightbirds are told their forebears wielded, but that they only have the embers of. Tiny sparks rather than the fire itself.

"They simply came when I called," she hedges. "I discovered the power quite by accident."

"And can you use your Nightbird gift as well?"

Matilde nods. The girls look stunned by the revelation. Nightbirds were once taught they cannot use their own magic. One of the many lies they were fed.

"You could, too, you know. But you would have to stop giving it away to others."

But it's more than that, she thinks. *To use your magic, you must own it fully. You must believe it's yours, and yours alone.*

The girls look at each other.

"Can you imagine what Marc would say if I cut him off?" Petra muses. "He'd have a fit."

Octavia nods. "Len too. Utter apoplexy."

"Yes, well," Sive says, smiling wryly. "You know what they say about boys and their toys."

They all laugh—*laugh,* as if none of this is of consequence. Suddenly they feel like strangers.

When Sayer and Æsa first became Nightbirds, Matilde wished they were these girls. She couldn't imagine Sayer and Æsa ever feeling like her sisters. But then they ran together into the Underground, forging a bond unlike anything she had known. It wasn't just the magic that bound them, but the sharing of their secrets. Matilde showed them pieces of herself she never thought she would reveal to anyone. Now she longs for Sayer's caustic jokes, Æsa's sweetness—even Fen's stoic brand of arrogance. What she wouldn't give to have them here beside her. In this moment, they feel more lost to her than ever.

"Now," Petra says, her soft voice growing pointed. "Tell us about Dennan Hain."

Matilde stiffens. "What about him?"

"How do his kisses rate on the Nightbird scale?"

"Pet," Sive says, frowning. "Really."

"What?" Petra bats back. "He's devilish handsome. Why shouldn't Tilde have some fun?"

"Because he's trouble as well," Octavia says. "Len says he's too reckless. And everyone knows he had a hand in his sister's death."

But not *just* him. A vision floods her: Epinine Vesten on the floor, touching her poison-slicked lips. The truth is that Matilde killed the suzerain, tricked into it by Dennan. She blinks hard, forcing the memory away.

"Don't say such things," Sive whispers. "Anyway, he is the suzerain now, which makes him the catch of the century. So tell us, Tilde: Is he your admirer?"

It's the word their Madam, Leta, would use when a gentleman applied for a Nightbird's hand. *It seems you have an admirer.* But they didn't admire *her*—they wanted the Goldfinch. Dennan is no different, no matter what he might claim.

"He is not."

Petra quirks a brow. "Then what is he?"

Dennan isn't her suitor. After the way he used her in his plot to kill his sister, he isn't her friend. But he is her clearest path to changing things in Eudea. As suzerain, he is one of the most powerful people in the Eudean Republic, and staying close to him means keeping his ear. It's a power she would be unwise to walk away from. That's what she tells herself in moments of doubt.

"Speaking of," Petra whispers, elbowing Matilde.

The band stops playing as Dennan steps up onto the

garden's small stage. He looks handsome in a pale suit that sets off his bronzed skin, the golden sash he always wears in public shining. Simta's first suzerain used to wear one just like it, and Matilde has to admit it makes him look the part. Every inch of him is sleek and polished, but there is still a flash of sea captain about him. His roguish charm is part of what makes him beloved amongst many of the Simtan people, despite the dark rumors that swirl around him about his sister's suspicious death.

"Welcome," he says, "and thank you for joining us this evening. I've enjoyed our conversations over cocktails. Though some of you are drinking more than your fair share, I'd say."

The crowd rumbles a laugh. Dennan's voice, clear and deep, circles the garden. He has a way of leaning toward a crowd, making it feel like he's speaking to each person directly. One of the girls beside her sighs.

"I know that many of you have fears and questions about our future. This is a time of change for us all. An unsettled time, with far too much division. But I believe in Eudea's strength, and that includes its magic. It is rising in Simta, and throughout our Republic, in a way we haven't seen in centuries. Such power should not be treated with fear or censure, but treasured. Just look at how Matilde Dinatris doused that fire in Pegasus, which might have ravaged our city. She has already lit the way."

Dennan's vibrant eyes find hers. She doesn't like the calculating gleam in them. It makes the hairs at the nape of her neck stand on end.

"Our church tells us stories of the Fyrebirds of old committing evil. What has been lost over the years is how much good they could do. Leaders and Fyrebirds worked together once to forge a stronger world. A better one. Which is why I am thrilled to announce that Young Lady Dinatris and I are getting married. The wedding will be on the last day of Risentide, and you are all invited."

Gasps cloud the air, a few claps, and a flurry of whispers. Matilde has to fight to keep her jaw off the floor. Sive covers her mouth with a gloved hand. "Ten hells, Matilde. Why didn't you tell us?"

Because this engagement is news to her.

Dennan's gaze has not wavered. *Play along,* it seems to say, or to demand. Anger flares, but to deny his claim here, now, would undermine him, and her powers by extension. She raises her glass and forces a smile.

Dennan raises his glass too. "To my bride, our union, and a brighter future."

Everyone toasts. She accepts her friends' enthused congratulations. But behind her mask, deep in her secret heart, she burns.

YOUNG LORD HEATH ROCHET
REQUESTS
YOUR COMPANY AT HIS
STAG NIGHT

WHICH WILL COMMENCE AT SUNDOWN ON
THE FIFTH DAY OF LARKSMONTH.

COME TO
801 LOOSEPETAL PLACE,
DRAGON QUARTER,
FOR A
NIGHTBIRDS PARTY.

DRESS TO IMPRESS AND
WEAR A MASK.

– CHAPTER 2 –
A SHADOW DOESN'T HAVE TO FEAR THE DARK

AYER SWAYS TO the music, making her stolen dress glimmer. Its sequins flash with the light of the candles, all trickster-kissed to burn a sultry red. Each dancing girl wears a feathered mask with dark mesh over the eyeholes. Sayer swore she would never put one on again. Yet here she is, playing at being a Nightbird. The irony isn't lost on her.

When the Nightbirds disbanded, the system that once kept their secrets safe unraveled. Old clients started talking. An anonymous lord even sold a tell-all to a newssheet: *My Evening with a Nightbird.* Now that all of Simta knows about the elite girls who once gifted magic with kisses, everyone wants a taste, real or not. Hence this new type of amusement: a so-called Nightbirds party. The evening's host, a House Rochet lordling, has brought his friends to an establishment on Smoky Row to celebrate his impending nuptials. The evening started with them going through the bawdy house's parlor, where a woman calling herself Madam Crow took their money. She introduced each girl by a code name: things like the Swallow, the Wren, and the Flamingo. None of these girls were ever Nightbirds, but that doesn't matter. The evening wouldn't be as thrilling unless it followed the entirety of the script.

The guests—all men—hover at the room's edges. A few are moving in, swaying and tipsy, doing their best attempt at the Deepwater Creep. The girls are doing a passable job of pretending to enjoy it. Sayer keeps her eyes on Iona, the girl she came for. Leta heard, through her web of spies and whispers, that she wants out of this brothel, but apparently her Madam has other ideas. After all, a girl like her is worth a fortune. This Madam Crow has promised her clients there is a truly magical girl at this party, a gold coin hidden in a stack of copper naves. The first to find her gets to claim her. Sayer's got to get her out before they do. This house, this city, isn't safe for girls with magic, especially those with no family. Pipers harass them, the church's Wardens arrest them, lords like these see them as fair game. So Leta uses her wealth and connections to help find and rescue girls who need it. Sayer spends her nights as their unforgiving blade. Still, for every girl she helps, another seems to slip through her fingers. For every man she makes pay for his crimes, another walks free.

We can't guard them all, Leta tells her, *and punish every villain who deserves it.*

She thinks of her sire. Anger crackles inside her. It's always there, a dark heart between her ribs.

Watch me.

Sayer dances closer to the girl they're calling the Flamingo. She flinches a little every time someone touches her, wiping a hand on her deeply pink dress.

Sayer is almost there when a boy wedges in, blocking her view.

"Pleasant evening," he says, thin lips framed by a goatee that reminds her of a hedge maze. "What's your name again, sweetling?"

She tilts her head coyly. "The Egret."

Lucky Sayer and the actual Egret have similar coloring. The girl was happy enough to let Sayer take her place tonight.

His hand snakes around her. "Tell me, little egret. Are you the one with magic?"

Sayer makes herself smile. "Wouldn't you like to know."

He laughs, though it's more of a bray. "Aren't you charming."

If only he knew she has a knife under her dress.

"I have to talk to one of the other girls," Sayer says. "Don't go away. I'll be right back."

Hedge Maze squeezes her waist. "Wouldn't you rather find somewhere private to continue our . . . conversation?"

Sayer finds herself wondering what Matilde would say to him. She often leans on her friends—in thought, at least—borrowing their charm or guile or kindness. She has to do it from memory, since it's been months since they spoke. Æsa is in Illan, as far as she can get from Simta. Matilde is cloistered at the palace, playing politics. Fen avoids her like some form of the pox.

She pushes that last thought aside. Matilde, she decides, would go on the offensive.

"I have a better idea. Let's play a game. You close your eyes and count to one hundred, then come find me."

With a grin, the boy dutifully closes his eyes and starts counting. Sayer turns, but the Flamingo is gone. The boys are starting to disperse, following the dancers into closets and other shadowed corners. She curses under her breath and goes on the hunt.

She slips down the main hallway, which is lined with gilded

mirrors. She doesn't look at them as she creeps up the staircase, calling on her magic to muffle her steps. Her air magic isn't as powerful as it was when the four of them were still together, not nearly, but her control over what she can do with it has grown. She can sharpen her hearing, deaden sound, and make herself invisible, though she doesn't want to risk it here—not yet. The house's upstairs level is dark enough that it's hard to see in front of her. No matter. A shadow doesn't have to fear the dark.

There's a shuffling in a room down the hall, a murmur of voices. Sayer stalks closer. She doesn't have to strain to make out their words.

"That is quite a gift," a male voice says. "How fortunate I am to be sampling it."

Quick as a breath, Sayer makes herself blend into the shadows, body and clothes all shifting to match the hall, part invisibility, part camouflage. She eases open the door and slips slowly inside. No one notices her entrance. The masked client is standing by the balcony door, flung open to the night. This bawdy house is on the end of Smoky Row, near the canal. Sayer can hear the water slapping gently down below.

The client pulls Iona close, hands sliding around her. Something about the way he touches her, almost proprietary, sends Sayer's mind tumbling back to that day she saw a man pin her dame to a wall. Wyllo Regnis was hungry for her dame's magic once, too. Sayer's estranged sire took and took, then left them both in the gutter. Thinking of him has her pulling out her knife. It's mostly for show: These days, she doesn't need it. She can do more damage with her magic than any blade, however sharp. But it reminds her who she was before she could bend the air and sink into the shadows. That even without it, she would still hold a lethal edge.

"What is it?" the man says as Iona pulls back.

"I told the Madam I would give you my magic. No more than that."

"Yes, but I've heard that more than a kiss is required to fully transmit it. The more contact there is, the longer it lasts."

Sayer frowns. The city's rumor mill has churned out all sorts of tales about girls with magic lately. Some call them wanton, selling body, magic, and soul to the highest bidder. Others make them sound like vampiresses out for blood. They'll give you magic, but it will cost you. They will drink your soul given the chance. She busted a piper the other day selling a vial of blood, which he said held the same magical properties as the girl it was drawn from. A dangerous lie. This one is, too.

"That isn't true," Iona insists. "A kiss is plenty."

"For you, perhaps. But I expect more."

She hates that men like this think they can take what they want without consequence. She hates that this girl, any girl, feels powerless to stop it. Sayer edges forward, ready to fight if she has to. Then the man smooths his lapels.

"Ah, well," he says, turning toward a sideboard. "I've rushed you. Let's have a drink and talk some more."

She watches him take off his mask and put it down beside the line of bottles. With a jolt, Sayer recognizes his face. He's the boy who tried to feel up a maid at Leta's Season-opening ball all those months ago. A part of her wants to stab him just for that.

"I could take you away from all this, you know," he says.

Iona grips the back of a chair. "What do you mean?"

"I believe you owe the Madam quite a sum. I could pay it off for you. Set you up in your own house with an allowance, plenty of finery. All I would ask is that you give your magic to me—only me."

"I . . . don't know," Iona hedges. "My Madam would be angry."

"I will persuade her, don't worry. I do hope I can persuade you, too."

As he talks, he pours their drinks. His back is turned to Iona, but Sayer can see his hands in the reflection of a mirror. He surreptitiously takes a small tin out of his pocket and pulls something free. It looks like a lozenge, about the size of a shill coin, but sickly yellow. He drops it into a glass, where it dissolves.

"Here," he says, holding it out to Iona. "Drink up. It will relax you."

She clearly doesn't want to, but takes it anyway. What choice does she really have?

Sayer moves, plucking it out of her hand before she can drink it. Iona gasps, eyes on the cup that seems to hover as if floating on the air.

"What devilry is this?" the client says, going crimson.

"The kind that will stab you if you move. So don't."

He sucks in a breath, his eyes trying to find her.

"You can shout for help, if you like," Sayer tells him, voice cold as steel. "But no one will hear you. I've made sure of it."

At that, the client's face goes from blotchy red to pale.

"I know who you are."

"Oh, yes? Who am I?"

"The one who's been causing us all so much trouble. The Storm Witch."

She lets her invisibility fall away. Her mask will conceal her, and she wants him to see the knife she's holding.

"I'm glad my reputation precedes me. That should save us some time."

"Why are you here?" he says. "My dealings don't concern you."

His voice is steady, all bravado, but his trembling hands betray his fear. Good.

"I beg to differ." Sayer sniffs the drink. It smells of char and algae, mixed in with something sweeter. It reminds her of the potion the zealot tried to give her on her last night as the Ptarmigan, sending a nasty shiver down her neck. "What did you put in this drink?"

His jaw ticks. "I don't know what you mean."

"Try again."

He doesn't speak, lips pinching. Then he turns and makes a dash for the door. Sayer concentrates until she can see the air, shimmering in bands of grey and blue. With a thought, she wills it to thicken around him, pushing him back into the chair. He grunts as he tries to pull his arms up, only to find them fixed to it as if by manacles. She has made sure the bands of air are good and tight.

"How dare you," he sputters. "Do you know who my sire is? He will—"

She cuts off his air, just to show him she can do it. From near the balcony door, Iona sucks in a breath. He chokes once, twice, before she lets him breathe freely again.

"I'll ask you nicely one more time." She circles, a tigren stalking her prey. "What did you try to drug this girl with?"

He wriggles in his chair, sweating now. "It's a party drug. Something to enhance the mood. That is all."

She slips the tin out of his pocket. He yanks at his restraints, his pupils huge.

"Put that back," he grits out. "Do you know how much it's worth?"

Sayer snorts. "I'm sure you can afford more."

"They're dashed rare. My sire will murder me if he finds out I wasted them both."

She opens it to see one yellow lozenge tucked in waxed paper. It's etched with a wilted-looking flower.

"What is it called?"

He doesn't answer. Sayer runs the tip of her knife across one of his hands, leaving a thin red line there. He jerks but is helpless to pull back.

"I recommend you spill," she says, all menace. "Unless you want to leave this room a lot less pretty than you entered it. I won't be shedding any tears over your fate."

His mouth works. "Sugar. It's called Sugar. It's meant to make a girl more . . . biddable."

And he waited to put it in Iona's drink until he knew she had magic. A suspicion creeps through her, spreading like a stain across cloth.

"It only works on girls with magic. Is that what you're saying?"

The boy grinds his teeth. A sinister wind cuts through the room, smelling of storm clouds. Iona gasps, but Sayer's gaze stays fixed on the client.

"It's . . . yes," he growls. "It only works on girls with magic."

"And where did your sire get it?"

"A friend of his. An important man." His lip curls. "One day soon, I hope he becomes your keeper. Someone needs to put you on a leash."

The church says girls like her are some great, corrupting evil. They post flyers portraying her, Matilde, Fen, and Æsa with wings and fangs and claws, as monsters. But it's boys like this who deserve to be shamed. As he speaks, his voice twists, becoming someone else's. Suddenly it's Wyllo Regnis in the chair. Sayer remembers the feel of his hands around her wrists on Leastnight, pulling a rope tight. Men like him—like this— are never made to suffer. Why shouldn't it be her who makes them pay?

Her fury spills over, almost blinding. Quick as lightning, she brings her knife down. It sinks into his hand, biting into the plush velvet of the armrest. He screams, high pitched, and yet it isn't enough. She presses down, imagining it's Wyllo panting in agony. Her rage is a storm that never dies.

"Please. Don't," Iona whispers.

Sayer sucks in a breath and steps back, pulling her blade free. The man screams again, then starts cursing. She gags him with another band of air.

"The Storm Witch," Iona breathes. "It really is you. What are you doing here?"

"I'm here to get you out."

"But my Madam. If I run, she will find me."

"She won't." She takes Iona's hand. "I promise."

A moment passes, then another. At last, Iona nods.

"I have a few more questions for this one," Sayer says, nodding to the client. "But then—"

The doorknob rattles.

"Little Egret," comes a slurred voice from the hall. "Are you there?"

Dash it: the client she left counting downstairs. She'd forgotten him. Just as she forgot to lock the door . . . It swings

31

open, and the drunken lordling stumbles into the room. Sayer pulls Iona behind her. There's a moment as he takes in his friend bleeding in the chair. She reaches out, hoping to muffle his voice, but it's too late. He shrieks loud enough to wake the dead.

"Witch!"

He lunges. Sayer uses her magic to push him up against a wall, pinning him there like a butterfly. The boy in the chair fights and writhes to get free. He is still bound, but it's getting harder to hold him now that she has two bodies to manage. Without the other girls near, her magic tires more quickly. It has limits, and she's stretched it too thin.

Footsteps pound through the town house. More boys are coming. She sheathes her knife and backs Iona toward the balcony.

"Can you swim?" she asks.

The girl's eyes are dark spheres in the moonlight. "Yes, but the canal's too far. We won't make it."

Sayer looks out over the railing to the cobbled street below. She's right: Even with a running start, which they won't have, they should hit stones rather than water. Or they would if she wasn't the Storm Witch.

"Trust me."

They scramble over the balcony's railing. Sayer clings to it with one hand.

"On three, we jump."

She will have to drop her fraying hold on the two boys before she tries this. The one in the chair has already broken free. Sayer pulls a small orb out of a pocket and throws it. The glass breaks on the rug, and both boys start itching madly, yelping as the alchemical makes welts spread like fire across their skin. That should keep them busy.

"One . . ."

She lets the last bands of air around the boys drop.

"Two . . ."

Sayer grabs Iona's hand, concentrating, tongue tasting of rain and wind and iron.

"Three."

A hand grazes Sayer's shoulder, but they're already falling. Sayer throws her concentration out into the night air, asking it to shape and bend. The air beneath them hardens, turning smooth as glass. They slide along it, arching over the street and toward the water.

"Gods." Iona's eyes, which had been screwed shut, shoot open. "Are we flying?"

More like sliding, but still. Sayer lets herself soar on the thrill of it.

"That's what clever birds do."

ALDRICK DORISALL, THE Red Hand, drums his burn-marred fingers on the table. He has never been a very patient man. As a boy, he was the first to reach for toys and whatever food landed on his family's table. As a young acolyte of the Church of the Eshamein, he was always grasping, eager to propel himself through the ranks. Now he is hungry for Simta to see his vision of their future. But the path to it involves many pieces, some of which have yet to fall into position. When it comes to patience, he is learning.

He gets up from his prayers. His new headquarters is much finer than he is accustomed to. All these gilded trappings, gaudy and cluttered, are needless, much like the lord who owns them. But both house and man have proven useful in their way. The quiet seclusion has given him time for contemplation, prayer, experimentation. To listen as his god whispered ideas into his ear.

He catches a glimpse of himself in the metal of the sword over the altar. He has never been a vain man, but the gnarled skin is arresting. His wounds from the fire at the alchemist's have only just healed. Old scars from a fire years ago have been twisted by new ones, all given to him by witches. Anger flares, to think of all the damage they have done. He warned the old Pontifex that witches were rising, but the man dismissed him. The Brethren sneered, refusing to heed his words. Now the Flame Witch poisons the new suzerain. The Storm Witch terrorizes the city's paters, while the Wave Witch is allowed to roam the world unchecked. None get under his skin like the Flower Witch. *Ana*. The girl he raised, and who betrayed him. The one he should never have let slip out of his grasp.

He makes his way down the hall of the mansion, heading for the cells set up in what was once a stable. There, he finds braziers of blessed witchbane burning. He also finds his subjects: five witches, all plucked from the streets of Simta by his Caska. People are calling them specters, he hears: a fitting title. But the Blades of Flame will not be ghosts forever. Soon they will rise.

"It is time," he says, pulling out a tray of lozenges, "to take your medicine."

One of the witches spits at his feet. They have all been troublesome, but in perfecting his Sugar, they have more than proved their worth.

"You watch," she says, not for the first time. "The Fyrebirds will come for us."

The Red Hand smiles. "Oh, I am counting on it."

The so-called Fyrebirds think they have beaten him; he is certain. They think no one can touch them now. But Marren has shown him the way to their destruction, and his ultimate salvation. His god will help him put them in their place.

– CHAPTER 3 –

PAYMENT AND PRICE

FENLIN **B**RAE HAS stolen many precious things in her time. Jewels and coins, artwork and secrets. The best thing she ever pilfered is only precious to her. Her name was stolen straight out of a book some do-gooder brought to Pater Dorisall's orphanage. Rankin didn't like how dark the stories were, but Fen found a kind of escape in the grim tales. She especially liked the one about Fenlin Brae, who snuck into dragons' caves and damsels' rooms, smiling and toothsome. Nothing ruffled the Sly Fox. Fen's spent years crafting a reputation to match. *You've got ice in your veins,* the Quick Cuts boss once told her. *You could stick her,* the Deep Seas boss joked, *and I'm not sure she would bleed.* Simta's only girl gang boss isn't moved by anything. It's a lie that's always suited her just fine.

She wipes the sweat off her brow. The rival gang's clubhouse is too full of bodies. With so many Quick Cuts boys on all sides, she can't relax. As she and two of her Dark Stars weave through, she counts them out of habit: one, two, ten. Most of the Cuts are taller than her, but size isn't what makes the difference in a street fight. It's skill, nerve, and control. Always control. Fen used to have that in spades, but not so much lately. Her temper, and her magic, keep slipping the leash.

"Some party," Hallie says beside her. "The crackdown doesn't seem to be hurting the Cuts any."

Fen rolls one of her shoulders. Her shirt is chafing at her clammy skin. "No indeed."

She's surprised to see that some of the Cuts have been indulging in magical cocktails. It's gotten more dangerous with the Wardens knuckling down. Since Leastnight, there've been more searches and seizures of bootleg magic, and more violence between the church and Simta's sandpiper gangs. It would take a deft hand to navigate the current restrictions on imports and exports. But then, Graff "Edges" Lanagan is bolder than most.

"You sure about this, boss?" Olsa, Fen's second, asks. "Taking jobs from the other clubs is always messy."

"For the price Edges is offering, it's worth at least a conversation."

After all, they lost a lot of money when the Underground flooded, taking their illicit plant business with it. They've had to return to their old tricks, thieving on contract. But the Stars are struggling to claw back what they lost, both in coin and reputation. It's getting hard for Fen to keep them afloat.

Hallie purses her lips. "Still. I don't like it."

Hallie scowls at a Cut who's giving her the fisheye. Her sweet, round face makes her one of the Stars' best secret gatherers; everyone wants to be alone with Hallie. She's a girl, though, so the other pipers weren't quick to see her value. It's the same with Olsa. He's all muscle and brass, but he's got a limp and a mighty fear of blood. The other bosses see her crew as castoffs and misfits, but Fen wouldn't trade them. She's done a lot of things for the Dark Stars in her climb up the ranks of Simta's most disreputable ladder. To keep them all together, she'll do a lot more.

"Why does he want you?" Olsa asks. "That's what I wanna know. Seems fishy."

"We'll find out soon enough," Fen says. "Until then, hold your fire, would you?"

But Hallie isn't done. "Our boss can't take a job from another one. It'll make us look desperate."

Fen's fingers curl into fists. "You think we aren't?"

Her irritation brings her magic running. She tastes earth and growing things on her tongue.

Fen bites down on her mastic. The witchbane tastes rank, but she is used to it. She's been using it to tamp down her magic for years. Fen figured out what the plant could do when she still lived at Dorisall's. He was always tinkering, looking for ways to draw magic out of a girl, to control it. Her 'spring-stained eyes—one brown, one green—made him certain she had magic too. She fought tooth and nail to keep it hidden, but when Dorisall was out, she conducted her own experiments. When she ran away, she took witchbane's secrets with her, but he got there in the end. She thought for sure he'd have told the church about it by now, but no Wardens have turned up in the streets with burning braziers. If they know about witchbane, they don't have access to it yet. It should reassure Fen: Maybe Dorisall really is dead. But she knows better than most how hard the man is to kill. She can't shake the feeling he is biding his time, lying in wait, and that she should do something about it. Right now, though, she's got more than enough on her plate.

They've reached the booth at the back of the club. Hallie and Olsa post up next to Edges's guards, knowing they won't be invited to this conversation. One of the boys pulls the booth's curtain back.

"Fenlin," Edges says, flashing his crowded teeth. "Enjoying yourself?"

"Well enough," Fen says, sliding into the seat across from him. "Bold, to be dealing so much magic, though."

"Ah, but it's danger that makes a party go down sweet."

Edges would know. He's the city's chief dealer in Mermaid's Dust, a popular alchemical that heightens the senses. Fen has never understood the appeal.

Fen was thirteen when she first met the boss of the Quick Cuts. She and Rankin were fresh to the streets, still learning its rules. They spent their days picking pockets, targeting rich-looking tourists. She was loitering outside a coffee shop when he walked in, wearing his signature silver suspenders. People moved out of the way, as if he had the power to make the world bend around him. She wanted to figure out how such a thing was done. So the next day, she went to the Cuts' clubhouse and offered to steal for Edges. All he saw was a girl, too thin and with only one eye. He threw her a challenge he didn't think she'd accept. *My lady covets a greenstone necklace she saw one of the Rochet girls wearing. Bring me that, and maybe we'll talk.* He was surprised, Fen could tell, when she pulled it off. She did jobs for him for years, some dirtier than others. He even tried to get her to join the Quick Cuts for real. But Fen wanted to make her own crew, a family where she'd never known one. A place where she could be herself.

But are you? The words come in Sayer's voice, sharp and accusing. *You hide your magic from them. You hide yourself.*

Some parts, yes. Other than Rankin, her crew doesn't know

about her magic. They don't know she's the one people are call-ing the Flower Witch. It's a miracle that no one recognized her in that courtyard, when she made the dashed vine grow up the side of the building. It's better no one knows—safer. Men like Edges would use it against her. It would threaten everything she's built.

Edges's raspy drawl brings her back. "What're you drinking?"

Fen wipes her brow again.

"Nothing for me, I thank you."

"Don't be dull, boy." Edges calls all pipers *boy*. Most of them are. "You're here for a good time."

"I thought I was here to talk business."

"Maybe you're in the mood for something stronger."

He snaps a finger. When the curtain parts again, Fen thinks it's going to be a waiter. Instead, it's three girls in various shades of silver, the Quick Cuts color, each with a dark red freesia pinned to her dress.

"What's this?" Fen asks, skin prickling.

"My newest jewels," Edges says. "Aren't they fine?"

Jewels. That's what some pipers have taken to calling girls with magic, as if they're something that can be judged on clar-ity and cut. Fen heard Edges has a group of magical girls on his payroll, playing Nightbirds, kissing people for a princely sum. It's no surprise. With the secret of magical girls out, the streets have grown more dangerous for them. Some are turning to the pipers for their Watch, their protection. And in return . . . well. They pay with what they have.

But there's a thin line between exchange and coercion. The girls don't look as if they're here by force. Still, guilt squirms.

She would've offered them Watch, not long ago, without making them work for it. But the Dark Stars are spread too thin to help them. Fen can barely manage to take care of herself.

"Come here, my beauty," Graff says.

The closest girl perches on his lap, leaning in to kiss him. Fen fights the urge to touch her eyepatch, silently commanding her own power to stay down. These days, it seems to want to break free whenever another girl uses magic in her proximity. Being near them makes it hard to keep hers under control. And as it rises, a shadow comes with it. Her vision is starting to go dark at the edges. Her hands, hidden under the table, start to shake. A whip cracks through the air. One of the girls frowns, as if she hears it. There is a flutter of leaves, a stab of dread.

Blazing cats, not this.

The nightmare first came in the days after Leastnight, when she lay in a fevered stupor at Leta Tangreel's. She dreamed of the orphanage: the *snick* of the basement door, the searing pain of a lashing, Dorisall's gravelly voice in her ear. *Pain strips a tree of its leaves and shows its true strength.* Her magic leaked out as she slept, bending the iron of the bedstead and making the potted vines grow around it. When she woke up, the things were everywhere.

Did she shout in her sleep? Did she cry? She hates that Sayer saw her like that, exposed and helpless. It's one of the reasons she's avoided her since. The visions come when she's awake now, threatening to swallow her. There's only one thing that seems to keep them at bay.

Fen yanks her silver tin out of her pocket. She should be more careful with her mastic, with her witchbane supply running so low. Most of it was lost when the Underground flooded, and it's not as if she can pick up more of the rare plant at a corner store. But that whip crack is still in her ears, and those leaves are still trembling. She needs it. Her magic is dangerously alive under her skin.

She bites down and sighs, long and low. The nightmare recedes.

Edges comes up for air at last, looking at Fen. "Take your pick. I'll give you the first taste for free, for old times' sake."

It wouldn't work—girls with magic can't gift it to each other. But Edges doesn't know about that, about Fen.

"Not tonight. I'd like my wits about me."

"Ten hells, boy, I thought you'd have loosened up by now. But you're still as cold a fish as they come."

A cold fish: That's how all the bosses see her. If only they knew how much longing she keeps hidden. Sayer's face flashes through her mind, there and gone.

"Nice a time as I'm having, Edges, can we get to it?"

He sighs, shooing the girls away.

"All right, then. Have it your way." He tucks his thumbs into his suspenders. "I got a tip that someone's peddling a new alchemical. Very exclusive, very powerful. Word is it's only being sold to fancy lords."

"What's this drug do?"

"You know Hypnotic?"

Of course Fen does. Put in a drink, the potion makes someone more susceptible to suggestion. It's most often girls in clubs who are dosed with it. Fen's heard horror stories she wishes she could unhear.

Edges cracks his thick knuckles. "It's like that, I hear, but it only works on girls with magic. Word is it might let someone control their power."

Fen goes still, fighting the shudder that moves through her. "What's this drug called?"

"My informant called it Sugar."

Fen, so hot before, goes suddenly cold.

Her mind reels back, back, to a hazy afternoon at the orphanage. She was six, maybe seven, sitting in Dorisall's greenhouse. His concoctions made her nervous, but when he asked her to try this one, she did it.

What does it taste like? he asked her.

Sweet. Like sugar.

Have some more. There's a good girl.

She stares Edges down.

"Why are you so keen on this Sugar, then, Edges?"

He chuckles. "Don't shoot me daggers, boy. I don't need to drug my girls, as you saw. But if this thing is real, it's worth a fortune. More than Dust could ever be. And the last thing I need is someone moving in on my patch."

"And why send me?"

"Because I hear the Dark Stars are strapped for cash. I figure you won't mind a side hustle."

Fen leans back. "Why not get one of your boys to do it?"

"Because, much as it pains me, no one's as good a thief as you."

And as far as Edges knows, Fen doesn't deal in magic: doesn't like it. Which means she won't try to steal this drug's secrets for herself.

"I've gotten wind there's going to be some kind of exhibition," Edges says. "At the Hunt Club. Seems the dealer plans to show the drug off. I trust you can find a way to sneak in. I want as much information as you can get me. Samples, too."

Fen tries not to look too keen. "That's a big ask. It would cost you."

"I expected you'd say that." Edges takes a small sack out from under the table. "This is half of what I'm offering. You'll get the rest on delivery."

Fen opens it, counting the coins. There are a lot of them.

Edges puts out a hand. "So, do we have a bargain?"

Fen tells herself it isn't a deal with the devil. That the Dark Stars need this kind of coin. But that isn't why she says yes: not truly. If this drug is legit, she wants to know more about it. If it does what Edges says, then Dorisall must be involved. And where he goes, witchbane follows. For that, she's willing to take a risk and pay the price.

I know we Fyrebirds must hide our magic. Hunted as we are, it is the safest course. But still, I fear what doing so might make us. What our magic, once so mighty, will become. The more of my power I give away, the more it seems to shrink, growing brittle. My fire, once so easy to wield, eludes me now. And yet I continue to play the Nightbird, in hopes it will protect the girls who come after me. I hope our daughters never have to sacrifice so much.

—FROM THE LOST JOURNAL OF DELAINA DINATRIS,
ONE OF SIMTA'S FIRST NIGHTBIRDS

– CHAPTER 4 –
WING-CLIPPED

WHEN MATILDE WAKES from the dream, she smells something burning. She looks down to find she's scorched the sheets again. Outlines of her fingers mar the fine cloth, charred where she gripped them most fiercely. The dream clings to her, still, like bitter ash.

It was the same as always: half memory, half nightmare. She watches Epinine Vesten claw at her throat, breaths ragged, as she chokes on the poison Matilde planted on her mouth.

You want power? she asks.

Matilde tries to speak, but no sound comes out. In this dream, she is always rendered mute.

You would have to burn down the world for it. But they won't let you. They will not suffer a Fyrebird to rule.

Usually she watches Epinine die again, powerless to change it. But this time, the suzerain started to flicker, guttering like a flame in an unsteady wind. Her face changed, becoming Phryne, the lost girl.

Find me, she croaked. *Help me.*

She sputtered, coughing up what looked like flamemoths.

The floor was littered with their fading, blackened wings. With another flicker, the face changed again, becoming Æsa's, then Sayer's, then Fenlin's. She was forced to watch them dying. Matilde's heart burned, but her arms refused to lift toward her sisters. All she wanted was to reach out, to hold on.

Open your eyes, they choked out. *Danger is coming.*

Their gazes drifted to something over Matilde's shoulder.

Matilde, look—

Now she stares at the gauzy canopy above, trying to calm her pounding heartbeat. It was just a dream, she knows, but she can't banish the dread. Her magic is restless, too. It's slipping out more and more as she sleeps. She tries not to use it, with so many judgmental eyes upon her. But the less she lets it out, the more her power seems to stir, growing wilder. For the thousandth time, she wishes she understood it better.

Dinatris family lore says the first Nightbird in their family kept a journal. If that story is true, the thing was lost long ago. Still, Matilde used to look for trick drawers in her family's cabinets and hidden boxes behind rows of books, hoping to find it. She longed to read about Delaina's days as a Fyrebird. Now she would give anything for that kind of guiding light.

She sighs, pushing herself groggily out of bed. She has never been a morning person. Her dark robe, made of Tekan silk, feels cool against her fevered skin. She pushes open the door and goes to the family's sitting room. Everything in their Winged Palace suite is richly appointed, velvet and gauze and soft carpet. It isn't home, though. This morning, it is empty—strange, for even Samson to be up and about at this hour. At least someone's refreshed the coffee service. She goes to make herself a cup, black, drizzled with cinnamon syrup. It's hot enough to scald, but she takes a big gulp.

She walks to the balcony, its doors left open to the morning. The rising sun turns the canals and the Corners into bright veins of fire. Her city will be waking up, starting to go about its business. Soon she will have to pull on her mask and hide her frustration behind it. But for now, her mind is still on the dream, and her friends' words. Did they reach out to her in sleep somehow? Is that possible? She still doesn't know much about the bond between them, or how far it might extend.

Krastan told her that, once in a rare while, a group of four Fyrebirds used to rise, more powerful than all the others. *Dendeal*, he called them: heart tied, bound and drawn to one another. When joined, body and soul, they were powerful enough to shake the world. When she joined hands with Sayer, Fen, and Æsa in the Underground, the story felt true. She can remember the feeling of fullness, of wholeness, it gave her. It's like when the sun leaves its image on your eyelids: an imprint. Except there's no way to blink it away. It burns.

But can they really be the second coming of those Fyrebirds? What might such a power let them do? She wants to test the bond they share, to understand it. Estranged as they are, perhaps they never will.

She pushes back a wave of sadness. No sense being maudlin.

The suite's outer door opens behind her, ushering in the scent of flowers. Dennan selects them himself, every day, and sends her a bouquet. Their cloying fragrance is more than she can stand.

"Take them away," she says without turning. "I don't want them."

"Not even when I deliver them myself?"

At Dennan's voice, she whirls around. He is wearing informal attire, rumpled shirt and linen trousers, and yet he looks annoyingly composed. The morning light wraps around his lean, taut frame, gilding his dark hair: It seems to love him. Matilde finds herself far less than charmed.

"It's a little early for calls," she says, pulling her robe tighter around her. "And hardly appropriate, given my current state of undress."

"Ah, but we're betrothed now. The rules are changing."

His words make her want to snap, but she doesn't. With him, she makes sure to hold her cards close.

He sets the vase on a low table. For Simtans, flowers are a language. Estaflower and bellenum, together, propose allegiance. Thistle and donellas might as well be a slap in the face. Dennan's bouquet holds winglily, House Dinatris's flower, their petals shining out against the dark greens of House Vesten's verdabloom. He has mixed in cowslip and sweet jasmine, for dedication and affection. Are they meant to soothe her? To sway her? All they do is make her want to smash them to the floor.

"Interesting, that," she says coolly, "as I don't remember you ever asking for my hand."

He grimaces. "I was going to. But Frey thought it would be better this way."

Matilde almost drops her cup. "You . . . talked to Gran about this?"

"Your dame as well. They agreed with me that a more formal alliance between us is the best course. They also thought it would be better to surprise you. Ask forgiveness rather than permission."

Her mind is whirring. The family matriarchs pushed her to settle down with an eligible bachelor when she was a Nightbird, but that was then. Why would Gran promise her to Dennan, after she watched him murder his sister? Surely she wouldn't do it without talking to Matilde.

And yet she, Dame, and Samson are all conspicuously absent this morning, as if they knew Dennan would come to see her. And there is that thing Gran said last night. *Soon, our family will have much to celebrate.*

There is a ringing in her ears, the sound of cage doors closing. She takes a long breath and tucks her panic away. It won't do to let him see her rattled. She stayed in the Winged Palace to play him, not the other way around.

"We agreed to be done with lies and trickery," she says, making sure her voice is smooth. "I don't appreciate being maneuvered like a game piece on a board."

Dennan rubs a hand over his mouth. "Ah. You're angry."

"No," she lies. "But you should have asked me before making such a declaration."

"Would you have said yes if I had?"

She puts down her cup. Her palms have grown so hot that the coffee's starting to steam.

"Something had to be done, Matilde. The other members of the Table are pushing back against having you at the palace. They say it creates too much strife with the church."

She rolls her eyes. "Kick the Pontifex off the Table, then. As I've told you."

When the old Pontifex was exiled to the Waystrell, she dared to hope whoever took his place would be less odious, but Pater Rolo is a constant thorn in her side.

"You know I can't. We were lucky to get the last one removed from his position. But Pater Rolo has the backing of the Brethren, and the people. The city is already fractured. I'm trying to unite us, not start a civil war."

He comes closer, jewel-bright eyes fixed on her. There was

a time when she found them hard to look away from, but now they only put her on her guard.

"With a little time, I think you will see why we need this. I am doing it for you."

"Excuse me?"

"I know you want a seat at the Table. You want more power, more sway. Taking my name will give you that, Matilde. They might deny it, but the Great Houses have long married Night-birds, and they understand the practice. They respect it."

Respect? An interesting choice of word, she thinks, for *exploit*.

"It will legitimize your place here. And once we're wed, I can share my seat with you. The first suzerain did so with his wife. No Table member will be able to turn you away."

Can that be true? She balls up her hands, willing her expression to stay neutral.

"What's in it for you?" she asks. "You share your seat with me, I share my magic with you? Epinine made me a similar proposition once."

He grips the back of a chair, arms flexing. His sister's name has brought an edge to his voice.

"That isn't fair," he says. "Have I asked you even once, since Leastnight, for your magic? Have I demanded you bring the other Fyrebirds into the fold?"

No. But then, he doesn't know the kind of power that the four of them can wield together: That secret died with Epinine. She doesn't want him ever finding out.

"You haven't helped me achieve my aims, either. Prohibition still stands. The city isn't safe."

"You're right. Girls with magic aren't protected. There are

more riots, more violence between the gangs and Wardens every day." He runs a hand through his hair. "But how can I make change, with the church still shouting about the escape of the Wave Witch, and the Storm Witch wreaking havoc every night? Half the city, at least, fears or distrusts you. They believe the church's lies. But I've seen the shrine they've built to you, Matilde. There are those in this city who revere you, and many more who love me. The Vesten name has power. And if a Vesten is willing to marry a Fyrebird, then surely you cannot be evil. It will legitimize you and others like you. If we play this right, we could finally shift the tide."

His words are jewelflower nectar, trying to lure her in, but she knows better. There is always a hidden, selfish angle. Dennan only truly cares about himself.

"You say you would share your seat. But you've made me lofty promises before, Dennan. Forgive me if I'm loath to take you at your word."

"This isn't just about you and me," he says, voice rising. "Open your eyes, Matilde. Don't you see how far from solid the ground beneath us is? You seem to think my power as suzerain is assured. It isn't. Half the people who walk these halls seek to replace me. The other half are jealous, or afraid, of you. The Houses are fighting amongst themselves about whom to back, me or the church, despite the way the old Pontifex persecuted them. Even those on our side are always squabbling."

He is pacing now, before the balcony's threshold, stepping in and out of the light.

"This wedding isn't just about making a statement in Simta. It's about creating union—stability. A fractured nation is a vulnerable nation, and our rivals know it. They are watching.

Planning. I'm getting reports from our spies in foreign courts. There are whispers from the Farlands about invasion."

"But . . ." Surely not. Matilde can't begin to imagine it. "We have one of the best navies in the world. They wouldn't dare try to take us."

"Why not? We are a lucrative port city, and we have something they don't. Something many of them covet."

Matilde swallows. "Magic."

Dennan looks back out at the Corners. "Our navy is struggling, with the influx of coastal raiders and the Tekans making trouble in the north. I've had to bring some in to help quell the violence in the city. Our forces are stretched thin. Too thin. And the longer the Table bickers and our city stays divided, the more likely an invasion gets."

"How will a wedding change that?"

"It will serve as a statement and a rallying point. We will start a campaign around it. We will invite all of Eudea, and delegates from all those foreign nations, to see a Fyrebird and a Vesten unite their power. Our enemies will think twice about challenging us."

He grabs her hand, squeezing it tight.

"Think of it, Matilde. United, we could do anything. Be anything."

He is standing too close, towering over her. Matilde wants to snatch her hand away.

The door to the suite clicks open, making her jump. They both turn, expecting one of Dennan's guards or a member of her family, but there is no one. And then Matilde feels a tugging at her chest. Prickles cascade over her skin, a sudden knowing. It makes sweat break out on the back of her neck.

Dennan is frowning at the door. She squeezes his hand, making him look back at her.

"All right, Dennan. I accept your proposal, inexcusably late as it is."

A smile curls his lips. "You do?"

She doesn't want to say it. But to get him out of here, she will. "I do."

He kisses the back of her hand. "You honor me, my lady."

"Now leave me in peace. I need to dress."

At last, he goes. She closes the doors to the suite, locking them behind her, and whirls.

"Dash it, Sayer. You know I hate it when you sneak up on me."

"Yes, well." Sayer's voice floats through the room, sharp and acerbic. "I didn't want to interrupt your romantic scene."

She watches as Sayer sheds her camouflage. It's not a sudden thing: She doesn't go from invisible to visible in an instant. It's more like sand being poured back into an hourglass, or smoke taking on a tangible shape. It's a marvel to watch, no matter how many times Matilde sees it. Having Sayer here, alive and well after the nightmare, fills her with a feeling she can't name. She wants to hug her. Instead, the two of them simply stare. The last time they talked, they argued. It doesn't look like time has softened her friend's mood.

"That coffee looks good," Sayer says at last, without preamble.

Matilde tries to sound nonchalant. "Shall I make you a cup?"

"As long as you make it right." Sayer drinks the dregs of Matilde's coffee, nose wrinkling. "You could send a barge to the Farlands with how much sugar you put in yours."

"If you ask me, you could use a little sweetening."

She makes them both fresh cups. Sayer likes hers with a boatload of cream and no sugar whatsoever. If Æsa were here, she would reach for the pot of fragrant tea. How does Fen like her coffee? Black, probably, but who knows: She might harbor a secret love of sweet syrups. She's tempted to ask Sayer, but thinks better of it. Matilde has a sudden image of them all sitting in her favorite coffee shop, Astraline's, talking over the sound of tinkling cups and bubbling foam. It pulls the thread of longing tight, but it's only a fantasy. In another life, maybe it could have come true.

Sayer leans against the windowsill in a familiar way, almost feline. A cat pretending it isn't getting ready to pounce.

"I suppose I should congratulate you on your engagement."

Matilde stiffens. "How much did you hear of that conversation?"

"Most of it."

"It's rude to eavesdrop, you know. And you shouldn't creep around the palace. It's dangerous."

Sayer arches a brow. "But not for you, evidently. You seem to be making all sorts of fancy friends."

Her tone needles Matilde. Who is she to judge?

"I am trying to navigate a complex situation. Not all of us can vent our frustrations through vigilantism, running around being a flayer of men."

The lines of Sayer's lovely face harden. "At least I'm doing something to make it safe out there."

"And I'm not?"

"All I see you doing is shaking hands and throwing parties."

The words threaten to cut her. Sayer's harsh truths often do.

"I am working to change things from the inside, where the big decisions get made."

"And how's that going for you?"

"I might be having more luck if you weren't terrorizing people nightly," Matilde retorts. "Every time you choke a lord or steal from a pater, you make my task harder. You're making us look like a threat."

"They *should* see us as one," Sayer says. "It would be safer. You haven't been outside these walls in months: You don't know what it's like. Girls are so scared, they are turning to the gangs for protection, because the law gives Wardens license to hunt them down. They're being arrested—tortured. Girls are going missing."

Matilde thinks again of Phryne, lost: taken.

"Yes, I know. I am pushing the Table to address the specters."

"The girls going missing are working class. As if the Table is going to give a toss about them. You might as well spit into the wind."

Matilde's tongue tastes of ashes. Something inside her, already brittle, threatens to snap.

"You think I don't long to act like the Storm Witch? You think I want to play this game? Sometimes all I want is to set it all on fire and walk away, but this is what duty looks like. It isn't easy, Sayer."

Sayer scoffs. "I think it's easy to stay here, safe and warm, rather than get your hands dirty."

"You're wrong. And I'm tired of cleaning up your messes."

Sayer's golden eyes flash. "I'm tired of fighting for us alone."

The words hang, a scythe hovering above them. How can she say so? Why can't she see Matilde is fighting too? The look on Sayer's face makes her think of Leastnight. That night, they understood—and loved—each other. At least, she thought so. But quick as it appeared, the look is gone.

At last, Sayer speaks. "As much as I've missed our playful banter, that isn't what I came for. I've got news you should hear."

Matilde sits down on the couch, accepting the fragile truce. "What is it?"

"I infiltrated one of those new Nightbirds parties last night."

She wrinkles her nose. "Why? They sound odious."

"Because there was a magical girl in there who needed help."

Sayer relates the story of her evening: the party, the girl, the drug. Is this what Simta's young lords are getting up to? Matilde shouldn't be surprised: They think it their right, to take such magic. Just thinking of it makes her chest start to burn.

"Is she all right?" she asks. "Iona?"

Sayer nods. "I took her to Leta. She'll find a safe place for her."

"It's good you were there." Matilde wishes she had been. "And what of this drug?"

"That's just it. The client only put it in Iona's drink when he knew for sure she had magic."

"So you think it's meant for girls like us specifically."

"The client said so."

Matilde thinks of witchbane being smeared under her nose, stealing her magic. Her skin crawls. "Do you know what it was meant to do?"

"Make a girl biddable."

"What does that mean, exactly?"

"I don't know. But he said he hoped the man who gave him the stuff would become my keeper."

Keeper. The word makes her think of lion tamers at a circus, making their animals leap through hoops.

"You think it allows someone to control a girl's magic."

Sayer's mouth twists. "Control it or take it from her against her will."

But no one can take a girl's magic by force. It's one of the cardinal rules of being a Nightbird, and one of the only ones that has held true. Is it possible?

"Did he tell you who the supplier was?"

"No. Just that it cost a fortune. Things got messy before I could get a whole lot more."

Matilde blows out a breath. "I'm loath to even ask what sort of mess."

It could simply be a new drug some piper is pushing. With any luck, it is all talk and no action. If it does work, though . . .

"If it's real, Fen will know. Have you asked her about it?"

Sayer goes very still. "Not yet."

The bond between them means Matilde can't read Sayer's feelings, but she can feel them. It's an interesting cocktail of anger, hurt, and desire. Something has clearly gone awry between the two of them. She would ask, but Sayer's expression is a padlocked door.

"Given who had it, I'm thinking it's exclusive," she says. "For lords only. I hoped you might have heard something at the palace, in the course of all your wheeling and dealing."

"It's news to me." And if it truly works the way Sayer thinks, who knows what's being done with it? She thinks of the missing girls. "But we'd better find out more."

Sayer pulls a tin out of her pocket. "Leta's putting feelers out through her whisper network to see what she can find out. I'm going to talk to the Dark Stars. Then I'll take the drug to Alec, see what he can make of it."

At his name, Matilde's breath catches. Her fingers find her locket, holding it close.

"How is Alec?"

Sayer hesitates. "He's . . . fine. Surviving."

Guilt digs in its claws. With his dying breaths, Krastan asked her to take care of Alec, and she hasn't. The last time she saw him, they tore each other to shreds. He walked away, and she has been too proud to chase him. Months later, his angry words about her choice to stay still sting.

She swallows. "Is he still staying at Leta's?"

"No. He's rented a room at the Bathhouse. That's where he's working."

Matilde frowns. "He's making cocktails for thugs now?"

"Amongst other things."

The city's sandpipers have been using more sophisticated weapons in their brawls with the Wardens lately. Smoke that causes waking nightmares, powder that burns the skin. Did Alec make them?

"Things like bootleg weapons?"

"I don't know. Why don't you ask him yourself."

She says it like a dare. Matilde takes the tin from her. The yellow orb inside looks like candy, innocent and sweet.

"I will. And I'll take him the Sugar in the bargain."

Sayer's eyebrows rise. "You're ready to leave your high tower, then?"

For this, yes. She longs to finally go out into her city. To face whatever dangers a night out might bring.

We reap what we sow,
We draw in the nets,
We light fires for our fortunes,
And we settle our debts.

—AN ILLISH SONG,
POPULAR FOR SINGING AT HARVESTTIDE

– CHAPTER 5 –
SHARP BARBS

THE CROWN ATOP Æsa's red-gold hair feels heavy. It's made of dried jinny reeds woven through with three plants: ice moss, purple thistle, and sea holly. Nothing delicate survives Illan's winds and waves. Unwed girls wear the crowns at Harvesttide to celebrate their own bounty. She can almost hear what Sayer would say, if she were here: *Or marking them as ripe to pluck.* She picks up a sprig of holly from the table to weave into a new crown. It's pretty but prickly, prone to snag on clothes and fingers. Her time in Simta taught her that unassuming blades can do a surprising amount of damage. That sometimes objects—and people—are more dangerous than they seem.

She, Mam, and Jacinta are working at the edge of the freshly shorn jinny field. They always celebrate the first evening of Harvesttide on Spard Deal's farm. He has had some local lads build a dozen driftwood bonfires, ready for lighting. They will be welcome later when the night starts to grow cold. Summer has faded, giving way to colder tides, longer evenings, and air spiced with the scent of curing jinny. She usually loves the week of Harvesttide, when fishermen tie up their boats and the Isles come alive with feasts and festivity. But she is having trouble sinking into the here and now.

She looks beyond the driftwood pyres to the cliff that drops off into the ocean. The setting sun has turned the Bluebottle Sea a brooding purple. It heaves and sighs, sounding like a sucked-in breath. Rock pillars jut up out of it like sharp teeth, their sheer edges full of nesting gannets. Some dive off and plunge into the waves in search of fish. The sound they make, much like a woman's scream, disturbs some people, but not Æsa. It is one of the many notes that make up the song of home. *Illish music,* her grandda used to call it. Yet even months after returning to her homeland, she can't quite catch the rhythm of it. She knows the tune but cannot seem to sing along.

Mam nudges her shoulder. "Quit your daydreaming, daughter."

"I wasn't." The words come out more crossly than she meant. "Just . . . thinking."

"Less of that, please. We need to finish these last garlands before the fires are lit." Mam puts down her garland. "We need more thistle, I think. You two keep on."

She walks away, toward another group of women. It's good to see the color back in her cheeks. That is why Æsa went to Simta: Her family was struggling, and being a Nightbird was supposed to change their fortunes. They thought she would marry some rich Simtan lord. She didn't, of course, but Leta has continued sending a stipend just the same. An inheritance, they've told Da, left to her by one of Mam's relatives. Æsa wishes Leta would send real news as well.

She looks back to the horizon, as she does often, searching for . . . something. A naval ship full of men come to arrest her.

One sent by the Pontifex to make her answer for her crimes. But none have come. It should soothe her, yet the silence makes her fractious. It's maddening not knowing what is really going on. Mail from the south, slow before, has diminished to a trickle. No word has come from Matilde, Sayer, or Fenlin. Not one. Given how things stood when she left Simta, she didn't know where to send them letters. She directed them to Leta, who sent a cryptic note back saying that missives entering Simta are being opened and scrutinized. She hinted, too, that the church has put out a bounty out for Æsa's capture. Better she stay silent and safe.

But she cannot shake her worries about the mess she left behind, or what trouble might be coming. Her gift for seeing visions of the future, always unpredictable, seems reluctant to come when she calls. Sometimes she reaches for the bond between her and her friends, but she can never feel it. Perhaps they are all too far apart. Her magic is less powerful, too, without them. It's beginning to feel as if she dreamed lifting that naval ship up on its swell. She has honed her command of water since, practicing with the fledglings in secret, but her magic feels less deep and vast. She would have been glad to feel it dim, once—even grateful. Now it only makes her feel estranged from those girls, and from herself.

"I had another run-in with your Pater Toth at the Hollow Tree," Jacinta says, putting down her finished garland.

"He is not *my* Pater Toth." Æsa's refused to go to church since they arrived, despite Da's coaxing. She can't find it in herself to sit through sermons about magic users poisoning the Wellspring. She has no patience for his moralizing now. "What did he say?"

"He asked a lot of pointed questions."

"About?"

"Who we are. Why we came."

Æsa's pulse quickens. When she washed up with a ship full of Simtan refugees, the Illish readily accepted them, but that was before the rumors about witches rising again. They have had to be so careful. She lives in fear of one of the fledglings doing magic where someone might see.

"What did you tell him?"

"I told him precisely where he could stick his nosy beak."

She looks at Jacinta. She has gotten thinner since their time in Jawbone Prison. Her most obvious wounds from their imprisonment have healed, but it's clear the Wardens left a lingering mark.

"Perhaps you shouldn't work at the Inn so much. At least until the rumors die down."

"They aren't going to die down, Æsa. If anything, they're getting worse."

She can't deny it. Wild stories are floating up from Simta. News washes into the Illish Isles slowly, but it's usually grown tentacles by the time it arrives. It's said the Bastard Prince has made himself into a king, with the girl they call the Flame Witch enchanting him to do her bidding. Others say the so-called Storm Witch murders paters in their beds. A week ago, Da came home with a tale about the Wave Witch. *They say she made a tidal wave rise in the harbor,* he said, *and used it to drown a ship full of sailors.* Æsa wanted to tell him she didn't kill any of those men, but she couldn't. He still has no idea the Wave Witch is her.

"I end each day with one of the girls coming to me in tears," Jacinta presses. "Boys chase after them, calling them names, or trying to kiss them."

Æsa gives her a sharp look. "Have any of them shown their magic?"

"No. But we're female refugees from Simta. That is enough to earn us all strange looks and hostile glares."

Æsa sighs. "The townsfolk may talk, but they're good people. None of them would hurt us."

"You love this place too much to see it clearly."

A prick makes Æsa flinch. The sea holly's cut her finger. It's gotten caught in her skin, a sharp barb.

"We should go back," Jacinta says. "To Simta."

Æsa wipes away the blood. "We sailed out of that city to escape danger. Now you want us to sail right back in?"

"It's not as if we're safe here either."

She tamps down her frustration. "Have you forgotten what I did to get us out? We are fugitives. If we go back, the Wardens will only throw us back into Jawbone."

"A fight is coming, whether we hide or run to meet it. Simta is going to need its Fyrebirds."

She knows Jacinta has had troubling visions about Simta's future. Æsa's divining happens less these days, but she has had them too. They are murky and confused, giving her nothing to hold on to, no clear course to set.

"I know you miss home, Cin. But for me, *this* is home."

"And what about the girls you left behind?"

Matilde, Sayer, Fen, all back in Simta. But surely if they needed her to come, they would write to her. Still, guilt is a gannet, always hovering, trying to find a place to land.

"I can't just leave. What would I tell my family?"

Jacinta leans in. "You could always try the truth."

She told her mam everything when she arrived: well, most of it. Mam just held her close and said, *Don't tell your da.*

She fears he won't take it well, with the rumors and Pater Toth's increasingly fiery sermons. It hurts Æsa's heart to lie. *Then don't,* Willan says. *Trust him to love you, even if he doesn't understand you.* But every time she tries, Da says things that make her bite her tongue.

I'm glad you're out of that city, daughter, he said just last night. *I wouldn't want you exposed to such evils.* The words stung worse than a kelden jellyfish, burning as they sank into her skin.

"Go if you must," she tells Jacinta. "Say what you like. My family needs me."

"Your family needs you to be the fragile flower you were, in need of tending. You aren't that girl anymore. You are a sheldar. A Fyrebird. It's about time you remembered it."

Æsa is about to bite back when Da and Mam arrive.

"Hello, girls," Da says. "Those garlands are looking lovely. Not as beautiful as you, of course, my love."

Da presses his bearded cheek to Mam's, his red-gold hair shining out against her warm brown locks. Mam giggles. They are always like this, as if they've only just started courting.

"How are things at the harbor?" Æsa asks.

"Busy," Da says, green eyes sparkling. "You'll never guess who the tide's brought in. Enis Dale."

"Oh?" she says, heart hammering. "I thought he was in Caggen-Way."

"He's finished his training, and he's going to start at the distillery soon. He'll be running that place before you know it."

Æsa's stomach is in knots, tighter than Enis's grip on her all those months ago. *The gods mean us to be together,* he whispered in the Nightingale's room. *I know it.* Willan said he raved about it all the way back to Illan. For many months, she has worried that her magic made him mad.

"How did he seem?" she asks.

Da frowns. "Seem?"

"Was he . . ." She fumbles for words. "Healthy?"

His face clears. "Ah. Your mam told you he was sick, then, did she? He's fine now. A bit less strapping, but that's nothing a few of his mam's best stews won't fix."

She lets out a breath. Da has always had a soft spot for Enis, the boy next door. She wonders what he would think if he knew that boy attacked her.

"Is he coming tonight?"

Da smiles. "If he does, I hope you'll save a dance for him, lass. He'd make a fine beau for you."

His words make her flush, but not with pleasure.

Mam elbows him gently. "Now, Brendan. That's enough of your matchmaking."

"What? Can't a father give his daughter a nudge?"

Da has already tried nudging her away from Willan. The one time she brought him to their cottage for dinner, Da questioned him like he was wrestling a troublesome fish. Who were his parents? Where did he come from? What did he do for a crust? Willan said he was an honest trader, but Da didn't believe him. *He reeks of trouble,* Da told her afterward. *Mind you keep some distance.* If only he knew how close she and Willan are.

Da and Ma chatter on as the sun fully sets. Æsa throws herself into finishing the garlands, then goes to help set up refreshments, hoping the tasks might calm her mind. Soon the fires are lit, turning the yellow stubble of the jinny field a ruddy red. The mood gets wilder as the field fills and the sky darkens. A boy saws at his fiddle, the song fast and lilting, and people dance, full of sticky seed cakes and spiced ale.

Several of the fledglings dance around the closest fire. Kadeel, one of Willan's men, is twirling Layla, making her crown bounce wildly. She's glad the crew have lingered in Illan. The sea raiders were wary of the girls at first, but these past months they have all grown fond of each other. The men are rough around the edges, but they look out for their girls. They've even taught them how to fight with swords. They meet at a sea cave where Willan's da used to hide stolen goods and spar together. *Treat your blade as a friend,* Willan's always saying, *and eventually it'll start to feel like a piece of you.* She was hesitant, at first, but she has come to relish the lessons. It's felt good to hone her body into something harder to break.

"Dance with us!" Layla calls to Æsa.

"Not with how fast you're spinning."

Her thoughts are whirling enough without their help. *You're a good girl,* Da whispered before, kissing her forehead. But Jacinta is right: She isn't the soft girl she was, who dreamed of being a doting farmer's wife. She struggles to picture it now. She closes her eyes, imagining a cottage by the seaside where she cuts herbs and hangs them up to dry. The door opens at her back: Enis coming home from the distillery. Except when he speaks, it's someone different. Willan's voice always sets her heart to dancing.

"Have you tossed in your wishes yet?"

She turns toward him and can't help but gape. Willan is wearing a finely woven green shirt a few shades darker than his eyes, a sprig of jinny blossom pinned to it. The firelight gilds his brown skin, making his jaw seem even sharper. Impossibly handsome. She finds she cannot look away.

"Not yet. Have you?"

"Nah. It's too early. I like to wait until the fire's good and hot."

It's a Harvesttide tradition. If you write your wishes down and throw them into the fire, they say the Wellspring will grant them.

"Go on, then," he says. "What did you wish for?"

"Now, Willan. You know it's supposed to be a secret."

"Ah, but I'm king at keeping those."

"All right then. I wished for kittens and an endless supply of seed cakes."

"You're as bad a liar as you are a swordswoman."

She makes a mock-affronted face. "I've gotten much better, I thank you."

"It sounds as if you have an excellent teacher."

Their conversation flows like water, as always. The pull between them since the night they met hasn't slackened. If anything, it only seems to grow stronger. They have spent many afternoons combing the dark blue beaches and rambling the cliffs together. Sometimes they climb aboard Willan's ship, the *Tempest*, and talk about all the places they might go. He inspires her to imagine a different life, a daring future. They laugh easily, talking of everything and nothing. Sometimes they simply watch each other. He has never tried to kiss her, though, and she hasn't dared take the risk. Matilde and Sayer have kissed people without hurting them, yet still she fears it. Especially with the vision haunting her thoughts. She has had it several times, always the same: Willan kisses her, and then the scene shifts, and he is stumbling, blood on his lips, coating his chest. He is dying, and somehow it is her fault. The devastation in his eyes keeps her awake at night.

Willan is frowning, though he cannot know her thoughts. She has kept the vision from him.

"Kilventra ei'ish?"

Are you well, heart in mine? He asked her that the first night they met, when she was a Nightbird and he was the Hawk guarding her door. No more rules keep them apart, but he still feels barred to her. Wanting him feels more dangerous than before.

"I am fine," she says. "But after a dance, I might be better."

He gives her his infectious pirate's grin. "I thought you'd never ask."

He takes her hand and leads her toward the bonfire. A new dance is just starting. It's a circle dance, where couples form two rings, facing each other. The fiddler picks up the rhythm. Willan dances like he spars, ever graceful, but he throws in little leaps that have everyone giggling. She twists and spins, hair getting caught on her crown.

The dance slows, bringing Willan closer. The two lines heave forward and back like crashing waves. Their chests brush once, twice. The feeling that rises in her is always the same. A sense of . . . rightness. Mam said it was like this with Da, her apselm: an Illish term for two souls meant for each other. *It felt like fate,* Mam told her, *guiding me toward him.*

Willan's sea-green eyes are a tidal pull she can't escape.

"I've never been here for Harvesttide," he confesses. "Da and I used to leave before the summer ended."

She smiles up at him. "I am glad you're here."

His smile dims. "The crew is growing restless, kilventra. They weren't designed to hold anchor forever. I don't know how much longer I can stay."

"Oh." She looks away, telling herself it is better for him—safer. It feels as if a fishhook has gotten lodged in her chest. "When do you go, then?"

"That depends."

"On what?"

"On you."

The dance pulls them apart. Æsa feels hot, almost dizzy, her magic rising with the sudden flush. When they come together again, Willan holds her closer.

"Will you come with me?"

Her breath catches. "And go where?"

"To the Spice Isles, or the Farlands, or wherever we like."

She should tell him about the vision of his death. Perhaps then he would leave her. But try as she might, the words won't come.

"I couldn't leave without the other girls."

"I know. And I could argue that you all should come because we can protect you, but I know you no longer need a guard." He looks away, almost bashful. "No. Truth to tell, I just don't want to be without you."

His honesty almost makes her stumble, but his hand is warm and sure at her back.

"Wherever I go, I will be hunted," she says at last. "I would make you into a target. You don't want that."

"I do." His gaze is like a lighthouse, filling her vision. "But I want to know what your wish is, Æsa. What is it that you really want?"

She is full of conflicting tides. Her desire for Willan to sail away to safety crashes against her need to keep him close. She wants to stay with her family and go back to her friends, to fight with them. To be a loving daughter, an apselm, and a sheldar, all at once. But can she? She takes a breath. They've stopped dancing. Sparks fly everywhere their bodies touch.

"Willan, I—"

Someone yanks them apart.

"*You.*"

Æsa blinks, trying to get her bearings. Enis Dale is there, chin raised, three of his friends standing around him. Their mottled cheeks make her think they have had too much ale.

"I hoped I'd seen the back of you," he says to Willan, "but here you are, grasping for things that're too fine to you."

Willan's tone, laced with quiet menace, makes her shiver. "I should've dumped you in a canal and left you there."

The fledglings have stopped dancing, and two of Willan's crewmen step closer.

"Shove off, boy," Kadeel says, pulling back his coat to show his knife. "Best go home to your mammy."

"Manners," Enis says. "Though I suppose we can't expect much from pirates."

"Enis," she says. He does look thinner than last she saw him, and less fevered, but something about the gleam in his blue eyes is the same. "What do you think you're doing?"

He keeps his eyes fixed on Willan. "I wasn't just going to stand by and watch someone dance that close with my betrothed."

"Enis Dale," Æsa snaps. "We are not betrothed. How can you say so?"

He finally looks at her. Something about him is . . . hungry. Too much like the boy in the Nightingale's room.

"Don't you remember what passed between us?" Enis says. "I do, and it's the kind of thing you marry after."

His friends laugh. She fears a crowd will start to gather from around the other bonfires. It's time to stop this before it gets any worse.

"Take it back," she says. "I'm not having this, Enis."

He lowers his voice. "I think you will. Or should I go and

tell your da the whole story? I think once he hears the full tale, he will agree."

Her magic flares, tongue tasting of brine and salt and outrage. Enis still wants her magic. He will tell her da about it if she won't go along. She struggles to accept, even now, that he would do this, but she is finished making excuses for him. She is done with letting men talk over her.

"That's enough," she says, stepping between them. "Walk away, Enis. I mean it."

"You think I would ever let you have her?" Enis says. He is playing to the crowd, his voice raised. "A fine Illish girl, courting some sailor's bastard? An outsider. A *cullcaila*. As if you could ever be worthy of her."

People gasp at the slur. It seems to make something snap in Willan. Æsa stumbles as he lunges forward, shoving Enis. He recovers quickly, throwing a punch that clips Willan's jaw. He hits back, knocking Enis sideways. His friends are grappling with Willan's crew now, fists and knees and elbows flying. Æsa can't take her eyes from Willan and Enis. It's like the night they fought in the Nightingale's room, history repeating. But she's no longer the girl who cowered on that floor and waited for it to be over.

"Stop it!" she shouts, pushing between them, but neither of them heeds her. She presses her hands against their chests.

"I said *stop*."

The words roll through her bones, a humming vibration. The ocean of her magic shushes and whispers in her ears.

Without thinking, she reaches for the streams of Enis's emotions. She hasn't done this since escaping Jawbone, but it comes easily. She can feel his longing and envy and anger, braided tightly. She wraps them all around her will.

"You are ashamed of what you've said," she says, voice rippling like it does in the sea cave, echoing off its craggy walls. "Apologize to Willan."

"I'm sorry, mate." Enis can't seem to say it fast enough. "I was only having a laugh. I didn't mean it."

Enis is fully in her thrall. There is a tenuous line, she's found, between feeling and thought, thought and action. With a twist of her power, he'll do anything she asks.

"Now apologize to me," she demands, pouring shame and the desire to please into him. His lips begin to quiver, but it's Willan who speaks first.

"I'm so sorry, Æsa. Forgive me."

She turns in horror to see him dropping to his knees. His eyes are glazed, swimming with painful remorse. Oh, gods . . . did she put it there? She didn't mean to. She wants to pull him up, to take it back.

But it's too late. Enis is on his knees, too, hands up as if in prayer to her. One by one, Willan's crew and Enis's friends drop down, too. Jacinta and the fledglings are all watching, wide-eyed. She always thought she had to touch someone to mold their emotions, but it's as if she has dropped a rock into a pond, her magic rippling outward, engulfing them. These boys can't help but bow to her.

She lets go of them all just as a familiar voice comes out of the darkness.

"Daughter?"

Da emerges from the shadows, fingers shaking as they make the sign of the Eshamein.

"Cal áina sléant agalle?"

What have you done?

Enis closes his eyes as if he wants to hold on to the feeling. Willan's hand goes up to rub his chest. But Da's face is the worst, so full of horror. It is more than she can bear.

She flees, weaving quickly between bonfires. She doesn't stop until she's found the cliffs and a path to the beach, stumbling down it, toes digging into the blue-black sand. The stars form a thick ribbon above her, lighting the tips of the Three Sisters. The water wets her hem as she sucks in heaving breaths.

When she was young and upset after a bad day, Mam would take her on a walk down this beach. *Look,* she'd say, pointing at the sand. *See how the sea scrubs the marks away, making it new again? Tomorrow you will write a different story.* But the marks she has just made won't wash away; they will stain.

Jacinta was right: The girls aren't safe here. And she, an Illish daughter, no longer belongs. She takes a step into the cold night sea, another. The water rushes in, up to her knees, caressing her waist. She hasn't gone swimming since arriving back in Illan. She closes her eyes, letting her body and mind drift. All at once, she feels a tumbling. All she sees are bubbles and foam. When her vision clears, she is standing on a stage, looking out at rows of angry faces. The vaulted ceiling makes her sure she's in a church. Fen, Sayer, and Matilde are all beside her, chained together. The sight makes her heart climb up into her throat. The scene tumbles again, breaking into many pieces. One piece shows Sayer twisted up in vines, struggling to break free of them. Another shows Fenlin lying in a tangle of roots. In another, Matilde is ringed by roaring flames, her eyes both flat and hollow. Another tumbling wipes them all away.

The vision splits. She is standing on some steps, seeing a girl bound in silver, but she is also on a high place watching ships fill Simta's canals. Their crimson sails fill the city in the hundreds—thousands. They are going to burn the city down.

At last she is released, but that future won't leave her. She struggles out of the ocean, wiping her eyes. Her heart feels like it's drowning. Those crimson ships roll over her still, a dangerous tide.

She takes a shaking breath, then a step, then another. Each one makes her surer of her path. She thinks again of the future Jacinta once gave her. *You will take a winding path, but eventually it will bring you home again.* Simta, she meant. Matilde, Sayer, and Fenlin. They are the home she must return to. The family she has to protect.

PART II

TO
THE
ROOT

My dearest Nadja,

Thoughts of you consume me. I can scarcely draw breath without wanting you back in my arms. When I think of your lips on mine, I feel invincible, my little dove. Your magic thrills me. Nothing tastes as sweet as you.

Yours,
W

—AN OLD LETTER FROM YOUNG LORD WYLLO REGNIS TO YOUNG LADY NADJA SANT HELD

– CHAPTER 6 –
A BITTERSWEET TASTE

FEN'S BROKEN INTO lots of places. There's a unique satisfaction in cracking open what's supposed to be impenetrable, a thrill when a complicated lock comes apart in your hands. But she's found that getting in is usually easy. It's getting out without being caught that's the art.

She carries her tray through the dimly lit Hunt Club. Clove smoke slithers through the air, wrapping around the dozen lords assembled. It's a select group: They had to bring an invitation and flash their House rings to gain entry. The men's-only clubhouse isn't as flashy as the Liar's Club, but it's preferred by some of Simta's stuffiest lords. Everything here is buffed and lustrous. Even the glasses are etched with the club's sigil, a stag shot through with arrows. Subtle. One of the creatures rears up on a pedestal, long dead and stuffed.

Fen is wearing the blue livery of the Hunt Club, lent to her by a gambler who owes the Stars a favor. She got a set for Rankin and Hallie, too, since they refused to be left out. Olsa's on the roof, ready with a quick and dirty escape plan if they need one. Fen would've preferred to take this risk alone.

They've all used some of Alec Padano's alchemical balms to disguise themselves. Hair darkened with Four Seasons, a bit of Swift Whiskers to give Rankin and Hallie the shadow of a beard. It was overkill, she thinks: No one's looked at them closely. To people like these, a servant's about as notable as the wallpaper. Still, Fen knew her eyepatch would attract too much notice, so Alec gave her some tinted film to make her bright green eye look the same brown as the other. Eyes like hers are called 'spring-stained, and superstition holds they're a sign someone has magic. That's why, when she escaped the orphanage, she decided to hide the more distinctive one. It was disorienting at first. She'd had a hard time judging distance, and the blind spot the patch created got her into trouble in a few fights. Now it's seeing with both eyes that makes her feel off-kilter. The green one's watering, but she can't let herself rub it. The colors in the room seem too loud, despite the dim.

A reedy lordling throws his empty glass down on Fen's tray, almost tipping it.

"I tell you, it was chaos. The girl tried to kill Heath. She had him bound to a chair with just a look and a thought."

Another boy shudders. "This Storm Witch does sound rather terrifying."

"She certainly knows how to ruin a good stag."

His words are clear enough. Sayer's been causing them trouble. Fen doesn't know whether to be proud or annoyed.

"You." One of the men points at Fen. "Find me some port, will you?"

She heads to the drinks table tucked against one wall. Rankin is there, holding a silver cigarette case. Freshly turned fourteen, his gangly frame has started to fill out these past few months. With his wild brown hair ruthlessly slicked out of his face, he looks older. But it's hard for Fen to see him as anything other than the scared boy he was when they ran from the orphanage. A baby brother, truly. She wishes he'd stayed home tonight.

"What's news?" Fen asks, voice quiet.

"Not much. The gents are all frothing for the thing to start, but the way they talk makes me think they don't know a lot more about the drug than we do."

Fen gets the same feeling. She hasn't heard anyone mention either the Red Hand or witchbane. She hopes the exhibition will prove more fruitful.

"What about you?" Rankin asks. "Hear anything good?"

"Only that the Storm Witch has been ruffling some feathers."

Rankin grins, revealing the gap between his front teeth. "That's our girl."

At the other end of the room, the main doors click closed. Fen flinches. It's fine: The servants are coming and going through a discreet door tucked behind a potted plant, beside one of the many suits of ancient armor. The main entrance was never meant to be their way out. Still, that *click* never fails to make her think of Dorisall's basement. He used to lock her in there, hoping to scare whatever magic she might have to the surface. It worked: She melted a spoon and forged it into a key, that first time. She was lucky Dorisall didn't catch her at it. He suspected, though, so she never risked using magic again to get free of that prison. That click makes her think of hours trapped in the dark.

Rankin shifts from foot to foot. "Do you think Dorisall will come tonight?"

"Unlikely."

Fen can't see him willingly giving anything to these men. They aren't zealots or abstainers, so not Dorisall's crowd. He's always believed magic should be given back to the Wellspring, not parceled out to lords like party favors. Fen knows the man won't have changed his tune. Still, something deep down tells her he's tangled up in this. If she can find out how, and nab some witchbane in the bargain, all the better.

"But if things get messy, remember what I told you."

Rankin's fake beard shifts as he sets his jaw. "I'm not a kid anymore. I'm not scared of him."

A lie. "You'll do what I tell you, Rankin."

"But—"

"Keep sharp," Fen snaps. "We've got work to do."

Rankin slinks away. Fen sighs: She didn't mean to lose her temper. It's just that sweat is trickling down her back, soaking her shirt, and her fingers are trembling. She's working without any mastic tonight. She only has one piece left, which she's saving for when she truly needs it. Maybe that's why she feels the sudden, familiar catch, like a key slotting into its keyhole. The feeling snags on her ribs and *pulls*.

Blazing cats, Sayer.

What in the ten hells is she doing here?

Head down, steps measured—nothing to see here—Fen carries her tray back toward the man who wanted port, surreptitiously studying the room again. There's no sign of Sayer, but then, you don't see the Storm Witch unless she wants you to. But Fen has made a habit of finding Sayer, of drinking her in when her gaze is turned elsewhere. There, on one of the wrought-iron staircases that spiral up to the library's second floor, something twists through the air, disturbing the clove smoke. The outlines of a shadow girl.

They met years ago, at Twice Lit coffee shop's back door, but Fen first saw Sayer maybe a year before that, at a night market. She was an accomplished thief by then, and made a habit of assessing everybody as a potential target. Something about the way she moved caught Fen's attention. It was held by the blaze of her honey-gold eyes. The long line of her neck, her graceful steps: Fen couldn't look away from her. And then she heard Sayer laugh at something a vendor said. That sound, like liquid light: She wanted to thieve it. Since then, Fen's often longed to steal a kiss from her . . . maybe a heart.

Let her skulk, Fen thinks as she edges toward the stairwell.

Leave her be, she tells herself as she creeps, hoping the lords won't see.

The stairs let out onto a carpeted balcony that rings the room, hemmed in by a wrought-iron balustrade lined with potted night vines. The glass-dome ceiling arches some ten feet above them in panes of muted olive green. Narrow paths lead off the balcony like the spokes of a wheel, each lined with bookshelves. Fen can see the heads of all the lords milling below. If they look up, they'll see her hovering. At least no one's lit any lanterns up here, keeping it in shadow. She's about to risk whispering Sayer's name when a hand grips her, tugging her down one of the paths.

"Fen," Sayer whispers. "Took you long enough."

Fen pulls out of her hold. "What are you doing here?"

"Same thing as you, I expect."

Sayer drops enough of her camouflage that Fen can see her dark bob, her slender neck, her dark grey mask. Her lips, too. Fen drinks in every detail, hungry for them. Knowing she can't get too close.

"What's that, then?"

"Don't play coy. Hallie told me about the exhibition. Did you really think I was going to sit this one out?"

Fen looks away. "She shouldn't have done that."

"Why not? The Stars still trust me, even if you don't."

The words cut into Fen, but she won't show it. She can't lose her focus now.

"Why didn't you tell me?" Sayer presses. "We could've planned this together."

"Because your plans tend to leave a mess behind, and I can't afford one."

A flash of something like pain. Fen steels herself against it.

"Anyway, my exit doesn't require any magic. Yours does, and I think they might have witchbane. This is dangerous."

She smiles. "Haven't you heard? I'm the most dangerous thing here."

Fen shouldn't find the words so dashed alluring. She wants to lean in. She needs Sayer to go.

"I've got this covered," Fen says. "Sneak out down the servants' hall when the thing starts and everyone's distracted. I'll find you after."

"Forgive me if I don't believe you."

The things Fen said to Sayer on Leastnight hover, ghostlike, between them. *I'll always find you. You're my shadow.* It was the most honest thing she'd ever said. But she can't let anyone all the way in, even Sayer. *Especially* Sayer. She steals too much of Fen's control.

"I'll consider doing as you say," Sayer says. "If you tell me why you've been avoiding me."

It's not avoiding. It is more like . . . abstaining. Knowing she will get addicted if she doesn't.

"I've been busy. The Stars need my full attention. It's not personal."

Sayer steps close, forcing Fen back against the bookshelf.

"Liar."

They're almost chest to chest, touching in too many places. Her closeness is drugging Fen's senses. All girls with magic make Fen's own harder to keep down, but this is different. Sayer's power feels like roots forcing their way beneath the armor she spent years crafting, threatening to rip it all away. A part of her wants to give in, to let go. But feelings—and magic—always cost her something. There is always some price to be paid.

And here it comes. Leaves shimmer at the corners of her eyes, the lights dimming. She hears the crack of Dorisall's whip. *Little thief,* he whispers. *You cannot hide from me. I see you.*

The nightmare is trying to swallow her whole.

She squeezes her eyes shut.

"Fen? What's wrong?"

Sayer's voice is soft. Fen can't take it. She pulls her silver tin out of her coat. The mastic is as rank as always, but nothing has ever tasted sweeter. The nightmare recedes, the darkness is banished. She takes a grateful, unsteady breath.

There is a pause, taut and trembling. Fen makes herself open her eyes and weather Sayer's horror.

"Tell me you aren't still using that poison."

This is another reason she's avoided Sayer. Fen knew she wouldn't understand. She hates this feeling creeping up the back of her neck, heavy with shame.

Someone below claps their hands, making them both start. Fen turns toward the room below, creeping closer to the balustrade; the lords have formed a loose circle around someone. Fen can't see his face at first: just his velvet suit coat and a head of slicked-back hair that's gone silver at the temples. He turns like a magician keen to show there's nothing hidden up his sleeves.

"Welcome, friends," he says. "Thank you for joining me this evening."

"No," Sayer whispers. "It can't be."

But they both know Wyllo Regnis on sight.

SAYER CAN'T LOOK at her sire's face. Instead, she looks at his hands, soft and manicured. A lord's hands, unused to toil. The first time she saw them was around her dame, pulling her close as he kissed her against the wall of their rooms above the silversmith's. She didn't know he was her sire then—just some man greedy for the last dregs of Dame's magic. He tried to steal Sayer's too, not long ago.

Fen rescued her that night. Wyllo was caged, but not vanquished. She vowed she would ruin him once and for all. She hasn't found a way to do it that won't also hurt the Regnis women, who don't deserve to go down with him, but she's used her gifts to chip away at his strength. The Storm Witch has stolen notes and ledgers, compromised his deals and investments. She even burned down one of his warehouses in Dragon Quarter.

Leave him be, Leta warned. *A cornered wolf makes desperate choices.*

But she wanted Wyllo Regnis looking over his shoulder, knowing the shadows held knives and a girl who wasn't afraid to use them. She thought she had him cowed. She should've known he was just sharpening his claws.

He smiles at the crowd. "In coming here, you have all been made certain promises. Let me assure you that those promises were good. I do, indeed, have something very special to show you. It is something new, and very powerful. Unlike any alchemical you will find in our streets."

That prompts a wave of whispers amongst the men.

"I'm surprised, Wyllo," a round-bellied man says. "I thought you were an abstainer."

Wyllo nods, the movement slow. "I am, in most cases. I do not believe a man should have to turn to magic for his fun or his fortunes. But I also believe in protecting our investments. The Great Houses cannot afford to lose the fortunes we have built."

His eyes are bright, full of promise. His voice takes on a storytelling lilt.

"Centuries ago, the last of the Fyrebirds came to Simta. The Great Houses chose to take them in when no one else would. We gave them everything: care, shelter, respectability. The Nightbirds system was created to nurture and protect them. Over the years, we shaped their power at great personal cost."

Cost? Please. The Houses only earned through that system. It's the girls within it who ended up having to pay.

"And now that system is broken, its secrets laid bare. We lords are accused of hoarding what doesn't belong to us. Matilde Dinatris says the magic in our bloodlines isn't really ours, despite the role we played in protecting it. We are told it is a crime to ask for a Nightbird's magic, when really it is ours by rights."

Several men make angry noises. Sayer grips the railing hard.

"The church preaches that magic is holy, and they are right, of course. It should not be used carelessly or lightly. That is why the Nightbirds system worked so well. Girls like that cannot be trusted with such power. It is not their fault; they are too weak to wield it properly. We have seen proof of what happens when Nightbirds are left to themselves. The so-called Flower Witch caused mayhem in the streets of Phoenix

Quarter. The Wave Witch broke out of jail and destroyed a naval ship. Matilde Dinatris has bewitched our suzerain, doing untold damage to our Republic in the process. And I have it on good authority she is responsible for Teneriffe Maylon's addled state."

More outraged noises. Wyllo lays his points down like krellen cards, showing his friends a winning hand.

"And the Storm Witch," he growls. "There is no end to her depravity. She spends her nights terrorizing paters and stalking self-respecting men with impunity."

A malevolent ripple moves through the crowd.

"The truth they don't want to admit is that such girls cannot control their power. They require a tight rein, a firm hand. They *need* us to guide them. Tonight, I have brought you a means by which to do just that."

Fen has gone completely still. Sayer finds she can't move either. Wyllo's words are venom seeping through her skin.

"This," Wyllo says, taking something from his pocket, "is Sugar."

He holds up what looks like a piece of yellow candy, just like the one Sayer took from the stag party.

"We know a Nightbird's magic can't be taken from her. It can only be given. But Sugar makes her compelled to give it to you. Or you can simply beckon her to do with it as you will."

Fevered whispers erupt, men elbowing each other.

"It will dissolve in any liquid. It's sweet, but otherwise untraceable. Once she's drunk it, you must be the first person to speak to the girl. In doing so, you will become her keeper."

Keeper. It's the word the client at the stag party spat at her. A word that means utter control.

"How long does it last?" a lord shouts.

88

"One dose will last up to a day."

More excited whispers.

"Must you stay close to the girl?" someone asks. "To keep your hold on her?"

"Proximity is no matter. She will stay under your sway for as long as the Sugar lasts. You can send her away with your words in her ears, your purpose. No one will be able to dissuade her."

Another voice, tinted with doubt: "But does it hurt them?"

"Oh no," Wyllo assures him. "It will leave them with a headache, just like any good bootleg cocktail, but I'm told the sensation is pleasant. The girls enjoy being led."

The lords drink in his words, nodding to each other. Their eagerness gives Sayer the crawls.

"Forgive me, Wyllo," a balding man says. "But this all sounds rather outlandish. I have never heard of any alchemical with such a power. Where is your proof?"

Wyllo flashes his white teeth. Then he goes to the door, beckoning to someone behind it. A girl walks out on his arm, steps uncertain. Sayer's stomach swoops like a plummeting bird.

Fen leans close. "You know her?"

"Yes." She swallows once, twice, bile rising. "Her name's Jolena."

The girl she promised to look out for, to protect.

Sayer has snuck into the Regnis house many times to check on her half sister. At first it was mostly to satisfy her curiosity, but despite herself, Sayer quickly found herself charmed. They sit on the roof outside her bedroom and talk into the wee hours. They have little in common, but never run out of things to say. At fourteen, Jolena is sheltered, but funny, curious, and guileless. Her eyes are a window into her heart. They always light up on seeing Sayer, even though she doesn't know the blood they share. Now, though, she is wringing her hands, clearly anxious. She looks so small amongst the men. So alone.

"*Your* daughter?" one of the men says. "She has magic?"

"Yes," Wyllo says, looking solemn. "A recent revelation."

But how did he find out? Sayer made Jolena promise never to do her earth magic at home, where he might see her. She should have taken the girl out of that place.

"In bringing her here, I hope to reassure you of Sugar's uses and its safety. You all know that I would never give my daughter something that might do her harm."

What flotsam. Sayer knows all too well the harm Wyllo is capable of doing to his daughters. But then, unlike her, Jolena is the family he chose.

"I think one of us should be the keeper," the balding man says, stepping forward. "The girl is already likely to follow your lead, Wyllo. We need someone she doesn't feel beholden to."

The lordling standing next to him raises his hand, fast and eager. "I can do it."

"Very well," Wyllo says, gesturing him forward. "Come, Owen."

Owen steps out of the crowd. With a jolt, she recognizes his awful goatee. It's Hedge Maze, the boy who tried to corner her at the stag party. The thought of him having any control over Jolena makes Sayer want to pin him to the wall all over again.

Wyllo hands Jolena the cup. She stares down at it, hands shaking.

"Drink up, child," Wyllo commands.

Sayer takes a step, ready to fight, but Fen stops her. She slowly mouths the words *Not yet.*

Wyllo and Owen have a quick whispered exchange. Jolena drinks. The men all watch, spellbound, as she puts the cup down, swaying slightly. Her eyes are glassy. The room is a collectively held breath.

"Heed me," Owen says.

Jolena's hands clasp together like an eager pupil.

"Yes, my lord."

Her voice still sounds like hers, but it is sanded at the edges. Almost flattened.

"Tell me, young miss," Owen says. "What is your magic?"

"I can talk with growing things. Plants, flowers. They respond to me. They listen."

"Give us a demonstration."

Jolena lifts a hand, and the potted night vines around the balcony start moving. As the men turn to look up, Fen pulls Sayer back and out of view. But she can still see how the vines stretch, growing so fast she can hear shoots splitting off from main stalks, almost snapping as they race for the floor below. She has seen Jolena coax plants into growing, but never like this: so many at once, blooming so fast it's almost violent. Is it because she and Fen are here, amplifying her magic? Or is the Sugar making her power more potent than before?

The vines have reached the ground floor now. Some have grown as thick as an arm, slithering between the men's polished wingtips. Owen looks drunk and giddy on his power.

"Use one of them to trap that server," he tells Jolena. "That one there."

One of the vines shoots out, wrapping its way up the body of the server standing closest. Sayer squints, looking past his scruffy beard. Is that—?

"Oy," Rankin says, struggling to free himself. "That's enough of that. Leave off."

Owen acts as if he doesn't hear. "Squeeze him."

The vine constricts. Rankin gasps as it presses down against his windpipe and presses in against his ribs. Beside her, Fen spits out her mastic. Sayer is spellbound by the scene. She can't tell if Jolena is disturbed by, or even understands, what she is doing. Her face, usually so emotive, is a blank page waiting for someone else's ink.

Sayer is about to intervene when Owen commands Jolena to release Rankin. He backs away, wheezing. The room is stunned to silence. At last, someone speaks.

"How much?"

Wyllo smiles. "All I ask is fifty andels and your absolute discretion."

A blinding sum, but still, hands fly up.

"How many do you have?" someone asks.

Wyllo pulls out a long box, the kind that might hold chocolates.

"One piece of Sugar per man."

The balding man frowns. "One each? Is that all?"

"Patience, my lords. The drug's chief ingredient is difficult to get out of the Callistan, and just as hard to smuggle onto our shores. But a shipment will be heading toward us soon. Rest assured, we will have more Sugar by Risentide. Just in time to celebrate our suzerain's special day."

The men are reaching for their wallets, loud and eager. They see nothing wrong with robbing girls of their will and their choices. Of course they want to drug Simta's daughters and steal their light.

Sayer's fury spills over, tasting of lightning. The shadows in the club start to deepen and stretch. The air changes, and a sudden wind knocks a decanter off its table. Men startle as it shatters. She wants to asphyxiate every dashed one of them.

Sayer concentrates on the feel of the air, trying to change it. Dropping the pressure in a room is a complex bit of magic, and she has never done it on this scale before. She needs more power . . . more.

"Fen." Sayer holds out her hand. "I need you."

Fen shakes her head. "Sayer, I can't . . ."

"Please."

After a beat, she takes Sayer's hand in her clammy one. Sayer hasn't done this with Fen, Matilde, or Æsa since they joined in the Underground. The feeling is the same: a tingling, an echo, a rush. Inside her, storm winds blow through leaves as their magic weaves together. It stretches as if waking from a long, troubled sleep.

When she goes to drop the pressure this time, it happens quickly. She creates small bubbles of air around Jolena, Rankin, and Hallie, carving out pockets of normal air for them. The rest she has no problem bringing to their knees. Several men double over, shaking and coughing. One throws up noisily into an ice bucket. She keeps going until most of the men are unconscious, sprawled like dolls across the floor. It's only then she makes a run for the stairs.

Tig, she hears Fen say. Her invisibility has faded, she knows, but her mask is on, and staying hidden doesn't matter. All that matters is getting Jolena away from their sire.

"Jolena?"

The girl looks up as Sayer touches her cheek.

"Sayer."

She lets out a relieved breath. "Yes. Come with me now. Quickly."

Jolena's eyebrows crease. "I don't know . . . I . . . ."

There's no time for gentleness. They have to get out of here. She pulls Jolena toward the servants' door, limp and slow-footed. No one stops them. But then she hears three choked, angry words.

"You will *stay*."

Owen's voice makes Jolena yank back so suddenly that Sayer lets go of her.

"Trap her!" he wheezes, high pitched. "Contain the Storm Witch."

Sayer takes a step, but something trips her. She falls hard, banging her head, only to be yanked upright by one of the vines. It moves so fast, twining up her legs, her torso. She slashes at it with her knife, but it's too quick. Her arms are pinned.

She looks wildly around. Hallie and Rankin run toward her, but several of the lords grab and subdue them. The vine is cutting off her air, her magic, her thoughts.

"Jolena," Sayer pleads. "Come on. You can fight this."

No response. Sayer's hold on the air pressure loosens. She tries to bring it back, but her head is still throbbing. She's so dizzy. Her magic feels as bound up as she is.

The men are starting to come to. Wyllo is up already, smoothing his rumpled jacket. He pulls a jar out of the breast pocket. She knows what it contains: She can already smell it. But she can't stop him from smearing the witchbane paste under her nose.

"You've overplayed your hand," he says, leaning in close. "And now you'll pay for it."

The horror of his words steals her voice. She is helpless. This feels like Leastnight all over again.

"Gentlemen," Wyllo says, turning back to the crowd. "I think it's time we find out the true identity of the Storm Witch. Wouldn't you agree?"

A round of croaky cheers. Sayer writhes, panic threatening. He reaches up to pull her mask away.

Before he can, there is a mighty clang as something shiny crashes into Wyllo, knocking him sideways. It takes Sayer a moment to understand what she is seeing: It's one of the suits of armor come to life. Wyllo rolls out of the way, cursing, as it brings its sword down over him. All around her, suits of armor lurch away from the walls. They lunge for the lords, swinging their morning stars and maces, pushing them back toward the edges of the room. Men throw glassware, which only shatter or bounce off their breastplates. The stuffed stag is knocked off its pedestal, toppling Owen. Rankin and Hallie cut her vine away. Sayer wipes the witchbane off her face, but her magic is still muted. Jolena is staring at them all, clearly lost.

"Sayer," Hallie says over the din. "Are you doing this?"

"No." She's only seen one person command metal on this scale. Sayer finds Fen still on the balcony, face sweat-streaked, eyes wild.

"Blow the whistle!" she shouts.

Hallie fumbles out a whistle and blows it. A hatch in the glass dome above them opens, revealing Olsa's bulky form. A rope unfurls from the hatch, and Hallie gestures Sayer toward it. She looks back at her sire on the floor. The suit of armor has a knee pressed to his chest, keeping him pinned there. The box of Sugar is still clenched in his hand. Sayer goes to him and peels his fingers back until he drops it, swearing.

"I'm taking Jolena too."

"Don't you dare," he spits. "She is *mine*."

Sayer bares her teeth. "We both know you don't deserve her."

Behind her, something shatters, and a black cloud rolls out around them: Nightcloak. It fills the room like dark, impenetrable ink. Sayer stands, head swimming: Where are her friends? How will she find them? But then she feels Fen stepping close. She tugs Sayer one step, two, through the darkness.

"Jolena?" Sayer gasps.

"We've got her," Rankin shouts. "But she's fighting us."

Sayer reaches for her flailing sister.

"Don't stand here like stunned mullets," Fen pants. "Climb the rope."

"No!" Jolena shouts.

How is Sayer going to get her out of here?

"Just go," Fen says, close to Sayer's ear. "I've got her."

"But how—"

"Trust me and *move*."

Sayer does, climbing hand over hand up through the Nightcloak, away from the chaos and the sound of Wyllo bellowing Jolena's name.

When she swings, I hear that music.
When she laughs, I feel that beat.
When we kiss, I feel that magic,
thrumming from my lips down to my feet.

—"MAGICAL GIRL,"
A NEW SIMTAN JAZZ SONG

– CHAPTER 7 –
MADE OF FLAMES

IT WAS EASY, in the end, for Matilde to leave the palace unnoticed. Sneaking out is rather a breeze when you can wear a face that isn't yours. She hasn't used this trick in months, but changing her appearance to look like someone else came without effort. She took the guise of one of her maids: the one with the pert nose, wild curls, and smattering of freckles. She was half tempted to walk out into the streets as herself. Maybe doing so would dare one of the so-called specters to try to abduct her. Let them try and see how far they get.

She strides down a street lit with green lanterns, her cocoon coat pulled in tight. She's been through Griffin's before—her carriage has passed through this Quarter to get to the Neck, the strip of land that connects Simta to the mainland—but only ever once on foot. It feels quiet. There are no street bands wailing on corners and hawkers selling sweet citrine. She wonders if it's because of the Wardens. They hover in clusters, sticking out in their uniforms emblazoned with the upturned cup. Some have their Saluki dogs, which Matilde makes sure to steer well clear of. Luckily, they don't seem able to scent intrinsic magic unless they get up close.

These streets felt different on the night she and Petra snuck out and came to Griffin's. They'd heard from their brothers about the high times one could have in the Green Light District, and they wanted to see what all the fuss was about. It was everything she'd imagined: roguish pipers, street musicians, loud laughter. They wandered into the first club they found and danced as if no one could see. They'd only been there for an hour before they were dragged home by a Dinatris footman. The evening caused one of her and Gran's biggest rows.

But that was nothing compared with their argument this afternoon about the engagement. She still can't believe how unrepentant Gran was. *You think your magic is enough to protect you?* she said. *You forget that it will leave you, eventually. You won't be like this forever. But tied to a Vesten, who is also the suzerain, you will always be strong. And so will we.*

Matilde railed against being forced into a corner. She can't forget Gran's parting shot.

It's time to grow up. Sometimes duty is sacrifice. For women like us, duty comes first.

She has a duty to her family: She knows that. But she has a duty to the girls of Simta too. She hasn't done enough to keep them safe from those who seek to harm them. If she can save them from this new drug, then she must.

She passes one club, two, wending her way to the door she is seeking. It's carved with wings and an eleven-pointed star. The Bathhouse is currently one of the most exclusive clubs in the Green Light, catering to lords and ladies who like a splash of danger and have money to burn. With a small sack of coins and a sweet smile for the doorman, she is ushered down a long, dimly lit hallway. Another takes her coat, revealing a dark velvet gown dripping with tassels. She may not look like herself, but she always dresses to impress. He leads her to a door that looks like the entrance to either a bunker or a storage cupboard. It swings wide, and she blinks against the dark.

The Bathhouse was designed for communal bathing, once upon a time. The main pool cuts right down its middle, orb-lights floating on its surface. Their light catches on the mosaics stretching up the pool's columns, making the mirror shards embedded in them shine. Revelers mill at the pool's edge, dipping toes in as they sip at their cocktails, while others dance up on the second-floor balcony that rings it. Looking up, she sees a dark-glass ceiling turned inky by the evening sky. But her gaze snags on the bar at the far end of the balcony. A barkeep works behind it, grinding herbs and pouring libations. For a moment all she can do is stare, transfixed.

Move, she tells her feet, stuck to the slick tiles. *It's just Alec.*

But seeing him like this, after so long, shakes her more than expected. Her heart seems to want to break free of her chest.

At last, she climbs one of the sets of stairs to the second floor. The bar offers one empty stool, which she slides onto. Alec has his elbows on the bar top, leaning in to talk to another patron. At least it gives her the opportunity to give him a good once-over. His pale blue shirt is fine, sleeves rolled up to his elbows, thin suspenders hugging his lean frame. His jaw is working as he chews what she assumes are frennet leaves. His curls have been cut short and slicked ruthlessly back. It makes him look different: Sharper. Warier. The way he works is the same, though, intense and careful. His forearms flex as he squeezes half a gulla fruit. The familiar sight makes heat dance across her skin.

At last, he turns her way. He won't recognize her: not with this face on. But looking at him, she feels exposed all the same.

"Pleasant evening," he says, grabbing a clean shaker. "What'll it be?"

The band playing in the corner is loud, but she still hears him crack one of his knuckles: an old habit. It takes her a moment to find her stolen voice.

"Something unique," she says. "I'm feeling experimental."

He nods. "Alcoholic or alchemical? The latter's scarce just now, so it'll cost you triple."

"You look like an inventive soul. Surprise me."

The corner of his mouth quirks. "That's brave, on so slim an acquaintance."

"You and I have always liked living dangerously."

He goes still at the words, a familiar jab between them. His dark, close-set eyes seem to burn. She doesn't want to have to announce herself; she wants him to see past her falsehood. To cut through the disguise and know it's her.

But then he turns, walking away.

Disappointment stings. Of course he didn't see her. But then he says something in the other barkeep's ear and slips out from behind the bar, coming toward her. He takes her hand, tugging her off the stool. "Come with me."

She follows without protest as he leads her through the crowd, around a corner. He pulls her into an alcove, shielded from general view. She assumes this must once have been a changing room. There are murals here, too, blue waves flecked with shards of mirror. The air is warm and strangely charged.

Alec drops her hand and steps back, staring. His posture is adamantine. He's holding himself like the figurehead of a ship.

"Tilde," he says at last.

Relief floods her at the pet name. But then he adds, "You shouldn't be here."

His accusatory tone raises her hackles. The speech she rehearsed all afternoon flies away.

"It's nice to see you too, Alec. I'm well, thank you for asking."

"I mean it. The streets are crawling with Wardens. I'm surprised the Bastard Prince let you out."

A defiant hand goes to her hip. "I am no pet. He doesn't own me."

"Really?" Alec crosses his arms. "Could've fooled me."

Her breath catches. Has news of the engagement reached him already? If so, he doesn't seem ready to say.

"And you? Talk about owned. I never thought I'd see you selling your skills in a place like this."

He shoves his hands in his pockets. "After the shop burned down, I didn't have a lot of choices."

The mention of the fire makes her pause, but she finds she has to say it. The wound is right there, begging to be pressed.

"You should open your own shop," she says. "It's what Krastan would have wanted."

"With what supplies?" he snaps. "And what money? I lost everything in that fire. *Everything.*"

His words fill the small space, sharp and accusing. Full of the hurt they both share.

"Dash it, Alec. I didn't come here for a fight."

"Then why did you?"

She should explain about the Sugar before this chat sours any further, but when she opens her mouth, that is not what comes out.

"I wanted to see you," she says. "We have never gone this

long without talking, you know. There's been no one around to remind me I'm not as special as I think."

He does not respond to the quip. She itches to muss his sad little curls and shake the reserve away. Instead she hits him with another, dearer truth.

"I wanted to spend an evening with someone who truly sees me," she says. "Sometimes it feels like you're the only one who ever has."

Her cheeks heat, but the words seem to knock the stiffness from him. The mirrors on the walls throw pinpricks of light over his face.

"How am I supposed to stay mad when you say something like that?"

She smiles. "You can't, I'm afraid. So you might as well have a drink with me."

"If I do, will you promise not to get me into any mischief?"

"Of course not. I have a reputation to uphold."

He heaves a dramatic sigh. "All right, then. One drink."

Just like that, he is her friend again. She lets out a breath as something inside her unspools.

He leads her back to the bar and convinces the other barkeep to cover for him. He makes them some searingly strong cocktails that go straight to her head. At first, they simply watch the crowd, making up stories about the people on the dance floor. The music is jumping, tempting her to join in. She should open the false bottom of her purse and take the Sugar out. But they have all night, and this fragile truce feels precious; she doesn't want to break it. She wants just one free hour with him, one dance.

She puts her empty glass down. "Dance with me."

He winces. "You know I'm just going to step on your toes, don't you?"

"Not if you let me lead."

She pulls him out into the sea of dancers. The brass band is playing something slow now, the singer's voice turning sultry and sweet. Matilde starts to sway, pulling Alec into her rhythm. This is how she first taught him to dance. She used to turn him around Krastan's shop, trying to show him how to make a frame for a partner. He often accused her of stealing the lead. He takes it now, though, pulling her closer. Time passes in a wild, delicious slide. How long has it been since she felt this unfettered? She is drunk on the feeling of acting without a sea of eyes watching and judging. No one knows who she is except for him. She tips back her head, letting the light play across her eyelids. When she looks at Alec again, he's looking back.

"I'm sorry for what I said on Leastnight," he says.

She looks away. "I can barely recall it."

A lie, of course. She could never forget his words about her decision to stay at the palace. *Krastan would shudder to see you play a Vesten's whore.*

"It wasn't right. I should never have said it."

She swallows. "We both said things we didn't mean."

They take a few more turns in silence.

"I was angry that night," Alec goes on. "Maybe I still am. But I've missed you, Tilde. Every day."

He pulls her closer. For a heartbeat, she thinks he might kiss her. Then he sees something over her shoulder that makes him freeze.

"Blazing cats and dash it *all*."

He takes her hand and tugs her through the swaying crowd of dancers. She stumbles just a little in her heels.

"What's wrong?"

"Nothing. Just don't look back. Tilde, you're *looking*."

What she sees is a bullish-looking boy in a blue-green vest prowling the dance floor. He has the thuggish mien and floral lapel pin of a piper. She sees a flash of something that looks like a dark metal tooth.

"What does he want with you?"

Alec hurries her toward a set of trellis stairs. He's gone up two when he swears again, catching sight of something he doesn't like coming down them.

"*Alec*," she insists. "Tell me."

"It's . . ." He's sweating now. "Gwellyn Mane, the Kraken boss's second. I owe him something. I don't want his boys to find me. Or you."

She blinks hard. Nothing sobers like the need for subterfuge. Matilde looks around, assessing the situation, taking in the settee in the darkness under the stairs. Pieces of past revelers' outfits dangle over it, hung up on the steps, creating a kind of scandalous curtain.

"Just follow my lead," she whispers, tugging him toward it. She pushes him down, hiking up her velvet skirt. A stockinged knee lands on either side of his lap as she straddles him.

"Tilde," he chokes out. "What in the ten hells are you *doing*?"

She grabs a top hat from the dangling wardrobe and pulls it over his shorn curls. "Alec. Stop talking."

She leans forward and captures his lips. There is a moment of stillness. Then he relaxes, lips parting. The kiss is like a long, perfect exhale.

The last time they kissed was in Krastan's shop, brief and searing. She has thought about it almost every night since.

What would it be like, to kiss him without the world burning around them? Would it feel as good as she has dreamed? Yes. Better. He tastes like frennet, sweet and fresh. She wants to devour him.

"Put your hands on me," she whispers.

He kisses like he brews, with complete and utter focus. His spellworker's hands travel from her shoulders to her hips, clever and sure. As he grips a hip bone through the velvet, she trembles. She finds herself stifling a very real moan. Her magic rises, wanting to pour into him. She has to concentrate to keep it down, and her disguise in place.

The Kraken boys clomp down the stairs right above them. She presses into Alec, curling over and around him, hoping her body and the hat will hide his face.

"He's not in his room?" someone calls, voice gruff.

"Nah, Gwell," one of the boys above them answers. "He's nowhere."

Gwellyn swears. "He's supposed to be behind the bar."

Matilde clutches Alec's neck. Why are they hovering?

"Oh, Peter," she says, breathy, but loud enough for them to hear. "That's it. Higher. Yes, *higher*."

Behind them, Gwellyn chuckles. "Ten hells, get a room."

Then they're off. Matilde keeps kissing Alec anyway, for good measure. She finds she doesn't want to stop.

When he pulls back, his dark eyes have grown impossibly darker.

"I think they're gone," he whispers, voice a little ragged. "I can't believe that worked."

"Of course it did," she says, breathless herself. "You're welcome."

He clears his throat. "They might hang around. We'd better make ourselves scarce."

They head up the stairs, which leads onto a flat expanse of roof. Matilde touches the glass dome, through which she can see the pool far below. Alec doesn't say a word as he leads her past what looks like a greenhouse and to the door of a free-standing shed. Inside, the space is neat as a pin, like his old room at Krastan's. It features a narrow bed, a few lanterns, one chest of drawers. The room feels bare, with so little in it. Krastan's shop was full of jars and feathers, bones and gems: of life.

She lets her glamour fall. Letting a visage go always makes her skin burn like it's being taken to with a hard sponge. With Alec watching, it feels more like being undressed.

She presses her back to the door. "What are Kraken boys hunting you down for?"

He blows out a breath, mussing his hair.

"I've been doing some alchemical work for them, here and there. Moonlighting."

Suspicion rises. "Tell me you haven't been making them weapons."

Alec's jaw sets. "I can't control what they do with what I make them. But if they're using it to push back against the Wardens, I'm all for it."

"Alec."

Krastan refused to work for the gangs. Even if they paid well, he said, they were crooked. He would hate this.

"What? You're the one who said I should open my own shop," he says, pacing the floor. "I can't do that without money, and I'll never get there on the wage this place pays. Getting ingredients has gotten even more expensive. Working for the pipers is the only way I get access to most of them. Do you know how hard it is to get frennet right now?"

The plant he needs to manage his sugar disease; he would die without it. But even so . . .

"It's the only way I can help Sayer," he goes on. "And what's left of the Underground. They need my skills."

"It's too dangerous, Alec."

"So is everything worth doing. I'm not afraid to take some risks for what's right."

The words sting, though she doesn't think he meant them to.

"If you needed help, you could've come to me."

His jaw ticks. "I don't need charity."

"It isn't charity, Alec. It's family."

"I don't have any family. Not anymore."

A lump rises in her throat. She cannot swallow past it. Krastan hovers between them, as real as any ghost.

"You're better than this," she says, fingers finding the chain of her locket. "Better than them."

He sighs. "What do you want from me, Tilde?"

She takes a breath. She should tell him why she really came here.

But all she wants is his lips on hers again.

She takes hold of his suspenders, pulling him in.

"I want this."

This. Her mouth melting into his, fitting against it. Him kissing her back with as much fire as she gives. They trade hot, open-mouthed kisses, as if they're trying to brand each other. It's like her fingers have a mind of their own, pushing his suspenders off his shoulders, undoing buttons. She isn't interested in being genteel or gentle. She bites his lower lip, making him gasp. One of her dress straps slides off, but she doesn't fix it. She wants to feel his lips against her skin. He kisses his way across her jaw, down her neck, lower. The flames of the room's two lanterns leap, making strange shapes.

"Is this all right?" Alec says against her bare shoulder.

"Very," she whispers.

She pushes them both back toward the bed.

"Are you sure, Tilde?"

She's sure she wants to push the world away, just for a moment. To take off the mask she has been wearing for so long.

"Yes. Are you?"

He strokes her cheek, her neck. "I've wanted this for as long as I can remember."

He sits down on the bed. Like before, she pulls her skirts up and straddles him, but nothing about this moment feels like pretend.

"If that's true, why didn't you say?"

His fingers wrap around her hips. She can feel the heat of them through the thin layers of her outfit. The searing look he gives her is almost more than she can stand.

"It's something Krastan used to say, when he caught me looking at you. 'Those Dinatris girls are too fine for the likes of us. Don't go wanting things you aren't allowed to touch.'"

Matilde's cheeks flame. "I'm not some delicate treasure on a shelf."

"I know. But you've always felt . . . untouchable."

His words threaten to bring all the reasons they shouldn't do this between them. She wants to peel every layer away.

"Take off your shirt," she commands.

He obeys, making quick work of the buttons, revealing a body that is lithe and finely tuned. Lean, but strong. He's wearing no jewelry except for a tattered bracelet. No: They're

109

braided ribbons. The same ones she tied there as Krastan's shop burned around them, in those moments before they kissed. Seeing them there, even after all these months, emboldens her. She pulls her dress over her head and lets it fall. Alec's eyes go wide at the sight of her in nothing but a silken slip. It's rucked up scandalously high onto her thighs.

He touches her again. Her breaths are shaking. As seasoned as she pretends to be, this is new. Even so, she doesn't want to stop. Not with the lanterns' flames catching in Alec's eyes, turning them molten, and his face tipped reverently up to hers. When they kiss again, it sends sparks cascading through her. Every part of her feels like it might be made of flames.

The door bangs open. Matilde jumps up, heart racing, as several people tumble into the room. For a moment they all simply stare, frozen by shock. It's too mortifying.

"Sayer," she says. "What did I tell you about sneaking up on people?"

Nature is neither kind nor malicious. It strives for equilibrium; for balance. It's said that where a toxin blooms in a plant's petals, the balm for it is often found in the roots. In alchemy, we often find that different parts of the same plant have opposite effects: This is balance. A mirror image forged in the same soil.

—A PASSAGE FROM ONE OF THE
YELLOW ALCHEMIST'S NOTEBOOKS

CHAPTER 8

TO THE ROOT

I T'S BEEN AN age since Matilde was last in Leta's study. It seems darker now, the deep mauve walls soaking up most of the light of the candles. This strange reunion is making her feel off-kilter. Leta's desk seems too large, the fire too bright.

When Sayer, Fenlin, some Dark Stars, and a confused-looking girl all busted down Alec's door, Matilde turned what must have been an unflattering shade of crimson. The memory of being caught undressed with Alec still has her flustered. At least the girl did her the courtesy of fainting in that moment, forestalling whatever remark Sayer might have made. That girl—Jolena—is on Leta's divan now, awake but looking worse for the evening's adventures. It's strange: Matilde knew Wyllo Regnis had two legitimate daughters, Lystra and Jolena, but she has never really thought of them as related to Sayer. Jolena has a rounder, sweeter face, with a smattering of freckles, but there's some resemblance in the almost-black hair and slender nose. The way Sayer holds Jolena's hand is shockingly tender. This clearly isn't the first time they have met, which is news to Matilde.

Jolena trembles a little as Alec coaxes her to drink a concoction he's just brewed. He didn't have what he needed at the Baths, which is what brought them to Leta's. Some of the rare plants in her conservatory, it seems, aren't just for decoration. He's used leaves from one of them to make some sort of tea. Matilde couldn't look away from his hands as he poured it. Those hands that, less than an hour ago, were on her skin. This is no time to dwell on what happened between them, but she can't help it. She can still feel his lips inside the dip at her collarbone, a ghostly brand.

"Are you sure the tea will help?" Sayer, who is sitting beside Jolena, asks.

"It should help flush out whatever they gave her. Though without knowing what was in it, I can't promise how long that will take." Alec frowns. "What did you say the drug was called?"

Sayer's golden eyes flash Matilde's way. "You had one job, Dinatris. Did you not tell him anything?"

Her cheeks flare. "I was getting around to it."

"The only thing I saw you getting around was—"

"Ladies," Leta interjects. "Not now."

Their old Madam is sitting behind her desk, as she used to during Nightbird meetings. Her gaze, usually cool and unruffled, is more troubled than Matilde has ever seen it before. She is watching Sayer, but her eyes keep straying toward the window, where Fen is standing. Since they entered, Fen has kept her back turned on the room. Matilde sees her face in the dark glass, though. It seems she *does* have two eyes. Is one of them a lighter brown than the other?

"Rankin," Leta says. "Why don't you introduce your friends?"

Matilde barely looked at the Dark Stars on their tense and

quiet ride over to Leta's. She already knows Rankin, who has grown at least a hand span since the last time she saw him. The other two are strangers. Olsa is a deeply bronze-skinned, hulking lad, while Hallie is trim, short, and bearded. On further inspection, she thinks the latter might be a girl.

"Facial hair doesn't suit you," she says without thinking.

Hallie gives her an imperious look. "I bet I pull it off better than you would."

Matilde almost laughs, despite everything. Hallie almost does, too, until her gaze finds Fen again. The Stars keep looking to their boss as if awaiting orders or an explanation. Fen doesn't seem inclined to give them either. She looks thinner than Matilde remembers, and hungrier. There is an edge to Fen that makes her think of fraying thread.

Matilde can feel her magic, too, from where she's sitting. It tugs at her, a tingling recognition, made stronger because Sayer is here, too. Matilde's magic hasn't pulsed so strongly since she, Sayer, Fen, and Æsa were last together. If Æsa were here, how would it feel? What might they do?

Jolena puts down the now-empty teacup, which rattles on its saucer. The poor girl blinks once, twice. "I'm so tired."

Sayer strokes back her disheveled hair. "Sleep, then."

Jolena lies down with her head in Sayer's lap. Her eyes flutter closed. But when Rankin lays a blanket gently over her, they open.

"I am sorry for what I did to you," she whispers. "But I had to. I *had* to."

Rankin doesn't reply. Simply stares at her, spellbound.

"It's all right," Sayer says. "It wasn't your fault."

But Jolena doesn't seem to hear. Matilde watches her breaths slow, trying to make her own match them. Even sitting, she feels unsteady on her feet.

For a moment, everyone is silent. Then Leta speaks.

"I think someone should tell us all what happened, start to finish."

After a beat, Sayer begins, describing what they saw at the Hunt Club. An exhibition of an alchemical with the power to make a girl do someone's bidding. Great House men clamoring to get some for themselves. An old, stubborn part of Matilde wants to close her eyes to it all, to deny it. After all, those men once swore to protect their Nightbirds, to treasure them. How can they think that makes the magic theirs to own?

But just as bad as what the drug can do is who was selling it.

"I can't believe it," Matilde says, skin crawling. "I know Wyllo is loathsome. But to subject his youngest daughter to this Sugar . . . It's . . . depraved."

"He has shown little care for the women in his life," Leta says, eyes hard and distant. "They are either an asset to him or a liability."

"I should've known he would find out about her magic," Sayer says. "I never should have left her alone with him."

How did *Sayer* know? She has kept so much from Matilde these last few months. How many other stories has her friend withheld?

"I'm surprised a House lord would risk selling something so hot," Hallie says. "The Wardens would skin him alive for it. The other bosses would happily rob him blind."

Leta taps her desk, deep in thought. "Wyllo lost some of his prestige after Leastnight. The man craves status, and he covets power. This drug, exclusive, rare, would offer him both. And it's not as if he has ever been a friend to the Nightbirds. He holds grudges. I told you not to poke at him, Sayer."

Sayer scowls, unrepentant. "You're right. I should have stabbed."

"But is he making this drug?" Alec asks, cross-legged on the floor now, knees pulled into the crooks of his arms. "Surely he doesn't have the skill to brew something like this."

"The Deep Seas might," Olsa cuts in. "It doesn't sound all that different from Hypnotic."

"But it only works on magical girls," Alec adds. "That's a complex alchemical. I've never heard of anything like it."

"Yes, you have."

Fen turns at last. She looks worse than she did when they stumbled through Alec's door at the Baths. Her color is off, forehead shining with sweat.

"Witchbane only works on girls with magic. I'm betting the two are connected. This is Dorisall's work. Has to be."

Sayer and Rankin both stiffen, as if they know who Fen is speaking of. Matilde feels like she's three steps behind.

"Who is Dorisall?" she asks.

Fen swallows once, twice. "You call him the Red Hand."

Matilde doesn't know much about Fen's past; she was never a Nightbird. They never had a chance to gossip and share secrets, and Fen is clearly not the secret-sharing kind. But from her tone, it's clear she knows the Hand more personally than Matilde does.

"Sayer told me he raised you and Rankin," Leta says. "Is that right?"

"I don't know if you'd call what he did raising," Rankin says. "That place was somewhere we survived."

That knocks the room properly speechless. Fen looks at her Dark Stars, then to Sayer.

"What else did you tell Lady Tangreel while I was sleeping?"

"Nothing." Sayer looks almost offended. "It wasn't my story to tell."

Fen slides her hands into her pockets. Then she fixes her gaze on the hearth and starts talking. It isn't a comfortable tale. Matilde can't imagine growing up under the same roof as the Red Hand, the kind of man who thought pain was the best path to obedience and fear was a tool to be used. Her mind tumbles back to that day he and his Caska cornered them in Krastan's shop. She had been too distracted then, too scared, to make much of the way he spoke to Fen. He called her Ana, she remembers. What else did he say? *I could never forget you. You who led me down this path.* Matilde shivers.

"He knew," Matilde says. "The Hand. That you had magic. Even back then."

"He suspected," Fen says, voice flat. All business. "And he didn't have anyone else to test his theories on. So I got a front-row seat to his experiments. He dedicated a lot of time to trying to force whatever magic I had out."

Olsa and Hallie are gaping at Fen as if this is all news to them.

"*You* made the armor come to life at the club," Olsa says.

Rankin speaks up. "And she made that vine grow in Phoenix Quarter."

Fen shoots him daggers, but Rankin looks relieved to have it out in the open.

"The Flower Witch." Hallie's voice has an edge. "That was *you?*"

The air in the room grows thick with silence.

"Why didn't you tell us?"

"We'll talk later, Hallie."

"But—"

"Blazing cats, I said *later*."

Hallie looks like she might argue, but then the iron grate around the hearth starts to tremble. Fen grips the back of a chair, taking deep breaths.

"Dorisall was always bringing home these tomes from Augustain's library," she goes on. "Old books about botany, stories about Marren. Always trying to sniff the truth out of the myths. Marren found a way to cut a girl's magic out, the stories said. Most of them reference a flaming sword, but Dorisall thought that was just symbolism. He got obsessed with the idea that Marren had some alchemical means of taking the power right out of her."

It comes as no surprise. Matilde grew up with stories of men killing witches, but also of kings wrapping them in chains. There have always been those who want to own them. It's why the last of the Fyrebirds hid in Simta, why they turned their magic inward. They thought pushing it down would make them safe.

"He thought *weil breamus*—witchbane—was the key," Fen goes on, "but he couldn't figure out how to work it. I did, though. I took that secret with me when I left that place. But Dorisall caught up in the end."

Matilde remembers the greasy, hollow feeling of the witchbane in her system. That was bad enough on its own. What if the plant can not only rob them of their power, but leash it? Control it? The ramifications are too bleak to contemplate.

"It can't be witchbane in this drug, though," she says. "It compels us to use our magic. Witchbane suppresses it. It doesn't make sense."

"It might," Alec says. "There are plants whose different parts have related but opposing properties. Two ends of a connected spectrum. Like my frennet. Its leaves help regulate my sugar disease, but the powdered roots make it worse."

Alec holds up the box Sayer gave him, looking at the pieces of Sugar nestled within. "This looks like a compound. He could've taken something like Hypnotic, say, which makes people open to suggestion, and adapted the recipe to include some witchbane. I'd have to look at it more closely to figure out what might be in it."

"But why would the Hand give it to Wyllo?" Matilde asks. "How do they even *know* each other?"

"I don't know," Sayer says. "But Wyllo had witchbane with him on Leastnight. He used it on me, in the palace. He tried to abduct me. I barely got away."

"He did *what*?" Matilde's hands have gone hot, her magic stirring with her agitation. "Why didn't you tell me?"

"You were busy."

Matilde glares. She is growing tired of revelations—of things she can do nothing to change.

"So Wyllo has known about witchbane for months," Leta muses. "Which means he has had some connection to the Red Hand. But neither he nor any of the Caska have used witchbane publicly, that we know of. And the Sugar seems to only just be emerging. I wonder why that might be."

"Maybe he needed an investor," Sayer says. "To finance his experiments. Someone with the power to get the ingredients he needed without anyone finding out. Someone has been keeping him and the Caska hidden. Perhaps the price was access to whatever he created."

"Why not take it to the Brethren instead?" Alec asks. "They have money and power, and he's a pater. Surely he'd want to get back in with the church."

"Because they didn't back him," Fen says. "When he told them about Matilde having magic. And then after the flood on the Underground, they let the Vestens pin the blame on him. No one holds a grudge like Dorisall."

"What's his aim, though?" Matilde says. "What is he trying to accomplish?"

They all sit with the question, though they all know the answer. The Hand wants what he always has: to bring them down.

Sayer looks down at Jolena's sleeping form, frowning. "At least the drug hasn't spread far. I took what Wyllo had at the Hunt Club, and he said supply is limited. He was only going to let the lords have one piece each."

Leta drums her fingers on the desk. "The Hand won't have given all his stock to Wyllo. Whatever his plan, Lord Regnis is simply a means, not the end."

Matilde's stomach twists. She has a heavy, sinking sensation, like someone's thrown her fully clothed into a canal.

"You say he used to test things on you, Fen," Matilde says. "It stands to reason that is what he has been doing since Least-night. Testing this drug. Trying to perfect it. Do you think that is where the missing girls have gone?"

"The specters wear grey, people say," Hallie says. "Same color as the Caska."

Fen closes her eyes. "I wouldn't put it past him."

Horror sinks in its claws. Matilde thinks of Phryne, the lost fledgling. What if she is locked in some dark cell right now, at the Red Hand's mercy? Caged and waiting for a Fyrebird to set her free?

"We have to stop this," she says. "Before it goes any further. We have to locate the Red Hand and put him down."

Leta nods. "We know Wyllo is involved. That is a starting place. But we need to find the root of this problem and cut off the supply."

"They're waiting on a shipment of the main ingredient," Sayer says. "Wyllo said it's supposed to get in just before Risentide."

"Could be witchbane," Rankin chimes in. "You don't think Dorisall has a local crop growing somewhere?"

"It's hard to keep alive out of its native soil," Fen says. "It grows best wild in the Callistan."

Leta's gaze has gone sharp. "Do you have any idea who might be selling it to them, Fenlin?"

"No. I never found out where he got his stuff from."

Fen grips the chair, knuckles starting to whiten. She really doesn't look at all well.

"We have a contact, though," Rankin says. "One of the Sythian clans has sold us plants before. Maybe he can help us."

Fen shakes her head. "The Sythians are wary of outsiders. I'd have to go and talk to him."

"Will you?" Matilde presses.

Fen sways again. She's sweating freely. Matilde thinks she might be sick.

Leta stands. "Why don't you sit down, Fenlin."

"I don't need to sit down."

"I'll just ring Alice for some—"

"Ten hells, I'm *fine*."

She stalks out without another word, looking at no one, leaving an uncomfortable silence in her wake. Olsa and Hallie pull Rankin into a corner and talk at him in hushed tones. Sayer stares at the doorway as if she might force Fen to come back.

Leta stands, pulling her robe tight around her. "I will be

back in a moment. You all stay put. I will send Alice in with refreshments."

She sweeps out of the room. Matilde turns her gaze on the crackling fireplace. It seems to have grown brighter in the last few minutes. Her frustration, which has been banking up, feeds the flames.

She looks to Sayer. "Why didn't you say Wyllo attacked you with witchbane? I could have gotten Dennan to bring him in for questioning. We might have nipped this whole thing in the bud."

"Would you have?" Sayer's voice is low so as not to wake Jolena, but it's pointed. "*Could* you have?"

Matilde crosses her arms. "Whatever you think, I do have influence. I swear, sometimes I wonder if you like going it alone."

Sayer's golden eyes turn molten. "What are you complaining about? You never have to get your hands dirty. You're too busy getting engaged to bastard princes."

Alec's eyes go wide. Matilde could rip Sayer to pieces.

"You're engaged?" he asks. "To him?"

The question hangs on the air, heavy with portent. She finds she can't make herself reply. For a moment, he just stares, as if trying to make sense of her. Then his dark eyes shutter and he stalks out of the room.

"Ten hells, Sayer," she says at last. "Must you cut everyone to ribbons?"

"The truth hurts," Sayer mutters. "I should know."

Matilde wants to go after Alec. She wants to tell him what is really in her heart. But what would it achieve? Tonight has shown her how little her efforts have changed things. Men like the Hand and Wyllo Regnis are still allowed to wreak havoc. The Table won't let her in, no matter how many parties she throws. What is it that Epinine Vesten told her? *A woman has to work twice as hard to make people respect or fear her. She has to be much tougher than the men.* Matilde needs to step out from behind her screen and make those men hear her. Married to Dennan, her voice isn't something they could deny.

Leta can tap into her spy network to try to find out where the Red Hand is hiding. Perhaps Fen can find out where the witchbane is coming from. But as the suzerain's wife, she will have power and influence. She can do so much more within that circle of light.

She looks at the doorway the boy she longs for just walked out of. Until tonight, she didn't know how much. *Duty is sacrifice,* Gran said, and Matilde didn't believe her. She fought the idea that her desires shouldn't come first. But what's at stake here is so much bigger than her wants, however much they burn inside her. As she tucks her heart away, it starts to ache.

※

FEN DIDN'T PLAN to go to the conservatory, but she let her feet carry her here: a mistake. There's too much greenery. She can feel sap humming through leaves, calling out to her. Trying to pull more of her magic out through her skin.

She wipes at her mouth. Blazing cats, she feels awful. She reaches for her mastic, but it's gone. That was her last. Somehow, she feels both sick and hungry. One of her eyes feels like it's filled with sand. She reaches up, plucking the colored film out, and blinks the pain away. Every inch of her feels scoured red raw. What she wouldn't give for the patch she stupidly left back at the Dark Stars clubhouse, that familiar barrier between herself and the world.

But she can't blame the world for tonight. She's the one who accepted the job, knowing the danger. She's the one who animated all those metal knights. She's the one who should have gotten rid of Dorisall years ago. Fen let herself hope he was defeated, after their fight in Phoenix Quarter: It was easier. But you can't pull a weed out by its leaves and expect it to stay dead. You have to yank it out by its roots.

She leans against the lip of the fountain. Water dribbles down the marble, its susurrus echoing off the tiles. The sound makes her think of Æsa, who caught Fen chewing mastic in the Underground once. She knew that secret before Sayer did. The words she whispered in Fen's ear are fresh still.

Tell Sayer the truth. She will still love you.

But Fen knew she wouldn't love that she's still chewing witchbane. The way Sayer looked at her at the Hunt Club, with disappointment—disgust, even—is part of why Fen's held her at arm's length. She didn't want Sayer to see how much she needs it. She can't understand; the Stars aren't likely to either. But this is how she became Fenlin Brae. To build a gang in Simta, you need brass and cunning. To keep it, you can't ever let down your guard. Her mastic has always been her armor, her shield, making her stronger. She doesn't know how to be the Sly Fox without it.

All around her, leaves shiver as if ruffled by a breeze. The light at the corners of her eyes starts to darken. Somewhere close, a heavy door clicks shut. She shakes her head, willing away the nightmare. She won't let it take her here. She *won't*.

Soft footsteps sound behind her. Fen curses.

"Not now, Hallie."

"It isn't Hallie."

Fen turns enough to see Lady Leta Tangreel.

Despite the fact this woman nursed her through an illness, she can count what she knows about Lady Tangreel on a hand. One: She was once the Nightbird's Madam. Two: She's rich, and apparently self-made. Three: Her network of spies and informants is one that any piper would covet. Four: Her stare is always unsettling. Keen enough to see through Fen.

"What do you want, Lady Tangreel?"

"I thought someone should make sure you haven't fainted amongst my potted plants."

"Like I said, I'm fine. I don't need looking after."

"We both know that isn't true."

At that, Fen turns. If Leta is surprised by her 'spring-stained eyes, she doesn't say so. She looks on, as polished and remote as ever. Fen remembers, vaguely, someone singing at her bedside during her fevered days here. Could that have been this woman? It's hard to imagine.

"I've heard that your gang are good at collecting secrets, Fenlin," she says. "I am too. Given the situation, I think it's time we pooled our resources."

Fen grips the fountain's edge. "What are you saying?"

"I'd like the Stars to help find the Hand's lair. I will pay handsomely."

The thought of her gang working for a Great House, even this one, raises her hackles.

"The Stars don't need your charity."

"It isn't charity. It is an honest offer. Which is more than I can say about any Edges Lanagan might make."

How does she know about that? Fen's thoughts are in pieces. She is nothing but a handful of raw nerves.

Leta tilts her head, as if listening for something. Then she takes a turn around the room, making Fen think of a stalking predator. Elegant, but deadly too.

"Did you know the Houses used to tell their Nightbirds that their magic would fade when they got older?" Leta says. "Mostly it's true. I suppose that is what happens when you give something away for long enough. But I never did what I was told. I never married. I kept my magic, and I've found that it has lasted. It isn't what it once was, but still."

Fen wonders if Sayer knows. This woman is clearly good at keeping secrets. She passes a cluster of closed flowers and they open, turning toward Leta. She runs a finger along a huge palm leaf, and it curls.

"I'm an earth girl, like you. My code name was the Bowerbird because of my gift for finding things buried and hidden. For seeing things that have been locked behind closed doors."

Hairs rise on the back of Fen's neck. The first night they met, Leta's first words were *Do I know you?* As if a Great House matriarch could ever understand her. But maybe she saw through Fen, even then.

"I was different from the other girls, though, in one respect. I was a dockworker's daughter. Before I was a Nightbird, I worked at a pleasure house on Smoky Row. In those years, I had plenty of chances to see what addiction looked like."

The silence stretches, but it feels full, almost expectant. It rubs uncomfortably against Fen's fevered skin.

"I'm not addicted to anything."

Leta nods. "Lots of the girls I worked with said that, too. They used Mermaid's Dust to help ease the burdens of our profession. But it got its hooks into some of them. I had a little trouble with it myself."

Fen wipes at the sweat on her brow. "What are you telling me all this for?"

"So you will believe me when I say I understand some of your struggle. You do not have to suffer it alone. Sayer cares for you deeply, and she is like a daughter to me. I would like it if . . . you could be my daughter too."

Her voice has turned dangerously soft. Fen can barely stand the pity in it.

"Sayer might be in the market for a dame," she spits, backing away, "but I don't need one. Never have."

Leta steps closer, her expression sad: almost wistful.

"Somehow I don't believe you, Ana."

Fen flinches. How does she know that name? Who told her?

Something touches her waist: a vine, wrapping gently around her. Plants are bending, responding to her fear. Emotions are blooming that she has no name for. The room is threatening to turn dark again.

"I don't want this," she says in a rasp. "Any of it."

"Wait," Leta is saying, reaching out a hand.

But Fen is already tearing out of the conservatory, with no thought other than running. She has to get out of this house, away, *away*.

She runs back toward the Dark Stars clubhouse, sticking to the shadows. Her thoughts are a maelstrom, her heart a ruin, but she didn't become Fenlin Brae by letting emotion rule. She can't let Leta Tangreel get into her head. What she needs is to get herself back under control. She has a crew to look after, bills to pay, and troubles to fix. She can't ignore Dorisall anymore, given what she now knows he's up to, but she can't face him—any of this—in such a state. There might be a way to thwart Dorisall's plans, get herself back in order, and shore up the Dark Stars' fortunes, all in one swoop. It might even be a way to help other girls who want to keep their magic under wraps.

She thinks through her next steps: Leave a note at the club-house, telling Olsa what to say to Edges to keep him off their backs about the exhibition, and telling him to accept the job from Leta Tangreel. She'll pack light and leave the city before anyone's the wiser. Sometimes a sly fox does her best work alone.

The Storm Witch is a plague in our city. She has stolen from me, which I cannot abide. Our precious daughter has been taken, and I fear she is in grave danger. How far must the witch go before our esteemed Table deigns to deal with this threat once and for all?

—AN EXCERPT FROM A STORY PRINTED IN *THE CROSSING*, A SIMTAN NEWSSHEET

– CHAPTER 9 –
CURSING THE LIGHT

SAYER CURSES THE light. It's found its way through the crack between her bedroom curtains, and now it's spearing straight into her eyes. She rubs at them, feeling groggy, as she tries to get her bearings. Something moves beside her, making her flinch. Jolena is all tangled in the sheets, her long, wavy hair spread out and wild across the pillows. There's a little crease between her brows as she sleeps.

When was the last time Sayer shared a bed with someone? She shared one with Fen once, the night her dame died. They shared one again after Leastnight, when Fen was sick and fevered, and she feared her best friend might never wake up. Sayer crawled in beside her, pouring confessions into her sleeping ears. *I'd be lost without my shadow,* she whispered. *I need you. Don't leave me.* When Fen woke up, Sayer thought, she would say it all again. She would blow on the embers of this thing simmering between them. Before she had a chance, though, Fen was gone. And she's stayed gone, without any explanation. *It's not personal,* Fen said last night. It feels personal. Even now, the words make Sayer's cheek sting hot.

Jolena stirs. Her dark eyes flutter open, wary, but she relaxes when she sees Sayer. As if she makes the girl feel safe.

"Where are we?" she croaks. "Is this your house?"

At least she sounds better than she did last night: less vacant.

"It's Leta Tangreel's house. But yes, I stay here."

Jolena sits up, wincing. "I always pictured the Storm Witch living somewhere dark and nestlike."

Sayer almost laughs. "I'm not a bat."

Jolena smiles, but the expression is fleeting. It slips off her face like water through a sieve.

"How are you feeling?" Sayer asks.

Jolena rubs at her temples. "Like someone's taken to my head with an anvil."

"Do you still feel . . ."

Compelled? Possessed? Sayer doesn't want to voice either.

"Drugged? No." Her normally open face shifts, collecting shadows. "But I still feel . . . I don't know. Dirty."

She hugs her knees up to her chest and shivers. Sayer tries to think of what to say.

"How much do you remember about last night?"

She swallows. "I remember the way it made me feel . . . eager. It's like nothing existed except that man's voice. Answering his commands became what I most wanted. I couldn't stop. It felt good to obey. It felt right."

Sayer assumed it would be like being trapped inside your mind, but this is worse, somehow. To make a girl obey your every word and like it: such violation. A knot pulls tight in Sayer's gut.

"How did your sire find out about your magic?"

"I know you said to be careful," Jolena says, turning her face away. "And I was. But I like to keep a journal. I write about my experiments, the things I've figured out about my magic. He must have found it hidden in the greenhouse. But I don't think he knew for sure until . . . he tricked me."

Sayer has seen Jolena wear many emotions: joy, eagerness, sorrow. She isn't sure she has ever seen her angry.

"At dinner, he collapsed. He was red and choking. It was awful. Dame said someone must have poisoned him, and we needed a doctor. But Sire said that, no, he needed me. And I realized that he must have read my journal, how I discovered I can extract poison from someone. He said I could fix him. I thought, maybe if I did, he would see me as something other than a nuisance."

But Sayer knows how Wyllo Regnis feels about daughters with magic, estranged or otherwise. She wishes Jolena hadn't had to learn that lesson too.

"I extracted the poison from his body. I was confused, because it wasn't a high enough dose to cause him true peril, and not enough to warrant his choking fit. But he seemed . . . pleased. I should have known, then. I should have suspected. But it felt too good to have him proud of me."

She wilts at that last, a shamefaced flower.

"Then, last night, he asked me to come out with him. He said he needed my help. I didn't want to make him angry." She twists her fingers in the sheets, then rubs her wrist. The first time Sayer met her, it held bruises. "I didn't know what the drug would do. I never thought he would hurt me. At least, not like that."

Jolena's words make Sayer ache. Before last night, she thought she hated Wyllo Regnis. But this loathing feels almost too big to contain.

"I should never have left you there," Sayer says. "This is my fault."

Jolena shakes her head. "If it wasn't for you, I would still be with him. You saved me."

She should have taken Jolena out of House Regnis earlier. Perhaps Sayer also should have told her about the blood they share. But it feels heavy, that truth: that they are sisters. Saying it out loud would mean explaining Sayer's own past, and she doesn't know how Jolena will take it. It still feels safer to keep it under wraps.

She stretches out her legs. There's no time to sit here brooding. She needs to go and see the Dark Stars, and start hunting for the Red Hand in earnest. She has to ruin her sire once and for all.

The bedroom door bangs open, loud in the tense silence.

"Say, listen—"

Rankin comes to a gasping halt by the bed. His brown hair is wild: He often looks a bit like he just came out of a washing mangle, but this is messy even for him.

"Do you mind?" she says: What is he doing back here? "We aren't even dressed yet."

His eyes have widened at the sight of Jolena in nightclothes. He's always had a penchant for posh girls. "Right. Well . . ."

Jolena tucks a strand of hair behind her ear. "It's Rankin, yes?"

He nods, a little slack-jawed. "John, actually. Johnny Rankin."

Sayer has never heard him introduce himself that way.

"Johnny. I am sorry about what I did to you last night."

He gives her a little bow. "It's no worries, miss. Wasn't your fault."

She smiles, and his eyes go puppy soft.

Sayer snaps her fingers. "Rankin. Focus. What's the problem?"

He shakes his head. "Right. Yeah, it's Fen. She's gone."

Leta appears in the doorway, rigid. "What do you mean, *gone?*"

"She left us a note saying she's going to the Callistan, to find out about the shipment Lord Regnis mentioned. See if she can sniff out where it's coming from. She went alone, but I don't think she should be doing that."

Sayer frowns. "Why not?"

He's wringing his cap like it's a dishrag. "She's . . . still sick. Been like that since Leastnight. Something's not right with her. She tries to hide it, but I know."

Sayer thinks of Fen in the stacks at the Hunt Club, pale and sweating. The way she screwed her eyes shut as if she was in pain. If she was still sick, why didn't she say so? Frustration and worry twist in her chest, a tangled vine.

Leta steps into the room, looking less polished than usual. Her dressing robe is rumpled and her feet are bare.

"That isn't the only problem we must deal with this morning."

She hands Sayer the morning's early newssheet, pointing to the story at the top of the page. Sayer reads it once, twice, feeling the words sink their claws in.

"What's it say?" Jolena asks.

Sayer's blood has gone cold, flowing too thick.

" 'Storm Witch Steals Beloved House Daughter.' "

The newssheet tells the story of the exhibition, but it's all wrong: In this version, there is no drug, and no drugging. Just a group of friends having a private dinner, one of their daughters in tow. Witnesses say they watched as the Storm Witch crashed in, injuring several lords without provocation. They also say she abducted Jolena. And then there's Wyllo's final, impassioned plea. *Our precious daughter has been taken, and I fear she is in grave danger. How far must the witch go before our esteemed Table deigns to deal with this threat once and for all? I ask my fellow Simtans to help us bring Jolena home, and the Storm Witch to justice.*

He offers a reward for Jolena's return: The sum is blinding. But what arrests her is the illustration below it of a girl with too-sharp teeth and dagger eyes. It's a twisted version of her face, all menace, but unmistakable. And below it, her name: Sayer Sant Held.

Sayer swears.

"Indeed," Leta says. "You neglected to mention, last night, that they unmasked you."

"They didn't," she says, heart pounding. "But Wyllo knew me." Her sire has known her true identity for months; it seems he's decided to out her. "But what's his game? Doesn't he know I can go to the papers, too, and tell them what he's been up to?"

"We have no concrete proof," Leta says, crossing her arms. "It's your word against his. He is clearly betting that no one will believe you about his selling Sugar. He has long been known as an abstainer and supporter of the church. But the Storm Witch: You have champions in Simta, but also enemies. This is a bid to further char your name."

Sayer paces the rug. It should be Wyllo's face on this page, his crimes emblazoned in thick, damning letters. She crumples up the paper and lets it drop to the floor.

"I can go to the papers," Jolena says, uncertain. "I'll say it isn't true."

"No," Rankin and Sayer both say at once.

"If you do," Leta says, "they will make you go back to House Regnis."

Jolena's face pales. "I . . . don't think I can."

"You don't have to." Sayer paces, thinking of all the ways she is going to hurt Wyllo Regnis. Leta takes Sayer's hand, making her stop.

"You should leave the city. For now, at least."

Sayer scowls. "I'm not going to let him send me running."

"All of Simta knows who you are, and they will come for you. Many will recognize your name and know that you're my ward. Wardens could show up here at any moment. We are lucky they haven't already."

Which means staying here is going to endanger Leta further. Still, she doesn't want to let Wyllo make her turn tail and run. Simta is her world: She has never been outside it. But she's on the back foot, and needs a new way to take him down. What better way than finding his supply line and disrupting it? And ideally some solid proof of his crimes. The kind he won't be able to wriggle out of.

Sayer pushes back her short hair. "Can you tell us exactly where Fen went, Rankin?"

He nods.

"Then I'll go after her."

Rankin frowns. "Not without me, you won't. Rafe won't talk to someone he doesn't know."

Jolena sits up straighter. "I'm going too."

"No," Sayer says.

"Why not? Sugar was used on me, and I know what it looks and feels like. I also know more about plants than you. I can help you find what you are looking for."

"It could be dangerous."

Jolena lifts her chin. "I'm not as soft as you think."

Sayer and Jolena don't look much alike. But just now, in her defiant expression, Sayer can see herself reflected. How is she supposed to say no?

She turns back to Leta. "But what about finding the Hand's lair? And the missing girls?"

"Let Matilde pick up that torch," Leta says, squeezing her hand. "She and I and the Stars. Go, Sayer. Find Fenlin and whatever else you can before Risentide."

She closes her eyes, battling back her rage. She wants to go to House Regnis right now and put an end to him. She doesn't want to chase after a friend who keeps leaving her behind. But Fen rescued her on Leastnight, even if she regrets it now. Perhaps it's time for Sayer to do the same.

PART III

TWISTS
AND
TANGLES

JOOST BRINGS HIS fur-lined cloak closer around him, blocking out the chill sea wind. The vessels before him are finely made, part of a fresh fleet of warships. To finish in time, his builders had to work at a frenzied pace. The port swarms with activity, the pounding hammers keeping swift time with his heartbeat. All of his desires are edging close.

"Are you warm enough, my dear?" he asks his new galgren.

Phryne shakes her head, making her pershain glimmer. The girl doesn't seem to like Trellane's crisp air— she is forever shivering. But she does look fetching in the silver chain. She was loath to wear it, at first. She has fought many of his edicts, for which he had to punish her. He does not like to see his magic girl weep. But at last, with some coaxing and a few promises, she told him about Simta's new Fyrebirds. It seems his galgren knows them better than any of his Simtan spies. Her tales of how they commanded fire, and made vines swallow buildings, and lifted ships, and conjured storms made him ache with longing. But what entranced him most was how they stopped a flood that swept through a place called the Underground. Phryne described how the four girls joined hands, calling up a power it warms his blood to imagine.

They are different together, she told him. *Stronger. They amplify the rest of us. They can do things most of us cannot.*

They are the stuff of his father's fireside legends.

Imagine how much more his new galgren could do, with the Fyrebirds to fuel her. Imagine having such a weapon at his command.

That is why he sent one of his best raiding ships ahead, to comb the Illish Isles for the Wave Witch. Phryne says the girl hails from those islands: It makes sense she will have fled back there. His men will find her and bring her to heel. Now that he knows what they can do, he will not settle for just one magical galgren, or one Fyrebird. Whatever it takes, Joost will collect them all.

He smiles. It seems like fate that he has just received an invitation to Dennan Hain's wedding. Instead of breaking down Simta's doors to seize his treasure, he will simply walk in.

"Never fear," he says, patting Phryne's hand. "We will soon set sail for your homeland."

His galgren's voice is small and tight. "And you will take me with you? Like you promised?"

"Of course," he soothes. "We must find you some friends."

– CHAPTER 10 –

THE KISS OF DEATH

ÆSA KNOWS HOW the Singing Isles got their name. It is because of the sound they make as the wind passes through their pine trees, whistling. Today, in the grey mist, they lie silent and still. The isles are sparsely populated, the waters quiet, but prickles still run down her neck like premonition. She can almost feel eyes watching from the fog.

They have dropped anchor near one of the smallest islands. She and Jacinta are sitting on some upturned barrels tied to the deck. On a clear day, they could see the northernmost part of the Callistan from here, but fog is smothering the coastline. The air, muggy and listless, has the feel of a storm that needs to break. This weather is making everyone fractious. Arjen is grumbling about his sweat-soaked shirt as he mends rigging. Kadeel has some practice swords out, sparring with one of the fledglings, but their lunges are half-hearted at best. Some of the crew have rowed out to the Singing Isles in search of replenishment. The ship feels empty without them.

"This is taking too long," she says. "We need to get moving."

Jacinta shuffles her oracle cards on the barrel between them. "It can't be helped. We need real food, Æsa. It won't matter how fast we get to Simta if we're all dead by the time we arrive."

It's only been a week since they left the Illish Isles: With Willan at the helm, and Æsa coaxing the waves to smooth and carry them, they have made good progress. But they left the Illish Isles with little but hardtack and stale biscuits in the *Tempest*'s larder. Jacinta is right: They needed to stop. But she keeps looking out over the rail, hoping to catch sight of the crew rowing back in their pinnaces. She does not like them sitting out here, so exposed.

"We should've gone by land," Æsa says. "There could be naval patrols, especially this close to Simta."

"Perhaps. But it would have been slower, and we don't have time to waste."

Going by land would also have meant parting with Willan. After what she did to him at Harvesttide, she thought he might sail away from her on his own. Instead, he insisted on seeing them back to Simta safely. To her surprise, the crew agreed without a fight. Since they set sail, she has avoided finding herself alone with Willan: an easy enough feat, on a ship this full of people. And yet she always seems to sense where he is. Her gaze finds him now, standing alone at the prow. The crew often stop there to whisper prayers and wishes down to the *Tempest*'s figurehead. She brings them luck, they like to say. Unlike Æsa.

Willan turns, as if he feels her watching. Their eyes meet, green on green.

"Have you kissed him yet?"

Æsa's gaze snaps back to Jacinta. "Why would you ask me that?"

"You think we can't all feel the smolder between you two? This isn't *that* big a ship."

Æsa grips the edge of her barrel. "My mind's on other things."

"You should enjoy each other while you can. Believe me."

A haunted look crosses her friend's face. She must be thinking of Tom, the boy she lost back in Simta. Æsa understands why she would offer such advice, but Jacinta has never addled anyone with her kiss. Her friends have told her it's possible to kiss someone without giving them her magic. But her head is too full of visions, and of what happened by that bonfire, to risk it. She can't stop thinking of the way her magic brought Willan to his knees.

And her da saw. He stared as if he didn't know her. She keeps hearing his words: *What have you done?*

She looks down at her thumb, at the old scar there. She got it the first time Da took her out on his fishing boat. He bandaged it up, kissing her hair. *Never fear, lass. We'll fix it.* But some wounds aren't so easily dressed.

After she had the vision on the beach, Æsa went to find Jacinta, setting their plans for flight in motion. But she could not leave the Illish Isles without seeing Mam and Da. When she got home, they were sitting at their battered table, eyes red rimmed. Da stood when she came near, his face drawn. Perhaps afraid.

Æsa opened her mouth, apology poised on her tongue, but she stayed silent.

I don't understand, he said at last. *How did this happen?*

Mam shook her head, as if to keep Æsa from speaking. But it

felt good to finally confess, like draining a wound. Painful relief. As she spoke, night began to turn into morning, the first streaks of light staining the dirt floor of their cottage. The four walls of her childhood, so different now. Herself, so changed.

When she was done, she waited for his judgment.

Can't you give it back to the Wellspring? Da said at last. *Perhaps Pater Toth will know what to do.*

No, she could not give her magic back—it was a part of her.

I do not condemn you for it. But I fear for you, daughter.

It was the first time she ever saw her da cry.

Before they went to bed, he hugged her tight. *Sleep, lass. We will make this right tomorrow.*

But she had other shores to sail toward. By the time they woke up, she was gone. What did they think when they found her bed empty? Will they love her, still, when more tales of the Wave Witch reach their shore?

Jacinta shuffles her cards, disrupting Æsa's thoughts. "Let's try again."

For the past few days, they have experimented with joint scrying. Æsa amplifies Jacinta's magic, and Jacinta seems to lend her better control. They hope that combining their powers will let them see more about the invading army: who they are, what they want, when they will come. Try as they might, their visions are fractured, broken into too many pieces. Scraps of a story that refuse to coalesce. At night, in sleep, is when she sees the future most clearly: Matilde jumping into a raging river, Fen rowing through swampland, Sayer struggling to get free of a net. Every dream ends with them all bound in a grand church, surrounded by censers full of witchbane. Then she sees the girl, her neck clamped in chains of silver, and the sea of ships with their angry red sails. They've come to Simta for her friends:

Somehow, she feels it. She jolts awake in her hammock every time, soaked in sweat.

Jacinta cuts the deck, handing one half to Æsa. They take turns flipping the cards over, slipping new ones on top of old. The Mountain, the Three Kings, the Tallship. None of them mean anything to her. Frustration flares. Why do the visions always come in waves, refusing to let her steer them? What good is such a gift if she cannot see what she most wants? She hates how they make it feel like someone else is dictating her life to her. As if she isn't the one writing her tale.

When she looks up, Jacinta has stopped flipping cards, gaze fixed on the ocean.

"You know, I haven't seen it in my cards," she says. "Not exactly. But a part of me feels certain I won't see Simta again."

Æsa starts. "Of course you will, Cin. Don't say such things."

Jacinta is silent for a long, pregnant moment. Then she cuts her cards and flips a new one over. It shows a bright bird, its wings aflame. She lets out a sigh.

"I am just glad I get to see you being brave at last. A Fyrebird. The four of you will find each other, Æsa. You will change things. I believe in that future, even if I won't be there to see."

Æsa takes Jacinta's hand, wanting to reassure her. A vision rises, swift and sudden, blotting out the muted fog. She is standing on another ship, and Matilde is there, wearing a dress that flashes like scales in sunlight. Fire surrounds her, taking on bestial shapes. The flames are hers, but it feels as if her friend is not controlling them. Æsa runs for her, crashing into Fen and Sayer. This future is rife with chaos and danger.

The vision dissolves, leaving her dizzy. When it clears, Jacinta's expression is vacant. It raises the hairs on the back of Æsa's neck.

146

Æsa shakes her lightly. Jacinta blinks once, twice.

"What did you see, Jacinta?"

Before she can answer, the cloud above them splits open. Sheets of soft rain silver down, sweeping over them in curtains. Æsa grabs for the oilskin lying near, throwing it over herself and Jacinta. Several fledglings flock over, trying to squish in underneath. The crew don't look distressed. One of them cups his hands around his mouth, gleeful.

"Shower time, boys!"

Someone whoops, and then the crew are rushing about, grabbing piles of clothes and cakes of soap out of buckets. Boots come off as they gather on the deck.

Jacinta shoves her cards into her skirt. "What's this, now?"

Æsa blinks, nonplussed. "I have no idea."

At least not until they start taking off their shirts.

"They're . . . washing," Layla says, voice halfway between fascinated and disgusted. "Why are they washing?"

The men laugh and shout, taking soap to grimy skin. Æsa flushes.

"Sailors do it on long hauls when it rains without storming. Fresh water isn't to be wasted."

"I suppose," Jacinta says. "Though I could've done without seeing Arjen in his jocks."

"Get in here, Cin," Arjen crows. "Scrub my back for me!"

"Scrub your own."

There is a round of raucous cackling.

"Drawers stay on, gents," Willan shouts. "No need to scar the girls' eyeballs."

Æsa's gaze snags on him as he approaches. The rain is soaking his clothes, making them look painted on his body. She can see all his taut, muscled lines. And then he yanks his shirt over his head. His torso is chiseled as if by a sculptor. Æsa's lungs have shrunk to the size of shelled peas. He picks up some soap and scrubs it over his shoulders, making suds trail down his body. What would it feel like, to touch him like that? To be those bubbles on his skin?

"If you don't want to kiss him," Jacinta murmurs, "I might have to."

One of the fledglings lets out a choked almost-laugh.

Æsa's mouth has gone dry. Her magic is stirring, trying to rise with her desire. She needs to slow it down, to rein it in: to stop wanting. The waves, no longer still, slap against the ship's sides. One of them rises to spill over the railing, sending some of the men off-balance. The fledglings look at her, as if they know she caused it. The crew notice, too.

"Was that you, sheldar?" Kadeel shouts. "Try not to capsize us."

It's only a jest, but it makes Æsa's chest hurt. She stands too fast and stumbles, but keeps on moving. She doesn't stop until she reaches the ship's hold, and the corner where the dry goods are kept. It's so dark here that she can barely see her hands, yet she doesn't look for a lantern. Better she is not able to see. She presses her hands to the hull, trying to calm her breathing. She doesn't want to cause a storm. The sea is vast, forever pressing its ear to the ship's side, listening. *Speak, sheldar. We hear, we hear, we hear.*

"Æsa?"

She whirls around. Willan is there, a lantern held high, still shirtless. He looks perfect, standing there, his sea-colored eyes shining. Her fingers twitch to touch him. She will not let herself reach out.

There is a story her grandda told her once, about the gods

who came before the Eshamein, and who some of the Illish pray to still. Ælish, a lesser goddess of tidepools, spent her days collecting shells and singing to crabs, contented with her life in the warm, shallow waters. But one day Glaum, a god of the deep seas, saw her there and fell in love. *You cannot have her,* the other gods told him. *She's not meant for deeper waters.* But Glaum didn't attend. He went to hold her and she dissolved, sand running through his fingers. He tried to gather her up, to make her whole, but too late.

What's the lesson? Æsa asked, so used was she to Pater Toth's sermons.

No lesson. Only a warning about longing for things we can't have.

"What's wrong?" Willan asks.

"Nothing," she says, a little breathless. She presses her back against the ship, glancing away.

"Don't hide from me, apselm."

That endearment—*beloved, fated*—is one he's never used with her before. Voiced in this small space, it feels more real.

"You shouldn't call me that."

"Why not? It's true." He touches her cheek, so gently. "Or do you not agree?"

"I don't know how I feel, Willan."

"I don't believe you."

She shakes her head. His nearness is doing something to her insides. She can smell him, salt and caramel and sun.

"Why aren't you afraid?" she blurts out.

"Of what?"

"Of me."

He is looking at her the way he did when they first met, as if she is a beacon he wants to swim out to.

"You've a mighty power. I won't pretend to understand it. But I'm not afraid of it."

She should stop, but the words are rising. They will not be held back.

"You should be. I meddled with your emotions, Willan. I reached inside and changed the way you felt."

She watches his face. He has known about her power since he was her Hawk and she his Nightbird, but knowing is different from having it used on you.

"You were only trying to stop the fight," he says. "I should've walked away and spared you from it. But when he called me cullcaila, I lost my temper."

Outside blood, it means. A term coined in a time when invaders from the Spice Isles tried to conquer the Illish Isles. It's considered a grave insult. It makes her cheeks flame to remember it said.

"Enis shouldn't have called you that."

Willan shrugs. "He isn't the first Illishman to do so. I never truly felt like I belonged there."

You belong with me, she wants to say, but cannot. Will not.

"Still, I'm sorry."

"Why? You didn't make Enis Dale into a greedy piece of flotsam."

She thinks back to her kisses with Enis, all those months ago. "I might have."

"Your magic didn't make him like that, Æsa."

She takes a long, slow breath. "Perhaps not. But my kiss has the power to change people's feelings. How do you know the way you feel for me is real?"

Willan rears back. "The way I feel has nothing to do with your magic. My feelings are my own. Surely you know that."

150

But when Willan is near, Æsa's emotions get away from her. He makes her feel as if her heart lives outside her chest. She cannot afford to lose control or get distracted with what she thinks is coming. Her friends need the sheldar in her, not the apselm. She does not know how to be both things at once.

"Don't you see?" she chokes out. "I am not good for you. I'm dangerous."

"I know you are," he growls. "And so am I."

There's a look on his face she's never seen before, almost haunted. His breaths are coming fast now, matching hers.

"I know how you feel about that boy you killed in the Underground," he says. "I know it haunts you. But you forget, I've lived my life as a sea raider. I've killed more men than you, and for less compelling reasons. But that isn't stopping me from putting my hand out. From offering myself, if you will have me."

The words steal her breath. But what if she is a deep-sea god, and he is one of shallow waters? What if trying to hang on to him will only be his end?

He cups her chin. "What is this really about, kilventra?"

"I had a vision," she whispers, the words like poison. "Of you dying in my arms. Dying *because* of me. I've had it many times over the months. Always the same. I'm afraid that if you stay, I will kill you. And I can't bear to live in a world where you are not."

For what feels like ages, he just stares, as if he's trying to see into the depths of her. And then he *shrugs*.

"I'm willing to risk it."

For a moment, his words shock her speechless. Frustration has her speaking again.

"How can you say that, Willan?"

"Because I've loved you since the first time I saw you. You know what I thought, that night? I thought, *This girl should never cower for anyone. I want to spend my life lifting her up.*"

A shiver ghosts across her skin. He touches her cheek again.

"I know you don't need me," he goes on. "You are strong enough to take care of yourself. But whatever is coming, I want to fight beside you. If it's my fate to die there too, that's all right. I'm not going to let a vision make my choices for me. I choose my own fate, and I choose you. But I will leave if you ask. I will never take anything you don't want to give me. And I won't kiss you unless you ask me to."

He turns and starts walking back toward the stairs. She tells herself to let him leave her. But this love is theirs, and she wants to claim it. Æsa wants to chart her own path, come what may.

"Willan."

He turns back. She takes a step, pulling him closer. And then she touches his chest, as she's longed to do, fingers spreading across wet skin. The only sounds are the rain pattering on the deck above them, Willan's lantern swinging on its hinges, and his heart crashing under her hand.

"Kiss me."

He leans in, slow, and Æsa rises to meet him. His lips melt against hers, sure and soft. Their bodies press close, molding together as if they were made to do it. As if they two were destined to fit.

There is a stretch of jagged cliffs where she used to play sometimes in Illan. They are called the Fangs because of the way they stick up out of the water, sharp enough to pierce the sky. The wind that howls up over them is so strong some days that it will hold a person's weight. She and her friends would line up on the grassy bluff, put out their arms, and fall into that wind, daring it to catch them. This kiss makes her feel the same: thrilled and held, alive and known. It feels like flying.

She reaches around his ribs to grip the winged muscles behind them, feeling them flex beneath her palms. Somehow they've turned so his back is the one against the ship, his arms around her. There's only the fabric of her dress between his chest and hers. She drinks him in, touching his face, gripping his shoulders, devouring. He consumes her just as hungrily in return.

Outside, the ocean roars, or maybe it's the blood rushing through her. Her magic is a torrent in her ears. A part of her screams to pull back, to protect him, but the wild abandon in this kiss feels too good, too right, to be denied.

"Æsa," he gasps, almost guttural.

Her mouth covers his, making him quiet again.

A wave slaps hard against the hull. There is a pounding above, then the rumble of thunder. Willan breaks their kiss, frowning a little, as if torn between her and the sound.

But she isn't going to let anything ruin this. She leans in, refusing to let the moment end.

His hands wrap around her hips, sighing into her.

Then someone above shouts loud enough to wake the dead.

"All hands!"

The everglade forests of the Callistan are vast, impenetra-ble by foot and hard to navigate by boat unless you know its pathways. Those who dare trespass without permission from the Sythians often do not make it out again. The glades are holy to them, the very heart of the Wellspring. There is a Sythian saying: Our glades eat the unworthy. *But they also say that when Fyrebirds once roamed, they were always welcome. The Sythians called girls with magic en-limned: blessed by the waters. They were not considered tres-passers, but pilgrims. Wandering souls returning home.*

—AN EXCERPT FROM THE TRAVEL DIARY
OF LORD ANTONY SILVEEN

– CHAPTER 11 –
WANDERING SOULS

W ELL?" FEN SAYS, wiping her brow. "Will you do it?"
Rafe takes a sip of hard cider. He's on his third,
since Fen's paying, but she'll be scraping the bottoms
of her pockets soon enough.

"I don't know." He raps on the bar with a knuckle. "It
would cost you."

"I figured."

Fen takes a pouch out of a hidden pocket. Rafe tips its yellow seeds out into the bowl of his palm and holds them up,
studying them as if they're diamonds.

"What's the mix?"

"We grafted Tigerlark with Midnight Sigh."

Rafe nods in approval. "Impressive, for a *gwythda*."

Gwythda: drylander. Too right it's impressive. It took Fen
years to hybridize the lilies, which she did in hopes of selling
them to Simta's upper crust. There's no magic in them, but rare
flowers are worth a lot of coin in Simta. These seeds are dear,
some of the only ones that made it out of the Underground.
What lies in the Callistan is much more precious to her now.

Fen wipes her damp palms on her trousers. The Speckled Hen is heaving, bodies crowded too close to where they sit at the bar. The inn is perched on the banks of one of Sarask's many waterways—the town has more rivers than roads, which boatmen like Rafe use to get in and around. A limp breeze wafts in through one of the windows, but Fen's still sweating. Since leaving Simta, she hasn't stopped. She spent the trip trying to block out the mess she left behind her. Not to think about Sayer or the Stars, Dorisall or Leta Tangreel, and focus on the task that lies ahead.

Rafe leans his bronzed, well-hewn boatman's arms on the counter. "These are good, Fenlin, but good isn't enough to get you passage into the glades. You know that."

"Why not? I'm no stranger. We've known each other for years. We're friends."

Rafe cuts her a look. "That's a stretch."

He's right, but she needs Rafe. It's not a feeling she enjoys. Years ago, he sold her the seeds that started up the Dark Stars' rare-plant business. His trust in Fen was slowly earned and hard-won. Worth it, though: Eudea's most valued magical plants come from the Callistan, which the Sythians call home and guard fiercely. They're touchy when it comes to selling plants to outsiders, and they let very few people into their sacred glades.

"What do you want to come into the glades for, anyway?" Rafe asks.

Fen doesn't want to risk telling him the whole truth before he agrees to take her. She takes a swig of water and tells him part of it.

"Someone's been smuggling something out of your glades and taking it to Simta. Something dangerous."

Rafe frowns. "What sort of something?"

"It isn't safe to talk about here. Your clan leader will want to hear what I have to say, I promise you. The quicker you take me to her, the sooner this ends."

"I'd have to get approval first. She'd skin me alive if I brought a gwythda into the glades without her say-so."

"I could buy a boat and go in without you."

Rafe snorts. "You'd get lost within ten minutes, Brae. Believe me. Spare me the sight of finding a roaming boat, someday, containing your desiccated corpse."

Rafe's probably right. The glades are an impenetrable maze to outsiders. If the Sythians don't get you, then the forest will. They say it swallows the unworthy. Plenty of poachers wander in and never find their way back out. But she'll risk it if she has to.

Something shatters. Fen shoots up, reaching for her knife.

"Easy, Brae," Rafe says. "Someone's just knocked a glass off a table."

Fen grips the bar, trying to hide her sudden dizziness.

"Yeah, well. You don't get ahead in Simta by being slow to draw a blade."

She sits down again. It's been a long few days, and she has slept very little. The light streaming into the bar is too bright. Someone laughs and Fen's vision swims, blurring. The laugh blurs, too, starting to sound like Dorisall's. *I see you, little thief.* She blinks hard, forcing the nightmare back. Without her mastic her magic is escaping more, and the memories with it. She needs witchbane. How much longer can she go without it?

Rafe's looking at her closely. Fen wipes her face clean of emotion, but she can't hide her sweaty brow or shaking hands.

"What's this really about?" he asks.

Fen can't tell him what she needs: She can't risk him turning her away before she gets it. It's time to play the only card she has left.

"I've heard Sythians will take any girl with magic into the glades, no questions asked. Is that true?"

"True enough," he says.

Fen grits her teeth. "Fine, then."

She looks around to make sure no one's staring, then peels off her patch. He stares at her eyes, one a warm brown, the other green, and taps his breastbone the way she's seen him do when handling a particularly magical plant.

"'Spring-stained eyes," he says, quiet. "You're *enlimned*?"

Fen nods, though the last thing she feels right now is blessed.

"Well, then," he says, leaning back. "That's a fish of a different color."

"You'll take me? Today?"

"I think I'd better."

Relief washes through her. She's going to get what she needs and finally take a full breath. After that, she'll be able to begin to make things right.

FOR FEN, LOVE and pain are often tangled. She loved the shadow of her dame, but then the woman never came to save her. She loved the stuffed dog some do-gooder gave her, then cried when it was taken away. Now she knows how love cuts, but she didn't expect to feel it in the Callistan. Her heart is throbbing in a way that makes no sense.

Rafe is at the back of the flat-bottomed boat, using a slender oar to steer them through the swampland. He seems to know the way, though Fen doesn't see how. It's all the same, wild tangle, trees reaching out of still waters. They're bigger than she expected, spreading in every direction. Moss hangs from their branches, swaying like ghosts. She never knew there were so many shades of green, dark and light, pale and shining. The air is making her teeth ache.

"What is that?" she asks.

"What?"

"That sound. The . . . humming."

Rafe keeps his eyes on the trees. "It's the magic that runs through this place. We call it the pulse of the Wellspring. All Sythians can hear it, as well as the *enlimned*."

It's too loud. Blazing cats, she needs her mastic. Her mouth is so dry, her skin so hot. She can see the swamp's silty bottom clearly, crisscrossed with interwoven roots. She sticks her fingers into the tea-colored water, hoping to steal some of its coolness. It's warm, but she shudders a little nonetheless.

When Fen was young, and things got bad, she used to close her eyes and dream herself into a forest like this one. It made her feel safe, somehow: protected. That dream place loved her. This place loves her just the same. Vines keep reaching out as if trying to caress her. But there's a hunger in the air, a watchfulness. The glades want something from her: She can feel it. The leaves whisper in a language she shouldn't understand.

We see you.

Her magic rises, bringing darkness with it, curling at the edges of her eyes. She hears a door click closed, a rasping voice. *Little thief. I see you.* The air is cut by the crack of a whip.

She grips the boat's sides. *Get it together.* She needs to keep herself from falling apart.

At last, Rafe stops rowing. He raises his hand, making some gesture at the trees. A voice floats out, and Rafe answers.

Finally. Then the air is ripped in two by a sudden *thwip*. An arrow streaks by, pocking the water not far from them. Then more come, *thwipthwipthwip*. Fen ducks down low.

"Ten hells," she growls. "Why are they firing on us?"

"They're not," Rafe says, pointing. "It's them."

Fen whips around to see the prow of a boat much like theirs, rocking sharply. Whoever's in it is mostly hidden by a tree, but Fen can *feel* her. How did Fen not clock Sayer before?

"Stop," Fen shouts. "That's my friend."

Rafe scowls. "Did you know they were behind us? For the love of the waters, Fen—"

"I mean it, Rafe. Call them off."

"They don't take their orders from me, mate."

More arrows fly, seeming to come from all directions. One lodges itself in the boat's side as it drifts closer, revealing Sayer, Jolena, and Rankin.

"Leave off," Rankin shouts, gripping his oar like a club. "We're with Fenlin!"

But the archers keep shooting, getting close—too close. An arrow forces Rankin to dodge, and Jolena catches him as he almost tips over the edge. Sayer starts working her magic. The light changes, making the water ripple all around their boat, the air shimmering darkly. The arrows flying toward them start to slow, caught in whatever barrier Sayer is making, dropping harmlessly to either side. But one breaks through: Sayer cries out, hand flying up to her shoulder. They've hit her. Fen sees blood between her fingers, bright against the backdrop of the leaves.

Her magic explodes, seeming to split her open. All around them, trees hiss and shudder, voicing her rage. Vines shoot out from the trees and roots reach out of the water, all twisting themselves into impossible shapes. They encase Sayer's boat, weaving into a dripping shield around it. Someone is screaming: She thinks it might be her.

The nightmare sinks in its teeth.

We see you, someone whispers.

I see you, Ana.

She tastes iron and helplessness and terror.

Then, all at once, the raging stops. She can barely feel her body. Rafe shouts something over the din, but the words make no sense. There is only the magic, and the voices, and the feeling of falling. The water wraps around her. She closes her eyes, lost to the dark.

Every chemical action has a reaction, every poison a remedy. But you must learn the language of our plants. It isn't enough to know their properties: You must dive into their history, their origins. Do not ignore the old wives' tales. They may seem fanciful, but they should be respected. Such tales have led me, time and again, to truth.

—A PASSAGE FROM ONE OF
THE YELLOW ALCHEMIST'S NOTEBOOKS

– CHAPTER 12 –
A TOXIN ENTWINED WITH ITS BALM

SAYER CAN'T COUNT how many times she's dreamed of adventure. She's never traveled—she and her dame could never afford to—so Simta is all she's ever known. But on nights when she couldn't sleep, she'd imagine what it might be like to pack a bag and walk out across the Neck and go elsewhere. She'd picture herself sailing to the Singing Isles, combing Faire's bright markets, or trekking up Stonington's chalk-white hills. She never dreamed herself here, into this place so few people ever see with their own eyes. She's too worried about Fen to take it in.

After Fen collapsed, their attackers called a sudden cease-fire. Small houseboats emerged from the trees, and Sayer watched a boy haul Fen out of the water and take her onto one of them. She wanted to shout as a woman took Fen behind its bright orange door, closing it firmly. But Jolena was pressing her hands to Sayer's bleeding shoulder, and for a while she was too dizzy to say much at all. One of the Sythians came to fish them out of their boat, which Fen's manic tangle of roots had torn several holes in. One of them even healed her wound. Sayer gritted her teeth as the Sythian girl put her hands over the gash, using some healing magic to make the skin knit back together. It burned. *I could have saved you the trouble,* Sayer snapped, *if you hadn't shot me to begin with.* The girl tapped her breastbone. *We wouldn't have, had we known.*

The clan is rowing their houseboats through the swamp now, taking them who knows where. They're being treated as guests, at least, and not prisoners. It hasn't made her feel less on edge. She, Rankin, and Jolena are on the houseboat they took Fen to, which the boy Fen came with is steering. As soon as they boarded, Rankin parked himself next to that closed orange door. Sayer can't stop glaring at it. She asked—demanded—to see Fen, and was refused. She came very close to ripping the thing off its hinges. *Seleese knows what she's about,* the boy, Rafe, assured her. *She's the best healer in the Callistan.* Whatever's wrong with Fen, Sayer doesn't like to leave her with a stranger.

Sayer huffs out a breath. If Matilde was here, she'd lighten the mood by making jokes and sultry comments to their boatman. Æsa would stroke her arm and murmur sweetly in her ear. *Fen will survive this,* she might whisper. *She is strong.* But Sayer keeps seeing her falling into the water, pulled down by it. She didn't look like Fenlin Brae at all.

A flash of pink makes Sayer turn back toward the prow. Jolena's coaxed Rankin away from his vigil at the door to sit beside her. She's pulled some bright, fragrant flowers from somewhere, and he's letting her braid them into his unruly nest of hair.

"Does it suit me?" he asks, perking up under her fixed attention.

"It brings out the lovely golden flecks in your eyes."

Rankin blushes at that. "I didn't know I had any."

"This place is making everything brighter."

Jolena sighs. Her face tilts up to the trees, a basking flower seeking sunlight. Despite everything else there is to worry over, it's good to see Jolena opening back up. Since leaving Simta, she's been withdrawn and quiet. Rankin cajoled a few smiles from her, but they never lasted. More than once, Sayer caught silent tears slipping down her cheeks, her gaze distant. But here, in the glades, she seems closer to her sunny self. It makes sense: She is an earth girl, which makes this place her element. It's Sayer who feels out of her depth.

"How do you know where you're going?" she asks Rafe. "All the trees look the same to me."

"That's because you're a gwythda," he says. "You wouldn't know a glade path from a sinkhole."

She watches him row, the movement making the braided reeds around his forearm ripple.

The boat they're in is much bigger than the one she stole from outside the Rover's Inn, and shallower. The water here isn't as deep as she would've guessed. The swamp has no roads: It's all water, dotted by the small islands choked with trees. It feels alive, this place, as if it has its own heartbeat. She can almost feel it trying to keep time with hers.

Jolena takes a deep breath. "The air here is so much fresher than in Simta. It's so peaceful."

Sayer slaps at one of the many biting insects. "I'd like it more if the place wasn't trying to eat me alive."

"Toothbalm," Rafe says, grabbing a few serrated yellow leaves off a trailing vine. "For every ill, the glades provide a remedy. Rub it over your skin. The oil should keep them off."

"How do I know this won't make me break out in pustules?"

Jolena laughs. "Sayer. Be nice."

But being nice is about making other people feel comfortable, and she's not in the mood.

Rafe just smiles. "Don't worry. I'm not trying to kill you. Don't need to. After all, that's what the gators are for."

As if to make his point, there's a slapping sound not far off. Sayer watches as a giant, scaly monster creeps onto a nest of logs, teeth glistening. It makes her think unpleasantly of her sire. That old, familiar rage blooms in her chest as she dwells on Wyllo Regnis. Have Matilde and Leta found where he's hiding the Red Hand? Have they cornered Wyllo and made him confess? If she was there, she would pin him to the wall and make him tell her. He shouldn't be allowed to walk around, free and clear. But that is part of why she came: to find out who's supplying him with witchbane and stop it from reaching Simta. She has to find out what these Sythians know.

Sayer leaps up as the woman reemerges from behind the orange door. She's perhaps Leta's age, plump and compact, her skin smooth and deeply tanned. Like Rafe, she has what looks like dried reeds braided through her hair and tied around her forearms. But like Fen, her eyes are two different shades. One is the same warm brown as the tree trunks around them, and the other is the burnt orange of the door.

"My name is Seleese," she says, voice smooth and deep. "Head of this clan. Welcome home, daughters."

The word makes Sayer tense.

"Where is our friend? What've you done with her?"

"She is sleeping," Seleese says. "I have given her something to keep her that way for a small while."

"Why?"

"It will help with her withdrawal. The poison's hooks are deep in her."

Rankin looks a little sick. "Do you mean the witchbane?"

Rafe makes a noise, *achfft*, halfway between a spit and a hiss.

Seleese folds her ample arms. "We call it venom vine. I hope your hearts aren't still set on poaching any from our glades. I assume that is what you came for."

Sayer shakes her head. "We didn't come to steal anything."

"Addicts will do many things to get what they need."

It's hard for Sayer to imagine Fenlin Brae needing anything that badly, even witchbane.

"You don't understand," Sayer says. "She can't be addicted. It makes us sick."

"But if you take it long enough, that sickness fades, and it has its attractions. Increased calm, sharpened focus. Most Sythians with magic in them know better than to be drawn in by its lures. We stay away from it. But I knew a girl once, from another clan, who chewed it. She had spent some time in Sarask, where a traveling pater convinced her that magic would corrupt her. For those who seek control, the plant holds a certain appeal."

When Fen popped the mastic in her mouth at the Hunt Club, Sayer was horrified. She can't understand why, after everything, Fen would still be inflicting it on herself. It's not like she has moral qualms about her magic, like Æsa.

She remembers what Fen told her, months ago, about her reasons. *All magic's ever done is cause me pain.* That night was the first time she confessed the lengths to which the Red Hand went to bring Fen's magic to the surface. Her life with him was dark basements, locked rooms, a whip hung on the wall. But Fen survived it all: None of it broke her. At least that's what Sayer thought.

"She's been chewing it a lot more since Leastnight," Rankin is saying, clearly troubled. "I tried to tell her not to, but she brushed me off. I kept tabs on her stash, though. It's only just run out."

"How long ago?" Seleese asks.

"Four days? Five?"

"I am amazed she arrived in our glades standing. Her withdrawal is very close to reaching its peak."

Dash it, Fen. Sayer's anger rears again, but it's like frost on a window. Scratch it with a nail and you'd find guilt lying beneath. She should have seen what was happening; but then, Fen could have told her. Sayer wants them to be done with keeping secrets from each other.

Seleese is whispering to Rafe, who changes course with his long pole.

"Can you help her or not?" Sayer asks.

Seleese nods. "Yes, I can. It will take several days, but she should recover fully. In the meantime, I'd like it if you told me why you've come."

Sayer takes a breath. Can she trust them? If she wants their help, she isn't sure she has much of a choice. So she explains about the Red Hand's witchbane, the exhibition, and the Sugar. Seleese's face quickly goes from calm to grave.

"My clan would never sell venom vine outside the glades," she says. "Such a thing spits in the face of the sacred."

"Maybe you wouldn't," Sayer presses. "But are there other clans who'd make a deal for the right price?"

"No," Rafe says at once. "The clans may operate independently, but we have laws. To sell such a plant would break them. No Sythian would sell something that might hurt the enlimned."

Sythians see girls with magic as sacred. *Daughters,* Seleese called them. But Sayer knows that such ties don't keep families from hurting each other. It doesn't protect them from betrayal.

"I have heard some troubling rumors," Seleese says. "About a Simtan cult making inroads with some of the clans. Convincing them the Callistan's riches should be used to fight the enlimned. I did not want to believe it, but if what you say is true . . ."

"We know the name of the buyer," Jolena says, expression darkening. "Wyllo Regnis."

"He's a Simtan lord," Sayer adds. "Have you heard of him?"

"No," Seleese says. "But I could speak to some of the other clan leaders. Quietly, mind you. These aren't accusations to be thrown around lightly."

"There isn't time to tarry," Sayer presses. "We think some men are being sent to pick up a shipment—a big one—any day. We have to stop them."

Seleese looks to Rafe in silent communion. At last, it seems a decision is made.

"We will help you stop them, daughter. We will not let venom vine leave the glades. But your friend will need to rest while we seek answers."

Sayer lets out a breath she didn't know she was holding.

"I want to see her."

Seleese's expression softens. "She asked that you all stay away, for now. And perhaps it's wise of her. She is going to get worse before she gets better."

Sayer's chest stings, a sudden burn. They are supposed to be each other's shadows. Why is Fen still hiding from her?

Seleese tells Rafe to slow the boat next to one of the small islands.

"See there?" She gestures toward a climbing vine with three-pronged leaves that's wrapped itself around a gnarled tree. Sayer doesn't know much about plants: This one looks like every other. But somehow, she can sense its ill intent. The undersides of its leaves are tacky looking, as if coated in resin. Its smell—smoke and decay—makes Sayer want to gag.

"That's witchbane," Jolena says, eyes haunted. "Isn't it?"

Seleese nods. "And the one growing next to it is what we've stopped for. We call it bleeding heartvine."

Sayer can see why. Its heart-shaped leaves are red, unlike so many of the other plants she's seen here. Its stems stand out against the tree's skin like brilliant veins. Seleese leans down, dipping two fingers in the water and whispering something. Then she peels some bleeding heartvine from the tree, careful not to touch the witchbane.

"It is for Fenlin," Seleese says. "Its vapor and oils are a restorative for the enlimned. It should help to build her strength up."

As Sayer watches, the vine starts to grow, wrapping around Seleese's arm. Jolena gasps. It's strange to see a woman as old as she is doing magic. Perhaps the Callistan has kept it alive in her. Or maybe it's just that, unlike the Nightbirds, she never gave it away.

Jolena reaches out to touch the heart vine. One of the leaves curls lovingly around her hand.

"How will you prepare it?" she asks.

"It's best if the leaves are young and fresh," Seleese says, clearly pleased at her interest. "We will grind some for a chest ointment and make the rest into a tea. You can help me, daughter."

Jolena's gaze has turned thoughtful. "One of my botany books says the best cure for one plant's poison lies in another that grows near it. *A toxin*, it says, *is often entwined with its balm.* Like fireweed and queen's lace. Fireweed will give you blisters, but queen's lace will cure it. It can even ward against the fireweed's effects."

Seleese smiles. "Clever girl. But bleeding heartvine doesn't nullify all of witchbane's effects. At least, not totally."

Sayer's skin is prickling now. "But you're saying it helps."

If bleeding heartvine can ease some of witchbane's effects, could it guard them against it? Could it make it so that Sugar wouldn't work on them?

Jolena grips Sayer's hand, seeming to hear her thoughts. "Maybe it could help us find an antidote to Sugar. It could make it so no girl will ever suffer like I did, ever again."

"It's a nice idea," Sayer says gently. "But I don't want you to get your hopes up."

Jolena's eyes are shining, coming alive. "What's wrong with hope?"

Sayer doesn't know how she can even ask, after what's happened to her. How she can still have so much faith when the world keeps letting her down. But her excitement is infectious, a growing thing. Sayer doesn't have the heart to squash it. She wants to hope, for once, instead of doubt.

Bright of mind, swift to fly.

—THE HOUSE DINATRIS CREED

– CHAPTER 13 –
A STOLEN GLOW

MATILDE STRAIGHTENS ON her pedestal, lifting her arms, as instructed. She flinches as one of the dressmaker's pins pricks her skin.

"The color isn't right," Dame is saying, scrutinizing the silk being slipped around her. "Red will make people think of mourning."

"But flames as well," Gran says, sipping her tea. "There will be many eyes watching. A reminder of her power might be prudent."

"Perhaps I should go naked," Matilde says archly. "That would give them something to talk about."

Dame frowns. "Tilde, don't joke."

She can't help but want to lighten the mood, just a little. So far, these wedding planning sessions have felt more like war councils than anything, though she supposes the event is part of her greater fight. Every detail will send a message, from the music to the flowers decking each chair. She needs to make sure they are the right ones. Now, though, she would really rather take a nap.

Dame holds up a few small swatches of fabric. She has waited years for Matilde to take the long walk down the aisle. *My daughter, wed to the suzerain,* she keeps crowing, forgetting she once demanded that Matilde stay away from him. Everything is different now.

The wedding's set for a few weeks from now, at the end of Risentide. The short engagement has her family and Dennan's staff in a tizzy. There is much to do, and not much time. It is just enough time for guests to travel from across Eudea. Luckily, the foreign courts got invitations in advance. It turns out they were sent out several weeks before Matilde knew anything about the wedding. She is furious that Dennan went behind her back so boldly, but has decided she's too tired to make a fuss.

"What about white?" Dame says. "A version of our House color."

Gran looks Matilde up and down. These past few days, she's always looking, as if she expects at any minute for Matilde to pick up her skirts and bolt.

"Perhaps green and white," she says. "A symbol of unity between our Houses."

"Gold might be better," Matilde muses. "It is the color of myth and legend. Of greatness. And it reflects the light beautifully."

Dame claps. "Dennan can dress to match. How you will glow!"

Smiles all around. Matilde tries to smile, too, but it's an effort. She is struggling to keep her eyelids aloft.

Dame frowns. "You really must get your beauty rest, Tilde. No one likes a bride with dark circles."

Matilde takes a careful sip of coffee. "Yes, well. I have a lot on my plate."

There is no time for sleep. During the day, she sits through hours of wedding planning sessions and listening in on Table meetings. At night, she heads out to hunt for the missing girls, Sugar, and the Red Hand's lair with the Dark Stars. Despite her low opinion of sandpipers, Matilde likes them—Hallie especially. The girl's gallows humor and penchant for knives remind her of Sayer. It seems Alec has been too busy studying the Sugar samples to join them. Or, more likely, he is using it as an excuse to avoid her. She tells herself it's better for them both to keep their distance. Most of the time, she almost half believes it.

Since Wyllo Regnis is their best lead, that is where they have concentrated their efforts. They follow him everywhere: to his club, church, the Merchant Bank, visiting other Houses. When she can, she pulls on someone else's face and goes in closer. She even snuck into House Regnis while the family was out, rifling through his desk, looking for any clues: nothing. He doesn't have one scrap of writing connecting him to the Red Hand. The man is clearly covering his tracks.

She would love to truss Wyllo up and simply make him confess the truth, but Leta thinks it a bad idea. She has grown more cautious since the Wardens stormed her house looking for Sayer. They subjected her to a proper inquisition, and though she gave them nothing, they have her under something close to house arrest. *We must use stealth,* she says. *Let Wyllo think he has bested us. It will make him more likely to let down his guard.* But if there is a chink in his armor, she hasn't found it. Her frustration is a banked fire, and Wyllo's antics have her itching to unleash it. She still can't believe the flotsam he published in the papers. He talked about Sayer as if she was a monster. Now the whole city is worried the Storm Witch will abduct their daughters from their beds.

The witch must be found, the Pontifex argued at a Table meeting this morning. *We cannot allow such crimes to go unpunished.*

Too right, added Sand Deveraux. *It makes us look like we have lost all control.*

She listened from behind her screen as the men debated. Most seemed intent on seeing Sayer wear a noose. Not Dennan, though; he is pressuring Matilde to invite Sayer to the palace, where he says he can protect her. Matilde finds that offer as disconcerting as the Table's threats.

This is why we need a registry, Sand said. *If we know who these girls are, we can regulate them.*

If we know who they are, the Pontifex added, *we can ensure their magic is used only for holy work.*

We should consult my betrothed on this, Dennan said. *After all, she has a vested interest. And it won't be long before she joins us.*

His words elicited a tense, simmering silence. One she wanted to fill with her own voice. *Someone is poisoning us,* she would shout. *It's them we need to punish.* Matilde can't pull up a seat at the Table soon enough. What would they say, if she told them about Sugar? If she demanded they find the Red Hand and bring him in? It feels more like a risk than a solution; she cannot trust any of them to fix her problems. They may not see Sugar as a problem at all.

Dame is talking about bridesmaid dresses. Petra, Sive, and Octavia have all agreed to stand up with her. How she wishes it was Æsa, Sayer, and Fen instead. Sayer wrote her a note before she left for the Callistan. *I'm sorry about outing the engagement to Alec. I was angry. I do believe in your power; don't be afraid to use it.* Matilde keeps it tucked in her pocket as a reminder that she isn't alone in this. But the knowledge that she is the only Fyrebird left in Simta hangs heavy, lead weights tied to her wings.

There is a knock on the door. Matilde sees a flash of violet as the Pontifex sweeps into the room without waiting to be asked.

"Excuse me, ladies," he says. "I don't mean to interrupt."

Please. That is exactly what he means to do, clearly. She smiles as if she doesn't have a care in the world.

"Pontifex Rolo," Gran says with a cool smile. "This is a surprise."

"It isn't proper." Dame jumps up, cheeks flushing. "My daughter isn't dressed."

Matilde takes her time reaching for her robe. Let him see she isn't flustered. "I'm sure our Pontifex won't take advantage. After all, Rolo loves only the gods."

His lips thin at the way she uses his name, not his title.

"I would like an audience with Young Lady Dinatris," he says. "Alone."

Matilde smiles on. "Of course. Do take a seat."

Her family files out, taking the dressmaker with them. Gran looks uneasy, but Matilde is curious. What could he possibly want? As the door clicks closed, Matilde stays up on her pedestal. She isn't ready to give up the high ground. Instead, she gestures toward the coffee service.

"The coffee is still warm. Help yourself if you'd like a cup."

"None for me," he says. "I try to limit my vices."

She winks at him. "If only I could say the same."

Rolo's mouth puckers. He is a softer presence than the last Pontifex, shorter, less manicured, with a rounded stomach and winglike ears. His shaved eyebrows give him an innocent air, but she knows better. He might not have tried to stab her, like the last one, but she knows he dislikes her just as much.

"A fine work," he says, gesturing to the painting across from her.

In her opinion, there are far too many images of gods in the Winged Palace. This one features Syme bathed in sunshine, holding his traditional sheaf of wheat aloft. How smug the man looks in his gold robes, his stolen glow. Clearly no one has ever found his power threatening, or questioned whether he should have it at all.

She looks down at her nails. "I suppose, if you like religious scenes. I confess I've lost my taste for them lately."

"I understand it was a gift from the church when the first Vesten became our suzerain. Something to remind him that miracles can be had if one is worthy." He folds his hands over his belly. "Do you know this story of Syme's?"

Matilde lifts an insouciant shoulder. "Something about making fields of wheat grow? Or perhaps it was about him stopping a plague. I can't remember."

"You should really come to church more often, Young Lady Dinatris."

"Perhaps I might be more inclined if you didn't preach that girls like me are evil. Alas."

He doesn't rage at her blasphemous talk. Just smiles, showing his teeth.

"This miracle of Syme's is one of my favorites. It was a time of war, of heartache, and the fruitfulness had drained out of the soil. Nothing would grow. People were starving. Some sort of blight had made all the seeds go bad. This painting celebrates the moment when the Wellspring rose up, gifting Syme with magic, and he was able to use it to talk the dried-up seeds into sprouting."

"Much like the Flower Witch made a vine grow on Leastnight," she muses. "How interesting."

"Except she used the magic for destruction. I would have such gifts used for good."

She takes an impatient breath. "What have you come to discuss, Pontifex? I assume it wasn't art history or religious doctrine."

He smooths his robes. "No. I simply wanted to tell you that I have spoken to our suzerain, and he has convinced me to officiate your wedding."

She tries not to let her surprise show. Dennan said he was going to speak to Rolo about it. *Having him marry us would be a sign of favor,* he said, *and of cooperation.* She never thought the man would agree.

"And what is to be the price for your services?"

He lifts his spotted hands. "These are troubled times, Young Lady Dinatris. I seek unity. You and I do not have to be enemies."

"I don't see how we could possibly be friends."

He moves closer. "It may surprise you to know that I don't believe in killing witches indiscriminately. The Wellspring gifts its holy magic with a purpose. To cast it back is an insult."

She almost laughs. "Really, Rolo. I thought the gods frowned upon telling fibs."

"I am in earnest, Young Lady Dinatris. I don't believe girls like yourself should be killed for what lives inside you. I simply don't think you were made to withstand its power. Most of us are weak vessels, unfit to carry the holy. Few of us are made to be gods."

"So you would have me give it to someone else," she says, thinking of Sugar. "Someone like you?"

"The people won't stand for the kinds of crimes Sayer Sant Held has been committing. They, and I, will fight what they see as blasphemy. But if such girls partnered with the church, we could use their power for something holy. In the right hands, you could perform all sorts of miracles."

She throws him what she hopes is an unfazed look, but her head is spinning. What is he truly saying? The words *in the right hands* are ricocheting through her head.

"I have graciously decided to put our differences aside and officiate your wedding," he says. "In return, I simply ask that you consider supporting a proposal Dennan will explain to you in due course. A registry of magical girls. If you were to become its public face, Simta's witches would be much more likely to come forward."

"And what would they get out of such an arrangement?"

"Knowledge." His watery eyes are sharper now, more calculating. "Our library holds all sorts of tomes about magic. There are recipes and spells for helping someone channel it, strengthen it. Sweeten it."

His voice doesn't change, but that word—*sweeten*—sends a chill right through her. Is it some sort of veiled reference to Sugar? Does he know about the drug after all?

Krastan said, once, the great library at Augustain's church held secrets in their archives. *We don't know what kinds of knowledge they might hold.* The paters of old found ways of controlling a girl's magic—of leashing it. Fen told them that most of the books the Red Hand used for his experiments came from there. Clearly, it holds treasures worth getting her hands on. Perhaps she and the Dark Stars have been hunting for answers in the wrong place.

"I shall think on what you've said," she says. "But for now, I must rest. I woke quite early."

And tonight, she plans to be out late.

– AQUAVERA –

ATTEMPT #3

GOAL: to let a person hold their breath for a prolonged period.

> ~~Full~~ half a dram of liquid aquavit
> 4 pieces ~~dried~~ fresh sleepweed
> ~~2~~ 3 dashes powdered blowfish
> 2 Illish brineweed roots (harvested at Risentide,
>   if available)

METHOD: Steep all ingredients in the aquavit for two weeks. Add fresh saliva, preferably from the person who is going to use the potion. Reduce over low* heat, stirring constantly, to a sticky paste. Works in capsule form.

RESULTS: Still choked after about three minutes, but no unsightly gills this time.

*Don't turn the heat above a whisper. Almost blew my face off. Eyebrows singed, but otherwise unscathed.

—FROM THE SECRET JOURNAL
OF ALECAND PADANO

– CHAPTER 14 –
HOLIER THAN THOU

MATILDE ADJUSTS HER robe in Augustain church's looming shadow. It swishes around her in diaphanous folds.

"I'll give it to the church," she says, voice deep and rasping. "These robes are ugly, but they're awfully comfortable. It's like wearing an oversized tent."

They borrowed their outfits from the Dark Stars, who seem to have a plethora of costumes at their clubhouse. She can't say she loves Alec in an acolyte's robes. He used some alchemical balm to make it look like his head and brows are shaved, like all paters. Without his hair, he looks little like himself.

"This is a terrible idea," Alec says. "I just want to say that again for the record."

"Come now. Where is your sense of adventure?"

"I left it at home, beside my sense of self-preservation."

She rolls her eyes. He's been grumbling since she showed up at the Bathhouse and cajoled him into coming, and yet he didn't tell her no.

"Look, the Pontifex knows more than he is saying. That library could hold the answers we need. We could find the recipe for Sugar there, or an antidote. That alone is worth risking it. We might even find out where the Red Hand is hiding." She touches her cheek. "How's my face?"

"Your face is fine," Alec says. "Though I still think it's the wrong one. Too recognizable."

"That is precisely the point." She can only borrow the guises of someone she knows, and she doesn't know that many paters. The Pontifex would've drawn too much notice. His secretary, though: the slight, unobtrusive man who often comes to Table meetings and scribbles in his notebook. A silent presence. "Garald's important enough to get us through any locked doors."

"Or get us caught when someone stops and asks questions you can't answer."

"If you're going to grouse, perhaps you should stay out here."

He scoffs. "You don't know the difference between a cake recipe and an alchemical gold mine. You need me."

It's true. He has a better chance of navigating Augustain's library than she does, but his disguise isn't as good as hers.

"I mean it, Alec. If you don't want to—"

"Tilde. If you're going, I'm going."

The words send a wash of relief straight through her. She doesn't want to do this alone.

"All right. Just remember, I'm a high-ranking pater, so you should stay behind me. Make sure to look awestruck."

He makes a sound that's almost a laugh. "I'll do my best."

They head toward the front of Augustain's church. Its vaulted doors are closed, but they will still be unlocked. The public section is always left open in case someone wants to come and pray.

"Don't swish your hips so much," Alec says.

"Excuse me?"

"It doesn't suit a pater." And then, under his breath, "And it's confusing enough seeing you like this without . . . all that."

His words are like sparks, though his tone isn't particularly warming. They haven't talked about their kisses in his room, or anything that happened after. He hasn't brought it up, and she doesn't know how. The engagement sits between them, a pet waiting to be acknowledged. Or readying to bite one of their hands.

Matilde takes a deep breath, then pulls one of the doors open. Augustain's public section is long and soaring, its ceiling so high one must crane their neck to take it in. It's all marble columns and long benches hewn of an unforgiving wood. The ornate windows look black at this time of night, obscuring the scenes etched into them. Most of Simta's windows are made of colored glass, but these are colorless, supposedly to let the gods see through them. Matilde's always suspected that it's truly to let the sun in, searing congregants to ensure they stay awake.

They move quietly down the main aisle, the air rich with incense and beeswax, past the pulpit ringed by elegant stone stairs. Fortunately, no paters hover near the whisperboxes where Simta's finest confess their sins. The only sounds are their footsteps and the trickle of water. Small fountains are placed along the aisle, meant to represent the Wellspring. Matilde touches one, letting the cool water bathe her palm.

Out of the corner of her eye, she sees a flicker. It's coming from one of four shrines along the walls, each decorated with a burbling fountain and a statue of one of the Eshamein. This one is crowded with offerings, every candle burning. She wonders if it's paters or congregants flocking to Marren's shrine. Either way, she doesn't like to see it looking so lively.

She leaves it behind, stalking over to one of the discreet doors near the back wall. The map she found in the Winged Palace's archives suggested one would lead them up to the belltower, while the other should take them into the inner, private bowels of the church. She and Alec slip through, into the vast complex where the Pontifex and his Council of Brethren hold their meetings, and acolytes train and eat and sleep. For a church that preaches moderation and abstention, it's richly appointed. They take one turn, two, winding past prayer alcoves and classrooms. In one hall, a series of what looks like human skulls shine like trophies. She wonders if they belonged to Fyrebirds.

None of that, she tells herself, shaking the thought away.

There aren't many paters afoot, just as she'd hoped. They like to rise early. A few do pass, nodding in greeting. She nods back, a bead of sweat tracing her spine. Finally, they catch sight of the doors to Augustain's great library. She lets out a breath: They aren't guarded.

She and Alec look at each other. When she pushes on the door, fortunately, it falls open.

The space is even more vast than she imagined. Lanterns line the main floor, but their light does not quite reach its upper levels. Matilde isn't sure she has ever seen so many books at once. Towering stacks fill the ground floor, rows and rows. It is a labyrinth. From what she can tell, they have it all to themselves.

The only sound is the constant rush of churning water. It's coming from a canal that enters the room at its far end, running down its wide center aisle before splitting into two channels that disappear through openings in the walls. Matilde has heard tales of the Maelstrom, which is supposed to be a proxy for the Wellspring.

"A bold choice," she whispers. "Building a river in a library."

"I've read the men who built it devised a pump to bring water up from the canals," Alec whispers back, "and another to make it rush like that. Quite a feat of engineering."

"I wonder where it leads."

"Back into the canals, I suspect. I've heard that acolytes jump into these before they're allowed to become paters. To prove their devotion."

The very thought makes her shudder.

A walkway takes them over the right-hand branch of the Maelstrom and into the labyrinth. As they weave through the stacks, Alec runs his hands over spines as if he can't quite help it, whispering to the books as they pass. She reads some as they go. Most have boring titles like *A Treatise on Agriculture in the Waystrell* and *Guidance in the Art of Focused Prayer*. After a while, they start to blur.

She leads them to the far end. There must be a restricted section housing the church's most precious treasures. The map she found made it seem like it might be somewhere back here. Yes: She sees an ornate door against the back wall, set deep into a bookshelf. She hurries over, almost tripping in her haste. Alec grabs a lantern off a hook, limning the design etched in the metal: a tracery of ornate waves encircling three words in old Eudean.

EN RECTA, VAILE.

In knowledge, power.

Anticipation dances down her skin in a rush.

She reaches for the wrought-iron handles. Alec stops her.

"Wait."

"Why?"

"Because I think there's a charm on it. See there?"

He circles the air beside one handle, where there's a hollow handprint.

"You have to put your hand in. If you're one of the people included in the spell, it will admit you. If not . . ."

Her heart pounds. "If not, *what?* Alarms? Dismemberment?"

He looks a little sheepish. "I don't know."

"Well," she says, trying for confidence. "We've come this far."

She checks her disguise, making sure it's firm. Then she puts her hand—Garald's hand—to the hollow. She counts: one, two. This will work. She won't let it do otherwise. This door will only see what she wants it to see.

At last, a *click.* The door swings open. They both let out a shaky breath.

The room inside is narrow, but long, and crammed with books. There are hundreds of them—thousands. So many secrets, trapped behind these walls.

Alec rests his hand on a shelf, soft and reverent. His voice is soft too.

"Krastan would love this."

Krastan, with his ready smiles and gnarled hands, and his belief in her. Tonight, she's going to prove his faith right.

After a beat, Alec starts sliding books out and leafing through them. Matilde stands near the door, keeping one ear out, and starts to peruse the closest spines. None of them seem particularly relevant to her interests. The titles don't help: They're all dry-sounding treatises. No *Helpful Hints for Warding Off Witchbane* or *Fyrebirds: A Comprehensive Guide.* Still, she picks one out and flips it open, looking for something: anything. It feels like looking for jewels in a dragon's hoard.

"I've never seen some of these recipes before," Alec says,

running a finger down a fragile-looking page. "There is a healing spell in here that can make bones grow."

She frowns. "You can't do that sort of thing with alchemicals, though, can you?"

"No. But this recipe's from before the Great Revelations. Krastan said magic was different then." He turns a page. "All this knowledge, owned by people who don't use it."

She recalls something her sire once said. *Buy up all the stock and you get to set its value. If you're the only game in town, you hold the power.*

"That's the point, I'm sure. They want to control it."

She wonders how many paters have played with magic while preaching it's a sin.

They are quiet for a time, both turning pages. Every few minutes, Alec scribbles something down in his notebook. They find no mentions of Sugar or witchbane. Perhaps the Red Hand stole all the books containing them? There are so many; reading through them all would take a lifetime. Impatience has her gripping the shelf's edge.

"Look at this," Alec says.

She goes to lean over his shoulder. The book he's holding seems to be some sort of a ledger, filled with cramped, spidery writing. At first, Matilde can't understand what caught his eye. Then she sees the drawing of two wings, and the lines scrawled within them.

If a sorceress's magic she will not submit, then witchbane's oil will banish it.

If magic and the soul do part, the sundering is healed with bleeding heart.

Matilde's pulse picks up. "What does that mean?"

"No idea. But it's something."

He copies the lines. She holds up the lantern so he can see better. In the recesses of the shelf, behind the place where his book just sat, something glimmers. She leans forward to see a slender volume, bound in dark blue leather. A tiny symbol is stamped on its spine with gold foil. Recognition jolts through her at the flying horse, so familiar. She has seen journals just like this before. Her tradition-loving family has had them handmade for generations, stamped with the House Dinatris sigil. What is one of them doing here?

She pulls it out. It's old, cracked at the edges. The leather feels like fragile skin left in the sun. The writing on the title page is faded, but legible.

"Alec," she whispers, holding it out. "Read this aloud. Tell me I'm not dreaming."

He sucks in a sharp breath. "The journal of Delaina Dinatris."

Her heart feels as if it's just caught fire.

This journal has never been more than a bedtime story. A tantalizing myth, its words lost to time. Not lost, after all, but stolen. She wonders who it was that locked Delaina's words, her thoughts, in here. Most seem to be diary-style entries, but there are recipes and loose pieces of paper. Every page is filled with writing. She leafs through it, fingers trembling, too excited to take in more than snatches of words.

"My daughter does not want to be a Nightbird," she reads aloud. "She does not want to give her power away. Imagine what she would say if I told her that, in gifting it to others, it will fade that much more quickly. The magic will not stay with her forever, as ours once did."

"So your magic may not leave you after all," Alec whispers.

"It did for Gran. It always has, for Nightbirds."

But she isn't simply a Nightbird. Matilde touches the page, as if she might be able to reach through it to Delaina. To ask her for her secrets and her aid.

Alec opens his mouth, but she puts a hand up.

"Did you hear that?"

Was it voices, or just the rushing of the Maelstrom? She hurries to the door.

"You have acceded to his request?" a raised voice says. "To marry them?"

She dares a peek. Alec comes to stand just behind her, his chest brushing her back through her robes. Outside are two paters, arguing in a reading nook some ten paces away from them. She can just make out their faces around the edge of a shelf. With a jolt, she recognizes them both. It's Kyr, the old Pontifex, and Rolo, the new one. *Ten hells.*

"He will marry the witch, with or without our blessing," Rolo says. "By compromising now, it will be easier to control them both later."

At the mention of the wedding, she and Alec both stiffen. He pulls just slightly away.

Kyr and Rolo have leaned close, voices lowering. She hasn't seen Kyr since he tried to stab her on Leastnight and Sayer stopped him with her wind and storm. Kyr was forced to step down; she was told he left the city. What in the ten hells is he doing back here? She can't make out their words over the rushing of the Maelstrom. She strains, listening hard. One of them says *witches*, and perhaps *Red Hand*? Then Rolo's voice rises high again, excited. "That is precisely what I am saying. We need that power inside the house, not out."

What power? Sugar? Is he working with the Red Hand? Alec is whispering close to her ear.

"We have to go. If either of them comes this way, we'll be cornered."

Alec is right. They can't get caught here, in the restricted section after midnight. Perhaps eavesdropping will be easier from out in the stacks. She shoves Delaina's journal under her robe.

"Follow me."

She slips out the door, creeping toward the shadows of the stacks. There is little to hide them between the door and safety: a few chairs, a low table, a pedestal, a standing globe. She hunches, creeping from one to another. She is almost there when she hears something clatter. She whirls to see Alec's robes have gotten caught on the pedestal, sending the book atop it tumbling. The two paters start, turning fast.

"Acolyte," Kyr snaps. "You should be in bed. What are you about?"

Alec drops his gaze. "I was . . . reshelving."

"At this hour?"

Matilde walks back, steps measured, heart racing. She simply has to brazen this through.

"Garald," Pontifex Rolo says, frowning. "What is going on here?"

Her smile is the thin, placid one she has seen the real Garald wearing. She makes sure her voice is his, deep and smooth.

"Apologies for interrupting, brothers. I woke up with a notion regarding the matter we spoke of earlier. I thought some reading might help me clarify my thoughts."

The men's stares move between them. She feels Alec shift behind her. She wills her glamour not to do the same.

"And the acolyte?" Kyr says.

"Some midnight reshelving. A punishment for an offense

against me. But you've paid your penance, haven't you, my son?"

Alec nods, keeping his eyes down.

"I will leave you now," she says, bowing. "May the Wellspring offer you its waters."

At last, they respond, "And may the Ones Who Drink share their cup."

She turns away, Alec just behind. They have done it.

And then the real Pater Garald strides into their midst.

Everyone freezes. The real Garald drops his pile of books, staring wide-eyed at his second self. Matilde hears nothing but her desperate, screaming heart.

"What sorcery is this?" Rolo demands as the real Garald says, "Who are you?"

"Who are *you*?" Matilde blusters. "Impostor!"

Kyr looks between them, gaping. Then Rolo shouts, clear and loud.

"WARDENS!"

Alec shoves the globe, sending it crashing into the real Garald. He falls into the other men, knocking them down. She and Alec run into the labyrinth of stacks, trying to lose them. She trips on her robes once, twice, as they sprint down aisles. They have to reach the door before any Wardens block their exit. But she sees them already, pouring in, their crossbows raised.

"Dirty shills," she swears. "I'll have to use my fire to get through them."

"*No.* They'll know it's you. They will arrest you."

"Not if they're busy putting out a library fire."

She can't let them get caught. They will send Alec to the gallows. Panic is climbing its way up her spine. But Alec is busy pulling off his robe, revealing the coat beneath, full of pockets.

"Tell me you have something useful in there," she says. "Some Nightcloak, or that green dragon, or . . ."

Alec is looking up at the balconies above them. His expression is the same one he uses when he's measuring ingredients, trying to ensure he has enough and not too much.

"Do you trust me, Tilde?"

She asked him the same, not long ago, and he said, *That feels like a dangerous question.* Trusting him has never felt dangerous to her.

"Of course I do."

He extracts a sachet from one of his pockets, shaking two capsules out onto his palm. "Then chew on this and follow me."

He pulls her to one of the sets of stairs up to the first-level balcony. They creep up and along it, skirting between shelves. The contents of the capsule taste like grass and salt, viscous and sticky. She tries not to think about what they might be as the Wardens fan out below, hunting for them. The Maelstrom's rush covers the sounds of their steps, at least, but the Wardens have lanterns: Any moment, they will look up and see them. They will be trapped.

At last, Alec pulls her to a stop.

"Make sure you take as big a breath as you can before we hit the water."

"Before we hit the . . . *what?*"

He points down toward the Maelstrom, rushing darkly below them. Her heart pounds.

"You must be joking."

"Don't worry. The Aquavera will let us hold our breaths for a long time."

"How long a time?"

"Three minutes? Four? It's . . . still experimental."

193

"Alec—"

"Shed the robe, Tilde. It'll only drag you down."

A panicked laugh tries to escape. "This isn't the time to undress me, Alec."

"Tilde—"

"Yes, all right."

She strips, silently thanking Sayer for introducing her to pants wearing. *Dresses weren't meant for fleeing,* she said once, on another occasion when they ran from paters. The memory makes her want to laugh and cry.

"Delaina's book," she says, clutching it tight. "I can't leave it."

"Give it here. My bag's resistant to water and fire."

She hands it to him. He gestures over the iron railing. She climbs, hanging on for dear life.

"On three," he says, taking one of her hands. "Don't let go of me."

She nods, heart screaming, as he starts to count.

"One . . ."

She looks at the water, wondering how dark it is, how cold.

"Two . . ."

A Warden is pointing up at them, shouting. She grips Alec's hand. *Don't let go.*

"Three."

They jump. Arrows fly as they fall, zipping close enough that she can feel them. With a shock of rushing cold, they plunge into the foaming dark. The Maelstrom sucks them down, tumbling them like jetsam in a storm. She grips Alec's hand, his arm, terrified of losing him. The sides of the channel bang and scrape at her skin.

Where is the water going to take them? It will spit them out in one of the canals, surely. The Aquavera seems to be doing its job. But she can't stop the fear that wants to flood her, to tell her they're heading for a watery grave. She knows how it feels to drown. The Underground flood almost consumed her. Water above and below, pressing her down. And the darkness: such darkness. She had never felt so helpless before then, so lost. But her girls were there to pull her out, hauling her up by the tether that bound them. And then Alec breathed into her lungs, giving her life.

The Maelstrom sweeps them on and on. She almost loses him as they rush down a precipice, and then the tumbling roil starts to slow. Alec is pulling, pulling, pulling her through the water. She feels his legs scissoring, and so she kicks hers too. And then there's a sudden undertow, a whirl. They break apart. Where is he? Her lungs are starting to burn. She needs to breathe.

She searches the dark for Alec, looking for anything. Far away, something glimmers. She kicks, kicks, kicks, fighting the urge to suck in air.

At last, she breaks through the surface, lungs heaving. Above her is a scattering of stars. For a moment she just breathes, looking up at them. Then, wiping water from her eyes and film from her lips, she looks around. To her left is Augustain's, lit up against the evening. She's floating in the Corners, where Simta's main canals all meet. A canal boat passes by in the distance, the men aboard it laughing. Panic has worked its way back into her heart.

"Alec?" she shouts, treading in a circle. Where is he? "Alec!"

"Tilde!" He swims toward her, splashing in his haste. "Are you—?"

In answer, she throws her arms around him. She can see his wet curls—feel them. Her disguise is gone, too.

"Tilde," he chokes out. "Let go. You're going to drown me."

"You almost drowned me first!"

His laugh is watery, but real. "You'll thank me later."

They swim toward the closest shore, which is Pegasus Quarter, and down one of the main canals. A line of boats is tied up next to an ornate bridge and under a flamemoth lantern, parked for the evening. They climb up into one and collapse onto their backs.

"The journal," she says, when she can talk again. "Did it make it?"

There's a crumpling as he pulls out his bag and opens it up. "It's all right."

They lie in silence for a beat, just breathing. Above them, the flamemoths flutter and crash. They really are beautiful, the way they shine together. Burning no matter how dark the night gets.

Alec sighs. "That was close. You love getting me into trouble, Dinatris."

"You know you wouldn't have it any other way."

He laughs again. She feels it rumble all through her. And then he rolls onto his side, looking down.

"Your face is showing."

"And looking about as pretty as a canal rat, I'd wager."

"You're beautiful, Tilde. In all your guises."

His fingers trace her jaw, her lips. Her cheeks heat.

"Exactly how much canal water did you swallow?"

The jibe floats away, leaving them staring at each other. His eyes, the darkest brown, caress her. She reaches up to smooth his hair out of his face. The flamemoths gild one of his cheeks and the corner of his mouth, still smiling. It's making something flutter wildly in her chest.

She should get up and head back to her bed at the palace. She shouldn't let this reckless, desperate want tug her in. But they are alive, and whole, and here together. She grabs his shirt, pulling him down. His lips taste of salt and whatever herbs were in the Aquavera. Their mouths collide like the flamemoths throwing light over them both. The feeling is so good: She wants it to linger. She wants this kiss—this fire—to be all there is.

I know you do not understand why I have left you, Kras. I know you think I do not love you as much as you love me. I do—I truly do. But what life could we have together? How could we ever take our love outside your attic room? You deserve someone who can stand beside you night and day, without secrets.

My family demands I wed another. I cannot refuse them. For women like me, duty comes first.

—AN OLD LETTER FROM FREY DINATRIS
TO KRASTAN PADANO, UNSENT

– CHAPTER 15 –
WHAT WE TREASURE

MATILDE HAS ALWAYS been good with words. Quick with a quip, a joke to fill any silence. But as she takes on the guise of her maid and hails a carriage, she says nothing. As they turn into the Garden District, walk the last few streets to the Dinatris mansion, and she extracts the house key out of its garden hiding place, silence reigns. It feels like, if they talk, the spell will be broken. She doesn't want to think about what any of this means.

They creep through Gran's garden. She hasn't seen it since she ran for her life all those months ago. It's a little less kempt than she remembers, wild in places. The winglilies have died back and the fountain is empty. Bits of what she assumes are broken bottles glitter like stars across the paving stones. The house itself is dark and cold, emptied of servants. It smells of flowers just starting to turn.

"Tilde," Alec says in a whisper. "Should we really be—"

She kisses him quiet. She didn't bring him here to think, or to question. It was simply a place she could be sure they'd be alone. But as she leads him up the stairs, she wonders if it was the wrong choice. Would it serve as a reminder of all the barriers between them—the things that will pull them apart?

Her bedroom smells a little musty. It is cold, too, the curtains closed.

"Do you have any matches?" Alec asks.

She smiles. "Why would we need them?"

She lets her magic rise. One by one, the tapers in the fireplace spark to life, gilding Alec. It's a thrill and a shock to have him here. When they were young, she spent many afternoons at Krastan's and thought nothing of spending time in Alec's room, but this is the first time he has ever been in hers. There is something intimate about him standing here, surrounded by mementos and the bed she used to dream in. A secret shared.

"We should get you out of those wet clothes," Matilde says, not caring how brazen she sounds. "You'll catch your death."

She pulls at his shirt, trying to tug it off him. He pulls her close and sighs. This kiss feels full of all the things they have no words for. It is stripped of pretense, of all their masks. Their fingers are their own language, painting desire over each other. Alec's spell worker's hands twine tight with hers.

When Gran first told her of her love affair with Krastan Padano, Matilde couldn't fathom it. A Great House daughter and an alchemist's apprentice: impossible. What might they even have as common ground? But the heart doesn't care about practicalities, station, difference. Right now, hers feels like an open wound.

"Wait." Alec pulls back, breaths rough. "Wait, Tilde. You're engaged."

"I . . . am," she says. What else can she say? "But . . ."

"But what?"

She flushes. "Do we have to talk about it?"

"Yes." He takes another step back. "Are you really going to go through with it?"

Her chest aches, as if her magic is trying to reach out to him. The candles tremble, twisting with her frantic pulse.

"I have to, Alec."

He looks as if she's run a blade right through him. Is this how Krastan looked at Gran, in the end?

"Why?"

"For one, because half of Simta already distrusts me. They will truly hate me if I jilt their suzerain."

"That isn't a good reason."

Matilde grips her locket. "I disagree. But I have others."

"Such as?"

An argument hangs, simmering like a potion. She can feel it gathering heat.

"Marrying the suzerain will show the people that magical girls aren't the enemy. And it will get me a place around the Table, so I can deal with the threats against us properly. A position from which I can finally make change."

"You don't have to marry him for power," Alec presses. "You don't need him."

"What about my family?" She is the reason they had to abandon this house, this life, and take refuge at the palace. "A connection to the suzerain will give them power, too. Safety. I owe them that."

"Not at the expense of your happiness."

When Gran told her about letting Krastan go, it shook her. Why would she let her sire choose a suitor for her when she'd already found love for herself? She said it was her duty, and Matilde hadn't understood it. But perhaps Gran was right: Duty does mean sacrifice. *For women like us, duty comes first.*

"And what about the missing girls? And all those people in the Underground? This is the surest way I can see to help them. To fight Prohibition and get rid of the Red Hand. I'll make it safe for you to make your potions, and for the girls to come out of hiding. I can change things. I thought that was what you wanted me to do. It's what Krastan wanted."

"What do *you* want, Tilde?"

Months ago, she would've chosen to shield her feelings from him. But they are beyond that. She wants her true self to be seen.

"I want Sayer, Æsa, and Fen back. I want to discover what the four of us can do. I want to own my power without having to bow to anyone. And I want *you*."

His expression changes, full of longing. He steps in close enough to touch. His hands flex, those fingers that have made so many potions hovering. She yearns for them to come to rest on her skin.

"It won't stop us from seeing each other," she says, knowing it isn't fair, but she is desperate. "You and I will find a way."

For a moment, he just stares. And then his mouth brushes hers, just once, all heat and tenderness. It fills her, lighting every nerve.

"I don't want you just at night," he says, voice husky. "I want you in the day, too. I want to hold your hand in the street with you wearing your real face. I want all of you, or none."

He takes a step back. She has to fight not to chase him. In the hearth, the candles stutter.

"Alec . . ."

She fights the urge to demand that he obey her. Alec isn't someone she can bend around her will.

"It's late," he says at last. "We should go, before someone at the palace misses you."

She doesn't move. If they leave things like this, it will be over. She breathes, in and out, until her magic calms and her pulse slows. Her hands go to her locket. It used to hold the potions Krastan made for her, and for Gran before that. It is perhaps her greatest treasure, the thing that sits closest to her heart.

She slips it off, settling it around Alec's neck.

"Keep it safe for me, will you?" she whispers. "Until I can come back for it."

He says nothing. Matilde can't bear this new silence.

And so she turns and walks away.

Those who seek the paths with an open heart will find them.
Those who do not will get lost in the reeds.

—A SYTHIAN PROVERB

– CHAPTER 16 –
UNLOCKED

FEN IS LOST. The space is dark, and smells of earth and metal. She crouches down and runs her hands across the floor. It moves beneath her, the dry, hot scales of a thousand snakes. No . . . They're vines, but they're writhing like snakes might, constricting. Panic has her by the throat. She tries to shout, but leaves are sprouting on her tongue, filling her mouth. They are gagging her. A raspy male voice slithers through the dark. *I see you, little thief.*

I see you—

Fen jolts back into her body, letting go of the tree roots she was holding. She's covered in sweat, her skin on fire.

"You aren't even trying, daughter."

Seleese's voice is calm, but relentless. They've been at this for hours.

"That's because I don't know what we're doing here."

Fen doesn't remember much of the last few days with any clarity. When she woke up after passing out in Rafe's boat, she found herself in unfamiliar darkness. It was a cramped space, too much like the orphanage basement, but there was a lantern

205

shining and a woman sitting beside it. Seleese has tended her for days, rubbing her chest with oil and making her drink foul-smelling concoctions. All the while, she shouted for witchbane instead. Fen hated how much she needed it. She's pretty sure that at one point, she begged.

I will not help you poison yourself, Seleese said. *But I will help you break free of it.*

Going without meant days of bad sleep and big sweats, of throwing up in buckets. And pain: so much pain, like her scars were turning fresh. There were the nightmares, too. Sometimes she woke up screaming. At least Seleese barred her friends from coming into the houseboat. For that, she's grateful. She doesn't know how she is going to face Sayer. She's feeling better now, but raw, like the skin of a new leaf. Fragile in a way she doesn't like.

She sits up, rubbing her green eye. "I don't understand the point of this."

Seleese walks out from behind one of the trees, the bells tied to her green skirts jangling. They're on one of the small islands dotted throughout the Callistan. This one is almost entirely circled by trees. Each one is so wide it would take all the Dark Stars joining hands to reach around it. The bases of their trunks are like wings, stretching out to form smooth walls around her, their roots woven into a kind of nest across the moss.

"You have loosened the venom vine's hold over your body. I want you to expel it from your mind."

"How is communing with trees supposed to help me do that?"

Fen looks into Seleese's eyes—one dark brown, one burnt orange. Two-toned, like hers.

"In the glades, no tree stands alone," she says. Her voice was made for stories, warm and lilting. "The ground here is too

206

soft to hold them. So their roots reach out through loam and wave, braiding together. They communicate that way, sharing stories and strength. They rely on that network to hold each of them up. They will do the same for you, if you ask them. They will help you."

Fen huffs out a breath. "Look, I am grateful for your help. I feel much better. But I don't need . . . whatever this is. I'm good now. I'm fine."

Seleese crosses her arms. "So you aren't having the visions anymore? They've gone?"

Fen clenches her jaw, saying nothing. Insects creak above them, hidden in the leaves.

"You cannot get strong when you refuse to face your demons. Until you do, daughter, you will live a haunted life."

Fen goes still. She read once that some creatures freeze to hide from predators. Hiding is survival: Fen learned that lesson well.

"Are you afraid of your magic?" Seleese presses.

"No," Fen lies. "I just don't like the way it makes me feel. Out of control."

"Being numb is not control. That is all the witchbane gave you." She leans a hand against one of the trunks. "The visions come as your magic does, yes? Have you ever wondered if your gifts are trying to help you deal with your past? To move beyond it?"

Having to relive those moments doesn't help her. Some memories are better left in the dark.

"Try again," Seleese says. "Let the visions come. Give your stories to the trees."

She disappears around a tree fold. Fen wants to call her back. But Fen is sick of hiding from her past, trying to outrun it. She needs to pull herself together. For the Stars, who depend on her to keep them going. For Sayer, who deserves a better friend. And Dorisall, who is her demon to slay. How can she face him if she hasn't conquered the visions? If she can't get a hold on herself?

She sighs, lying back on the mossy earth. Branches arch above her, a living ceiling. The canopy is so thick with leaves she can't see the sky. If she lets herself, she can feel the trees' heartbeats, the sap moving under their skin. The nest of roots is smooth and cool, inviting. Tentatively, she wraps her hands around them, holding tight.

The lights dim, surrounding her in murky darkness. The nightmare starts to rise again. It begins with the sweet scent of flowers, a haunting note of safety, before shifting into something else. She feels Dorisall pouring boiling water over her fingers. There's the crack of a whip, a burn at her neck. It's not the memory of the pain that skewers her. It's the helplessness she felt—the dread. Dorisall used to feast on her reactions, on any sign of emotion. He was always trying to get her to feel, to react. So she learned to push it down, to lock it in. It was safer. But she makes herself open back up for this.

More memories rise, wrapping their tendrils around her. Their thorns have started piercing her skin. She tries to pull her hands off the roots, but they seem hewn to them. Dorisall's voice slithers back in.

Pain and deprivation are the true path to the Wellspring. It is only when you strip a tree of its leaves that you can see its strength.

She feels picked clean. There's a dank smell in the air, jawbone algae, rancid water. Once again, she's in the orphanage basement. Maybe she never truly left.

"Take it away," she whispers, voice hoarse.

The tree roots only seem to push in more, seeking, probing. She doesn't want to be seen like this.

Another memory crawls out of the dark. It's old, but somehow worse than the beatings . . . worse than anything. She watches from its edges like a ghost.

Dorisall is at his desk, scribbling in his private notebook. A much smaller Fen—six, maybe? Seven?—sits on an upturned pail. Her hair is still long, her back bony through her work dress.

"Give me your finger," Dorisall says.

Fen does, and he pricks it. She doesn't make a sound. He pats her shoulder, almost gentle.

"You're a good girl, Ana."

She feels her small self light up at the praise.

Fen wants to cry out, *Don't,* but she can't save that girl. Dorisall killed her. All around her, leaves are shivering, pressing up against her skin.

More memories rise: The times she tried to lean her head on his shoulder. The times she tried to reach up to take his hand. She wants to wretch at this brutal truth, so long buried. The knowledge that she loved him once.

It's love that breaks you.

"Please," she rasps. "Don't make me see this."

The trees whisper, *You must.*

In this life, Fen's been two people: Ana, the girl she was before, and Fenlin Brae, the one who came after. But the roots bind them as one, wanting to stitch them together, ripping open all the doors she's kept locked.

But she isn't alone. She sees herself reading aloud to a much younger Rankin, doing voices for him. She sees evenings with the Dark Stars, laughing over one of Olsa's badly cooked meals. There is Leta Tangreel singing by her bed, and Æsa and Matilde teasing and coaxing. And Sayer, always Sayer, her best friend, her shadow. The girl she would give anything to hold.

Fen lets out a ragged sob. The noise is like fabric ripping through the darkness. She can hear someone banging their fists against a door. Then voices come: Sayer, Matilde, Æsa. Her friends have come to unlock it. She opens her eyes. *Let me out.*

Flamemoths shine as they do because of a unique mix of chemicals in their abdominal cavity. Alchemists have tried to extract and bottle it, but its properties do not seem to last. The flamemoth holds the key to that alluring brightness. The glow can only be created within, and by, them.

—FROM THE *ENCYCLOPEDIA OF EUDEAN INSECTS*

– CHAPTER 17 –
THE LIGHT BETWEEN BRANCHES

SAYER DOESN'T KNOW why they call this place the Tangles. It's the only place she's been to in the Callistan where you can see a wide expanse of sky. The lake is round and fringed by jungle, large enough to hold some fifty houseboats. They've all parked in a circle, with planks set up between each craft so people can walk between them. Floating bridges connect some of the boats to the tiny island at the Tangles' center, a grassy knoll they've lit with lanterns. Beyond the boats, the jungle is dark.

The clan spent a whole day rowing here for a meeting. Seleese had quiet talks with several of the other clan leaders about who might be selling witchbane to someone outside the glades. *They were offended by the accusation,* she said. *As they should be.* They all said they would never do such a thing. But they, too, have heard rumors about a religious cult making inroads with a few clans. After Sayer testified to what's been happening in Simta, one of them pulled her and Seleese aside and told them she knew more. She has a sister who married into another clan and is worried about her beloved's sudden religious fervor. The sister, shamefaced, told them where the deal would be going down. *Do not judge my man too harshly,* she said. *He has lost his way, is all.* It sounded like something Æsa would say.

The shipment will change hands tomorrow morning, not far from here. Seleese has pledged her help in intercepting it. Sayer is relieved, but edgy too. She wants to go now: to get answers. But it isn't safe to navigate the glades at night, and it's not as if Sayer can make it there without them. She has no choice but to wait for the dawn.

The meeting is starting to turn into a party now. Over on the little island, people are drinking some kind of spiked tea and dancing. Rafe's out there with his betrothed, a boy named Tryste, spinning him, laughing. As if loving and being loved is an easy thing to do.

"There," Jolena says, triumphant. "All done. You look beautiful."

Sayer touches the flowers in her hair. "Somehow I doubt it."

"Stop that, now. I'll think you're fishing for compliments."

Jolena is wearing a pretty yellow dress, borrowed from one of the girls in Seleese's clan. It's hung with little bells that jingle, light as laughter, as sweet as the dusting of freckles across her nose. These past few days, she has continued to blossom. This place has worked a kind of magic on her. Sayer is amazed by how openly she seems to love, despite her recent experience. She flirts with Rankin, who is completely besotted. She grabs Sayer's hand and hugs her for no reason at all.

"Sayer?" Jolena says, voice turning serious.

"Yes?"

"Thank you for saving me."

Sayer tugs the end of one of her braids. "You don't need to thank me. I'd do it again in a heartbeat."

"I don't just mean from . . . what happened that night. I mean when you first came to see me. When you came to my house. I love my dame and sister, but they don't understand me. Before you came, I felt so alone."

Sayer remembers that feeling. It's haunted her often. She reaches out to squeeze Jolena's hand.

Now is the time to confess: *We're sisters.* But that would mean telling her the whole, ugly truth of Wyllo Regnis. The man's hurt them both enough without that.

Instead she says, "You aren't alone. I'm here. I always will be."

The music circles the air, settling like dragonflies on the water. When Jolena speaks again, her voice is sure.

"When we go back to Simta, I won't go back home. I can't."

The words make Sayer's chest ache. Memories of her dame circle, touching down soft. She's never thought much about what it must have felt like to run away from her Great House family. Pregnant at seventeen, Sayer's age, she must've been so frightened. But she still chose to do it, for her. For them.

"You can live with me," Sayer says, swallowing hard. "If you want."

Jolena rests her head against Sayer's shoulder. Her heart feels like it's growing wings.

A few boats over, the orange door on Seleese's boat opens. Fen appears, wearing a loose flax shirt and simple trousers. Seeing her makes Sayer's heart thud, much too fast. These past few days, she's only seen her from a distance. Seleese told her Fen was improving, but she couldn't trust it until she saw her with her own eyes. She's pale, still, but does look better. Even from where she stands, Sayer can see the way her eyes shine, full of life. All at once, the knot that's taken up most of her chest since they arrived releases. She's really going to be all right.

Fen catches her eye. Something pulls tight between them. Sayer tells herself to move, but finds she can't.

"Why don't you just tell her how you feel?"

There Jolena goes, disarming her.

"It isn't that simple."

Jolena frowns, looking genuinely puzzled. "Isn't it?"

Sayer remembers all the things she whispered in Fen's sleeping ear after Leastnight.

I'd be lost without my shadow. I need you. Don't leave me.

And then Fen stole her heart and ran away.

"At least ask her to dance," Jolena says.

"If Fen wants to dance, she can ask me. I'm done chasing her."

"She probably thinks you'll say no. You don't make it easy. Sometimes you can be so . . . I don't know. Closed."

Before Sayer can reply, Rankin swaggers up to them. He's been playing his trumpet with the band, but now it's strapped to his back.

"Evening, Say," he says, giving her a little bow. "Jolena, can I beg a dance off you?"

Jolena nods, and Rankin lights up like someone's just crowned him king of Simta. They skip across one of the bridges toward the island, hand in hand. Jolena throws Sayer a sly grin over her shoulder as if to say, *See? Simple.* Sayer finds herself turning back toward Fen.

When she was young, her dame would tell her love stories

at bedtime, threading them through with whimsical confessions and soft touches. Gallant boys who kneeled at the feet of nice girls who smiled and sighed. At some point, Sayer said she didn't want to hear them anymore. When Dame asked why, Sayer said, *Because they're lies.* None of them felt like they could ever be her story.

You'll find your match someday, Dame told her, *and then you will see the truth in them.*

This look passing between her and Fen, this heat, feels true enough.

Sayer takes one step, another. The pull between them beats fast as a pulse.

"Fen," Sayer says.

Fen smiles. "Tig."

"Seleese said you didn't want to see me."

Fen runs a hand through her hair. "I didn't want you to see me like that."

"Like what?"

"Broken."

The word, raw and real, robs Sayer's anger of its heat.

"You should have told me. You and I aren't supposed to keep secrets."

"I know . . . but I don't know how to do . . . or what you want."

Fen doesn't stumble over her words. She doesn't do uncertain. It's as if she doesn't know how Sayer feels. How can she not?

Jolena's words float back. *You can be so closed.*

She takes a breath. Back in Simta, everything between them felt so twisted up, hopelessly tangled. But maybe here, it doesn't have to be.

She holds her hand out.

"Come on. Dance with me."

Fen takes her hand and Sayer leads her toward the dancers. The music has slowed to a sweet, lilting melody. All around them, couples pull each other in. She slides her arms around Fen's neck. After a beat, Fen's hands land on her hips, light as feathers. Inch by inch, they start to close the gap. She catches sight of Jolena and Rankin, awkwardly swaying. Both of them wearing their hearts on their sleeves. Sayer feels like one of the flamemoths flying above them, chasing starlight. The moment feels too vast. No words seem right.

She looks up at the sky. The night is moonless, speckled with more stars than Sayer's ever seen. A city girl, she's used to weak pinpricks trying to muscle their way through lamplight. These hang in swirls and clusters, denser than the labnum seeds in one of Simta's starcakes. *You are a constellation,* Leta told her once. *One everyone will want to wish on.* If she ever wished on stars, she'd wish for courage.

"Do you remember the first time we danced?" she asks.

Fen's lips curl by her ear. "You mean the night you bullied me into it?"

Her breath doesn't smell of mastic now—just the sticky cakes Seleese made for the party.

"I don't think that was *me*."

It was late, after one of her shifts at Twice Lit. The shop had been closed for hours, but the street band in the pavilion was still wailing, and some of the Dark Stars were drinking spiked citrine at the tables. Sayer was just getting to know the gang, to see how much they all loved each other. They heckled Fen until she agreed to dance a reel. She spun around Sayer the same way she did during their sparring lessons, quick and graceful. Someone tried to trip her, and she laughed, loud and unguarded. That was the first night she wondered what kissing Fen would be like. She's wanted to kiss her almost every day since.

"I wanted to dance with you like this," Fen admits. "Close."

Sayer's breath catches. "Why didn't you?"

"We had a good thing. I didn't want to ruin it."

Every slow turn brings their bodies closer, closer. A thumb traces Sayer's spine, so light it might be her imagination. She lets her fingers ghost over the back of Fen's neck.

"I know you didn't come to the Callistan just for me," Fen says at last. "But I'm glad you came, Tig. I'm sorry I didn't bring you with me. I never should have left you in the dark."

Sayer feels like a knife sliding out of its scabbard. A secret part of her unsheathed.

"Run all you want," she says. "I'll always find you. You're my shadow, Fen. And I am yours."

FEN STOPS DANCING. She barely notices the way partygoers bump and press against them. There's only Sayer, waiting for her to say something. All Fen wants is to get her alone.

"Come on," Fen says, taking her hand.

Sayer follows without question, letting Fen pull her through the crowd and to the little boat tied behind Seleese's bigger one. Neither of them speaks, like it might fracture this thing unfurling between them, which feels thin enough to see through.

She takes the oars and starts to row them out of the Tangles. She won't take them far: She doesn't want to get them lost in the dark. The star beetles give off enough light that she can see the outline of one of the glade's little islands, which she pulls them up next to. It holds a single singing willow, its dripping arms a delicate screen.

Fen pulls Sayer out of the boat and under its branches. Even here, Fen can't find words, heart in her throat. Sayer's eyes flash, transmuting from a hard gold to something softer. She raises her hands, resting her elegant fingers on Fen's face. With her thumbs, she slowly traces a circle around Fen's brown eye, then the green one. Fen shivers, hard, but doesn't pull away.

"Are you ever going to show me what's under there?" Sayer whispers.

It's the question she used to ask when they sparred together. Fen's eyepatch is gone now, and most of her armor, leaving her all too exposed. But this is Sayer, standing with Fen under these branches in a different world.

"What is it you want to see, Tig?"

"Anything. Everything."

Leaves rustle around them, an encouraging whisper. The air between them hums, green and alive. Yet even now, the part of Fen that's kept her safe all these years screams, *Hold back, stay hidden.* But she's tired of burying her feelings in the dark.

She backs Sayer up until she's pressed against the lichen-crusted trunk. Her lips part in surprise as Fen puts her hands on either side, bracketing her body.

"And what if you don't like what I have to show you?"

Sayer doesn't look away. "Try me."

She leans in, slow, and brushes her lips against Sayer's. They part easily, two petals opening out. The kiss starts soft, but soon it's wild with everything they've hidden. Tongues touch, a desperate heat, making her sigh. Her hands slide down Sayer's sharp shoulders, across her ribs, pulling her closer. Fen isn't sure she's ever touched this much of anyone. It feels like she won't ever get enough.

Her magic rises up, strong enough to be dizzying. Her earth and metal crash into Sayer's wind and rain. Her bones vibrate as their magic joins, weaving together. She doesn't try to push it down. The leaves dance over their heads in a soft breeze, reaching down to caress them. Behind them, water ripples, moved by them, by the moment. This kiss is everything at once.

When Fen pulls back, eyes closed, her eyelids glow with sudden brightness. She opens them to see flamemoths and star beetles flooding the tree, fluttering close. A few have touched down on their skin, shining like jewelry. Are they attracted to their magic? Maybe it's Sayer's incandescent laugh, free and bright and joyous. It's the sexiest thing Fen's ever heard.

"Leta called me a walking constellation once. And now I am one."

"You are my wish come true." Fen leans in, kissing her cheek. "I've wanted to kiss you like that for a long time."

Sayer flushes. "How long are we talking?"

"Every day. Every hour. Forever. I wanted it so much it scared me. The things I love always get taken away."

For a long moment, Sayer just stares at her, pensive. And then she leans downs and kisses one of the scars on Fen's neck. She flinches, but Sayer's soft lips keep moving, leaving hot trails across her vulnerable throat.

"I'm scared too, you know," she whispers.

Fen can't speak. Not with Sayer's mouth on her scars, kissing them as if she thinks she can heal them. She swallows, making the words coalesce: "Of what?"

"Of living with my heart outside my body. Of having it crushed."

The words sear through Fen. She takes Sayer's hand and presses it against her breastbone.

"I'll keep it safe, Tig. I promise you. I hope you'll have a care with mine."

Sayer kisses her again. Around them, insects light up the darkness, leaving her with nowhere to hide. But it's all right. There's something freeing about stripping off her armor. A beauty in being, at last, truly seen.

The tides, they rise,
Lifting us above our troubles.
The tides, they pull,
Tugging us toward our fates.
The tides, they turn,
Bringing us into new seasons,
filled as they may be with wind and storms.

—AN ILLISH SEA SHANTY

– CHAPTER 18 –
SNAKE IN THE NEST

THE CALL RINGS through the ship: *All hands!* Willan springs toward the stairs, Æsa following close behind. When they emerge on deck, all is chaos. The girls are clinging to the rails, pointing, as crewmen run between their stations. When one of them sees Willan, he stops short.

"What is it, Arjen?" Willan asks.

"We've got company," his first mate says. "Lookout didn't see them through the weather. But they're heading our way fast, and I don't like the look of them."

Willan takes out his spyglass, turning to look off the starboard side. Æsa peers through the mist and sees the dark outlines of a ship. The rain has stopped, but it's still difficult to make out its details.

"Is it a naval ship?" she asks, skin prickling. "From Simta?"

"Don't think so," Arjen says. "It's not the right shape."

Willan speaks again. "It looks like a Trellian raider."

"Who are the Trellians?" she asks.

"Farlanders. And not the kind we want to meet with."

His voice has gone tight. Æsa's heart starts to pound.

"Have you hailed them?" Willan asks.

Arjen shakes his head. "We put up the flags for parley, but they aren't responding."

Willan lowers his spyglass. "They clearly don't want us to know their business."

But why? The ship is closer now, hurrying across the water toward them. She squints at its sails. Are they . . . red?

Dread crawls up her spine. "Have any of the girls been doing magic?"

"No," Arjen says. "But . . . well, I don't know what you were up to in the hold, sheldar, but it made the rain take on strange shapes. Anyone who saw it would know it was magic."

Æsa bites her cheek. Her magic, always heightened by emotion, must have slipped when she kissed Willan. And now Farlanders are stalking toward them like a shark toward waiting prey.

"What now, Will?" Arjen asks. "Fight or flee?"

Willan shoots a glance at Æsa. "Tell the boys it's time to run."

"But the crew," Æsa says. "Half of them haven't come back yet."

"We'll be back for them later."

Arjen turns and runs down the deck, shouting orders. Willan squeezes her hand, then runs for the wheel. Æsa hurriedly rounds up the fledglings. Jacinta's already got most of them together by one of the smaller sails.

"What's going on?" a fledgling asks in a squeak. "Is that ship coming for us, Æsa?"

Æsa makes her voice calm. "I don't know, but we aren't going to wait to find out. Jen, can you help pick up the wind a little?"

The air girl nods, balling her fists. Æsa and Jacinta cajole the others into going below, making them promise not to come up until they say so. The ship's anchor rises, and after a moment they're turning, heading toward the Callistan's still-distant shore. Æsa reaches out, coaxing the waves to speed their passage, and Jen's wind picks up, stretching the mainsail taut. Æsa stands close enough to amplify the girl's magic, but she will only be able to sustain it for so long. As the minutes pass, her wind starts to sputter, tiring. Æsa's magic isn't enough to speed them away. Willan's men scurry from line to line, unfurling sails, trying to coax the ship to go faster. The Farlands ship seems to devour the waves.

"This isn't working," Jacinta says. "They're going to catch us."

"They haven't fired on us," Jen says. "That's good, isn't it?"

Jacinta's face is grave. "That just means they don't want to damage their prize."

Æsa can make out the faces of the ship's sailors now, pale and fixed on the *Tempest*. Their sails look like fresh blood in the mist.

"Points out!" Willan shouts. His men scurry for the ballistas, small crossbows affixed to the ships' railings. The Farlands ship is busy, its sailors clustered around what look like metal tubes, long and dark. Matilde's brother, Samson, told her about these weapons. Cannons, he called them. *They use some sort of powder inside the cylinders,* he said. *A controlled explosion.* She thought he was telling tales, but these look real enough.

Æsa grips the rail. She has to do something. Before she can think what, one of the Farlands ship's cannons bucks, cracking like thunder. It shoots something at them that almost looks like a cage. She dives for cover as the cage smashes into the rigging, shrieking as it bursts above them. The air is filled with clangs and scrapes as pieces of whatever it contained rain down, pounding the deck. Æsa pulls Jacinta and Jen tight against the ship's side as a chain lands near them. She reaches out, then yanks her hand back. The metal is hot, almost scalding.

"What in the ten hells—?" Jacinta says.

"It's grapeshot," Kadeel shouts as he grabs for a length of rope. "Meant to take out sails and rigging. Slow us down. They mean to board us."

His words make her blood roar in her ears.

Æsa looks to Willan. He is still clutching the wheel, teeth bared as he turns it.

"Fire at will!" he calls, and flaming arrows fly from the bal-listas. Æsa watches as most land in the water, hissing as they hit the waves. Those that do hit the other ship don't seem to slow it. They are almost beside the *Tempest* now.

"Go to the other girls," she tells Jen. "Tell them to stay hidden."

The air girl, pale faced, staggers toward the door to down below.

Æsa thinks of her vision of the future, of that sea of red, malevolent sails. She doesn't know what they want, but it's clear this ship means to take them. Jacinta reaches out and grips her hand.

"Those men are going to take the girls," she says, "unless someone stops them."

She looks at Æsa, waiting for their sheldar to emerge.

Not long ago, Æsa would have said it was too much to ask, too much to hold. Such gifts should not be used as a weapon. But to save her friends, she will fight with everything she has.

226

"I can." She nods, steeling herself. "I will."

The smoky air stings her eyes as she stands. Her magic rises, tasting of brine and salt. What should she ask of it? Months ago, she called up a wave in Simta's harbor, using it to lift a ship up and move it. But that was in a sheltered port, not open ocean. Can she command such power out here?

She throws her mind into the waves, letting it spread through them. She tries to hold the sea the same way Willan taught her to hold a sword. *Treat your blade as a friend,* he's always saying, *and eventually it'll start to feel like a piece of you.* But the ocean is so vast, almost fathomless. It takes all her strength to bend it to her will.

Another cannon fires. On instinct, Æsa throws out her hands, shouting in Illish.

"Granye."

Protect us.

In response, a glistening creature leaps from the waves. The water monster looks part fish, part horse, part nightmare. It wraps its watery teeth around the flying cage, pulling its quarry down, crashing back into the waves in a mighty flash of foam. Willan's men cheer, but she can't attend them. If she loses her focus, her control will go too.

More flaming arrows fire from the *Tempest.* Cannons boom, their deathly metal arcing high. She makes more watery creatures leap up to consume them, all smoke and steam and foam. But the Farlanders keep coming, keep firing, relentless. She can feel her magic starting to tire. At last, she asks her water monsters to swim toward the Farlands ship. Perhaps they can clamp onto the ship's side and pull it over, capsize it. The creatures begin to rise, hungry, but sluggish. She feels herself stumble, even as Jacinta holds her. Her strength, her will, is not enough. Suddenly she longs for Matilde, Sayer, and Fen so fiercely. If they were here with her, she could do this. If they were here, they would win.

The *Tempest* shudders, rocked by impact. Above her, something explodes. Sudden pain and a bright light blot out her vision. For a moment everything is a white, churning blur. Then she blinks once, twice, and the world starts coming back together. She is sprawled on the deck. How did she get here? Why does it feel as if the ship has slowed?

"Æsa." Jacinta is hovering over her, hair loose and wild. "Blazing cats, *say* something."

She tries to sit up, then slumps back down. "What happened?"

"A cage broke against the rigging. Something hit you as it fell."

She puts a hand up to her throbbing head, trying to still it. Her thoughts are full of chaos and smoke. Pain sears, white hot, up her right arm. There's a shard of metal lodged in one of her biceps.

"Stay still," Jacinta says. "This is going to hurt."

Before Æsa can ask what she means, her friend yanks the metal out. Her vision goes dark as she tries not to scream. There is the sound of fabric ripping. Jacinta wraps something tight around the wound, catching the blood.

"Can you stand?" she asks.

Æsa doesn't know. Her thoughts are fractured and swimming, the scene around her refusing to make sense. Boots pound across the deck as Willan's men try to rally. Some of the fledglings have come up on deck: Didn't she tell them to stay hidden? A man is moaning, a truly horrible sound. Æsa looks up to see the mainmast is gone, snapped in half. The *Tempest* is dead in the water. Which must mean . . .

"The Farlanders," she breathes. "They're coming."

She pushes herself up, hands slipping. Dark rivulets of something wind their way across the deck. The pattern they make feels familiar. She has seen them before, she thinks, in a dream. No . . . a vision. Panic grips her. Her chest, hollow before, starts to ache.

And then someone staggers through the smoke toward her. His steps are unsteady, his breathing ragged. His chest, still bare, is covered in blood. *I have seen this future,* she thinks, dazedly, and now it is the present. Knowing it was coming does not make it hurt less.

"Willan," she sobs.

He drops to his knees. The expression in his sea-green eyes spells ruin. She is not going to let his life run through her hands.

"You can't die," she commands. "I won't let you."

Her hands search for a wound to close, a hurt to salve, and find nothing. He pulls her tight against him. His breaths are coming in painful, rattling gasps.

"I'm not dying, kilventra."

"The blood," she chokes out. His usual scent is masked by the tang of metal. "Where are you hurt? Show me."

"Æsa." He takes both her hands in his, slippery. "It's not mine."

She sucks in a breath. A wash of relief shudders through her, but horror follows quickly in its wake.

"Then who—?"

There is a clang of metal hitting wood. At one side of the

ship, she sees claws catching on the ship's railing. *Birds,* she thinks, but then she sees they're hooks. The Farlanders are reeling the *Tempest* in, pulling them closer.

"Swords out," Willan shouts, voice raw. "They're going to board us."

They get to their feet. Jacinta steps up beside them as what is left of Willan's crew fans out, weapons raised. Someone passes swords to her, Jacinta, and the fledglings. The Farlands ship is beside the *Tempest* now, less than a sail's length between them. Sailors crowd its deck. There are fewer than she thought at first, but still too many, and all holding weapons. Several are up in the rigging, gripping ropes, ready to fly.

"If you're going to drown them," Jacinta says, low, "now is your moment."

"I don't think I can," Æsa says, still so dizzy. "My magic is . . . quiet."

Is it the blow to her head, or did she expend too much of it? Her magic is not inexhaustible. There is nothing to do but wait for it to come back.

A plank is slid between the Farlands ship's rail and the *Tempest*'s. One of the Farlanders walks across it. His skin is pale, like hers, almost translucent. She can clearly see the rivers of his veins.

"Which one of you is captain?" he says, in heavily accented Simtan.

Willan steps forward. "I am. State your business."

"I would think it fairly clear." His eyes are a flat, matte blue. When they land on Æsa, they brighten. "We have come to claim the witches. Do not stand in our way, and we will let your crew live."

The fledglings all press closer to Æsa. The crew shift, forming a tight ring around them.

"If you want them," Willan says, "you will have to go through us."

The Farlands captain doesn't seem concerned by the threat. "The Wave Witch," he says, pointing at Æsa. "Yes?"

She does not answer. It seems he doesn't expect her to.

"I have a sketch of you. The likeness was not so good, though. In person, you are much finer."

His eyes devour her. Æsa squares her shoulders.

"You have made a mistake. I am not who you think I am."

He wags a finger. "No tricks, Wave Witch. Our king sent us to the Illish Isles just to find you. You were already gone, of course, but some of your villagers were helpful. They told us where you likely sailed, and in what vessel. Now we have you. And all these magical galgren too."

"Try to take her," Willan growls. "Come on. I dare you."

But he is swaying a little on his feet: Most of his men are. Fear clears her mind and sharpens her focus to a sword-blade point. Her magic is still quiet, little more than a dull ache. For now, it cannot help her. But she can use one of the skills she learned as a Nightbird: She can pull on a mask and tell some lies.

"You saw the magic I did before?" she says, loud and commanding. "That was nothing. Leave now, and I might not send your ship to the deep."

The Farlands captain does not quail. "If you could, you would have done it. You have already lost this fight."

His words hang on the air, barbed and prickling. Then Willan raises his voice.

"Wave to wave."

His men respond: *We ride together.*

They raise their swords and rush for the railing. The Farlands captain merely smiles.

On his signal, the Farlanders in the rigging swing from their ropes, crashing down onto the *Tempest*'s deck. They collide with Willan's men, blades clanging. She sees Willan spinning left, right, so much faster than when they practiced, his sword like liquid light and certain death. His men fight with all they have, but they are outnumbered. Their tight circle becomes a messy crush.

Æsa grips her sword as one of the Farlanders breaks through them.

"Do not fight," he says, smiling at Jacinta. "I will be gentle."

Jacinta raises her blade. "Touch me and I'll gut you like a fish."

She jabs at him, but he bats her sword aside. Æsa steps and swings into the fray. He seems disconcertingly relaxed for someone fighting two on one. He blocks their thrusts as if they are nothing more than vexing flies. Æsa steps, lunges, steps, trying to remember Willan's lessons. She steps in close, trapping his blade, wrenching his wrist.

Don't hesitate, Willan is fond of saying. *Death lies that way.* Jacinta doesn't pause as she runs the man through. He screams, gripping his gut as her friend pulls the blade out. Æsa staggers back, trying not to be sick.

The man falls. But there are more: so many. The crew are scattered, their circle of protection broken. Around them people scream and bodies fall. Her friends are dying. The ones who followed her, trusting her to protect them. The ones whose faith made her believe in herself.

Please, she pleads with her magic. *Come back.* It is there, but faint, a flickering thing. If she can just dig down deep enough . . .

Through the smoke she sees Layla, one of their fledglings,

holding a small ball of fire. She is about to throw it at a Farlander when another one grabs her from behind, throwing her over his shoulder. The fire sputters out. She screams, eyes wide.

Jacinta speaks close to Æsa's ear. "When this is over, remember how much there is to fight for. Don't ever forget how strong you are."

Before Æsa can stop her, Jacinta is running. She slashes at the man holding Layla, making one of his legs buckle. Layla falls and scrambles out of reach. Jacinta and the sailor crash to the deck, a tangle of limbs, grappling, swearing. Jacinta has managed to get on top of him now. She raises her sword, ready to plunge down and through him. Her scream of rage is cut off by something Æsa can't see.

"No!" she screams, but it is too late. Jacinta is crumpling. One of the Farlanders is dragging Layla away.

Æsa reaches down, down into her depths for her magic. It will heed her now—it must. With the last gasp of her strength, she makes long tendrils of water rise over the ship's sides. They loom there, full of her rage, ready to strike.

She feels no remorse as she gives them their instructions.

"Kaila," she commands.

Destroy.

They lash out and wrap around the Farlanders. Some bash the men against the deck, like a gannet trying to break open a mollusk, while others drag them into the maw of the sea. Their screams scrape at her skin, but she shows them no mercy. She will not stop until she's punished them all.

At last, the captain is the only Farlander left. One of the crew wrestles him down, pulling his hands behind him. Æsa stumbles to where Jacinta lies, so still. There is an awful gash at her neck where the Farlander must have cut her. Her dress, brown before, is red, the color of mourning. Dyed that way by her blood.

"No," Layla chokes out, gripping one of Jacinta's limp hands. "She can't be. She can't be."

Jacinta's eyes are open, staring at nothing. Her fierce friend, silenced and still.

Æsa swallows a sob. "She is gone."

Jacinta said, before, that she didn't think she would ever make it back to Simta. Did she know it was her fate to die like this? And yet she fought anyway, with everything she had, with such courage. Æsa wants to call her back, to bring her home.

She turns to Layla, stroking her dark hair once, twice.

"Leave her with me. Take the other girls below until we know it's safe."

Layla goes, trying to scrub her tears away. Æsa closes Jacinta's eyes. She stands, dizzy again. Willan is there to catch her. For a moment they just hold each other, silent and close. He presses his lips to her temple. She leans into his neck and sobs, just once. Then she sucks in one breath, two, tucking her grief away. There will be time for it later.

"Where is he?" she asks, pulling back. "The Farlander?"

He guides her toward the prow. The ship is in ruins, but at least it is still floating. She tries not to look at the bodies strewn across the deck. The crew are tending to their wounds. They all touch their foreheads as she passes, a sign of respect, of worship. She fixes her eyes on the prisoner, trussed and tied. Kadeel stands nearby, glaring down at him. The man's fine clothes are bloodied now, his face wan.

"Such a pretty thing," he croaks. "I did not think you had such violence in you."

Æsa refuses to look away. "If you answer my questions, there need not be any more of it."

The man coughs, a wet sound, and spits blood onto the deck. "I do not answer to galgren."

That word again, said with such contempt. She wonders what it means to him. She crouches down, wrapping her fingers around his wrist.

"You want to answer our questions honestly. You want it more than anything in life."

Her magic is sapped, making it difficult to twist the streams of his emotions. And yet his fingers start to quake.

"Who is your king?"

"Joost Tharda," he answers. "Son of Djorn. King of Trellane."

She does not know that name.

"And what are his plans for Simta?"

He pants and writhes, fighting her hold.

"Is he planning to invade?"

"Yes," the man grates out.

"Why?"

"He wants witches. He wants to bring the glory of your magic to our shores."

Again, she sees those ships with their red sails, the girl in chains. She shivers.

"When does he plan to attack?"

"Soon, galgren. Very soon. You cannot stop him. You will feel the pershain around that lovely neck."

He says something Æsa doesn't understand: almost sings it. Then there is a crunching noise, glass on teeth. The man starts to convulse, lips foaming, black liquid dripping from his mouth.

Willan swears. "He's eaten a glass bead."

It is the same poison Sayer's long-ago client used to end his life, ensuring he could not spill any secrets. The air fills with his terrible, choking breaths. Then he is silent. But his words still hang, a heavy, dreadful weight.

At last, Willan speaks. "Do you know what he just said, Kadeel?"

He scratches his beard. "My Trellish is rusty. But it was something like, 'The snake is in the nest already. Curled up in the walls, ready to strike.'"

What does it mean? She does not know, but one thing is clear to her. Her friends in Simta are in even greater danger than she thought.

PART IV

BURNING

IT

DOWN

HESTER:

What is the cost, for this treasure so fine?

FASTEN:

The payment is that you will make yourself mine.

HESTER:

You've steep demands, Fasten, but I cannot be caught!

FASTEN:

Yet even the most priceless fish can be bought.

—ACT I, SCENE 5
OF THE *SIMTAN COMEDIES*

– CHAPTER 19 –
THE RISING TIDE

MATILDE WAVES AT the crowd on the banks of the canal, keeping her smile on. Tonight, she cannot let it slip. She and Dennan are in a canal boat, being rowed toward an event in Griffin Quarter. The canal is fast and swollen with the Alta Dai, or the High Tide, which brings Simta's water levels to their peak once a year. The flooding that ensues can be a nuisance, but Risentide is full of revelry. It is a time of reversal, when paupers become masters of ceremony and Great House lords dance at balls with kitchen maids. A time when anything might come to pass.

Matilde trails her fingers through the water, thinking of Æsa. She would have loved to share this festival with their water girl. Matilde would much rather be here with her.

Seated beside her, Dennan is dressed simply, in clothes that any navalman might wear on shore leave. He is kitted out like one of the people in an attempt at banking up some good-will. Some of them are staring at their suzerain from the canal bank, waving. When he waves back, they cheer: The people love their Bastard Prince, despite the rumors about him killing his sister. It helps that he poured so many funds into this year's Risentide celebrations. He has hired bands to play in every Quarter, paid for free-flowing citrine stalls and wine sellers, and served as patron of many of the theatrical performances being held throughout the city. He wants Simta at its best and most cheerful as wedding guests arrive. The streets are full and buzzing, and she is glad to see it. But there is something in the air that sets her teeth on edge.

"Stay close tonight," Dennan says, waving at a group of women screaming his name. "I don't want us getting separated."

As if she could escape, with all the guards he's brought along.

"I am no damsel," she says. "I don't need protecting."

"And yet I still want to be sure you stay safe."

She tamps her annoyance down. After all, she is the one who pushed for this outing. How can the city trust her when she never walks amongst them? she argued. How can they cheer for their wedding when they never see her and Dennan side by side? It wasn't a lie, but it wasn't the only reason she wanted to get out of the palace. Truth to tell, she is starting to feel the walls closing in.

The night she and Alec broke into Augustain's, she was able to sneak back into the Winged Palace without anyone the wiser. But the next day, the Pontifex made it known their sanctuary had been breached. The Wardens went on even higher alert, and the paters raged on about how a witch must have done it. Thankfully, they don't know about Matilde's ability to change her visage. They don't know it was her who stole from them. She denied any involvement to Dennan, who pretended to believe her. But she has found things in her room rearranged, as if someone has been through it. Dennan's guards have stood by her family's doors every night since, hemming her in. Sneaking out has become impossible. All she can do is send notes out through her most trusted maid.

Every day, she writes to Alec, but her missives go unanswered. She doesn't know how he can have nothing else to say. Leta only wrote back once, in code, saying it was too dangerous to send notes with her house so closely watched. She also said the Dark Stars have still not found the Red Hand's lair: The man is nowhere. Wyllo Regnis also continues to prove elusive. They are no closer to finding Sugar or the missing girls.

During the day, she goes to final dress fittings and discusses seating charts with her family. She tells herself the wedding is still the best way to quell the threats, to make things better, though it's starting to take on a panicked edge. At night, she pores over Delaina's journal. She has devoured every page. She writes about the Fyrebirds of old waging war, parting seas, and shaking mountains. How big their magic was—how vast.

The journal only has one story about heart-tied Fyrebirds. She has read it so often it is tattooed onto her mind. It speaks of a Tekan fleet that attacked Eudea once, their sails stretching out to the horizon. The church says it was one of the Eshamein who destroyed it, but Delaina's version tells a different tale. She says that four Fyrebirds joined hands, somehow combining their elements. *One of the girls pulled their power in, becoming their conduit. In her, their magic mixed and pooled, becoming one. She used it to burn the fleet of ships to ash, but a price had to be paid. Such power required sacrifice. Their magic burned her up.*

What does it mean? Matilde cannot stop thinking of it. Imagining those four girls fighting back a foreign power.

Their boat bumps against the dock, pulling her out of her thoughts. They have arrived. The guards tie the vessel up at their mooring, and Dennan helps her out onto the shores of Griffin's Quarter. Together, they join the flowing throng. People gawp at them, pointing and whispering, as they walk toward the Trill. The guards fan out, forming a watchful ring. The Wardens are everywhere, keeping their eyes out for lawbreakers. But what about En Caska Dae? Are any of them hidden amongst the revelers, looking for girls with magic? Are any of those girls here, waiting for her?

Dennan takes her hand.

"Remember to smile. You're grimacing like you have a toothache."

Matilde wants to pull away but won't in front of all these people. Better to smile and wave.

The stage has been set up at the Trill, the city's oldest outdoor amphitheater. The seats are packed with people, but two lavish chairs have been set up on a dais for the guests of honor. She and Dennan will be perched up there for all to see.

Heads turn as they take their seats. These are the people of Simta, its citrine sellers and flower girls and alchemists. The emotions on their faces as they look at her are varied. She sees reverence, fear, shock, disgust. Somehow, their stares are harder to bear than the lords and ladies at her garden party. Perhaps because so many of them look to her like Phryne's dame.

At last, the master of ceremonies strides out onto the stage. It is to be the *Simtan Comedies* tonight. He is donning the blue gown Fasten always wears, and his velvet top hat. His mustache twitches as he smiles.

"Pleasant evening, all," he booms. "And happy Risentide. May the risen waters sate you."

His audience knows how to answer. *And may your cup be filled.*

"Before the play commences, I would like to thank the patron who has made this evening possible, including the free drinks you're all imbibing."

A smattering of applause. As he gestures at their dais, it grows louder.

"It was my lady's idea," Dennan says, taking her hand again. "Give her your thanks."

They clap and shout, though not as loudly as they did for Dennan. She hears a few of what sound like jeers. But the master of ceremonies bows as if he means it.

"Lady Flame Witch," he says. "You honor us."

She nods in thanks. His expression turns mischievous.

"Will you honor us further and be our Queen for tonight?"

Matilde goes still. The part of the Queen is always chosen from the audience, but usually she's a working girl, not someone from a Great House. What is the master playing at?

Dennan leans close. She's sure he is going to say she shouldn't. She raises her voice, not looking at him.

"I would be delighted."

A few guards flank her as she goes. People reach around them as they pass, straining to touch her. She hears one of them say a quiet prayer. Up onstage, the master takes her hand, bowing over it. He leads her to the tower where the Queen always stands. She has no speaking parts; her only real role is to look on in silent judgment. The irony of playing a voiceless woman in a tower isn't lost on her.

The play begins. She has seen the *Simtan Comedies* many times, though never from this vantage point. Fasten and Hester make their deal, then fall in love against their better judgment. Hester is tricked into marrying another. Fasten and Gulle plot their revenge, which goes hilariously awry. Through it all, the players offer the Queen flowers and paper stars, bloodied kerchiefs and promises. Matilde knows her task: to stand mute and removed.

But somewhere in the third act, something changes. Gulle says something she has never heard him say before.

"This world is cruel," he opines. "Will my pleas never be heard?"

Fasten looks woeful. "If only we had a Fyrebird."

Both men's faces turn up toward her. Matilde's breath catches.

"But Fasten," Gulle says, "such girls are long since dead."

"No, my boy. They walk amongst us, filling their enemies with dread."

Someone cheers. A few people shake their fists at the play's change in direction. Around the Trill, Wardens are starting to bristle. Dennan has gone rigid in his chair.

Gulle leaps from foot to foot.

"Did the Flame Witch really bring the Yellow Alchemist's shop down in flames?"

"Nonsense," Fasten booms, arms akimbo. "She is the one who made them tame."

The day Krastan's shop burned, the crowd stared like this, as if unsure whether to stone or praise her. Matilde sees someone make the sign of the Eshamein, while others bow their heads.

"The church says she's a witch," Gulle insists. "One we have reason to fear."

"Mark me, she is a savior. A gift we should hold dear."

That is too much for the Wardens. Several shout, looking like they might storm the stage. Gulle and Fasten look at her as if it's her line, but what is she supposed to do? Make a speech?

Start a fire? She can do neither. And yet her magic quivers under her skin, begging to be seen.

The two men bow. The curtain closes. Beyond it, music swells, signaling the show's intermission. Fasten beckons her down a hall into the bowels of backstage.

"Come, Flame Witch," he says. "Quickly. You have a visitor."

She should demand he explain himself, or simply refuse to follow, but a feeling in her chest urges her on. She knows this soft, relentless tingling. She trips over her feet in her haste.

Fasten pulls back another, smaller curtain, ushering her into a changing room. Costumes hang from slender mirrors, all feathers and sequins. There, half hidden amongst them, is a girl. Her hair is covered, face obscured by a mask, but Matilde would know her anywhere.

For a moment neither moves, as if afraid they're dreaming each other.

"Such subterfuge," Matilde says. "I see you remembered my lessons."

Æsa's arms wrap around her. "Oh, Matilde. I have missed you."

For a moment, Matilde simply hugs her back, trying not to let any tears escape. Their magic weaves together, wave and flame, a tender relief. But then danger creeps in. She pulls back, heart pounding.

"What in the dark depths are you doing here?"

Anyone in Simta who sees her will know her as the Wave Witch. The Wardens in this crowd will arrest her on sight.

"It's dangerous. The church still has a warrant out for you."

"Never mind that. There are things I must say."

She whispers to Fasten, still hovering. He nods, walking out, and Æsa takes off her mask. She looks the same, but the way she holds herself is different. The last time Matilde saw her, when she gave herself up to the Hand, her shoulders were stooped, defeat curling her inward. This version of Æsa looks ready to fight.

Matilde opens her mouth, brimming with questions. Æsa speaks first.

"A Farlands king is going to invade Simta."

That knocks Matilde speechless. "What? Who?"

"Joost, the king of Trellane. He has a mighty fleet of ships, Matilde. So many. I don't know when it will happen, but soon. Very soon."

She blows out a breath. "How do you know this?"

Æsa drops her voice, low and urgent. "Willan and his crew brought us back by ship. Me, the fledglings . . ." She swallows. "Jacinta. Along the way, a Trellian ship attacked us. They knew I was amongst them. Their king sent them to capture the Wave Witch."

Matilde's stomach swoops. "Ten hells. Are the fledglings all right?"

"Most of them. They came so close to taking us. But we subdued them in the end." Æsa looks away. "We were able to question one of them. He told us this Joost would invade Simta for its magic. He wants girls with it, Matilde. He kept calling us *galgren*."

Matilde winces. "An awful term."

"What does it mean?"

"Beautiful chained."

The galgren are the most prized slaves in Trellane, and always women. Joost is a fool to think she will let him bring the custom to her shores.

"The sailor confessed all this?"

246

A pause, loud and full. "Some. But I have also seen it. Sometimes I see the future."

Matilde starts. As far as she knew, Jacinta was the only one who had such visions. But in the Underground, Matilde heard her say she and Æsa were birds of a feather. Is this what she meant?

"When did that start?"

A familiar expression clouds Æsa's face: guilt.

"Before we went to the Liar's Club. I saw Tenny kissing you, and the chandelier breaking. But I thought it was nothing more than a dream."

But that was months ago, when they were still Nightbirds together. Resentment burns, flaring bright.

"Really, Æsa. I thought we said no more secrets. But then, I suppose we were sisters when we made that pledge."

Æsa looks stricken. "We are still, Matilde. Why do you think I came back here? I had a vision in Illan of what was coming. I wasn't going to let you fight this alone."

Matilde closes her eyes, takes a breath. They already have too many troubles to contend with, but this feels big enough to swallow them all.

"We had to abandon Willan's ship," Æsa goes on. "It was ruined. We commandeered the Farlands vessel and came as quickly as we could. Willan dropped us off near the Neck, the fledglings and me. The girls all went home, and I came to warn you. He and his crew found papers aboard that hinted at where the fleet will be docking. He is going to see what he can learn."

How to proceed? She could tell Dennan, or she could try to go around him. Matilde's mind whirs with possible scenarios, trying to puzzle out what move to make.

"One thing is certain," Æsa says, taking her hands. "It's going to take all four of us, together, to stop them. I have seen it."

Matilde thinks again of the four Fyrebirds from Delaina's story.

"But Sayer and Fen aren't in Simta," she says. "They left."

"What?" Æsa sounds truly alarmed. "Where are they?"

Matilde's shoulders sag, the weight of the past months suddenly heavy.

"Oh, Æsa. I have no idea where to start."

She is about to when the curtain parts. Dennan is there, cool and collected. Matilde's skin prickles, hands going hot.

"Young Lady Æsa," he says, smooth as silk. "We meet again."

Dennan sweeps into the cramped space. His gaze on Æsa has the focus of a lighthouse, almost blinding. He steps forward, taking her hand. How long has he been standing there, eavesdropping? How much did he overhear?

She wills her voice to come out calm. "I assume you heard Æsa's news."

Dennan nods. "An invasion."

So he heard everything. Including the names of her friends.

"Thank you for coming to us with this," he says to Æsa.

Not us, Matilde wants to snap. *Me.* But there is no time.

"We have to cancel the wedding," she says.

Æsa's brow furrows. "What wedding?"

Dennan gestures between them. "Matilde's and mine."

Æsa's mouth goes slack. It seems her visions didn't forewarn her of the nuptials.

"We can't go through with it now," Matilde says. "Not with an invasion coming. We need to squash this threat before it has a chance to land."

"No." Dennan's eyes have gone vague, as they used to when

they played games together, as if trying to see all the moves he might make. "It's too late to cancel. Most of the guests are here, and everything's in place. Changing course will make us look unsure to the people and scared to our rivals. Including the Trellian king."

Matilde shakes her head. "I will not smile and swear vows in front of a king who plans to put me on a leash."

Dennan lowers his voice. "Look, I know Joost. He visited Simta when we were both boys, and even then he was obsessed with magic. He covets it. And now he sees us as vulnerable. If he wants to attack, there will be no dissuading him. Better we not tip our hand. Let him think we are none the wiser as we prepare to fight him."

"But you will tell the Table," Matilde says.

"Yes, but without concrete proof, they will be leery. War requires funds, and they won't want to pay unless they have to."

"I can tell them what I've seen," Æsa says. "Surely that is proof enough."

"And risk them carting you back to Jawbone? No. Never."

There is a possessive edge to his voice that makes Matilde's skin prickle. He is pacing now, hands clasped behind his back.

"We don't need the Table. I will talk quietly with my captains. They will listen. In fact, an invasion could work to our advantage."

Matilde crosses her arms. "I fail to see how an invasion could be good for us."

"Nothing unites a nation like a shared threat. People will look to us for leadership. And it will let me claim the right of entre dicta."

Æsa frowns. "What is that?"

Matilde remembers the term from her history lessons.

"*Right of rule*. It's something a suzerain can claim if Eudea is attacked. It lets them make quick decisions without having to consult the Table. They become a ruling general."

Dennan nods. "It would allow us to take control, defeat this enemy, and claim complete power. If we play this right, we won't have to give it back."

She understands his fervor now, sees his move.

"You would use this to make yourself a king."

He looks at her, eyes burning. "And you my queen."

There is a charged silence. Æsa looks worriedly between them. Matilde reaches for her locket, but it's not there.

"I will start rallying the navy," Dennan goes on. "Æsa, did you find out anything about where the fleet will approach from?"

Æsa looks at him, eyes wide and wary. Matilde feels just as unsure.

"From the north," she says. "Toward Fennis End. My friend Willan has gone with a few of his crew to find out more."

"Good. Their navy is strong, but ours can match it, as long as we know where to meet them. We will go back to the palace. You will get Fen and Sayer and ready them, too."

Alarm bells ring inside Matilde. "Ready them for what?"

"For battle."

She has seen Dennan wear this expression before. It's the one that says he will stop at nothing to get what he wants, damn the consequences. It conjures up a ripple of fear.

"We aren't soldiers, Dennan. You can't just stuff us into uniforms and send us into war."

He brushes off her concern as he might an errant moth.

"You will be fine; I will protect you. The four of you can

show the city what you can truly do. Imagine it: four Fyrebirds and the suzerain, saving Simta. They will love us."

He wants to wield them like tools: his weapons. Force them to wear a different kind of leash. But what can she say? Matilde looks to Æsa, but it seems she doesn't have the answer. She wishes she didn't feel so out of her depth.

WILLAN FIXES HIS spyglass on the horizon. He needs to look ahead, not behind. But it's hard not to turn back toward Æsa, though he knows he will not see her. It's been like that since the night he stepped into the Nightingale's room. He remembers it so clearly: her curled by the fireplace, eyes closed, hands in her hair. Even then, he could feel the strength in her, the loyalty, the fierceness. To him, she's always burned like a beacon through a stormy midnight. Even now, he can't help but want to seek out her light.

"Let's get some canvas on," he calls. His remaining crew rush to oblige him. They scramble up rigging, releasing ties, sails unfurling. They open with a crack, filling with wind. He lets out a long breath, feeling the ship sway beneath him. The Farlands vessel is a sleek beast, though it could never feel like home the way Da's ship did. It broke his heart to leave the *Tempest* behind. If only Da could see him now. Willan wonders what the mighty Serpent would make of his son sailing toward a fleet of enemy ships without any real plan for what to do when he finds them. Somehow he knows what Da would say. *Don't be a hero, lad. They always end up in early graves.* But he's not about to let anyone put chains around his girl, or any of them. To prevent that, he will give everything he has.

He thinks again of Æsa, heading into Simta without him. Falling for her wasn't a choice, but loving her is. He will choose it every day, despite the dangers, and gladly. Perhaps, in leaving her, she will believe it too. His fingers reach for the note she pressed into his palm before he left her. He doesn't need to unfold it now to know what it says. *Whatever fate has in store, I want to greet it with you, Willan. So, as soon as you can, come back to me.*

He will fight tooth and nail to do as she bids him. He will brave any storm to get to her.

– CHAPTER 20 –
PREDATORS

S AYER STALKS THROUGH the reeds, parting them sound-
lessly. The water sluices around her chest. It's clear enough
that she can see down to the glade's silty bottom, but she
fights the urge to look for yellowed teeth.

"No gators," Fen whispers, reading her thoughts. "Seleese
says they don't come this close to the coastline."

"Good. Because I have no interest in meeting one."

"You and me, Tig. We're the predators today."

She sounds assured, but Sayer knows what this trip could
cost Fen. She's only just gotten over her addiction to witchbane, and the men they're sneaking up on have a ton of it. What
will happen if they use it on her? *Like shadows, remember?* Fen
said, taking Sayer's hand amongst the nest of blankets they'd
made on Seleese's houseboat. *I'm coming with you.* She should
have made Fen stay back with the clan.

The deal is going down near the coast, where some tributar-
ies of the Callistan's fresh waters flow out to mingle with the
Bluebottle Sea. It's an easier way to access the glades than by
way of Sarask, if you know its tangled paths. Especially if a Syth-

ian is willing to ride out to guide you in. Sayer can see a Sythian riverboat ahead, tied up to a larger boat with holes for oars. She's seen boats like this skirting around Simta's coast: long-boats, good for both shallow ocean-faring and narrow water-ways like this one, fringed on either side by jungle. It won't be able to get away quickly. All the better.

Seleese's clan is nearby, tucked out of sight and waiting on her signal. They didn't want to swim in. Rafe said it's fine for the two of them, being enlimned, but Sythians don't like to pollute what they believe are the Wellspring's holy waters. Sayer can see why now: Or rather, she can feel it. In the water, the tingling hum she's felt since they arrived is stronger, a vibration. It's sharp enough to make her teeth ache.

She and Fen creep closer, closer, pausing behind the last clump of reeds between them and the vessel. The trees are thinner this close to the ocean, but the sun is only just starting to come up. The light is low, and on board they still have a few lanterns burning. Their light makes the passengers' pale grey cloaks glow.

Sayer grips Fen's arm. *Caska,* she mouths. It's no surprise, but it still makes Sayer want to hit something. They don't belong here, in this magical place. A few boys seem to be patrolling the edge of the boat, crossbows trained on the jungle. She just hopes they don't think to look further down.

Sayer glances at Fen again, chewing her lip. Is she up for this? Seeing her worry, Fen nods. The magic between them prickles, wind and earth. If Fen says she's ready, then Sayer trusts her. As one, they suck in breaths and sink down, trying to swim close to the swamp's murky bottom. The silt stings her eyes as a school of fish darts by, flashing silver. She can't let any air bubbles escape and rise, where the Caska patrols might see them. They can't stop until they get up next to the boat.

At last, she emerges slowly through the surface. Fen comes up beside her with barely a ripple. The water is deeper here, which means they have to tread. They swim slowly as they press up close to the boat's stern. Its side is curved, jutting out just enough that it should shield them. No one above will see unless they lean out over the railing. And if they do . . . well. One fight at a time.

"Come on, boys," someone aboard is saying. "We need to shove off before the tide changes."

Which means it's time for Sayer to pull on her disguise. She reaches for her magic, watching as her body blends in with the water, the leaves, the air. Invisible. Magic is easy here, especially with Fen. While Sayer is up on deck, Fen is going to scupper them. She's already pulling out some hole-boring tool Seleese gave her.

Sayer presses close.

"Stay out of sight," she says, barely a whisper.

"You too," Fen whispers back. "And just remember. I'm here."

Sayer takes a breath and climbs the wooden rungs nailed to the boat's side, a makeshift ladder. She scales them just enough to see over. A bunch of boys are moving crates: Three wear grey robes, and two wear shades of green and gold. They must be Sythians, and yet they don't seem to be in charge. An older Caska man is directing the action, pointing. She doesn't see her sire or the Red Hand. Not that she expected to: Of course they would send errand boys to do their dirty work. She's only here to look for evidence of their involvement, to steal as much information as she can.

When the guards pass, she climbs onto the deck. She creeps

over to what looks like the captain's cabin, which is empty, walking through as silently as she can. It is small, but tidy: no letters or missives left behind for her to pilfer. But then she turns and sees a coat hanging from a peg. She picks its pockets, finding a letter tucked in one of them. Its blue wax seal is stamped with a familiar Eudean timberwolf. She looks around one more time, then breaks it open. Reading quickly, she sees it's a shipping document, signed by the ship's owner. Even seeing his name written down—Wyllo Regnis—makes her recoil. This paper claims the ship is carrying jinny, a smoking herb, and states its destination as an estate in the Waystrell. Blazing cats, is *that* where the Red Hand is making Sugar? Would Wyllo really let the Red Hand use his country house to make his drug?

A shout from outside makes her start, shaking her focus. There's no time to dwell on her sire: His time is coming. She stuffs the letter in a waterproof pouch Seleese gave her and goes back out on deck.

"Is this all there is?" the Caska in charge is saying to one of the Sythians. "I was expecting more from you."

One of the Sythians worries the collar of his shirt. "It is not so easy to harvest without the other clans knowing. They would have my skin for this."

"They do not understand our mission," the Caska says, softening. "But Marren sees your holy work and will reward you."

The Sythian straightens, making a sign at his breast. "Thank you, brother."

Sayer pads over to one of the crates, easing it silently open. Ten hells, it's *full* of witchbane. Even without it burning, the smell almost makes her gag. Sayer can see the dark, oily-looking leaves, their roots packed tight in bulbs bound in burlap. Some other plants are mixed in amongst them. Are they part of what goes into making Sugar? She leans in closer, trying to see.

A light flashes behind: The two Caska guards are circling close, lanterns in hand. They're about to walk into her. She hops up on one of the closed crates, out of their path.

"You shouldn't complain," one says, frowning at the crate Sayer left open. He puts his lantern down on its lid. "This is a holy mission."

"I know. But I hope we get back in time for the wedding. I would hate to miss such a historic event."

Sayer frowns. He must mean *Matilde's* wedding. Her friend hasn't called it off, then, even after the way she kissed Alec at the Bathhouse. She will never understand Matilde Dinatris. But why would this Caska want to see it? He can't have made the guest list.

"The Red Hand told my brother what's to happen," he says, clearly excited.

"He did not," the other says. "What did he say?"

The first boy leans in, speaking in whispers, but Sayer hears him. Dread crawls like a spider down her neck. Then something crashes down over her head, pulling tight around her. She topples off the crate as she tries to break free. It smells of algae and fish: It's a net. Someone is dragging her across the deck, into the open.

"Fools," he says. "You have allowed a witch amongst us."

One of the boys makes the sign of the Eshamein. "How did you even see her?"

"I didn't. She left footprints."

Sayer curses herself. She tries to roll, to reach her knife, but the Caska's hold is unforgiving. She calls on her magic, shifting the air, making it taste of lightning. She will choke them if she has to. But then the Caska bends down, groping until he finds her chin, and quickly smears some foul paste across her mouth: witchbane. Her magic, and her camouflage, stutter out.

Caska faces stare down, seeing her now, full of hatred.

"By Marren's grace," one says. "It is the Storm Witch. It has to be."

She spits and spits, trying to get rid of the witchbane. One of the Caska is smiling now.

"What a gift for the Red Hand. He is going to bless us all for this."

Sayer writhes. Where is Fen? The Sythians, hovering behind the Caska, look unsettled.

"She is enlimned," one murmurs, tapping his collarbone. "The glades won't like this."

Sayer bares her teeth. "You're right. They won't."

With all the breath she has, she whistles. Seleese's clan starts firing. Arrows fly from every side, thunking into crates, rails, and barrels. The Caska duck down, firing back, spreading out. The two Sythians run by her, crouching low and praying. Sayer writhes like a fish, but the Caska holds fast. She takes aim and kicks, trying to dislodge him. He rears back, an arm going out to catch himself, knocking into the crates. The lantern falls into the one she left open, breaking, and the witchbane inside bursts into flame. Blazing cats, it catches fast, even as one of the Caska boys tries to smother it. The smoke makes her feel wretched. She is glad, now, Fen hasn't come.

"I have your witch," her captor shouts, loud enough for Seleese's clan to hear. "Cease fire, or I will slit her throat. I swear it."

The firing stops. The crates keep burning.

"Let go of her," Fen growls, "or die."

Sayer gapes at Fen. She is standing at the rail, dripping with water, her eyes as sharp as the knife in her hand.

"Another one!" the Caska shouts. "Take her."

"Go, Fen," Sayer says. "Please. The witchbane . . ."

It will ruin her. But Fen doesn't move as the Caska take aim.

Sayer's magic is gone: She can no longer feel it. But she feels Fen's fury rolling off her in waves. The air drips with it, the glades responding to Fen, adapting. The jungle seems to bare its teeth, unsheathe its claws.

Branches shoot out to knock away the Caska's weapons as vines as thick as her arm drop from the canopy. Her captor's eyes bulge as one wraps around him, lifting him up. It carries him away, slamming him back against a tree trunk. More tie him there, smothered in spine and thorn and leaf. He kicks and thrashes, but the glades want to devour him. It's like watching a spider wrap up a fly. Every Caska is entombed against a tree now, nothing but their faces visible through the greenery.

At last, the tumult stops. Fen is beside her, yanking the net away.

"You all right, Tig? Did he hurt you?"

"You shouldn't have come," Sayer croaks. "The witchbane. You should have left me."

Fen touches her cheek. "A promise is a promise, Tig."

There's no time to talk. The boat is burning. A few of Seleese's clan climb over the rail, working to put the fires out. The two rogue Sythians are helping too. Oily smoke curls around them. Sayer's stomach is a twisted ruin, but Fen . . . she seems fine.

"I don't understand," she says, throat raw. "How did you use your magic?"

Fen's expression is raw, too. "I don't know."

They get up and help douse the flames, throwing buckets

of water. At last, the fire's out; this witchbane won't make it to the Red Hand. But still, Sayer's dread won't be smothered. Not with the words the Caska boy whispered about the wedding, set to take place just days from now.

By the end of it, the Flame Witch will be ours.

Life is fine in Simta. My sisters and I spend our days in relative comfort, our nights with those who come to claim a Nightbird's gift. It is safe. But when I think of the sort of magic we used to wield, sometimes I tremble. We lit the way for so many; we were a torch held high against the night. And now the church is twisting our legends, making up lies about us. They blame us for every evil in the world. They write over our stories, and I can do nothing to stop it. Women with power are easy to condemn.

—FROM THE JOURNAL OF DELAINA DINATRIS,
ONE OF SIMTA'S FIRST NIGHTBIRDS

CHAPTER 21

THE FINAL HOURS

T O THE FUTURE," Dennan says.

To the future, the guests echo. Matilde raises her glass for the toast. Around the ballroom, hundreds of flames bend and shimmer. The fires in every chandelier and candlestick change from yellow to a sparkling white. She makes them shine like moonstones as the guests gasp and titter. It is a pretty piece of magic, reminding them of what she might do without being threatening. All at once, she lets her hold on them go.

Guests clap and exclaim, crowding in too close around her. She cuts a swath through them with small smiles and waves. She comes to stand beside Leta, who is positioned by a gilded mirror. In it, Matilde sees hundreds of eyes fixed on them. The palace's ballroom is swimming with wedding guests, here for dinner and dancing on the eve of the big event. Representatives are here from all over Eudea and every nation on the map. They all seem to want something from her. Laughter cuts through the room, the sound grating on her nerves.

"Are you sure you don't want to make a quick escape?" Leta says behind her glass. "I'm sure I could arrange it."

Guests have been peppering Leta with pointed, often callous questions about Sayer. Matilde is surprised her old Madam has stayed at the party this long.

"You always did delight in rejecting suitors for me. I'm not sure I ever thanked you properly."

Leta touches her arm. "No need. I was meant to protect you. I'm only sorry I couldn't do a better job."

She takes a fortifying breath. It's nice to have Leta here beside her. But she wishes Sayer were here to bicker with, or Æsa, whom she left tucked up in her room. She even wishes for Fen, who might offer to knife the diplomat who keeps ogling her cleavage. If they were here, she might feel stronger.

"You have always had a strong will," Leta says, as if reading her mind, squeezing her hand. "Do not let this marriage change it. Don't you ever bow to him or anyone."

Matilde squeezes back, throat tight. "I won't. I promise."

The band strikes up a tune. Dennan comes striding toward them.

"Will you honor me, my lady?" he asks, holding a hand out.

She doesn't feel like dancing, but they are supposed to appear a united front. The Vesten and the Fyrebird: a power couple, not to be trifled with. It's becoming hard to keep that mask on. To remember what game is being played.

She lets him sweep her out onto the floor, smooth and assured. From his fresh face, you would never know he has spent the past few nights arguing with the Table. Matilde listened through her grate during this morning's Table meeting, in which Dennan didn't mention the Trellians once. When she confronted him about it, he said that involving them would only slow down preparations for the battle. When she pressed him to let Æsa speak to the Table, he refused, saying they would not believe her. Matilde suspects he simply wants to win this fight without them, assuring his rise and their fall. That, and he doesn't want to share Æsa with them. She doesn't like how Dennan seems to want to keep Æsa so close, within his sight.

"You look beautiful," Dennan tells her. "As always."

"You would say that." Her gown is the same purplish blue as his eyes: Dame's idea. Something to make them look like a matching set. "I'm wearing your color."

He smiles. "It suits you."

But does it? His eyes made her think of fire once, but now they seem cold to her. They have long since lost their power to draw her in.

He sweeps her through a turn, hand low on her back.

"I remember when we used to play at the outskirts of these parties," he says. "And look at us now. At the heart of it."

Her stomach roils to think of those nights. He felt to her then like a puzzle she was slowly solving. She wonders if she ever really knew him at all.

Over his shoulder, Matilde can see her family looking on at them, smiling. It gives her a haunting sense of history repeating. It was like this at Leta's Season-opening ball, where she danced with Tenny Maylon. Gran smiled at her then, too, hoping Matilde would finally settle down with an eligible suitor. Like then, Matilde is having reckless thoughts.

"This feels wrong," she says. "Dancing and feasting while an army sails toward us."

"Our navy will be ready," Dennan says. "Never fear."

He has been having secret meetings with commanders, convincing them of what's to come. Scouts have been sent out, and ships prepared. None of it has truly eased her mind. She keeps thinking of what the captured sailor said: that the snake was in the house already. For all they know, the Farlands king could have allies in the city. No new visions have given Æsa a clearer picture of how and when they might attack. Her Hawk should have gotten back by now, but they've had no word from Willan. Matilde can tell Æsa is worried, but how can she reassure her? She doesn't want to lie.

"Still, Dennan. We have no idea what Joost might do at our wedding. Perhaps we should postpone. It's not too late."

Silence reigns for a moment as they spin again. The frame of his arms has the feel of a cage.

"It is all right to be nervous," Dennan says. "I expected it. Or is it Alecand Padano who is giving you cold feet?"

She misses a step, almost stumbling.

"Why would you ask me such a thing?"

"You two were close once," Dennan goes on. "I'm sure he still wants you. And your missives made it clear you are carrying a torch for him."

He speaks as if this is a casual conversation. Heated embers stir to life deep in her chest.

"You've been intercepting my notes."

"Your maid was reluctant to share, but I convinced her it was for your safety."

So Alec never got her letters. Dennan read the words she meant only for him.

"You had no right."

"I beg to differ."

His fingers curl around her waist, gripping her tight.

"Think what would have happened if he had taken them to the newssheets, or they had fallen into one of our enemy's hands. They would have made our union look like a farce. I couldn't have that."

His voice is smooth, but she hears the jealousy in it. Something crawls straight down her spine.

"I've heard some troubling rumors about your friend Alec," Dennan says. "Apparently, he has been making weapons for sandpipers, which have created quite a lot of problems for the Wardens. It would be a shame if he was arrested. A crime like that could lead him straight to Gallows Row."

She goes stiff in his arms.

"Is that a threat?"

"I'm simply saying that he is in a precarious position. As suzerain, I could help him. And I would do so, for an old friend of my wife's."

The music plays on, but Matilde's feet feel as if someone has wrapped them in chains. She can't believe she ever felt safe to play games with him. That she didn't see every game for what it was: a trap.

"He has confused you," Dennan says, voice softer now. "I understand that. But you need to keep your eye on the prize, Matilde. Your vision needs to be as big as mine."

His expression is sincere, coaxing her to believe him. Dennan has a way of making his vision, his truth, the only one.

"I know this wedding is political for us both. But the truth is that I want to marry you, Matilde. I would want you regardless. I will do anything to keep you by my side."

His eyes on her are burning like they did the night he murdered his sister. The bright conviction in them makes her blood run cold.

The last notes of the song ring out. There is a round of

clapping. Matilde fights the urge to turn and run. Before she can, a new song starts. Someone taps Dennan's shoulder.

"Excuse me, suzerain," the man says, accent heavy. "May I take a turn with your lady?"

Dennan goes rigid, jaw ticking. He looks close to refusing. But Matilde wants to take this man's measure.

"I would be happy to, King Joost."

She lets the king of Trellane sweep her into the dance. He is taller than Dennan, with long, slender fingers. His skin is so pale, almost colorless. His cropped hair reminds her of frost spread over yellow glass.

"This is a gift to me," he begins. "What a treat to finally meet the famous Flame Witch. Though I confess, I am disappointed not to see more of your magic this evening. I have heard such exciting tales."

She flashes her teeth. "I assure you, the tales of my power haven't been exaggerated. I can burn a man alive with little more than a thought."

Joost does not look afraid. If anything, he seems delighted.

"A mighty weapon. The suzerain is lucky to wield it."

"No one wields me. You are far from home, King. You forget that in Simta, we do not keep slaves."

He sighs. "Eudeans do not understand our ways. You see galgren as enslaved, when in fact they are protected. They know their role and are grateful. Some are meant to rule, and some to serve."

Matilde fights back a shudder. She lowers her voice, keeping it sweet. "I rule here, Joost. And I will destroy anyone who tries to put a pershain on a girl with magic. I hope you will remember that."

Her hand heats as she presses it to his fine green tunic.

Beneath her palm, the embroidery starts to melt. It will leave a scorch mark, but she doesn't stay to see it. If she did, she might burn the man to ashes. The room has grown too hot: Her head is spinning. She desperately needs some air.

She moves through the crowd, losing the guards meant to be keeping an eye on her, and slips behind a curtain. At last, she finds her way onto a balcony, breaths coming fast. Her magic, stirred by her anger, is restless. She wishes she could let it pour out.

For long moments, she just breathes, looking out at the Corners. It is usually filled with small boats ferrying people across the city, but they have had to make way for the structure floating there. It took many of Simta's carpenters a full two weeks to build the wedding venue. Half ship, half ballroom, it's perched where everyone can see. It sits empty now, lit only by flamemoth lanterns. She can almost smell the verdabloom and winglily twined around its railings, a haunting perfume.

She takes a breath, another. *I will be married in the morning.* If she says it to herself enough times, perhaps she will believe. How did she let things come to this? She stayed at the Winged Palace to change Eudea from the inside. It was the only way, she thought, to claim real power, to break the cage so many people have tried to put around her. And yet here she is, a Fyrebird, sitting behind a screen, bound and silenced. Being passed around a dance floor by men who see her as a tool.

She closes her eyes. *What do you truly want, Tilde?* Alec asked. What she has always wanted: to choose her own path. But Dennan made it clear he will hurt Alec if she doesn't go through with the wedding. He knows the Fyrebirds' identities, too, and there's no telling how far he will go to bring them into his service. Perhaps she has gone too far down this road to turn back.

This afternoon, she sat with Æsa on her bed, whispering secrets. It took them hours to share everything that had happened in their months apart. Matilde made sure not to hold anything back. She told Æsa about the engagement, the Sugar, the church heist. About her feelings for Alec, and Delaina's secret journal. The hardest confession was the one about falling out with Sayer. But sharing it all was a relief, too, a storm finally breaking. She didn't know, before, quite how lonely she has felt.

Should I go through with it? she asked at last. *Marrying Dennan?*

It took Æsa a long time to reply.

Only you can make that choice, she said. *But whatever comes, we will face it together, the four of us. You will not be alone anymore.*

Matilde looks out again at the wedding barge, its flamemoth lanterns shining out against the darkness. They are beautiful alone, the moths, the way they shimmer. But in a group, they become a beacon. The Fyrebirds were like that too once: a light that people followed gladly into battle. What did Delaina call them? *A torch held high against the night.*

The words make something move through her, new and fragile. Conviction, finally unfurling its wings.

All these months, she has been trying to change things from the inside. To make the Table listen and get Dennan to bend around her will. But she's been doing it as a Nightbird might, with words and charm and deception. She was trying to work inside a system that was not designed for girls like her.

To change things, she cannot play by the old rules. She has to break them. All of them.

She takes a breath, another, a great weight lifting. She isn't going to marry Dennan.

She and her girls are going to fight on their own terms.

A noise comes from behind her. As she starts to turn, someone grabs her from behind, wrenching her head back. Liquid pours fast down her throat. She tries to cough, but a hand has clamped her nose shut. All she can do is swallow.

"Matilde Dinatris," a man says at her ear. "You will heed me."

She blinks, once, twice, and then she nods.

"Yes. Of course."

YOU ARE CORDIALLY INVITED
TO THE JOINING OF

LORD DENNAN VESTEN,
SUZERAIN OF EUDEA,
&
YOUNG LADY MATILDE DINATRIS

IN MARRIAGE

AT NINE CHIMES
ON THE LAST DAY OF
RISENTIDE.

– CHAPTER 22 –
EVERYTHING BREAKS

MATILDE HAS NEVER fantasized about her wedding day. While her friends swooned over dresses and mused about their future husbands, she dreamed up ways she might avoid the whole affair. And yet when she looks in the mirror now, she sees a bride. She feels removed from her reflection, as if that girl is someone else entirely. But she must admit she looks the part. Her dress was made in the newest style, with thin straps and a drop waist, its soft layers flowing around her. Its golden silk and metallic silver thread will shimmer nicely in the sunlight, turning her to liquid fire. How fitting.

"You look perfect," Dame says, clutching her hands. She is crying.

"Agreed," Samson says, kissing her on the cheek.

Matilde smiles, though in truth she barely hears them. Her thoughts have already walked away, down the aisle.

Gran shoos them both away to take their places. It won't be long until the ceremony starts. Matilde can hear the string music and the footsteps of the guests above them. She has feelings about it all, but she feels untethered from them. Her lips are numb, her mouth so dry. She sips some water, but it doesn't rinse the film on her tongue away. Powdery sweet, she tastes it still.

Gran touches her arm, a slight crease between her brows. "Are you nervous, darling?"

"No."

The crease grows deeper. "You don't need to pretend with me. It's only natural. I was a nervous bride as well."

She imagines what Gran would've felt, the day she chose to walk toward a Dinatris boy instead of Krastan Padano. Just like Matilde is walking toward Dennan instead of Alec. The thought makes something inside her tilt. She blinks once, twice, a ship that's lost its bearings. But then she remembers why she is here. What she must do.

"I feel fine," Matilde says. "I know my duty."

At the words, Gran seems to relax.

"I know that duty can be a difficult path to walk at times. It takes strength, which you have in abundance. I hope you know how proud of you I am."

Gran hugs her, bringing her familiar scent of lilies. Then, at last, they make their way down a dimly lit hall. Dennan had a warren of rooms and passageways built beneath the wedding platform, meant to let servers and guards move around unseen. The bridal suite is on one end, and the groom's is on the other. She hasn't seen him since last night, when they danced.

Gran leads them to a set of stairs. A doorway sits open at the top, letting in music and sunlight. Her chest burns with the desire to be above. Her old Nightbird sisters, serving as bridesmaids, ascend first, each blowing back kisses. Dame makes sure Matilde's long, sequined cape is fanned out properly before she follows. Gran settles Matilde's golden veil into place, eyes shining. And then Matilde is alone.

She takes one breath, two, preparing. The music swells as she steps into the light.

It's a fine morning, crisp and blue. The barge's top level is like a stage, but rimmed with railings bedecked with flower garlands. Swaths of fabric stretch above the sea of seats, shading the guests without blocking the view. Through the shimmer of her veil, she can see the crowds lining the Corners, waving flags and cheering. Matilde is going to give them quite a show.

She walks down the carpeted aisle toward the dais. The guests stand, watching as she goes. She sees people she knows: family friends, Table members, Leta. She sees some she loathes, including King Joost of Trellane. But there is only one person here who matters. He seems to shine, brighter than any star. He gives her a subtle nod as she passes. Her sense of certainty, of rightness, swells.

At last, she gets to the dais, where Dennan is waiting, shimmering in a cream suit, golden waistcoat, and sash. The Pontifex stands just beyond him, as self-important as ever. She climbs the short set of stairs and joins them, steps measured and sure.

"Welcome," the Pontifex begins, gesturing for the guests to sit. "You have gathered today, from near and far, to celebrate this union between Dennan Vesten and Matilde Dinatris. One that promises to be both joyous and fruitful."

The Pontifex gives a speech about harmony and duty. Matilde hides her intentions under a serene, unruffled smile. There is a flash of gold as Dennan lifts her veil and settles it behind her. He smiles down as if he didn't threaten the boy she loves just last night. She has feelings about that, too, but they feel far away.

At last, the Pontifex holds up an ornate blade. It plays a part in every Eudean wedding: a symbol of strength and fidelity, meant to forge a union into something unbreakable. But even metal breaks if you hit it hard enough.

"Dennan Vesten," the Pontifex intones. "Do you swear to protect and honor this woman?"

"I do."

"And do you, Matilde Dinatris, swear to honor and obey this man?"

That word—*obey*—makes something inside her recoil. And yet she says *I do* as Dennan smiles on.

The Pontifex puts the hilt in her hand, then wraps Dennan's fingers around it. He pulls a length of cord out from his robe and holds it up.

"With this cord, I do bind."

He starts to wrap the cord around their joined hands and the hilt.

"Once for promise, twice for dedication, three times for a union that will endure."

The crowd is silent as the Pontifex knots the cord tightly. Matilde takes a fortifying breath.

"Matilde, don't!" someone screams.

The voice tugs at her heart, but she cannot falter.

The sun catches the blade as she stabs the Pontifex.

———— ⚑ ————

ÆSA YANKS DOWN her sky-blue veil as a palace guard rows her across the Corners. She found the dress and large hat she is wearing in Matilde's cluttered closet. It isn't the best disguise, but needs must. The veil obscures her vision like her Nightingale mask, giving her a strange sense of dissonance, of time running too fast, running out.

"You want to hurry," she urges the guard, squeezing his arm. "Everything depends on it."

He rows harder, panting with effort. She feels guilty for meddling with his emotions, but she can't afford such scruples. Not when the wedding music has already begun.

She didn't see Matilde after the function last night, or this morning. She had wedding duties to attend to, and Æsa's presence was deemed too great a risk. So she situated herself on the balcony of the Dinatris apartments, avoiding Samson's longing stares and Oura and Frey's pointed questions, and fretting about why Willan hasn't come. From there, she could see the crowds teeming around each of the Corners. Most of the city must have come out to watch. For such a public venue, the barge's floating nature meant the guards would have an easier time seeing guests—and threats—coming. Everyone would be checked for weapons. Anyone who stepped aboard would be closely watched.

She was sipping her tea, wondering how Matilde was feeling, when the vision came. It was short and sharp, and one she's had before. But this time, she saw it much more clearly. This time, she recognized the stage: not a ship, but a barge. Now she is here, hoping to prevent that future. But she fears she isn't going to make it in time.

At last, they pull up to one of the landing platforms floating around the wedding barge. Æsa's guard speaks swiftly to another, then hurries her forward, up one of the gangways. It seems the ceremony is already underway. They skirt the railing, as if looking for a seat. With a whisper, the guard leaves her standing by the base of an awning, partially hidden from the seated guests by a large vase of flowers. Not that anyone is looking her way. Their attention is firmly fixed on the couple up on the dais. Matilde's metallic dress is shining, almost hard to look at. The way she stands means Æsa can't see her face.

The Pontifex starts to wrap a cord around the couple's hands.

"With this cord, I do bind."

She looks around, frantic. How can she stop this without making a scene? She reaches for the bond that ties her and Matilde together. It should be easy to find, this close, pulsing like a shared heartbeat. Æsa can feel it, but it's . . . slippery. She cannot seem to yank it tight.

"Once for promise, twice for dedication, three times for a union that will endure."

The crowd is silent as the Pontifex knots the cord. Æsa takes a step, still reaching for that bond between them. She cannot let her friend do this.

"Matilde, don't!"

But it is too late. The knife flashes, and the Pontifex staggers. He clutches at his chest, where a dark stain is blooming. It spreads and spreads, swallowing his pale purple robes. With a guttering breath, he crumples. No one moves, as if suspended by the shock of it. Dennan stares down at their joined hands and the knife, open-mouthed.

Æsa takes another step.

A deep, gravelly voice cuts through the quiet.

"Shame."

It comes from the far end of the aisle, where the Red Hand has appeared out of nowhere, surrounded by several boys in grey.

"Shame," he says again, pointing at Matilde. His face is shiny with new scars, a red handprint smeared across it, eyes shining with that same old zealous light. "Is there no end to your depravity? That you would attempt to murder the voice of the gods?"

Dennan has pulled free of the rope and crouched down, but the Pontifex's chest has stopped rising. Matilde, standing over them, looks strangely unmoved.

"It had to be done," she says, voice flat. "The church's reign over us is over. It's time we burn it down."

Horrified cries float from the crowd. The Red Hand rises to meet them.

"Do you see, now, what En Caska Dae have tried to show you? No good can come of letting witches walk free. They corrupt what should be holy. They are a danger to us all."

The words are smooth, as if he has rehearsed them. This whole exchange feels like lines from some play. And then Æsa understands: The Red Hand must have planned this. He must have slipped Matilde some Sugar, somehow. How did no one see him coming? How did he get onto this barge, and to her?

"Just look at her," he goes on. "She does not regret this. In her quest for power, her thirst for blood, Matilde Dinatris has proven her wickedness. And she has bewitched our suzerain into aiding her crime."

"No," Dennan says, standing again. "I had no hand in this."

"You have been corrupted, Dennan Vesten," the Hand says. "You can no longer be trusted to serve as Eudea's suzerain. You and Matilde Dinatris are both under arrest."

"Try it," Matilde shouts. "I dare you. See how quickly I can set this barge ablaze."

Æsa feels a pulse of heat. The small flames around the

barge grow and leap, as if they've sprouted wings. They fly to Matilde, merging above her, forming a kind of halo. Dennan takes another step away. Several guests shriek, staggering back and cowering. The guards' weapons, once trained on the Hand, swing toward the bride.

"Caska!" the Hand shouts. "Light the witchbane."

The boys in grey pull censers out of their robes.

"Stop!"

Salt coats her tongue as Æsa calls on her magic. A wave rises over one of the railings and pounds across the wood. Guests scream, diving out of its path. They needn't bother; it only wants the Caska. It crashes into their censers, dousing the contents and curling tight around them all.

When she first came to the Dinatris house, she was given a lovely room to sleep in. A glass case sat perched on the mantelpiece. It was shaped like a bell, clear and smooth and perfect, encasing a trio of artfully posed moths. It seemed cruel, somehow, though the insects were well beyond caring. Forever stuck staring out at the world, flightless and still.

That is the shape she conjures now. The water arcs around and over the Caska, smoothing into a glassy sheet, and freezes. The Red Hand bellows, but the thick ice dampens the sound.

Æsa throws back her veil. There is no point in hiding. The crowd is whispering: *The Wave Witch, the Wave Witch*. She raises her voice to be heard.

"This isn't Matilde Dinatris's fault. She has been forced to do this."

Dennan is breathing hard. "What do you mean?"

"The Red Hand has created a drug," she hurries on, "that can compel a girl with magic. It's called Sugar. Girls under its influence have no choice but to obey."

The Red Hand shouts, but his words are muffled. Someone else—a dark-haired man—speaks instead.

"You would say anything to save her. But you are as bad as she is, Wave Witch. We cannot believe your poisonous lies."

An ominous murmur from the crowd. Æsa will not let their censure cow her. She stares down the man.

"This is no lie. The Red Hand wants to make Matilde look like the villain. He wants to turn you all against us."

People shift and whisper. There's a crack as one of the Caska kicks their cage. It won't hold for much longer. The guards' crossbows whip between Æsa and Matilde, unsure which one to aim at. They look to Dennan, but he seems lost.

"She speaks the truth, Lord Vesten."

The new speaker stands. It's Leta, regal and fearless.

"I have seen Sugar's effects with my own eyes. This zealot has tried to use it to poison us against the Fyrebirds, discredit our suzerain, and get rid of our Pontifex, all in one fell swoop."

"Of course you would defend her, Leta Tangreel," the dark-haired man snaps. "You were the Nightbirds' *Madam*."

There are sharp, scandalized gasps, but Leta doesn't shrink from them. If anything, she stands up straighter.

"I was," she says, voice as cold as Æsa's ice. "And I did my best to protect them from those who sought to harm them. Men like you, Wyllo Regnis, who seduced Nadja Sant Held for her magic, then left her and your daughter in the streets."

More gasps and exclamations. Sayer's sire goes purple.

"How dare you spread such falsehoods," he spits. "I will—"

Leta raises her voice, talking over him. "These men seek to discredit our girls simply because they will not bow to them. But I believe them, and I will always stand by them. Any Great House member worth their salt should do the same."

Æsa looks again to Dennan. His vibrant eyes are fixed on Matilde, seeming to register the way she looks around, vague and confused. Her halo of fire has shrunk down to fireballs floating just above her palms.

"Matilde," he says, taking a step. "You should have told me."

Æsa feels a surge of hope. He *believes*. Perhaps they all will. They can still pull this wedding back from the brink.

But then Matilde nods, and the fire above her palms sparks and swells. The air seems to shift. Something tugs at Æsa's ribs as the sky around the barge starts to darken. A wind kicks up, ripping at the wreaths of flowers.

"Leave her *alone*."

There is a commotion amongst the guests. People in the first few rows of seats are falling, as if pushed aside by something. Wyllo Regnis is knocked clear off his feet into the aisle. Æsa can almost see fists raining down, hitting Wyllo. He writhes and bucks, and then he shrieks: *"Kill her!"*

Many things happen at once: Crossbows click, guests shout, glass shatters. Dennan grabs for Matilde, spinning her as if they're dancing. An arrow punches through his back. There is a moment where he stands there, swaying, before he staggers and falls off the stage. Matilde blinks down, staring at him. When she looks up again, her eyes are burning.

Her fire leaps back to life, swelling and wild. Æsa has seen this future.

This is the moment when everything will start to break.

※

SAYER IS CLOSE: almost close enough to touch Matilde up on the dais. She has to snap her out of her trance. At least the Hand is trapped: He won't be able to compel her further. Her friend's gaze isn't fixed on him, though, but on the guests. No, just one, who stares fixedly back, all concentration. Sayer's skin crawls as her sire mouths the words: *Show your fire.*

Matilde nods, an eager gesture, as her small fires spark and flare.

Wyllo's lips curl into a smile. It makes something snap in Sayer.

"Leave her *alone*."

Sayer runs, heedless of the bodies between them. She pushes and leaps, knocking them all aside. She doesn't stop until Wyllo is on his back, pinned beneath her. A sound like thunder booms as she pounds him with her fists. There is nothing but her rage, her need to break this man to pieces. Her hands reach for his throat as he shouts, *"Kill her!"*

A weapon fires, a body falls, a fire is raging. Sayer feels its searing heat against her cheek. She springs up and wheels toward the dais, calling the air to arc and harden around her. Matilde has sent fire flying toward her, clawed and bestial. Sayer drops to a knee as it crashes into her shield. She tips the shield, trying to send the fire ricocheting toward the water. It rips through an awning, setting the whole thing ablaze.

All is chaos. Guests scream and shove, scattering chairs as they try to flee. Wyllo is gone, but Sayer can't afford to look for him. Every time she tries to send one of Matilde's fire creatures over the side, away from the wedding guests, it only seems to hit cloth or wood. Her magic feels swollen, almost erratic. Having all four of them on this barge is amplifying it, but it isn't a good thing. It feels like oil thrown onto an already raging flame. They're going to rip this place apart. Sayer trips, falling backward as another fire creature rears above her. She throws up her hands, trying to rebuild her shield. Æsa sends a watery serpent crashing into the fire and they roll across the barge like feral creatures, turning into a cloud of hissing steam.

But Matilde isn't done. The flames come fast and hot, relentless.

"Blazing cats, Dinatris," Sayer shouts. "Stop fighting me!"

If Matilde hears her plea, it makes no mark.

MATILDE IS BLAZING with her newest purpose. Her chest, so numb before, is on fire.

Kill her.

The words are like a brand, searing through her. The need to obey them is all she can feel.

It's hard to see. Hot steam and smoke swirl all around her. A blast of wind howls across the dais, catching her skirt. Something is heightening her magic, making it stronger. It stretches in her blood, desperate to fly.

Kill her.

Matilde wills another of her fire creatures to run at Sayer. It doesn't just bare its teeth: It roars. It has been months since she felt like this, so powerful. It feels so good to finally burn.

"Blazing cats, Dinatris," Sayer shouts. "Stop fighting me!"

"You don't want to do this," Æsa pleads. "Matilde. Please."

She feels a dizzying tilt, something inside her revolting. But the desire to do as she was told smothers it all.

FEN FIGHTS THROUGH the crowd. People are running, tripping, rushing toward the gangways. Some are simply leaping off the barge's sides. She throws a few elbows, but it's like swimming against a raging current. It keeps taking her away from where she wants to be.

Where are the girls now? She can feel them as they circle in the smoke; it seems they're amplifying each other's magic. They've turned this barge into a chaos of flames, and storm, and carnage. The awnings are rags of fire, sending embers falling down like snowflakes. Æsa's waves keep crashing over the railings, filling the air with steam so hot it burns. Somewhere to her right comes the sound of glass cracking, then shattering. Or is it ice?

There is no time to go after Dorisall. She promised Sayer she wouldn't leave her. Fen isn't about to go back on her word.

There is a mighty crack as a beam splits, crashing downward. She dives out of its path as it falls. She hits the deck hard. She's on her back, somehow, fuzz in her ears, lungs searing. Everything smells like melted flowers.

Move, she thinks, but she can't seem to do it.

Get up, she pleads as a scarred face looms close.

"Little thief," Dorisall growls, pressing a blade to her throat. "I have you."

She has to fight, but his voice has bound her. He is worse than any nightmare. He is every fear made flesh.

Dorisall bellows, falling sideways as something smashes into him. Leta is there, holding the remnants of a flower vase. The woman's hair is wild, cheeks streaked with soot, as she reaches out to Fen. A shadow moves behind her as someone steps in close. Before Fen can shout, Leta makes a pained noise, slumping against him. Wyllo Regnis doesn't catch her as she crashes to the ground. Fen can't stop staring at the bloody knife he holds, slick and gleaming. Dorisall is getting up again. The two of them are closing in.

Fen explodes. She pounds her fists against the deck, willing the nails there to rip free and go flying. The men shriek as metal pierces their skin. More planks peel up, smashing the two men sideways.

Fen scrambles to Leta.

"Go," she croaks. "The girls need you."

Leta coughs, painting her lips a violent red.

"What about you?"

"I've done my part. It's up to you now, Ana."

Leta reaches up a shaking hand and strokes her cheek, so tender. She exhales, long and ragged, and her hand falls to the wood. Fen is frozen, watching the life as it leaves her. A terrible ache throbs in her chest.

She hears a shout of pain: It's Sayer. She staggers up and runs, leaping over chairs and bodies, until she finally reaches the dais. Æsa and Sayer are on their knees, arms wrapped around Matilde, who fights like a demon. Fen feels like she is back in the Underground, in that moment when Æsa reached back her hand. *Please, Fenlin,* she said. *We need you.* This time, she goes to them without having to be asked.

When she throws her arms around them all, something happens. A shiver, a push, a quivering rush. The barge shakes as their magic twines, weaving through her blood and sinew. Fen is no longer just her heart, her body. She can't tell where her power ends and theirs begins. They are a thicket of leaves and branches, pulsing with life. But there's a blight amongst them. It feels almost familiar. Fen's magic reaches out, a trembling vine, curling around it. She pulls back hard and yanks it out.

Matilde blinks once, twice, breaths heaving. Her eyes begin to clear.

"Oh, Sayer," she croaks. "I'm so sorry."

They need to get up. Out of the corner of Fen's eye, around the flames, she sees grey. The Caska are there, crossbows raised, poised to take them. But Fen isn't going to let them lock her up.

She grips the girls tight and calls on her magic. When it rises, it feels like it's more than just hers. Leaf tangles with fire, wind with wave. She tastes ash and brine and lightning. The force of it is almost more than she can hold.

Planks scream as they are pulled free from their moorings. Shards of metal melt and lift. Fires twist and waves crash, swirling around them. Caska leap out of the path of the churning mass. It lifts and spreads, stoked by Sayer's howling wind: a maelstrom. The four of them are the eye of the storm. The thing she's made stretches high above the barge, flashing fire and lightning. It's a tempest she doesn't know how to control.

Something explodes. Fen is back in her body. There is pain and, all at once, the world goes dark.

IT HAS BEEN years since Joost spent a night out in Simta. He remembers that evening with his father so well. They visited bars and dance halls, seeking magic. Before Eudea's Prohibition, it could be found without a hunt. There are no signs of it now. The cocktail the barkeep pours, pale and tinny, holds nothing special. He prefers to drink in the bar's gossip instead. The men at the table behind him are swapping stories of the wedding.

The Flame Witch burned the Pontifex alive, one says. *I hear she laughed while she did it.*

Flotsam, another says. *The Wave Witch drowned him where he stood.*

The Storm Witch struck the suzerain with lightning, one adds. *Didn't you see it?*

But it was a simple arrow that pierced Dennan's heart. Joost saw it happen. Then he crept through all that smoke and carnage to ensure the suzerain was truly dead. He wasn't quite, and so Joost helped him on his journey. What a boon, that his rival should be gone, and this city so fractured. He could not have planned it any better.

The men in the bar have moved on to the elemental storm that swirled above the wedding. They speak of how it broke the barge apart.

They must've killed hundreds, one says, voice trembling. *If they wished, they could destroy us all.*

But it thrilled Joost, to see such power in action. He watched from a canal boat as it rose, crackling with menace, a force that made the whole city seem to shake. Such a weapon is a precious thing: rare and priceless. And these people want to lock it away. Such a waste.

He nods to his men, who get up and move to flank him as they pour back into Dragon Quarter. They are all disguised in drab cloaks, stripped of their Trellian finery. Few people give him more than a cursory glance. *It is good to learn an enemy from the inside,* his father told him as they roamed these streets all those years ago. *To understand the house you might someday raid.* And so he notes the chaos on every corner, the fear, the anger. Simta's people do not seem to know what will come next. But Joost does.

He and his men stop near a bridge, congregating in its shadow.

"You know your missions," he says. "Stay the course. Do not falter."

He shakes each of their hands.

"To victory," each captain says before they leave him.

Joost answers in kind. "And to our glory."

When all but his most trusted guards have gone, he takes a deep breath. The light is fading now, purple and bruised. His gaze is caught by a nearby lantern: one of the ones Simta is famous for. No mothman has come to refill it with fresh flamemoths. The ones from last night lie dead inside, dusty and still.

He thinks of those winter hunting trips with his father. How Joost used to long for the Fyrebirds from his stories, even knowing they were gone. But they are here, and ripe for the taking. Soon all of that power will burn just for him.

– CHAPTER 23 –

INTO THE CAGE

WHEN MATILDE WAS seven years old, a traveling circus came to Simta. Her sire liked the dancers best, while Samson favored the fire-eaters. But it's the Hall of Beasts Matilde could not forget. The tent was full of cages of all different sizes, each containing some exotic marvel. There was even a striped tigren, restless and lithe. She was mesmerized by the way the cat's muscles rippled as she paced her enclosure. Her amber eyes, so like Matilde's, were glazed, the pupils blown out. When she asked her sire why the tigren looked like that, he said, *She must be hungry.* But she knows now what those eyes really held: desperation. The manic helplessness of a wild thing put in chains.

The Fyrebirds' cage is larger than that tigren's, but not any nicer. Jawbone Prison is as awful as she imagined: wet stone, rancid straw, cold metal. There is the horrid stink of witchbane, too. Smoke from two censers twines through the bars of the cell, thick and pungent. It makes her stomach roil and twist. Unfortunately, the only thing to be sick in is a single wooden bucket. Matilde has used it twice already. A bunch of Caska boys and Wardens watched from the hall as she retched, pointing and taunting. She feels too hollowed out and tired to mind their sting.

How did they get here? One minute she was blinking as the Sugar drained away, and the strange storm raged around them. In the next, the storm died, Fen collapsed, a net came down: They were surrounded. The Caska rowed them away, hands bound, as the barge burned.

She looks at her friends. The chains that tether them to the wall are heavy. Every time one of them moves, they clink. Æsa is staring into space, as if trying to divine their futures. Sayer has turned her back on the oglers and positioned herself to block Fen from their view. Fen hasn't woken up—a worrying sign, Matilde imagines. At least she's still breathing. Not every wedding guest can say the same.

"As happy as I am to see you all," she croaks, "this isn't quite how I imagined our reunion."

Sayer sighs. "You and me both, Dinatris."

Matilde has the wild urge to laugh, or maybe sob.

"How did you all manage to get onto the barge?"

"I compelled a guard to take me," Æsa whispers.

"Fen forged an invitation," Sayer says, "and rowed us over. I snuck on while she argued with a guard."

"But *why* did you come?"

"Why do you think?" Sayer says. "To save you."

Instead, because of her, they are in chains.

Matilde grips a tattered corner of her wedding dress. It is heavy with water, clinging in cold sheets to her skin. A spear of sun from the only window catches its sequins, making light dance across the dank walls. They make her think of a false sky full of stars.

"A bride and a widow, all in one morning," she says. "I must have set some sort of speed record."

"I don't think such vows count," Æsa murmurs, "if you're drugged."

Perhaps, but they were still her words, her hands, her magic. Matilde closes her eyes, then wishes she hadn't. Again, she feels the knife sink into the Pontifex's body. She sees her family's smiling faces turn to masks of terror. There is Dennan whirling her around, taking the arrow she assumes was meant for her. She can feel the thudding impact of it still. She feels it all more keenly now, without the Sugar inside her. There is nothing to tamp down the horror she couldn't feel while under its spell.

Sayer pulls her knees up to her chest. "How did my sire get to you?"

"He was at the palace last night. He must have seen me step out onto the balcony. I was lost in my thoughts. He forced me to drink it . . ."

She reaches for the comforting weight of her locket, only to end up clutching empty air. Alec has it. She wonders if she will ever see him again.

"I haven't slept since. Wyllo compelled me not to. I suppose he worried the Sugar might wear off before the deed was done."

"And the Hand was hidden somewhere on the barge," Sayer says. "Waiting in the wings for you to . . ."

Matilde swallows back bile. The canal has washed her hands clean of the Pontifex's blood, but still she rubs at them. She wishes she could wipe her mind and heart completely clean.

"Did either of you see my family?"

"I'm sure they're fine," Æsa soothes.

"But did you *see* them?"

Matilde lost them in the smoke. Did they get free before the barge burned? Her heart is a stone, heavy with dread. And what about the rest of the guests? Most were Great House families, people she has known all her life. She is sure Leta will be fine: She is a fighter. But Petra has never been much of a swimmer. Sive was wearing so much heavy tulle.

"How many people did I hurt, I wonder?" she muses. "How many do you think I killed?"

Æsa squeezes her hand. "That wasn't you. Not really."

"It was, though. I destroyed the barge. I almost flambéed you, Sayer."

"No," Sayer seethes. "That was my ratbag of a sire."

"This isn't your fault," Æsa presses. "You aren't the villain."

"But that's what everyone will make us out to be."

"Æsa told them about Sugar," Sayer says. "And Leta too."

"They won't believe us," Matilde says. "Not after what just happened."

What is it Delaina wrote? *They write over our stories, and I can do nothing to stop it. Women with power are easy to condemn.*

"We will make the truth known," Æsa says, fiercer than she was months ago. "We will make them hear us."

"Hard to do," Sayer says, "when we're stuck in here."

A wave of despair threatens to overwhelm her. Matilde closes her eyes, but the truth won't be denied. These past months, she has worked so dashed hard to change things. She smiled and argued, charmed and cajoled. She has behaved, believing that if she just showed Simta's people that girls like them aren't a threat, they would believe her. She wonders now why she bothered to try.

There is a commotion beyond the bars. The sea of Wardens is parting, making room for two new men. For an instant, Matilde thinks the Pontifex and Dennan have come to life again. But it's the Red Hand and Wyllo Regnis, decked out in full regalia, both of them wearing dead men's clothes.

The pater put Vivienne on trial. There was no real jury: Those people had all condemned her already. None of them would listen to a single word she said. When Marren pulled his sword from the brazier, I could not save her. All I could do was watch my sister burn.

—FROM THE LOST JOURNAL OF DELAINA DINATRIS, ONE OF SIMTA'S FIRST NIGHTBIRDS

CHAPTER 24

FUTURE'S PAST

ÆSA HAS SPENT so much time contemplating the future. But now, she feels like she's reliving the past. She is back in Jawbone Prison, surrounded by men who hate her. Except this time, she has no way to escape.

"You must be joking." Matilde's eyes, dull before, are back to burning. She's glaring at the two men at the bars. "The Table and the Brethren put *you two* in charge?"

The men look nothing alike. One is polished and tanned, the other bald and scarred, but their expressions are the same, all satisfaction. The Red Hand puts his hands into his violet robes.

"Our Republic needs leadership," he says. "After the shocking murder of Pater Rolo and the demise of Dennan Vesten. A new and clear-eyed vision to steer us through these troubled times. The Brethren see now what a danger we have let grow amongst us. And that I alone have the means to bring it to heel."

The Hand's gravelly voice seems to shake Fen out of her slumber. She opens her eyes, trying to sit up.

"And you?" Sayer stands, looking at Wyllo. "How did you slither your way into that golden sash so quickly?"

"Someone had to take charge," Wyllo says. "And I have written for months about the danger you posed to us. After this morning's disaster, many see me as a visionary. In fact, you made me a popular choice."

Æsa looks between Sayer and her sire. She sees little resemblance. Except, perhaps, for the brittle hate in both their eyes.

"That will change," Sayer says, "when the city finds out you've been running a drug lab at your country house and selling Sugar to the highest bidder."

Wyllo's expression loses some of its polish.

"You have no proof of that."

"Want to bet? By now, our friends will have been and gone from there already. No matter what you do to me, the truth will come out."

He grips the bars, cheeks going red. "Where is Jolena?"

"As if I'd tell you."

"You listen to me," he grits out. "I have arrested Leta Tangreel. Tell me where my daughter is, or I will ensure she goes down with you."

"It's a lie," Fen says, reaching for Sayer. "Leta's dead."

The room spins, everything inside Æsa tilting. Matilde makes a choked noise. Sayer's face goes very pale.

"No," she says. "She can't be."

Not Madam Crow, Æsa thinks, who always seemed so strong. Nothing could touch her. If she is gone, then anyone can break.

"I was with her when she died," Fen says. "She was trying to help me. But then your sire . . ."

Leta's unspoken end hangs in the air, sharp and pressing.

Sayer jumps up and throws herself at the bars. When she runs out of chain, still she fights, kicking and clawing. Æsa feels her pain from where she sits.

"It wasn't enough to kill Dame," Sayer growls. "You had to take Leta too. Is that it?"

"The meddling whore got what she deserved," Wyllo seethes. "And so will you."

"Enough," the Hand cuts in, touching Wyllo's arm. "Go. There is much to be done before tomorrow, Lord Regnis. The people need to see their suzerain."

Wyllo takes a few deep breaths, putting away his anger. He smooths his golden sash.

"Indeed they do."

He walks away. The Red Hand looks at each of them in turn, as if savoring the moment. His cold brown eyes remind Æsa of a snake's.

"Hello, Ana. Marren has reunited us again. My god is bountiful."

Fen, sitting up now, doesn't respond.

"Now, now, little thief. I know how you love to hide in silence. But I see you."

Fen's lip curls. "You don't see anything, old man."

The Hand taps the bars. "Oh, but I do, Ana. Or is it Fenlin Brae? That is what your Dark Stars call you."

Fen shows no sign of emotion, but Æsa can feel it there, under her skin.

"You have built quite a little cult. That club of yours was full of your acolytes when my Caska raided it earlier. Little Johnny Rankin cried for you, I hear, before he died."

Fen's expression fractures like a cliff face tumbling into the sea.

"You're lying," she growls. "Rankin is fine. They're all *fine*."

Æsa grips Fen's hand, wanting to soothe her. The Red Hand looks like he's just won a prize.

"Enough games," Matilde says, drawing his gaze. "You have us right where you want us. The least you can do is tell us how you pulled off this little coup."

"No," he says coolly. "I owe you no explanation."

"Come now. I assume you won't give us a chance to repeat anything you tell us. You might as well rub your victory in."

Æsa sees what she is doing. When they were Nightbirds, Matilde schooled her in how to extract a client's secrets. She sees it working on the Hand despite himself. A light enters his eyes, bright and fervent.

"The fire at the alchemist's left its mark," he says at last. "For a time, I thought I would not survive. But Marren teaches us that fire purifies, distilling a thing down to its core. I was forged anew in those flames. Remade by them. They clarified what my god wanted me to do.

"Leastnight taught me that you were a bigger threat than I had imagined. I knew I had to vanquish you once and for all. But simply killing you might have turned you into martyrs. There are those who cling to stories of the Fyrebirds being saviors, despite the church's teachings. I had to find a way to ensure the people feared your power, rather than worshipped it. So I focused on honing a recipe I had all but given up on. You might remember it, Ana."

Fen looks away, jaw clenched tight.

"No? I tried some early versions on you. I thought it might allow me to force your magic to the surface. But then I realized it might also bend it to my will. But such a grand vision requires funds and ingredients. It calls for test subjects for trials. My Caska combed the streets for witches who would serve the purpose. They were easier to find after Leastnight, grown wanton with their magic."

"The missing girls," Matilde breathes. "The specters. That *was* you."

"They proved quite useful in helping me perfect Sugar's usage, to test its limits and power."

Revulsion grows inside Æsa. "Where are they now, these girls?"

"Some I sold to foreign buyers to help fund my venture. You cannot believe the fortunes Farlanders will pay."

He *sold* them? To whom? Æsa remembers the girl from her vision, wrapped in a chain, and those Farlands sailors and their talk of enslavement. *You will feel the pershain around that pretty neck.*

"And the rest?" she asks, dreading the answer.

"I returned their magic to the Wellspring."

He killed them, then. Æsa closes her eyes, wishing she could change it. Hurting for all those girls lost to the dark.

"Pretty rich," Fen says, "for a man who says *all* magic should be returned to the Wellspring to give it away to Farlanders and let lordlings steal it."

The Hand's expression curdles.

"It's true, what you say. But every mission requires sacrifice. I needed funds, a reliable supply of witchbane, and somewhere to conduct my experiments in peace. Lord Regnis provided much of that. In turn, I let him sell some Sugar, though I never let him have the recipe. Only I know that." His gaze goes distant, as if seeing beyond the bars and stones. "I did not plan to kill Dennan Vesten: only discredit him. But Marren had a grander plan than even I could conjure. Now Lord Regnis is in charge, and he is loyal to my interests. A man of greed is easily led."

Despair floods Æsa. For all his shortcomings, at least Dennan believed her about the Farlands threat. He was willing to rally the navy. But that fight, and their defense, just died with him.

For just a moment on the barge, Æsa caught a glimpse of King Joost of Trellane. She knew him by his pale skin and hair, so much like the Farlanders who attacked her. Unlike the other guests, he looked delighted by the chaos: elated. He stared at the Fyrebirds as if he might swallow them whole.

Æsa thinks of the Trellian fleet sailing toward them. Of the king who must know how very vulnerable they are. And they are prisoners, helpless to stop him. She has come too far to give up now.

She stands. "Enough. There is no time for this nonsense. You need to let us out."

The Hand laughs. "And why would I do that?"

"Because a battle is coming. One that threatens all of us."

She walks toward the bars, as close as she can.

"The king of Trellane plans to invade Simta. The same king who just watched Eudea lose its Pontifex and suzerain. He knows the city is in disarray: He saw it. There will never be a better moment to strike."

She doesn't point out that Joost is coming specifically for girls with magic, or that he will likely want Sugar and witchbane now, as well. Perhaps he will strike a deal with the Hand when he conquers them. And the four of them are locked in here.

"Lies," the Hand says. "A pathetic attempt to distract me. It will not work, witch."

If only she could reach through these bars, like she did all those months ago. If only she could touch him and compel him to believe.

"Joost has thousands of ships. He won't stop until this city is in ashes."

"Even if any of this were true, why would I let you free?"

"Because we have the power to stop him."

The Hand sneers. "Lie all you want, witch. I will not let you lead me from my mission. Tomorrow, your power will be sent back where it belongs."

The faint hope that made her speak is crushed, fading to nothing. He isn't going to heed a word she says.

"There will be a witch trial," the Hand intones. "Like those the paters held during the Great Revelations. You will confess your crimes in front of the city and its leaders."

"We will confess to nothing," Sayer says, voice like iron.

"With Sugar in your veins, witch, you will do as I tell you. You will say whatever I whisper in your ears."

Æsa thought that, with the power of her visions, she could save them. That together, they could do anything. But now they are trapped, back in the place she once escaped from. Nothing she does can save them from this fate.

WHEN ALEC'S DAME died, he wasn't with her. She was traveling with her dance troupe, seeking fame on the stages of Lyra. Instead, she got the Tekan plague and never came home. At eight years old, it seemed impossible that she could disappear like that. He kept expecting her to dance back into his life.

When Krastan was killed, Alec didn't get to hear his last words. There was too much smoke in the shop, so much noise. By the time he got to his side, Krastan had flown away forever. The man who made him who he is, there and gone.

When Matilde got married, Alec wasn't there to see it. He was too angry to join the crowds and watch her walk down an aisle toward someone else. A part of him still held out hope she wouldn't do it. He should have known she would, in the end. Years ago, when his gaze started lingering on Matilde Dinatris, Krastan warned him. *Those girls aren't for us, lad,* he used to say, not unkindly. *Best set your cap for a more achievable dream.* But Alec has always reached for life's high shelves, wanting to make improbable concoctions, believing in things he can't quite see.

He's spent most of the day pushing through the panicked streets, asking people what happened, trying to sort wild tale from truth. The Pontifex murdered, the suzerain dead, the Fyrebirds captured. The Red Hand lording over it all. The last rumor was the worst. *I hear the Flame Witch was possessed,* one shopkeeper told him. Was it Sugar that compelled Matilde down the aisle after all?

He went looking for answers at Leta's house and found it empty. He went to the Dark Stars and found their clubhouse in ruins. It was only when he got back to his room that he knew why. That's where he found Rankin and Jolena slumped against his door, pale and grim.

Raided, Rankin said. Even his sentences were broken. *Said we'd been hiding the Flower Witch. Some got away. Some . . . didn't.*

Jolena gripped his hand and handed Alec a sack of plants, badly withered. Bleeding heartvine, she told him. Something to help them fight the Sugar. But antidotes take time to test, and they have none of it. He doesn't see how it will help them now.

He rubs his temple. Rankin and Jolena are in his room, sleeping, he hopes. He's in the Bathhouse's rooftop greenhouse, which the owner let him turn into a makeshift lab.

"We have to break them out," Willan says, not for the first time. He showed up an hour ago, with tales of a Farlands fleet that made Alec's skin crawl. The pirate hasn't stopped his pacing since.

"It won't work," Alec says. "Jawbone's too well guarded. Our best chance is going to be at the trial."

He brews every quick-and-dirty potion he can think of. He reads everything he can find on bleeding heartvine, which isn't much.

He opens one of the only books he found intact after the shop fire, running his finger over Krastan's spidery script. He had a habit of annotating recipes, treasures tucked between the printed words. It reminds Alec of another annotation: one he saw in Augustain's. He finds it in his notebook. *If magic and the soul do part, the sundering is healed with bleeding heart.* It's a strange turn of phrase. Healed *with* bleeding heart, as if it were an ingredient. But it doesn't tell him how it should be used. What he wouldn't give to have Krastan with him now, to guide him. He has no recipe for what comes next.

In the end, he brews some Estra Doole. It's the potion Krastan used to make for Frey Dinatris, and later Matilde, when they were Nightbirds. She'd use it to calm and coax confessions out of clients, keeping it in the locket that is slung around his neck. He tinkers as he goes, swapping out the letha for brighteye and taking out the sleepweed.

Careful, he hears Krastan saying. *It's dangerous to stray too far from a recipe.* But Krastan also taught him that alchemy is as much art as science, requiring intuition. Sometimes you have to craft a potion by feel. So he adds some bleeding heartvine, leaves and stalk, and brings the pot to a simmer. It stains the contents of the bowl a deep red.

Matilde used to tease him about brewing up love potions. There is no such thing: Love isn't something you can bottle. But still, he stirs some into the brew, hoping to strengthen it. He whispers his love as he pours the potion into her locket.

He doesn't know how, or if, it might help Matilde.

But Alec isn't ready to say goodbye to her.

– CHAPTER 25 –

OPENING DOORS

FEN WISHES THERE were moonlight streaming through the one high window. Something to cut through the gathering dark. It keeps trying to drag her back to the nightmares. Those orphanage days when sometimes Rankin was the only bright spark. *Rankin*. Fen's chest shrinks, trying to guard her heart, but it aches for her brother. Dorisall was lying about what he did to the Dark Stars. He had to be. He just wanted to make her react, and she did.

She takes another deep breath, another. The air is rank with witchbane. It is still burning, smoke circling the cell. Her friends all look pale and drawn; Sayer keeps touching her stomach. But besides dry mouth and exhaustion, Fen doesn't feel a thing. Her magic is quiet, worn down by the storm she made, but still there. She's suspected this since they left the Callistan: hoped for it. But it's still a shock, to feel the witchbane take no hold.

She needs to tell the others, but there are too many Wardens still hovering. She focuses on gathering her thoughts and making plans. At last, as night deepens, their jailers and gawkers start to thin out. She waits until she hears their boots on stone but can't see them. She is about to speak when Matilde pipes up.

"I keep thinking about what happened, when we all came together. That burst of power, the sudden storm. It reminds me of something Delaina wrote. I wonder if she can help us."

She tells them about the journal she found at Augustain's library, written by some Dinatris ancestor. Fen listens, rapt, as she tells them a story about four heart-tied Fyrebirds destroying an enemy fleet.

"So the bond between us doesn't just amplify our power," Æsa says. "It lets us share it."

"It's more than that," Matilde says. "She says that one of the girls pulled their powers in, becoming a conduit."

Fen swallows. "I think that's what I did. That's what it felt like."

"The storm?" Sayer asks. "That was you?"

For a moment, they all sit with that possibility. Then Matilde frowns.

"Is that what broke the Sugar's hold, do you think?"

"Perhaps our bond diluted it," Æsa says, "and it nullified the poison."

Fen's heart is beating wildly. "No. That was me."

The three girls all look at her, waiting. It shouldn't be so hard to explain. It's just that she's spent so long holding herself apart and separate. But she sees, now, the power in opening yourself.

"I chewed witchbane for years." Fen swallows. "To keep my magic down. I ran out of my stash, just before I went out to the Callistan, and I got sick. The Sythians helped me get over the addiction. And now . . ."

Fen looks to the bars, to make sure no one is watching.

Then she looks down at the manacles gripping her wrists. She can feel their subtle workings, their contours. They click open with a quiet pop.

"Ten hells," Sayer whispers. "You *are* immune."

Fen nods. "We know that witchbane is the key ingredient in Sugar. If I'm immune to one, it stands the other doesn't work on me either. I could feel the Sugar in you, Matilde, on the barge. I thought I somehow pulled it out of you. But if we can share our powers, then maybe I gave you my immunity. And if I could do that . . ."

She reaches for their hands. As they touch, Fen feels a wash of nausea, an emptiness: an echo of the witchbane in their bodies. She can't believe she used to inflict this poison on herself. A part of her wants to pull back, to turn away, but it has no power over her. Instead, she imagines the Callistan's trees.

No tree stands alone, Seleese said. *Their roots reach out through loam and wave, braiding together. They rely on that network to hold each of them up.* Fen imagines them all as trees, twining together. Her roots wrap around theirs and hold them tight. She can feel their magic buried behind walls, locked deep inside them. She has to throw open the doors, let in the light. She imagines her immunity like that: as light that she can throw over the three of them. She offers it freely, holding nothing back.

Matilde takes a shuddering breath. Æsa lets out a small sob.

When Sayer speaks, her voice is choked. "I can't feel it anymore. The witchbane's gone."

The silence hangs, ringing with the sound of their freedom. Then Matilde says, "Let's get out of here."

Æsa and Sayer both stand. They want to run: Of course they

do. But Fen spent years running from Dorisall, hiding behind an eyepatch, the mastic, a stolen name. She was always looking over her shoulder, afraid he would catch up with her. But that nightmare was with her all along, keeping her chained.

"Or we could stay."

Her words are met with blank stares from the others.

"For the trial?" Sayer says. "Why?"

"If we run, everyone will believe the lies they're being fed about us. It'll look like we have something to hide."

"We will be free to fight the Farlanders," Æsa insists. "That is all that matters."

Matilde tilts her head. "But is it?"

Of the group, Matilde is the one Fen knows least. She didn't think a gang boss and a rich, spoiled Great House girl could ever find common ground. But Fen recognizes the calculating glint in her eyes now. She can almost read her thoughts.

"A lot of people will come to the trial," Matilde says. "Wyllo and the Red Hand will want as many people as possible to witness it. Especially since they think they have us well in hand."

"But they don't," Fen says. "I can make it so we're free to turn the tables. We'll expose them for the monsters they are."

It's a risk. They might not win this gamble, but Fen would rather fight than flee.

"I had a vision of us all in a church," Æsa says. "Perhaps that means we're destined to do this. But the Farlanders are coming, and we have to be ready."

"I'll get us free," Fen says. "One way or another."

Matilde looks her way. Her amber eyes are shining. It's as if something has lit her up from within.

"We've been playing their game," she says. "Now we have

a chance to turn their rules against them. Together, we can do anything."

Fen has feared dark, cramped spaces for as long as she can remember. She dreads being locked up and confined. But here, with them, she feels freer than she has in a long time. Like something inside her is finally unchained.

PART V

OUT
OF THE
ASHES

PATER DORISALL SENDS out a prayer of thanks to the Eshamein. At last, he will vanquish these Fyrebirds, as Marren once did. This morning, he feels closer to his god than ever. He could almost be a god himself.

All is prepared: the church, the trial, the crowd, the judgment. The only thing left is to prepare the witches themselves. He mixes the Sugar into four cups of water, stirring each until the lozenge dissolves. The guards have been sent away: He does not want to risk any of them knowing about this, even his Caska. This close to victory, he is taking no chances.

When he arrives at the cell, the girls stand. They have been given floor-length red robes of the kind witches used to wear at trials during the Great Revelations. He wants a sense of history repeating.

He passes the witches the keys to their restraints. Once they are free, he pushes the cups between the bars. They resist, at first, which is no less than he expected. But they change their tunes when he tells them what he will do to their friends and families if they do not obey. He watches them pick up the cups, at last, and swallow their contents. A righteous fire is spreading through his chest.

"Hear me," he says, becoming their keeper. He has found that girls on Sugar have a keen, silent attention. It is gratifying to have them all so in his thrall. Ana's disconcerting eyes are on him, waiting. This strange girl who set him on this path, then almost ruined it so many times. Having her here feels like divine providence.

He unlocks the cell door and steps inside.

"Bow to me, Ana."

She goes to her knees.

"Kiss my hand."

A moment's hesitation before she does that, too.

"Repeat after me. All of you."

He has them say Marren's prayer, relishing the sound of their surrender.

> *We light Marren's candle*
> *And kindle his sword,*
> *flames chasing shadows,*
> *burning darkness away.*
> *We make a fire,*
> *a mighty fire,*
> *a cleansing fire to cleanse the world.*

Then he pulls out the candle he brought, taken from his shrine to Marren, and lights it. This will be the ultimate test of Sugar's power.

He holds it out. "Show your devotion, Ana. Hold your hand over the flame."

Ana's hand does not shake as the flame licks her palm. Most acolytes can't stay silent as their skin burns, but Ana makes no sound: She rarely did.

He uses a new set of shackles to bind them, one to another. He tells the witches what will happen at the trial, what they will say. He spent all night coming up with it—a lifetime. They barely breathe as he speaks, listening hard.

"You will confess," he finishes. "And accept your just punishment. Do you hear me?"

They nod. He turns. The time has come, at last, for his ascension. He will finally become Marren's Red Hand.

FEN WAITS UNTIL Dorisall has turned his back. Then she wipes her lips, trying not to spit. His hand was papery and scarred where she kissed it. The feel of it was worse than the fresh burn on her palm.

She has to be quick. Not far away, Wardens are marching. Her friends are all staring at the bars, glassy eyed. With a quaking breath, she takes their hands. Her burned palm aches, but she doesn't cry out. If Dorisall taught her how to endure anything, it's pain. She can feel the Sugar swimming through the three of them, viscous, like treacle. Can she cut through?

She reaches with her magic, will, and heart, holding back nothing. What belongs to her has to belong to them all. She tastes iron and dirt, feeling the sting of Sugar's poison. She wills them to come back . . . to wake up.

Something shifts. Leaves whisper in her ears, even though there are no plants here. She swears she almost hears them sigh. Then Æsa, whose hand was limp before, squeezes hers. Matilde is sighing. Sayer's lips curve in their wickedest smile.

– CHAPTER 26 –
HE SAID, SHE SAID

MATILDE'S BARE FEET slap against the stone as Wardens tug her up the steps of Augustain's. The other girls, chained as they are, follow behind. It seems the Hand has decreed they should be led to their trial not through the church's internal doors, but around the front, where the city will see them. He clearly means to put them on display.

More Wardens line the steps on either side, keeping the crowd from surging forward. Boats fill the waters of the Corners, too. Most of the city seems to have shown up, bristling with excitement. She straightens her spine as some of them shout and jeer. She knows what they see: four girls who would destroy this city and everyone in it. But there must be some people here who know better. Her eyes search the crowd, looking for a friendly face. The bright light makes it hard to decipher anyone's features. Their audience is nothing but a faceless, seething sea.

But then she thinks she sees a flash of curls between the Wardens. Before she can even think his name, Æsa voices another. His name is like a prayer on her lips.

"Willan."

Some of the Wardens lift their crossbows as a dark orb comes crashing down against the stones. Her eyes sting as the roiling cloud of darkness swallows them. She stumbles, feeling her chains pull tight. Everything is shout and shove, but then someone's arms go around her, bringing the scent of rumfruit and frennet. Matilde can't stop the sob that escapes.

"Tilde," Alec says over the din. "I'm here. Come with me."

"I can't," she chokes. "Not yet."

He tugs her arm. It feels so much like Leastnight, when he tried to save her. This time, they have to stay to save themselves.

"Go, Alec. We have a plan. I promise."

"Tilde." His voice cracks. "I can't lose you again."

Her lips find his. For a moment, there is nothing but the two of them against the darkness. She whispers in his ear.

"Trust me."

She feels a cool, familiar weight slip down the front of her red robe: her locket. He kisses her again.

"I do."

Alec is yanked back. The Nightcloak has dissipated enough that she can see the crowd, pushing and screaming. She thinks she sees Willan punch one of the Wardens and hurry Alec off and through the throng. Then someone is tugging on their chain, hurrying them forward. She keeps her eyes on Alec for as long as she can. *See me,* she thinks, as she has so many times before. She hopes he can feel the way her heart beats for him.

And then they step into the church, the mighty doors closing behind them. It's time to focus on what lies ahead: Their jury is watching. She has to wear a mask, just one more time.

In the daylight, Augustain's is magnificent. Sunlight streams through the high windows, beaming down on the pews. They are heaving with people, so packed they spill into the aisle. Wardens stand around the edges of the space, holding their crossbows. She looks around for her family, her former Nightbird sisters, the fledglings. But their captors will have barred anyone who might speak for them. The Fyrebirds are going to have to face this alone.

The Warden tugs hard on their chain, yanking her up to the sanctuary. Æsa, Sayer, and Fen have no choice but to follow. Usually, this is where the pater stands to give his sermon, but they have replaced the pulpit with some kind of stage. They are led onto it and made to stand there, facing the crowd. It's fitting, she supposes. This is essentially a play, with them the actors. This church will serve as backdrop, reminding all present of the virtues of gods and vices of Fyrebirds. The stage is set with props befitting such a trial. Witchbane burns in censers at three of the platform's four corners. The fourth holds a brazier burning with fire. Beside it sits an ancient-looking sword, propped up so that the crowd can see. Matilde supposes it's meant to represent the one Marren used to burn the magic out of witches. Perhaps it *is* that sword.

She thinks back to that story of Delaina's about her friend who was put to a witch trial. *All I could do was watch my sister burn.* At the thought, her pulse stutters. For all their planning last night, there is much about this trial they couldn't account for. It's hard to plan your moves when you cannot see the board.

To their right, the Table and the Brethren are seated in the choir loft, where boys usually sit to sing the hymns. The Brethren are in their usual purple robes, their bald heads sweating in the sunlight. Wyllo Regnis is wearing a fine blue suit and the suzerain's gold sash. He is the only Table member who will meet her eye. Matilde looks at these men, all of whom were at the wedding. They must have heard what Æsa said about the Sugar. Do they know what a farce this is? Do they care?

One of the Table members stands and rings a bell, calling for order.

"This trial will now begin," Wyllo says. "All rise for our newly appointed Pontifex."

The crowd does, some making the sign of the Eshamein. As the Red Hand walks onto the stage, his pale robes glow like a moonstone, the crimson handprint on his face as dark as blood. He must be loving this. Matilde fights to keep disgust off her face.

He gestures for the crowd to sit. His voice, gravel and salt, was made for preaching. It rolls easily through the vast, vaulted space.

"First, let us acknowledge the great loss of Pontifex Rolo. It is an honor to be chosen to take up his mantle, especially at such a dangerous time. It is a mighty task we have, to stop the rising tide of evil in Eudea. But no one need fear the witches here today. Marren, in his goodness, has granted me the gift of precious witchbane. The plant has the power to suppress a girl's magic." He motions to the braziers. "With it, I have ensured these witches cannot harm you. That none will ever do so again."

The crowd murmurs and gasps. This is the first time most will have heard of witchbane. It will seem like a miracle to them.

The Hand raises his palms high. "Today, we sit in judgment of these witches before us. We ask the gods to make them face their crimes."

Some members of the crowd cheer, raising their fists in the air. *Justice!* The Red Hand makes a calming gesture until they're silent again.

"Everyone here saw what they did aboard that barge in the

Corners. They broke it apart, condemning many of the souls aboard. I, and every member of the Table, can attest to what happened. We all saw Matilde Dinatris murder our beloved Pontifex, then turn her wrath on our suzerain. These girls ended the Vesten line that has so long served us. If not subdued, they would have ended many more."

The crowd shifts, a wave of angry sound.

"But they have committed other crimes," the Hand continues. "We shall hear testimony for each of them."

Thus begins a stream of witnesses. None of them surprise Matilde. First comes Lord Heath Rochet, who accuses Sayer of having almost killed him in the middle of a stag party. Second comes Lord Ansel Broussard, who tells of the Storm and Flower Witches attacking the Hunt Club. Then comes a fresh-faced Warden, his expression fixed and stony. When he steps up to speak, Æsa stiffens.

"I was tasked with guarding the Wave Witch at Jawbone Prison," he says, cheeks reddening. "But she bewitched me. She . . . she took over my mind and bent it to her will."

He tells the crowd how she manipulated his emotions. To her credit, Æsa doesn't lower her eyes.

On it goes. Each piece of testimony is a thread, weaving over their stories, twisting the truth into an awful tapestry. And then another witness is brought forward, led by an older man. It's Lord Maylon, holding Teneriffe Maylon by the elbow. Heated whispers rise: No one has seen this boy in months. Tenny looks awful. His complexion is sallow, his gaze confused.

"The Flame Witch lured my son in with her magic," Lord Maylon booms. "She bewitched him until he was addicted. And then, when she was through with him, she addled his mind so he would never spill her secrets. She left him broken."

His finger shakes as he points.

"She ruined him."

She did no such thing. Matilde wants to protest, but she cannot give the game away. She must wait until it's their turn to speak.

The Maylons go back to their seats. The Red Hand takes the stage again, face solemn.

"This testimony is heavy indeed," he says. "It shows us all the ways in which these girls have broken our laws and corrupted the Wellspring. They have used magic to lie, coerce, and seduce. Some members of our great city were taken in by it. They built shrines to these witches, believing them worthy of worship. But we see them now as they are: false gods. The danger they pose to us is beyond reckoning. They are everything Marren tried to save us from.

"But the gods are just. Before we pass our judgment, we shall give these witches a chance to speak. Matilde Dinatris, you told me of your wish to confess your sins here, before these people. Will do you so?"

The crowd is silent. She can hear her own breaths, and those of her friends beside her. Her heart is a bird beating its wings against her chest. The Table members and the Brethren lean forward, eager. The Hand, meanwhile, looks perfectly composed. She knows her lines, and he trusts she will repeat them faithfully.

He doesn't know Matilde's voice is still her own.

"No."

The Hand's expression flickers. "No?"

"I will not confess to things I had no control over. Things I was forced to do."

Some of the color bleaches from his features.

"How dare you say so," he says. "When there are people here who saw you murder our Pontifex! You lie even now, while the gods look on."

She faces the crowd. "I didn't like our old Pontifex much. I can admit it. But why would I stab the man at my own wedding, in front of so many people? Why would I do something so damning? I wouldn't, unless I was compelled to. This man wanted everyone to turn on me, on us, and take control of the church in the bargain. In drugging me, he managed to do both quite neatly."

"Poisonous lies," the Red Hand spits. "I will not permit them to be spoken."

Matilde turns her gaze to the Table members and the Brethren. Some look angry, others wary. Wyllo's face has started to go pink.

"This is a trial, is it not?" she asks, loud enough for the crowd to hear. "And in our Republic, every person has the right to make their own defense. Even witches."

The crowd looks between the girls and the jury. They could so easily be robbed of their chance.

"Let them speak!"

She eyes the man now standing on one of the pews. It's the master of ceremonies from the play she attended. His deep voice echoes through the church, slowly fading. Then another voice takes up the call, another. *Let them speak!* So they are not completely friendless. The chanting threatens to bring her to her knees.

A member of the Brethren calls the Hand over. Wyllo is already arguing with the other members of the Table, seeing the danger, but the Hand did invite the girls to speak. Will he confess he did so only because he's drugged them? Of course not: just as Matilde suspected. He has backed himself into a corner.

At last, Sand Deveraux stands. "The witches will be heard. But order must be maintained."

Matilde looks to her friends, drawing strength from them. She touches her locket through her robes.

"Someone drugged me the night before my wedding," she says. "Using an alchemical called Sugar. The drug allows someone to compel a girl with magic. All he needs to do is slip it in her drink, and she has no choice but to do as she's bid. The Red Hand told us himself that he tested it on magical girls plucked from our streets by En Caska Dae. They are the so-called specters who've been stealing Simta's daughters."

Gasps rise from some of the crowd. One of the Brethren starts coughing.

"But he didn't do it alone," Sayer says, loud and clear. "A House patriarch funded the project, and has been selling Sugar to some of the rich lords in our city. He drugged Matilde. And I watched him drug his own daughter just to prove to his friends how it worked."

She raises one chained hand, pointing at Wyllo. His eyes go wide, neck flushing red.

"This is outrageous," he says, standing up. "I did nothing of the sort."

"You did," Sayer says. "You drugged Jolena. And then you used her to try to smear my name."

The crowd is jostling, whispering, restless now. Do they believe her?

"As if anyone will believe such filth," Wyllo sneers. "Is there no end to your deception? Where is your proof?"

"I am here."

Matilde looks out at the crowd to see it parting. Fen and Sayer both let out unsteady breaths. Jolena and Rankin appear. It is clear that most of those assembled recognize Jolena. Illustrations of her pretty face appeared in the newssheets for weeks, next to headlines proclaiming she was stolen by the Storm Witch. She's become a poster child for all that is wrong with the Fyrebirds.

"The drug is real," she says. "My sire, Wyllo Regnis, used it on me at the Hunt Club. It does just what the Fyrebirds say it does. The Storm Witch didn't kidnap me that night. She saved me."

Matilde can scarcely breathe. She looks over at Sayer. Her golden eyes are shining, brimming with tears she won't let fall.

"Come now, dearest," Wyllo calls. "You are confused."

"I am not." Jolena tilts up her chin, defiant. "I see you clearly. And what you've done to us is wrong."

Some of the Table members are looking, shocked, at Wyllo.

"The Storm Witch has bewitched my daughter," he shouts. "She doesn't know what she is saying."

But the crowd seems less sure of him than before.

"There's more," Rankin shouts, making room for two more people. A deeply tanned boy, with what look like reeds tied around his forearm, and a fragile-looking girl he has to help stay on her feet.

"We've just come from the Regnis mansion in the Waystrell," he says. "We found a lab there, full of Sugar. And we found some girls locked in the stables."

He coaxes her to step forward. She is thin, and squinting as if the light hurts her. The Hand didn't kill the missing girls after all.

"The boys in grey took me," she says, barely audible. "They threw me in a carriage and drove me far away. That man up there, the Red Hand, tested the drug on me. He wouldn't give me food unless I took it. He . . ." She chokes on her words, starts again. "He made me do such horrible things."

A few people shout in outrage. The crowd is shifting, simmering. A tide starting, perhaps, to turn.

"It isn't true," the Hand seethes. "This is pure trickery. Every word these witches speak is poison in our ears."

"We aren't poison," Æsa says, eyes shining. "That is only what they want you to see when you look at us. All we have ever done is defend ourselves, and others like us, from those who want to hurt us. Men like these, who want to strip us of our power."

The Hand's bald head is sheened with sweat, his face contorted. At last he snaps, losing control.

"Don't you see? It does not matter that I compelled these witches. They are evil. Marren gifted me the drug so I could show you what they are."

More shouts. Some of the Wardens look poised to fire their weapons. Violence hangs like a promise on the air.

Matilde raises her voice. "The church has long blamed Fyrebirds for every ill that befell Eudea. They wrote over all the good they did. But those women fought for us, and for those who needed their protection. They used their power to do good."

She thinks of Krastan saying that Fyrebirds used their power to shape the world and make it better. She thinks of Delaina's words, her strength, passed down.

"A Farlands king is coming for Simta," she goes on. "He

means to attack us, to take us. But we won't let him. The Fyre-birds will fight for you."

Her words ring out into the breaths-held silence. A sudden, strangled shout makes Matilde jump. The Red Hand is grabbing the ancient sword from its stand, pushing it into the flaming brazier. When he yanks it out, the blade is on fire.

The wicked prince locked up his palace. He charmed the doors and thought his treasure safe. But Fenlin Brae, clever and sure, found a chink in his armor, and widened it. She smiled her fox's smile, and then she sank in her teeth.

—AN EXCERPT FROM "THE CLEVEREST THIEF,"
PUBLISHED IN *AROUND THE TWISTED TREE:
OLD EUDEAN TALES AND FABLES*

- CHAPTER 27 -
A CLEANSING FIRE

T HE FIRST TIME Dorisall ever lit this sword, Fen thought it was magic. One Marren's Day, he brought it burning to their supper table, a miracle meant to scare them into saying their prayers. *Holy fires cannot be quenched,* he said, sticking the blade into a tub of water. No matter what he did, it still burned. She learned later that he had coated the metal with a resin that kept the blade aflame, but at the time they didn't know that. It terrified Rankin. It scared her, too, seeing a miracle made real. If Dorisall could do such things, she thought, he could do anything. It made him seem almost like a god.

But he is a man, nothing more. Nothing less. He's lost his power to awe her.

"By Marren's flaming sword," he shouts, "I will destroy you!"

He turns, raising the sword up high.

Marren teaches us that fire clarifies, he told them, *distilling a thing down to its core.* Maybe it's true, because she sees what she needs to do so clearly. In the light of this fire, she feels remade.

Fen drops to her knees and lifts her hands, a prayerful gesture.

"Marren, protect us!"

The words make Dorisall pause. His eyes burn into Fen's, almost a touch. Fine: Let him see her. Who she's become, both because of and despite him. That he couldn't break her after all.

She concentrates on the fiery metal. With just a thought, it starts to melt. The crowd, Fen hopes, will think it Marren's doing. It softens quickly, silver dripping down the hilt onto his upraised hands, then lower. Dorisall shrieks, trying to drop it, but the sword is hewn to his skin. The pale cuffs of his robes are alight now. The resin will ensure they stay lit.

"Marren, deliver me!" he howls.

But his god isn't listening. The smell is awful. Fen can barely see him now, amidst the flames.

Dorisall stumbles back, off the stage. He tumbles into the aisle, plunging himself headlong into a fountain, but it does not quench him. Marren's flame is eternal. He lurches through the crowd, who shrink away. No one helps him as he weaves, burning, screaming, toward the main doors. The Wardens swing them wide to let him out. He staggers down the steps, toward the water. Fen doesn't know how his legs can still carry him. He always was a stubborn man. At last he tips, plunging into the canal, but it's too late. There is almost nothing left of him.

For a moment, all is stunned, quivering silence. The other girls pull her up into a hug.

"Good riddance to bad rubbish," Matilde quips.

Fen isn't sorry he's dead. Still, she feels something like a sob climb her throat, but she can't fall apart now. Not with the Brethren and Table members staring at them, slack-mouthed, and a few Caska looking up, eyes full of rage. The Wardens' crossbows are still turned on them.

Fen concentrates on their chains, making them all click open.

"Now what?" she croaks.

"We fight our way out," Sayer says, "if we have to."

Her last word is trailed by a sound like thunder. It echoes off the stone, filling the church. Outside the doors, on the steps, a commotion is rising. The crowd in the pews turns as the air is filled with screams. The throng outside is pushing at the Wardens guarding the doorway. With a panicked shove, they break through, pouring into the church and down the aisle. Another boom comes, shaking the stones beneath them.

"Oh, gods," Æsa says. "It's starting."

Her words are drowned out as the church explodes.

Flying high or running low,
The sheldar's enemies will slow.
Voice at a whisper or raised up to a shout,
The sheldar will be heard, have ye no doubt.

—AN EXCERPT FROM AN ILLISH LYRIC POEM,
"THE SHELDAR WILL BE HEARD"

CHAPTER 28

PEACE AND WAR

ÆSA CROUCHES DOWN as the church rocks and trembles. The chaos moves as if she's drunk some Clockman's Bane, the world slowed down. The explosion knocks the running crowd askew, throwing them in every direction. The sky outside is blotted out on a cloud of searing smoke. The people in the pews huddle down, screaming. Another huge boom shakes the stones, another, another. The windows shatter. Shards of glass catch the light as they fall, like deadly stars.

Fen throws her hands out. Æsa feels her magic slowing the shards, making them coalesce and crumble. They float down, harmless, looking like snow. And then, all at once, the chaos stops, leaving a ringing silence. Her ears are ringing, too—is that the pounding of her heart? No: Distantly, she hears the bells of the harbor sounding a warning. Invasion is coming, they seem to scream. But too late.

Æsa looks around. The four of them are still huddled together. People are crouched down low, afraid to move.

"What was that?" Matilde says, voice trembling.

But Æsa knows. She has heard that booming sound before, on the *Tempest*.

"Cannons," she chokes out. "The Farlanders must have fired on us."

"But . . ." Matilde shivers. Æsa told her what the cannons did to Willan's ship. "All those people."

They all turn toward the church's gaping entrance. Bodies lie littered around it: people who must have been in the doorway when the blasting started. The thundering has stopped, but the smoke still hangs thick. When it clears, will she see Willan's body, lifeless? Did he make it back to her just to be lost after all?

Æsa closes her eyes. She knew this future would arrive, and yet she does not know how she will face it. Her foresight has not made it easier to bear.

And then someone says her name.

"*Æsa.*"

Her heart beats wildly as Willan throws his arms around her. For a moment she knows nothing but the blessed feel of him, here, alive. With her.

"What in the ten hells was that?" Fen asks. "Did you see?"

Willan's expression is sober. "The Trellians. They're here, and they're beating up our navy. And while they're caught up in the battle in the harbor, more are sailing in down the canals."

"But they can't," Sayer says. "The canals are too shallow for sea boats."

Matilde blanches. "The Alta Dai. The tide might just be high enough."

"The bridges, though," Fen says. "How did they—?"

Willan says, "They've been blown up."

King Joost. While they were chained up in their cell, he

must have done this, dismantling the city from inside. *The snake is in the nest,* that Trellian sailor said. She should have stopped it somehow. She should have known.

"Willan," Matilde is saying. "Where is Alec?"

"I don't know." He rubs his face. "We got separated."

Sayer grips Matilde's arm as she sways.

Just then, a group of soldiers marches into the church, boots ringing. The crowd shrinks back to let them pass. They move in time, each wearing some sort of cured leather armor, a cruel-looking sword strapped to their belts. The soldier in front, stocky and grizzled, comes toward them, stepping over the prone bodies in the aisle. Some twenty paces away from them, he stops and speaks.

"My king, Joost of Trellane, has this church surrounded. Do not fight, and there will be no more violence. My king requests a parlay with the Red Hand."

Æsa and the others stand. The church is so silent now that you might hear a pin drop. All eyes are fixed on the stage and the choir box. One of the Brethren stands.

"The Red Hand is dead."

The soldier nods. "Then we will have your suzerain."

Wyllo simply stands there, mouth opening and closing. One of the Table members gives him a shove.

"My king also requests the Fyrebirds."

Æsa looks to her friends. They seem as unsure as she does. But what choice do they have? The crowd stares on as they make their way down the aisle, followed by Wyllo. Some make gestures as they pass, as if praying. Their eyes seem to plead, now, instead of condemn.

They walk out onto Augustain's steps. They were white before, but now they are grey with soot, broken in places. Æsa can't look away from all the bodies strewn across them. People lie twisted on the stone, many still and silent. Some don't even look like people anymore. Others crouch over them, trying to stanch their loved ones' wounds, some of them keening. Blood runs in rivers down the ruined stairs.

Beside her, Matilde gasps. There, not five steps away, lies Frey Dinatris. Samson is clutching her tightly. Matilde goes to her knees beside them both.

"I told her not to come," Samson says. "I told her."

Matilde takes her gran's hands in hers, gripping them hard.

"If you die," she says, "I will be extremely vexed with you."

"My fierce girl," Frey croaks. "Don't be afraid."

Frey goes still. Samson bows his head, eyes streaming. Matilde lets out a horrible sound.

There should be time for her to grieve, to mourn this loss. But there isn't. The canals are filled with Trellian ships. Through the lingering smoke, Æsa sees their soldiers, their cannons, poised and ready. They've made a mess of the crowded canals. Simtan boats are overturned, their occupants swimming frantically for safety. Others float, arms outstretched, faces down. The Trellians' red sails stretch across the sky like the blood on the church steps. A violent, overwhelming sea.

The soldiers have marched to the edge of the water, stopping at the base of a gangway. It slopes up to a longship that has pulled close to the shore, red sail flapping. A tall, regal-looking man stands at its prow. Æsa recognizes Joost from the wedding. Atop his white-blond head sits a gleaming crown. Beside him stands an olive-skinned girl. She has a silver chain around her neck, which it seems the king is holding.

"Blazing cats," Sayer says, stunned. "Is that . . . Phryne?"

One of their fledglings from the Underground. Æsa saw this in her vision on the beach: a girl in chains, enslaved in silver. She never wanted to see such a thing come true.

The king holds something up to his mouth. It looks like a trumpet, but curved, and larger. It sends his voice booming, his words coming loud and clear.

"I am King Joost of Trellane," he says, in heavily accented Simtan. "Where is the Red Hand?"

"Dead," his captain shouts.

The king looks displeased by the news, mouth thinning. He turns his frosty gaze to Wyllo Regnis.

"I have taken your city," Joost says. "Meet my demands, and I will sail away in the morning. Do not, and I will sack Simta and leave it in ruins."

Wyllo puts up his hands, eyes glazed with panic. His legs are wobbling like a newborn colt's.

"What do you want?"

"I want the drugs the Red Hand used at the wedding. All of them. And I want the city's witches rounded up and handed over by nightfall."

"Take these!" Wyllo shouts, moving as if to cower behind them. "And leave the rest of us in peace."

Joost holds out his pale hands.

"Come, Fyrebirds. You will be the first to join me."

Matilde stands, blood on her robes. Æsa can feel her fury.

"We have been forced to bow to too many odious men today," she shouts. "We aren't about to do it for you."

"You have a simple choice," the king says. "Come willingly, or I will kill every person inside that church. Submit to me or watch your city burn."

Sayer takes Matilde's hand. Fen takes Sayer's, then Æsa's, linking them all together. Through their bond, she feels her friends' magic stirring, joining. The ocean of her own swells and crashes for release. But if they fight here, like this, they might never free Phryne. The Trellians will fire on the church, on their city. How many will die before the battle is done?

"Wait," she says. "We should go onto his ship."

Matilde frowns. "You mean surrender?"

Sayer and Fen both snap, "No."

All her life, Æsa was told that to use magic is to corrupt something holy. That a woman with magic is a poisonous thing. It isn't true. The Wellspring gave them these powers for a reason, and yet she has always felt more cursed than blessed. Why give such holy gifts to her? Her friends are fierce, but she has always shied away from violence. She has always wanted peace, not war. Is that why she, out of them all, was trusted with the power to sway emotion?

Perhaps the Wellspring blessed her for this.

"I can end this," she says, "without bloodshed. And I can make sure Phryne gets off that ship alive."

Matilde shakes her head. She knows what Æsa is thinking.

"Please," she begs. "I have to try."

There is a moment when she thinks they will deny her. But then, one by one, her friends nod.

"Æsa," Willan says, stepping close. "Don't do this."

She looks into his eyes and wonders why she ever believed she could be only one thing. Nightbird or daughter, sheldar or hashna, warrior or girl. She is all of them, and each piece of her is worthy. Each one gives her strength.

"You said I was strong," she whispers in Illish. "You made me believe it. I need you to believe in me now."

He takes a shaking breath. "I do, kilventra."

She steps away. He watches her go.

Æsa leads the other girls down the stairs, not looking at the broken bodies. Æsa keeps her eyes fixed ahead, on the king. One step, two, past the Trellian soldiers, who close ranks behind them, a wall between them and escape. Her instincts scream at her to run, to turn away from this mistake she is making. But Jacinta's words are in her ear: *Remember how much there is to fight for. Don't ever forget how strong you are.*

At last, they step onto the prow of the longship. A clutch of soldiers stands back by the ship's mast, watching. Joost eyes them like a starving man before a feast.

"At last," he says. "You are mine."

Beside the king, Phryne quivers.

"I'm sorry," she says. "I should never have told him—"

Joost yanks on the pershain, choking off her words. He doesn't even look at her. Just holds out his hand, as if he expects Æsa to kiss it. He underestimates her power. They always do.

She takes his hand and reaches for the streams of his emotions. With her friends so close, it is almost effortless. His feelings are like pine resin left to dry in the sun, hard and brittle. Triumph, eagerness, hunger, more fixed than any she has yet encountered. Still, she starts to bend them to her will.

"Oh, Joost," she says, voice pitched so only he will hear. "I sense you start to doubt your plans for Simta. You do not want our magic after all."

He frowns. "But I do."

"No, you don't. And you know this invasion will ruin you. All you want is to turn around and go home."

He shakes his head. "I have come so far. I cannot turn back now."

His feelings are iron, fired in a kiln of his conviction. She tries pouring terror into his veins instead.

"If you do not leave, we will destroy you. Hunt you. It is your greatest fear."

Joost's face drains of color. His hand goes slack around the pershain. Sayer reaches out to Phryne, who lets out a strangled sob.

"Æsa," Fen says. "The others."

Behind him, Joost's soldiers have sensed something amiss. They step forward. Æsa extends her magic's reach, letting it wash over them, weaving their feelings together like a bunch of errant threads. There are so many: Alone, she isn't sure she could hold them, but her friends are with her. She feels their power now, deep in her bones.

"Will it hold?" Matilde whispers in her ear. "If you leave?"

Æsa doesn't know. She should stay with Joost, to ensure he sails away from Simta, but that would mean leaving her sisters behind. A wash of indecision floods through her. And then, from behind, someone shouts.

"To the king!"

Footsteps pound behind them: the Trellian soldiers on the steps. She forgot them. Æsa whirls to see some of them fighting to get back to the gangway. A ring of Simtans blocks their way. People have poured out of the church, striking the Trellians with makeshift weapons. Willan is there, too, swinging his sword. One of the Trellians steps close, blade poised to impale him. Her panic sends a wave of water crashing up out of the canal to knock him down.

She turns back to see Joost shaking his head.

"You," he says, voice darkening. "What did you *do to me?*"

One of the girls pulls her back and down the gangway. Æsa

senses Sayer throwing her magic out, holding the king at bay. When they're all back on solid ground, Matilde sets fire to the gangway. The king is roaring, fire in his eyes.

"Come back," he shouts. "Or I will destroy you. All of you!"

Æsa reaches for her friends, ready to pull his ship apart, to stop this.

And then, all at once, the world goes white.

Leta begs me to come and make a home with her. I know she means well, and so I smile and nod. I am lucky to have a sister like her, so fierce and loyal. Knowing she is on my side makes it all easier to bear.

—AN EXCERPT FROM THE JOURNAL OF
NADJA SANT HELD

– CHAPTER 29 –
A HEALING BALM

S AYER GASPS, LUNGS burning. Everything is painted in a painful, too-bright light. Why can't she see? Panic threatens, but then the whiteness starts to fade, hearing returning. What weapon did the Trellians just set off?

She blinks hard, trying to get her bearings. How did she end up on the ground? She scrambles up, but a searing pain makes her bend over. Something is wrong with her ribs. Every breath brings a spear of agony. Swords clang, too close, as people fight. A Trellian throws a Warden down, sending him tumbling by her. Someone shrieks. She has to move.

She climbs the steps, trying not to trip on bodies, searching their faces for ones she knows. She saw Jolena and Rankin near the door before: Are they all right? What were they thinking, coming out here? Where are the girls? She feels for their bond, pulling it tight, trying to follow it. Behind her, she hears a wall of battle cries.

"Retreat into the church!" someone shouts: Willan? "Quickly!"

Sayer slips in blood. Her balance feels off somehow. She is

lost in this world of white, alone. Then someone hits her shoulder hard, knocking her over. Suddenly she's on her back again. A Trellian looms, teeth bared in menace. She's about to lash out when someone knocks him to the side. It's Fen.

"Come on, Tig," she pants. "Hurry."

They stagger the last few steps into the church. Matilde and Æsa are there, waving them on. Several people pull the church doors shut and throw the bolts.

Sayer wraps her arms around Fen, breathing hard. "You found me."

Fen kisses her cheek. "Always."

Sayer takes one breath, two, wanting to melt into her. Later. She makes herself pull back and look around. She can't see Wyllo: With any luck, he's locked outside with the Trellians. Æsa is comforting Phryne. Samson and Willan are holding a sopping-wet Alec up between them.

"Alec. You. Dashed. Idiot," Matilde says between kisses. "You almost exploded us."

"That was you?" Sayer says. "Ten hells. We had it handled."

"The other longboats were pulling in," he croaks. "Their cannons were smoking. I panicked. I figured they wouldn't shoot at what they couldn't see."

Sayer looks back at the pews. Behind them, the church is full to bursting. Simtans huddle there, eyes huge, so many. She scours their faces but can't find Jolena's or Rankin's. The Trellians are hammering on the doors, making them creak. How long before they break them down?

"We need to end this," Sayer says. "Before they do any more damage."

Willan nods. "If we could scupper their ships, that would finish their cannons. It would take them out at the knees."

"How, though?" Fen asks. "We can't go out there now."

"We don't need to." Matilde's expression is the one she wears when she's plotting. "We just need to get up high enough to see. The belltower—"

"Yes," Æsa says. "That is exactly where we go. I've seen it." Another bang on the doors, and the sound of wood splintering.

"We'll hold them off down here," Samson pants. *"Just hurry."*

There is no time for debate. They take off running down the aisle, but there are so many people. Sayer's ribs scream with every step they take. At last, Matilde leads them to a door behind the stage, tucked into the back wall. It opens onto a curving stone stairwell. Matilde, Fen, and Æsa go through, sprinting up. She's about to follow when she hears a scream.

"Let her *go!*"

Twisting around, she sees Rankin through the crowd, running at Wyllo. The man swings something at Rankin, who goes down hard. He tries to get up, but Wyllo is already slipping through another door, yanking Jolena behind him. Her half sister, seeing Sayer, screams her name.

Sayer takes off, pushing through the bodies toward the door, barreling through it. The vaulted hallway is empty, but they can't have gotten far. One corner, two, and then she sees them, grappling underneath a wall of human skulls.

"Stupid girl," he is shouting, gripping her wrist. "Stop fussing."

"Let me go," Jolena shouts.

"Do as you're *told.*"

Sayer's vision bends. She see herself bound by this man, too, made helpless. She sees her dame.

Then Wyllo raises his hand.

Her magic has always been a stealthy thing, a power that

very few people can see. Anyone watching now would think Wyllo has simply lost his balance. They wouldn't see the bands of air she bends around him, throwing him against the wall of skulls. Two of them fall and crack, turning to dust. Free again, Jolena stumbles back as Sayer compresses the bands around him. He gasps for just the smallest sips of air.

She steps in close. "It's over, Wyllo. I hope you've said your prayers."

"Please." His voice is small, almost a whine. "Spare me, daughter."

That word on his lips sends fury howling through her. She robs him of the last of his air. His mouth opens, soundless, lips going blue. His eyes are bulging and awful. She isn't going to stop until he's gone.

"Don't," Jolena begs.

But he has to pay for everything he's done to them.

"Sayer, please. He is our sire."

Wyllo splutters as her hold on him loosens. She looks to Jolena, beside her now.

"You knew?"

"I've known for months that you're my sister," she says. "I would love you even if you weren't."

Sayer has spent so much of the past few months in shadow, settling scores, exacting justice. Anger has been both her sword and her shield. But this girl's words cut through it all, spreading inside her. They seep into her chest, a healing balm.

"He doesn't deserve to live," she seethes.

"I know. But you aren't a killer."

Jolena threads her arms around Sayer.

"Please, sister. Let him go. Do it for me."

When her dame died, Sayer thought she would never again have a family. She thought it best to close her heart and fight alone. But then came Leta, who took her in and tended her. And this girl, pushing past her walls of thorns. Fen and Matilde and Æsa are her family, and they need her.

This man who sired her doesn't matter at all.

He collapses to all fours, pale and gasping.

Sayer takes Jolena's hand and leaves him there, not looking back.

One of the girls pulled their power in, becoming their conduit. In her, their magic mixed and pooled, becoming one. But a price had to be paid. Such power required sacrifice. Their magic burned her up.

—FROM THE JOURNAL OF DELAINA DINATRIS,
ONE OF SIMTA'S FIRST NIGHTBIRDS

CHAPTER 30

BURNING BRIGHT

MATILDE SHIELDS HER eyes, looking over her city. From the belltower, most of Simta is laid out before her, Corners to edges. She can see Simtan warships fighting Trellian ones out in the port, and losing. It looks like half the navy's ships are on fire. But the canals are almost worse. There must be hundreds of longboats in them, thousands. They're firing their cannons now, smashing into buildings. How many will it take to rip the city apart? She thinks of all the girls out in those streets, alone and frightened. She thinks of Gran, her eyes gone dull, her light gone out.

A clatter from the stairs: It seems Fen has found Sayer.

"Finally," Matilde snaps. "Did you have a more pressing engagement?"

"I'm here now," Sayer pants. "What's the plan?"

"We have to sink their ships," Æsa says. "It's the only way to stop them."

"But can we?" Fen asks. "From up here?"

Matilde thinks of Delaina's stories of parting seas and

moving mountains. She reaches for their hands. "We're Fyrebirds. Of course we can."

Again, they touch. Again, that flush of power, of growing things and rushing waves, lightning and fire, all bound together. She can breathe again, every piece of her expanding. But still, her thoughts are pierced by doubt. They have had no chance to practice this power, to truly wield it. But she won't let the Trellians destroy her world.

She takes a deep breath. "We have to pool our power to pull this off. Let me be our conduit."

Æsa frowns. "Why you?"

"Because I have a plan."

In their cell, she related Delaina's story about the Fyrebirds who destroyed the Tekan invasion. She recited the words, engraved on her mind. *One of the girls pulled their power in, becoming their conduit. In her, their magic mixed and pooled, becoming one.*

She lied about the story's end.

A price had to be paid. Such power required sacrifice. Their magic burned her up.

Did that Fyrebird die? Will *she*? She has no way of knowing. But if she fails in this, then all is lost.

She thinks of Gran's words about the importance of duty. It felt like it was code for letting others run your life. But now she understands. Sometimes, duty is about seeing the bigger picture. Duty is fighting for more than just yourself. That's what the Fyrebirds did once. They pulled on armor and fought, risking their lives to save others. And then they sacrificed that power to try to keep their daughters safe.

To save her city, she is willing to sacrifice.

To protect her girls, she will give everything she has.

She looks at Fen, Sayer, and Æsa one last time.

"I love you all," she says: one last secret shared. "I'm glad to call you my sisters."

Then she sucks in a breath, digs down, and pulls in.

Alec told her once how some stars die. *When they get near the end, the pressure of the sky becomes too much for them. The star collapses. Then it explodes, throwing itself out through the dark.* When she draws their magic in, she feels like that: compressed. It's all the elements at once, heating her core, a thousand sets of wings burning. Their power burns in her, lighting her up.

Far below, soldiers are heaving at the church doors, trying to burst through. Small fires are burning on the steps; she feels her own pulse within them. She wills them to rise out of their ashes and swell. Ribbons of water leap from the canals, crashing onto the steps, twisting strangely. They seem attracted to the fires, moths to a flame. They wrap around her fires, seeming to guard rather than quench them. Out on the closest boats, cannons melt, their liquid metal flying to join the other elements. She wills it to form a kind of skeleton. Spine, arms, legs, wings: the foundations of a monster. She wraps the blazing fires and water around it, turning them into its muscle and skin. Matilde's flames form a head, giving it a mouth to shriek with. Sayer's air magic shapes its spikes and talons, making their monster grow and swell. It's half the size of the church, hulking and huge, hungry for nothing but destruction. All she needs now is to bind it to their will. She adds her cunning, Sayer's fierceness, Fen's strength, and Æsa's courage. She pours their bond, their rage, into its fiery heart. This is their monster. An impossible, elemental bird of prey.

At last, it stretches out its wings, streaked with storm and lightning. It turns its head and screams, breathing out fire.

It turns on the Trellians at the church door. The men try to flee, but the monster swipes out a wing. She hears faint screams as bodies scatter and fly into the water. And then, with a whoosh, their bird takes flight. It circles the Corners, its shadow shining on the water like a terrifying flamemoth. All at once, the creature dives for Joost's longboat. She can see the king's terror through the monster's fiery eyes. Its talons spark as they wrap around him and slam his body to the deck. Lightning crackles around her, passing through Joost. His frost-tinged eyes have gone lifeless. The king is dead, but the battle isn't yet won. The bird takes flight again, crashing into the other longboats, punching through sails and exploding hulls, devouring. She feels each impact like a blow deep in her chest.

When all the ships in the Corners are wrecked, the bird wheels, still hungry. And then, with a roar, the creature splits. It becomes two fiery birds, three, smaller than the first, but just as deadly. One of them cries out, the sound of metal on metal, hungry for Farlander blood.

The birds each wheel and fly down a canal, swooping and burning. Matilde can still see through one of their eyes. She is that creature, tearing through each enemy ship, destroying it. The metal in her bones crashes through their hulls and cracks them. Lightning from her wings strikes their masts. A few brave Trellians fire on her, but she only absorbs what they throw at her. The water cannot douse her; no wind can diminish her. Their power, made whole, cannot be tamed.

But the farther she flies, the more of her collapses. Pieces of her wings are dripping off, peeling away. She is a dying star, running out of heat to burn with. Before she goes, she's going to win this fight.

At last, she's at the port, swooping low over the warships. With a shriek, she wraps her talons around one of the Trellian ships. It seems to melt beneath her, burning bright, pieces exploding. The other fiery birds have come to tear more down. Before long, the Farlands fleet is nothing but smoke and floating debris. Simtan navalmen stare up, pointing and shouting, but none of the monsters burn them. She hopes that they will all remember that.

And then the world starts to blur. Far away, someone is shouting. She thinks they might be calling her name. But she has no voice. Her body is burning to ashes. Her heart is beating slow, stuttering out.

THEY WERE BARRICADING the church doors with more pews when Alec heard the roaring. He thought it was the cannons at first, but it sounded like an animal, loud enough to shake the stones. There was a flash of light, a burst of shrieks, and the pounding on the door stopped. Alec peered out a hole the soldiers managed to make in one, gaping at the thing crouched on the stairs. It was a phoenix, beaked head and wings and claws, its spiked tail slashing. He watched as it took flight and fought for them.

Now he's stumbling into the light up on the bell-tower. The sky is bright, streaked with smoke and fire: The fight is over. Joy swells, filling him up.

"You did it," Willan crows. "You truly did it!"

The girls don't look up. They're half collapsed against each other. Why is Matilde lying down like that?

A sinking feeling rips through his gut. It's the one he gets when he's brewing a potion that's turned sour on him. He stumbles toward them, falling to his knees. His hands search for a wound to heal, a hurt to salve, but there is nothing. Matilde's skin is like parchment, dry and hot.

"What happened?"

"She collapsed when the birds did," Sayer says, expression bleak. "We can't wake her."

It's eerie, how still her body is. Her pulse is faint, barely there.

He pulls the golden locket out from under her robe, unscrewing it with frantic fingers.

"Tilt her chin back."

Slowly, Alec pours the potion on her tongue, hoping she won't choke. Bleeding heartvine is supposed to heal a girl. It has to. He isn't going to let her die.

Matilde lies still. They wait and wait, but nothing happens. Her chest rises once, twice, and then . . . it stops.

Fen grips Sayer's hand. Æsa reaches out to smooth Matilde's hair. One of them makes a painful, keening sound.

No one moves, their silence big enough to crush him.

Then Æsa takes a deep, steadying breath.

"This isn't how our story ends."

She looks at Fen and Sayer.

"We three are going to call her back."

She lays her hand on Matilde's chest, fingers splayed. Sayer lays hers on top, and then Fen, palm to palm, pressing together. Alec holds his breath, afraid to move.

Most of his best recipes involve an incantation. *Words have power*, Krastan told him. *They are their own brand of magic.* It's the girls who speak now, casting a spell.

"Come back, Matilde," Æsa says.

Fen bends her head. "Don't leave us."

"Please," Sayer chokes. "We need you."

The seconds pass, silent and still. Alec feels for a pulse, but there is nothing.

Nothing. *Nothing.*

Alec doesn't want a world without her light.

– CHAPTER 31 –
ETERNAL FLAMES

MATILDE FINDS HERSELF in a finely appointed bedroom. Her Goldfinch mask sits atop the velvet sheets next to a tray of glasses and a bucket of cool blush wine. Another Nightbird sits across the way. Her mask, blue and shimmering, is in her lap. Her eyes are the same amber as Matilde's, glowing in the nighttime shadows. She is smiling. Somehow Matilde knows exactly who she is.

"Tell me a secret," Delaina Dinatris says. "Something no one else knows."

"I fear death."

"Everyone fears death. Tell me something dearer."

"I fear losing my magic. I don't know who I will become."

"You will be just as fierce and strong without it," Delaina says. "Stronger."

"But will I be enough?"

Delaina puts her hand out, pressing it against Matilde's breastbone. Inside her, something flutters in response.

"You are more than your magic," Delaina says. "You are

your dreams. Your deeds. Your love. Your courage. No one can put out those fires in you."

The fluttering inside her spreads, growing stronger. It feels like flamemoths alighting on her bones. She tastes something herbal on her tongue, almost familiar. And then a sudden, aching tug around her ribs. Far away, someone is calling her name, telling her to come home to them. Her soul is such a tired and leaden weight. She cannot make it alone, but perhaps they can carry her. She closes her eyes and lets them lift her up.

The light changes. Delaina is gone, and she sees her friends instead. Fen, her two-toned eyes bright and shining. Æsa's sweet smile lighting up her face. Sayer is scowling down, tears flowing freely.

"Dash it," she says. "Come on. *Say something.*"

Matilde's voice, when it comes, is low and scoured.

"Stop blubbering, Sayer. It's going to make you blotchy."

Sayer hiccups a laugh, and then a sob.

The girls help her sit up. Alec takes her hand, squeezing. Arms go around her, pulling her close, keeping her safe. She should be glad. Her sisters are here, and they've saved their city. She is alive against all odds. But grief still rings through the hollow places where her magic should be. She cannot feel it. The fire that filled her once is gone.

Out of the ashes she rose, fighting our enemies.
Out of the ashes she flew for us all.

—A NOTE LEFT AT THE FLAME WITCH'S
SHRINE IN PEGASUS QUARTER, ON THE SITE WHERE
KRASTAN PADANO'S SHOP USED TO STAND

CHAPTER 32

THE FINAL SPARK

MATILDE HAS ALWAYS enjoyed making an entrance. When she sweeps into the Hall of Countenance, mounting the stage, all eyes are upon her. Thousands of Simtans have come to hear the announcement. Tonight, she wears no mask. She is herself.

After the battle with the Farlanders was over, the wreckage was cleaned up, and the remaining soldiers dealt with. With King Joost dead and most of their ships destroyed, they surrendered without much of a fight. The city was grateful to the Fyrebirds. Their deeds that day helped change many hearts and minds. It's helped that word has trickled out about the lengths some of Simta's finest went to in order to discredit them. Articles have been pouring out in all the newssheets, long exposés about the Red Hand and his Sugar, and Lord Wyllo Regnis's role in helping him create it. The truth about it all, out at last.

Still, not everyone trusts them—women with power will always have detractors. But most people no longer want to see them caged. The magical girls locked up in Jawbone Prison have been released, and the Wardens have been disbanded.

Most agree the church was wrong, at least about some things. Stories of corruption in the church have made their way into the newssheets, too, as well as calls for reformation. No one condones the Red Hand's actions except his most ardent acolytes, who have been rounded up and arrested. Even some paters have come forward to condemn what he did. Meanwhile, the small shrines that sprang up to them after Leastnight have grown, swelling with offerings. Matilde is no goddess, but she could have used the goodwill to make herself a queen, had she wished. But she isn't Epinine and Dennan, clutching onto power with both fists for its own sake. She wants to empower others to choose their own fate. She doesn't want to rule, but to serve.

"All rise for the suzerain," one of her new guards—Hallie—says. Matilde likes how fierce the Dark Star looks in her uniform. She also likes how everyone stands as their suzerain steps up to the podium, waiting to hear what she will say.

She smears some Echo Oil onto her throat to make sure the crowd will hear her. Alec brewed the paste himself: *I know how you love the sound of your own voice, Tilde,* he teased, pairing the jibe with a kiss that made her knees buckle. He's in the front row of seats, next to Dame and Samson. When she smiles at him, he throws her a wink. Sayer and Fen are there, too, wearing the uniforms Matilde commissioned for the Fyrebirds. The suits were made by Simta's finest tailor, the lapels embroidered with vines and storms. *I expect you won't complain,* she told Sayer, *given they're pants.* Sayer didn't complain about the duties Matilde assigned to her, Fen, and Æsa either. They may not want seats at the Table, but they've promised to keep fighting beside her. After all, they are stronger together.

"Good evening, friends," she says, her voice filling the vast space. "Thank you all for joining me on this historic occasion. It has been hard-won, this end to Prohibition. But one that's going to benefit us all."

She looks at the faces in the first four rows, filled with members of the Table. It's much bigger now, with far fewer Great House lords. All she wanted, once, was to claim a chair amongst the few on offer. Now she sees how badly the whole system needed to be smashed. The first thing she did was push the old guard out. *Clean up your house,* she told the newest Pontifex, *and perhaps you can join us.* For now, she would rather keep church out of state. Gone are the days when a few rich, privileged men decided Eudea's future. There are representatives from every Quarter on the Table now, and not just ones with money. Cobblers and alchemists, men and women, young and old: Alec is also a member. How Krastan would smile to see them now.

"As a Nightbird, I was told to keep my magic a secret," she continues. "To hide it behind masks and pretty lies. It was supposed to keep us safe, but hiding only ever made us weaker. No girl should be ashamed of such a gift."

The new Table has passed laws that will protect girls with magic. They cannot be coerced into using it or made to share the power in their veins. But there is so much more to do in remaking Eudea. A part of her worries she isn't up to the task. Who is she to mold this Republic's future, to help decide what its new rules should be?

But why not her? She thinks of Krastan, telling her to be brave with his dying breaths. She wraps herself in Gran's final words. *Don't be afraid.*

"Magic is a part of who we are," she goes on. "It is a strength. We should be proud of it. Today, we bring it back into the light."

The words aren't so different from ones Dennan once uttered. For all his many faults, Matilde thinks he would be glad of this.

The air shifts, tasting of rain and thunder. Slowly, the light begins to change. Sayer bends the air, making thousands of orblights dance above them. Fen sends colored sand rising from buckets, winding through the swirling sea of lights. It's beautiful to watch, but it makes Matilde long for her magic. Channeling the Fyrebirds' magic up in the belltower burned it out of her. Try as she might, it hasn't returned. She wouldn't change what she did to save her city, but the absence of her power still pains her. Other fires burn in her now: the desire to love who she wants and choose them freely. The drive to build a better, freer world. And moments like these, so full of hope, are starting to fill her empty spaces. They make her feel like she is who she's meant to be.

"COMMANDER?"

Æsa turns to face the naval officer standing behind her. "Yes, Cousins?"

"The port's not far off. Do you want us to strike sail?"

"No." She once thought you had to be loud to be a leader, but she doesn't have to raise her voice to have it heard. "Leave them flying."

He hurries off, readying the huge ship to reach harbor. The *Justice* is new, and this its maiden voyage. She almost called it the *Jacinta*, but thinks her friend would like this name. The figurehead looks like her, fierce, eyes fixed on the horizon. Unblinking and brave as she faces what will come.

Æsa shakes her hair, letting it catch the sea breeze. She's

braided some of it, as is the way of the sheldar. The sea glass wishes in it have mostly come true. Her friends are safe, and the fledglings can live freely. The Trellians are defeated. The ones who survived limped home and didn't look back. She's sure all those wedding guests took tales of the battle back home, spreading them across the seas in all directions. Others will think twice before they attack Simta's shores.

Especially with tales of the Wave Witch leading their navy. Many of their ships were scuppered at what's being called the Battle of the Phoenix Fires, their force depleted. The city's shipwrights are working hard to build their numbers up again. Some of Simta's alchemists, including Alec, have created alchemicals for use in future battles, from resins that make an arrow's fire burn hotter to potions to keep sails from fraying. But no weapon is revered quite so much as the Wave Witch. She prefers to think of herself as a protector, but one who will do what she must to keep them safe. Foreign powers will come again, she is sure, to pillage their coasts, hungry to steal Eudea's magic. When they do, she will fight them with all the power she has.

She touches one of the buttons of her topcoat. The Simtan naval uniform had to be tailored, of course, to suit her. It wasn't designed for generous curves. She is working to ensure that more women will be welcomed into the ranks, including some of Simta's water girls. She plans to send ships to foreign courts in search of any girls the Red Hand may have sold. Perhaps she will scour the seas for them herself. The world is wide, and she wants to see more of it. From now on, she is going to chart her own course.

"Kilventra ei'ish?" comes a deep voice from behind her.

Æsa smiles. "Of course I'm well, now that you're here."

Willan puts his arms around her, pulling her close. It must

be something of a shock, to some, to see two of Simta's naval commanders canoodling. If the ship's officers are bothered by the sight, none of them say. One—Kadeel—whistles from where he's climbing in the rigging. She is glad to have men she trusts with her, during this time of transition, and that Willan's been given a ship of his own. One of Matilde's first acts as suzerain was to ensure he was given a full pardon for any past sea raids, as well as a ship even finer than the *Tempest*. He will work alongside Æsa to protect Eudea's shores. They can even plunder foreign merchants, if they suspect any of smuggling magic out of the Republic. *Sea raiders aren't bad,* Matilde told them, *so long as they're pirating for us.*

So now they fight together, she and Willan. And for each other. She wouldn't have it any other way.

"Could I convince you to come back to our berth?" he says, voice playful. "This lot can dock without us."

She laughs. "Willan, really."

"What? I will have to share you with your friends soon. A man can covet some alone time with his lady."

Her cheeks flush. "You will have to share me with my parents too."

She wrote to them about what happened—all of it. She wanted them to hear the truth from her. She didn't know what Da would think of his daughter battling men with her magic. But just before they made this trip, she received a letter from him. *Your grandda was right. You are a sheldar, strong and blessed. And I am proud of you, daughter.* They will have arrived in Simta by now. They will be waiting for her, as will her sisters. The thought makes her heart lift and fly on the wind.

At last, they round the final headland. The Simtan Rim looms up before them, along with the ship she raised and placed up on its cliffs. It was a scandal once: a talking point for those who argued girls like her could not be trusted. Now it's seen neither as wreckage or ruin. It's turned into a symbol of their strength.

She raises her hands, letting her magic rise with them. Waves form on either side of the *Justice*'s prow. They look like a bird's wings, outstretched to catch the sun, which makes them glisten.

She is more than ready to fly home.

NIGHT IS COMING on as Sayer walks through the Green Light, no part of her hidden in shadow. She knocks on the Garden Club's dark green door. Two short taps and a cascade of fingertips: the same pattern Sparrows once used with their Nightbirds. It opens onto a foyer, revealing a guard.

"The password?" Olsa demands.

This club only admits girls with magic, and whichever friends they feel are worthy. It isn't any special words she needs, but action. She calls up a wind, blowing out the light above.

"Will that do?"

Olsa laughs. It's a nice sound, and it pleases Sayer to hear him make it again. Since the Caska attacked the Stars' club, laughter's been rare. "It's better than that time you tried to choke me."

"You had that coming."

"Fair enough. Onward you go."

He opens the inner door. It leads into a hallway, then a stairwell. She pauses at the threshold of the club's high-ceilinged lounge. They built the Garden Club in one of Griffin's oldest buildings, which used to house a flower market. Its dome is made of amber-colored glass, much like the one in Leta's conservatory. She wishes their old Madam could see this place.

Sayer doesn't know when, or why, she changed her will. *I leave all my worldly goods to Sayer Sant Held and Fenlin Brae,* the document said. *My daughters.* Sayer still misses her. She thinks Leta would approve of this place she helped them make.

Since Risentide, more and more girls have stepped out of the city's shadows. The laws are in flux, the rules about magic still changing, but in ways that mean they feel safe out in the open. That doesn't mean there is nothing left to fear. Not everyone likes the changes sweeping through the city. Some of the pipers don't like magic going legit. Matilde gave Sayer and Fen the Table-sanctioned task of making sure Simta's gangs weren't bullying any magical girls into staying in their service. *Do what you must to get them out,* Matilde quipped, *but don't cause too much mayhem.* It isn't Sayer's fault some of the piper lords needed a forceful hand. But she can't stop them from coveting girls' magic. She's sure there are those who want to resurrect the Red Hand's cause. Danger still lurks in their streets for girls like them; perhaps it always will. But in this club, they know they'll always be safe.

She strides into the room. Her friends are still setting up the party. It's the Garden Club's opening night, and everything is sparkling with newness. She and Fen chose every glossy bar and velvet seat. There are plenty of lush touches, but nothing that might put off a humble coffee girl. They want their patrons to feel that they belong.

Nectar hangs on the air. Vines climb around the many beams and columns. Fen has encouraged them to bloom, releasing their scent. Jolena fusses over a patch of moss, coaxing it to spread across a bar top. Rankin holds her hand, not caring who sees. It's not as if anyone here is going to stop them. Wyllo Regnis has no power anymore.

After the battle, he was caught trying to flee Simta. A mob

brought him to the Winged Palace and tied him, shouting, to its doors. The Fyrebirds all laid official charges. He cried conspiracy, but the evidence was stacked against him. It helped when his friends started turning on him. They told the newssheets the real story of the exhibition, hoping it might buy them some forgiveness. No one in Simta approves of such a drug now. Fortunately, there will be no more of it. Seleese's clan destroyed what was left of the lab at the Regnis country house. The remaining Sugar was burned up, the recipe lost. The only one who knew it was the Hand, and he can't hurt them. His poison secrets died with him.

Wyllo is in Jawbone, pending trial. Sayer thinks he deserves a noose instead, but she's glad she didn't kill him. She would have missed watching him stripped of everything he loves most. His position, his wealth, his good name. It must burn him to know that Minna Regnis heads his House now. It's a better revenge than anything she could've planned.

Jolena has invited her dame and sister tonight. *Can I tell them who you really are?* she asked Sayer, the question cautious. She clearly thought Sayer would say no. But she doesn't want to hide, and Jolena loves those women. Maybe it's time to meet the family. Sayer's learning what it takes to build her own.

Behind the bar, someone straightens. Fen looks at home, arranging the many bottles in neat rows. Sayer used to dream about them owning a bakery, but this place suits them better. They share an apartment in the back, where they whisper all their secrets. There are still nightmares to banish, but now they fight them together. When Fen has bad dreams, Sayer wakes her with a kiss.

Fen's two-toned eyes find Sayer. She grins, making them glimmer twice as bright.

"Tig. I've got that delivery you were waiting on."

Sayer walks behind the bar. "And just in time."

She kisses Fen, even though half the Dark Stars are watching. It's a heady thrill to love like this, out loud. Someone whistles, but Fen only leans in closer, not holding anything back.

Blushing now, Sayer turns to the box. Between its slats, she can see the flamemoths glowing. There must be hundreds tucked inside. A whimsical touch, but one she's sure will please the guest of honor. Sayer smiles, feeling smug. For someone who prides herself on knowing everything, Matilde has no idea what's in store tonight. She hopes no one's ruined the surprise.

Together, she and Fen open the box, letting the moths fly. They circle above them, as if drawn to the Fyrebirds, and then begin to find their own paths. Many land on the flowers, drinking in their nectar. Sayer finds herself drinking in the moment as well. They have lost so much, but the shadows make the lights burn so much brighter. Sayer's heart is shining, full of what's to come.

MATILDE HOLDS UP her crown. It's like cobwebs, made of twisted strands of gold and copper. The flamemoths all around the club seem to light it up. There is something thrilling about seeing them here, free to fly together. Just as her sisters are surrounding her now.

"You truly made this, Fen?" she asks.

The girl winks. "It was Sayer's idea."

"You swan around like a queen." There is no heat in Sayer's words: only teasing. "I figured you might as well look the part."

"Well, you know how I feel about sparkle. The more the better."

Alec kisses her cheek. "As if you need a crown to shine."

Sayer groans.

"Forgive my paramour," Matilde says. "When he asked what I wanted for my name day, I told him to shower me in sweet nothings."

"I'm running out," Alec laments. "I don't know how many more I've got in me."

"Willan can help," Æsa says. "He has plenty."

Several people groan. Willan shakes his head, laughing. "That's my cue to go get drinks."

He weaves toward the bar. Matilde watches the crowd, most of them chatting and drinking, swaying in time to the lively brass band. It's strangely lovely to see her old Nightbird sisters dancing with some of the fledglings, and the Dark Stars playing krellen with some of Samson's friends. Dame and Samson are here, too, talking to Phryne and her dame around a table. So many disparate pieces of her life, all in one room. But nothing feels as good as having her sisters here beside her. With them, she feels more like herself.

Willan puts a tray down, passing the cocktails out amongst them.

"Alec dreamed up this one himself," Sayer announces. "Just for us. It's called the Fyrebird."

She strikes a match and holds it over her glass. Tiny wings rise on the vapor. They glow, as orange as the drink itself.

"To you, Matilde," Æsa says. "Our favorite Fyrebird. Now and always."

They all repeat the toast, lighting their cocktails. *Now and always.* Even though she has no magic. She swallows down the lump in her throat.

Alec reaches out to light her drink.

"Wait," she says. "Let me."

She doesn't take the match he offers. His eyebrows crease, knowing what she intends. It is foolish, she knows. She burned up all her magic. But with her sisters here, she feels so much stronger—braver. Why not try it? She dares to let her hand hover over the glass. *You are more than your magic,* Delaina said in that shadowy dream place, hovering with Matilde between life and death. *You are your dreams. Your deeds. Your love. Your courage. No one can put out those fires in you.*

It's those fires she calls on, asking them to burn brighter.

She waits, knowing nothing will happen.

But then, from deep inside, rises a spark.

– ACKNOWLEDGMENTS –

IT TURNS OUT that writing your second book can be a challenging business. I'm not sure I could have done it without the many brilliant people who helped me out along the way. All the fancy bootleg cocktails go to my agent, Josh Adams, his partner in crime, Tracey, and Anna Munger for working tirelessly for me and my novels, and for being there through thick and thin. A huge thanks to my editor, Stacey Barney, for continuing to love and champion my magical girls no matter what level of chaos I have them getting up to. Thank you to everyone at Penguin Young Readers who gave this series its wings: Nancy Paulsen, Caitlin Tutterow, Jenny Ly, publicist/ sorceress Olivia Russo, Felicity Vallence, Shannon Spann, and everyone from the marketing team who've worked their elemental magic to get these books in front of readers. I'm so grateful. A shower of sparkles upon Jessica Jenkins for another incredible cover, Suki Boynton for the lovely internal design, and Sveta Drosheva for the beautiful maps I still cannot get over. A huge thanks to the copyeditors and proofreaders who made sure this book was ready for its red-carpet debut: Cindy Howle, Laurel Robinson, and Janet Rosenberg. A bottomless cup of thank-yous also goes to Molly Lo Re, Sarah Jaffe, and everyone at Listening Library. Seeing this story brought to life as an audiobook has been nothing short of magical; Saskia Maarleveld, someone should give you a crown.

Thank you to all the publishers who have brought this series to their readers in countries outside my own. It's been wonderful to see my words translated into multiple languages, flying into the hearts of readers who may not have found them otherwise. A special thanks to my Australian publisher, Allen & Unwin: You are all such a delight to work with.

This story owes big debts to the talented friends who helped me figure out how best to tell it. Their magical powers know no bounds. Thank you to Lili Wilkinson, who made me promise her big magic, and C. S. Pacat, who showed me where the real conflict was. I thank my lucky stars for the House of Progress crew and their collective wisdom, care, and insight. Much love to Ryan Graudin, whose writerly wisdom always make my stories better, and Amie Kaufman, who saved me with note card sessions and well-timed pep talks more than once. Bottomless gratitude to Miranda, who has read this book at least as many times as I have and whose insights shaped it profoundly. I am also grateful to Anna McFarlane and Arundhati Subhedar, who swooped in like the Fyrebirds they are when I asked.

Thank you to everyone who's joined Amie and me over on *Pub Dates*, the podcast that traced this series's journey to publication and took you behind the scenes on its creation. What an unexpected joy it's been to have you all with me, cheering me on every step of the way. Thank you to *The Exploress* listeners amongst you for your continued support and enthusiasm. A special thanks to Carly Quinn, research queen and beam of sunshine, who has brightened my creative life in all sorts of ways.

As I wrote *Fyrebirds*, I thought a lot about the lives and trials of women, past and present. I want to thank some of the incredible and powerful ladies who've shaped mine. The friends who always answer the call to my banner: Lyndsey, Eve, Lauren, Tori, Lori, Claire, Misty, Bel, Anna, Loran, and Nadja. A special thanks to Kaitlin for loving this world and these girls from the start: This one's for you. The clever, take-no-prisoners women I grew up with: Anna, Jacque, Caroline, and my aunties, Louisa, Joan, and Karen. And Grams, who I thought about a lot while writing this. I miss you.

Thank you to the Armstrongs, Chevaliers, Gablonskis, and all the extended friends and family who've cheered for me so loudly. Special thank-yous to my niece, Victoria, for loving this story (and convincing me that Alec needed to do a little groveling); my dad and Carol for their unflagging support; and my brother, John (I couldn't have asked for a better hype man). Thank you to my mom, Edie, who brainstormed with me in the early stages, made me dinner when I was deep in revisions, and reminded me to trust myself.

To Galahad, my best boy and most loyal writing companion, who we lost while I was drafting *Fyrebirds*. I miss you every day, my noble boy.

To Paul, the love of my life and excellent whisperer of sweet nothings. Thank you for supporting my dreams, no matter how wild they get, and for knowing just what sorts of snacks to bring up to my writing shed.

Finally, I want to thank all the booksellers, librarians, and readers around the world who have loved and recommended *Nightbirds*. Seeing my book pop up in your window displays, featured in your book clubs, and captured so fetchingly in your feeds has been a beautiful part of this adventure. Your support means so much, and I can't thank you enough.